Zara Cox's wr... eventually realis... Call in 2012. Za... kids and an endl...

Maisey Yates is ... of over one hundred romance novels. Whether writing strong, hardworking cowboys, dissolute princes or multigenerational family stories, she loves getting lost in fictional worlds. An avid knitter with a dangerous yarn addiction and an aversion to housework, Maisey lives with her husband and three kids in rural Oregon. Check out her website, maiseyyates.com or find her on Facebook.

Robyn Grady has sold millions of books worldwide, and features regularly on bestsellers lists and at award ceremonies, including The National Readers Choice, The Booksellers Best and Australia's prestigious Romantic Book of the Year. When she's not tapping out her next story, she enjoys the challenge of raising three very different daughters as well as dreaming about shooting the breeze with Stephen King during a month-long Mediterranean cruise. Contact her at robyngrady.com

Sins and Seduction

Sins and Seduction:
The Ruthless Rival

ZARA COX

MAISEY YATES

ROBYN GRADY

MILLS & BOON

First Published in Great Britain 2023
by Mills & Boon, an imprint of HarperCollins*Publishers* Ltd,
1 London Bridge Street, London, SE1 9GF

www.harpercollins.co.uk

HarperCollins*Publishers*
Macken House, 39/40 Mayor Street Upper,
Dublin 1, D01 C9W8, Ireland

ISBN: 978-0-263-31848-7

ENEMIES WITH BENEFITS

ZARA COX

To authors everywhere who have to deal with a
'birthing-a-pineapple' book every once in a while.
I took one for the team with this book.
You're welcome.

CHAPTER ONE

'I CAN TRUST you to behave yourself, can't I?'

Shit.

I dragged my gaze from the statuesque brunette weaving her way through the one-hundred-plus guests sipping vintage champagne on a chilly autumn evening. The five heating towers positioned around the terrace and immediate lamplit grounds of the Surrey mansion were doing their damnedest to warm up the abysmal temperature and failing, but I, for one, didn't need their help.

My body had heated up the moment I spotted Wren Bingham, wearing a clingy jumpsuit that lovingly followed every curve of her spectacular body. Fringed, shoulder-length jet-black hair brushed the frilly-looking scarf wrapped around her shoulders. Stilettos on her feet and a diamond bracelet circling her wrist completed her outfit. Her guests wore double and triple layers but she was obviously nowhere near cold, either.

I didn't mind one bit because she looked fuckable in the extreme—

'Jasper?'

I reeled myself in at Aunt Flo's sharper tone. An apologetic glance her way showed pursed lips and a disapproving glint in her eye. I was usually more circumspect but being in the same vicinity as Wren Bingham always scuppered my concentration.

I cleared my throat. 'Of course I'll behave. Scouts' honour.' The woman who'd been more of a mother to me than my own living parent snorted her disbelief.

'As if they'd have let you anywhere near a Scouts camp. You'd have scandalised them all within an hour.'

I grinned at her no-nonsense reply because her tone was couched in familiar, reassuring warmth. Warmth I let wash over me to disperse the soul-shrivelling chill that came from thinking about my birth mother, which inevitably led to thoughts about my father. Specifically, their arctic wind of rejection, far more brutal than any winter I'd experienced since their desertion. No, tonight most definitely wasn't the time to dwell on that noxious period of my childhood and how it'd ruined not just me but my siblings, too.

Tonight was about bringing recalcitrant business partners to heel. Mostly…

After another search failed to reveal my elusive prey, I focused once more on Wren, that compulsion since Aunt Flo and I had walked through the impressive double doors of the Bingham mansion in Esher forty-five minutes ago pulling at me.

So far I hadn't spotted Wren's brother, Perry Bingham, my primary reason for being here. Sure, I'd nodded and reassured my favourite aunt that accompanying her to this soirée was my pleasure and the right Mortimer thing to do. Also because, on some weird rota only Aunt Flo was privy to, it was apparently my turn to escort her to another social function. What I'd failed to mention was that I was on the hunt for Perry Bingham, CEO of Bingham Industries, who had stopped answering my calls for nearly two weeks, thereby threatening to throw one serious spanner into my latest project.

With my patience wearing thin, I'd grasped the opportunity to track him down at his family estate. Except it looked as if he was a no-show here, too.

But Wren was here, and I intended to drill his sister about his whereabouts. My choice of words brought an inner smirk I wisely kept off my face as I downed my whisky and turned to my aunt.

'Can I get you another drink?' I indicated her half-empty glass of sherry.

Several waitstaff circulated with trays of drinks but I didn't plan to grab one from them. Not when Wren stood next to the bar, chatting with two of her guests. As I watched, she threw her head back in laughter, her smooth, swanlike neck thrown into perfect relief.

Immediately, I imagined my lips there, beneath

her jawline, tasting her silky skin, then lower, tonguing her pulse. Would she cry out in delight or moan with pleasure?

'We both know that's an excuse to get away from me. Go on, then. Just don't do anything we'd both be ashamed of come morning, would you? I could do without a Mortimer tabloid scandal before Christmas,' Aunt Flo said.

Brushing a kiss on a well-preserved cheek, I muttered, 'You've taught me the importance of not making promises I can't keep. Don't make me start now.'

She rolled her eyes but her smile deepened.

I grinned again as I made a beeline for the bar, and I wasn't one little bit ashamed to admit that I was hard as stone.

I made sure to wipe the smile off my face, my eyes settling in the middle distance to prevent business acquaintances engaging me in conversation. A few feet from Wren, I paused to ponder why this woman, amongst so many others, had fired me up ever since she'd crossed my path five years ago.

Perhaps it was discovering that, far from being a superficial heiress and supermodel flitting around the globe between the ages of nineteen and twenty-three, she'd attained a master's degree in business while slaying the runways of the fashion capitals of the world. More besides, she'd graduated top of her class and was, at twenty-eight, now on course to become one of the youngest power executives in the city. Or perhaps it was some twisted attraction born from our family being embroiled in a generations-old feud, which dictated we should hate each other on sight like some pathetic Roman tragedy.

Whatever. All I knew was that Wren had intrigued me with increasing intensity over the past few years.

Intense empire-building in order to establish my role in my family's company as President of New Developments in Europe, Africa and the Middle East, and perhaps even the arrogant belief that our chemistry was a passing whim and wasn't worth turning my family upside down for, had so far kept me from pursuing Wren, but each encounter only deepened whatever this phenomenal chemistry was that stopped me from seeing any other woman but her whenever we were in each other's orbit.

Lately, I'd accepted that it simply wasn't going to go away by itself, as I'd assumed. Not until I did something about it.

I realised my motionless state was drawing curious attention from nearby guests, not to mention Aunt Flo's disapproving glare from across the terrace.

Discarding my glass, I stepped beside Wren. 'Good evening, Wren. You look incredible.' I said, my voice pitched low.

She tried not to stiffen, but didn't quite succeed, nor could she disguise the flare of awareness in her vivid green eyes when she turned to me. She didn't reply immediately, instead she scrambled for the jaded expression that had been her trademark in her modelling days.

I stifled the urge to tell her not to bother. Witnessing a demonstration of her fiery passion and stiletto-sharp business acumen five years ago across a boardroom table for an unforgettable fifteen minutes had etched a different Wren Bingham in my mind from the façade she wore for the public.

'Jasper Mortimer.'

The way she said my name, striving to be curt when different textures sizzled beneath, ramped up my temperature. I wanted her attempting to say my name just like that while she was tied to my bed with silken restraints, naked and wet.

'I don't recall seeing your name on the guest list.'

Pausing just as long as she did before answering, I snagged a glass of champagne from the bar. 'Because it wasn't there. I'm privileged to be my aunt's plus one. What I haven't had the privilege of is being acknowledged by the hostess since my arrival. I'm feeling sorely neglected.'

She tried to look through me, as if that would stop the arc of electricity zapping between us. As if she hadn't performed a quick once-over of my body as I got my drink. I planted myself in her line of vision until she had no choice but to focus on me, her nostrils flaring slightly as her green eyes—alluringly wide and sparkling with an interest she was trying to hide—connected with mine.

I barely heard her guests murmur their excuses and drift away, leaving us in a tight little cocoon.

'Perhaps I would've already greeted you, if you hadn't arrived half an hour late.'

I curbed a smile, inordinately pleased she'd noticed my arrival. 'I'm willing to make amends by doubling my donation to tonight's cause.'

One elegantly shaped eyebrow arched. 'Name it.'

I frowned. 'Name what?'

'The beneficiary of tonight's cause. What's this mixer in aid of?' she challenged.

Crap. I'd tuned Aunt Flo out when she'd mentioned it in the car, my frustrated attention on the echo of the ringing phone Perry was—yet again—refusing to answer. 'Something to do with pandas in Indonesia?' I hazarded.

Sparks gathered in her eyes. 'Why am I not surprised you don't know?'

Heat surged through me. 'That suggests a curious level of personal knowledge. Have you been attempting to get to know me behind my back, Wren?'

She gave the smallest gasp, then tried that bored look again. 'I've no idea what you're talking about. I can't help it if others feel the need to gossip about you Mortimers.'

'Oh, yeah? What else do they say about me? What else has that brilliant brain of yours retained?'

Her nose wrinkled in distaste. 'Nothing worth repeating.'

Unable to resist, I stepped closer. 'Are you sure?

I'm happy to hear you out, set a few things straight if you get anything wrong.'

She didn't reply. After an age of trying to decipher which I liked more on her skin—the scent of bergamot or the underlying allure of crushed lilies—I looked up to catch her gaze on my mouth.

Hell yes, that insane chemistry was still very much alive and well—and sizzling, as usual.

'Stop that,' she said in a tight undertone.

I raised my glass, took a lazy sip before answering. 'Stop what?'

'That extremely unsubtle way you're looking at me,' she hissed in a ferocious whisper, then glanced around. Thankfully, the music was loud enough for her words to reach my ears only. 'The way you look at me every time we meet.'

I laughed under my breath. 'And how do I look at you, Wren?'

'You might lure some women with those come-fuck-me eyes but I'm not one of them so stop wasting your time.'

My laughter was a little louder, genuine amusement reminding me how long it'd been since I'd enjoyed the thrill of a chase outside the boardroom. 'Come-fuck-me eyes? Really?' I didn't bother to keep my voice down.

Several people stared but I watched Wren, keenly interested in her next move.

She flashed the patently false smile she'd been doling out all evening but I caught the strain beneath the thousand-watt beam. Taking in the rest of her, I sensed tension in her lithe frame, in the fingers that clutched her glass a little too firmly. For reasons I suspected went beyond our conversation, Wren was wound extremely tight tonight.

And I was curiously concerned about it. 'Is everything okay?'

'Of course. Why shouldn't it be?'

I shrugged. 'You seem a little…stressed.'

Her chin notched upward. 'You don't know me well enough to make that assessment.'

'Ah, but I've attended enough of these shindigs to see when the hostess is fretting about the vegan-to-carnivore ratio of her canapés, and when it's something more. This is something more.'

Her delicate throat moved in a nervous swallow, but her gaze remained bold and direct, swirling with a deep, passionate undercurrent I craved to drown in. 'Even *if* it's the latter, it's none of your business. Now, if you'll excuse me—'

'Where's Perry?'

She froze mid-brush-off, her eyes widening fractionally. 'What?'

No, she wasn't as carefree as she pretended.

The rumours that Bingham's was in trouble had been circulating for a few years now. The veracity of those rumours was partly why I'd initially been reticent about joining forces with them. But, hell, call me a sucker… I'd always had a thing for the underdog.

Maybe it was a hangover from my daddy issues.

Or a tool I used to my advantage when idiots under-estimated me. Either way, my instincts hadn't failed me thus far.

There were certain family and board members who considered me, at thirty-one, too young for the position I was in, notwithstanding the fact that my older brother, Damian, and my cousin Gideon had been wildly successful in their newly minted co-CEO positions of the entire Mortimer Group despite being only a few years older. Or that my cousin Bryce was acing his similar position as President of New Developments in Asia and Australia. Even my sister, Gemma, and my cousin Graciela, who'd both resisted joining the board until recently, were excelling in their chosen areas of expertise.

I was damned if I'd let Perry Bingham's antics prove them right. Especially after going against all my business instincts and signing him onto my deal.

'There's nothing wrong with your hearing, Wren. Where's your brother?' I steeled my voice because, however much I enjoyed this erotic dance with her, Perry was at risk of tanking everything I'd worked for during the last eighteen months.

Several expressions filtered through her eyes—alarm, worry, irritation, mild disappointment. She finally settled on indignation. 'Is that why you came?'

'I told you, I accompanied Aunt Flo—'

'A ruse to hunt down my brother,' she interjected.

'That implies awareness that he's hiding. Is he?'

A look flickered across her face, gone too quickly

but revealing enough to intensify the unease knotting my belly. 'Tell me where he is, Wren,' I pressed. 'He's been avoiding my calls for almost two weeks and it's getting really old.'

'I'm afraid you'll have to do your own hunting. I'm not Perry's keeper.' Her tense reply gave her away. As did the minuscule tremble in the fingers that held her glass. Both intrigued and disturbed me but before I could push for more, she added, 'You've monopolised me quite enough. Enjoy the rest of your evening, Jasper.'

Just for the hell of it, and because something wild and reckless yearned for another demonstration that she wasn't immune to me, I brushed my fingertips down her arm. 'This isn't over.'

She attempted to cover her tiny shiver of awareness with a wide sultry smile that diverted my attention to her luscious lips. 'How can something be over when it didn't start in the first place?'

With that, she sailed away, her hips swaying in that unique way that'd held male and female gazes rapt during her modelling days. Since then, Wren had gained even more confidence in her womanhood, and left a swathe of admirers slack-jawed in her wake. I wracked my brain, trying to recall if she had a current boyfriend. The gut-tightening rejection at the idea of her being attached made me grimace into my champagne.

Until my gaze fell on the woman who placed herself directly in Wren's path before manoeuvring her away from the nearest guest.

Agnes Bingham—Wren's mother and powerhouse socialite in her own right.

The tall, slim woman was what Wren would look like in thirty years. Except where Agnes's beauty was classically cool, Wren was vibrant, passionate, even though she seemed hell-bent on suppressing it.

Why?

None of your business.

But I wanted to make it my business. I wanted Wren in my bed and damn all the consequences to hell. And more and more I suspected I wouldn't get over this fever in my blood until I'd had her.

Tension of a different kind raced up my spine when mother and daughter glanced my way. The touch of rebellion in Wren's gaze made me raise my glass in a mocking toast, even while I observed the animosity emanating from Agnes Bingham.

Bloody hell.

Family feuds, Perry Bingham going AWOL and now Agnes Bingham. Three stumbling blocks in my intent to have Wren. But despite the damning words my father had taken pleasure in decimating me with as a child, I wasn't afraid of a challenge.

All the same, my gut twisted as I made my way back to my aunt, the thought of broaching the subject of my father making my stomach curdle.

'Everything okay?' Aunt Flo asked, after smiling an excuse to the guest she'd been chatting to.

I let her fondness wash over me for a moment before I pulled myself together. Wishing her warm concern came from a different female voice had been fruitless when I was a child. It was even more foolish now. The woman who'd given birth to me wasn't interested in taking up her maternal role. Not for her first or second born, and certainly not for me, her third child. My arrival had spelled the end to her obligation and she couldn't get away fast enough. Years of hoping, of saving my allowance in a childish hope of enticing her financially had been laughed off. I was no longer ten years old, fighting to stop myself from crying as Damian advised me to give up my foolish hoping.

'George Bingham. I need to know the full story,' I said to Aunt Flo, my low voice brisker than she deserved.

'What's brought this on? You've never wanted to know before,' she said after eyeing me in frowning silence.

I shrugged, moving her away to the more private edge of the terrace. 'I've never cared enough about the finer details. Now I do because whatever happened all those years ago is endangering an important deal and I've just about had it.'

'Dear boy, money isn't—'

My bitter laugh stopped her. 'Do me a favour, please, and don't finish that sentence, Aunt Flo. We both know money is definitely everything to any red-blooded Mortimer.'

She harrumphed. 'Well, I don't agree but, since you seem to have a bee in your bonnet about it, I'll let it go. To answer your question, it was your father's last deal before he and your mother stepped away from the company, and the family. He and George Bingham were supposed to go fifty-fifty but George messed up somehow and could only come up with a fraction of the investment by the deadline date. There was a clause in their agreement that it was fifty-fifty or nothing and that loophole gave your father the right to cut him out regardless of how much money he'd pumped into the deal up to then. He didn't take it well. He wasted money he didn't have trying to sue your father. But Hugh was a brilliant, if somewhat ruthless, businessman.'

There was no *somewhat* about it. I'd come across some of his deals while my father had actively worked in the family firm. His cut-throat antics were legendary. If you liked blood and gore with your negotiations.

A memory shot through my head. 'Was closing that Bingham deal part of my father's walking-away package?' I asked.

Aunt Flo sighed. 'Yes, it was. Back then, every deal closed by a member of the board came with a ten-per-cent profit bonus. Cutting out Bingham and making it an exclusive Mortimer deal meant Hugh received a bigger bonus. About two hundred million.'

And he was probably in such a hurry to walk

away from his family that he'd been unflinchingly ruthless. 'I see.'

'What's going on, Jasper?' Aunt Flo asked curiously.

The cocktail of bitterness, anger and arousal swirled faster inside me as I looked over her shoulder to find Wren watching me. 'It's just business.'

'No, it's not. You're not cut-throat like your father. But you're just as dogged. I had my reservations when I heard about your deal with Perry, considering his problems,' she murmured. 'But knowing you, you'll move mountains to make it work.'

'Forgive me if I don't welcome the comparison to Hugh,' I rasped.

Her eyes clouded with momentary sadness. 'His blood may run through your veins but you're your own man where it counts, Jasper. Whatever you're getting involved in, just…protect your heart. I don't want to see you hurt again.'

Another harsh laugh bubbled up, but I swallowed it down. And just about managed to stop myself from telling her that, while I'd struck a deal with Perry Bingham in a moment of madness, perhaps even a sting of conscience and despite Perry's rumoured drinking problem, somewhere in the mix was the reasoning that it would put me in a good position to strike a better deal with Wren in the near future. Business-wise and in other ways, too.

'You have that gleam in your eye, Jasper. Am I

wasting my breath by telling you to be a dear and spare my nerves?' Aunt Flo asked.

I couldn't promise that. Hell, I *knew* there would be plenty more fireworks between Wren and me in the future. 'I can promise dinner at The Dorchester as soon as my schedule lets up a little. I know how much you like their new chef. We can check out the competition in the process.'

She smiled. 'Cecil is a culinary genius. And very easy on the eyes. I'll hold you to that promise,' she said, just before another acquaintance snagged her attention.

Briefly alone, I tried to suppress the tangled emotions churning through me.

I don't want to see you hurt again.

As much as I wanted to put my parents out of my mind for ever, to rub them from my existence as much as they'd rubbed me from theirs, the ten-year-old boy's anguish from relentless rejection, which I'd never been quite successful in smothering, wouldn't let me. But it was a good reminder not to count on anyone but myself. Not to let frivolous emotion get in the way of business.

I wanted this deal with Bingham because it was sound and profitable.

I also wanted to fuck Wren Bingham, once she got over the pesky family-feud thing. The two were mutually exclusive enough not to cause me to lose any sleep.

Which was why when Wren hurried away from

her mother, her shoulders tight with barely-harnessed emotions, I followed.

She was heading towards the far end of the grounds, her heels sinking soundlessly into the grass. She didn't hear me until I was six feet from her.

'Wren?'

Her head whipped around. 'Are you following me?' she asked sharply. But then she trembled. A tiny reaction, but, coupled with the slight wobble of her mouth, it hastened my steps, the peculiar punch in my chest unsettling me.

'What's wrong?'

'Other than the fact that you're stalking me now?'

'Hardly. You just seem—'

'There's nothing wrong. Just leave me alone, please?'

I looked beyond her to the high hedges of what looked like an elaborate garden. 'If everything's fine, why are you running away from your own party?'

'I'm not running away. And it's not my party—' She caught herself and snatched in a deep breath. 'Why the hell am I explaining myself to you?'

'Because sometimes it helps to vent.' Not that it'd done me much good. Ever. All my good intentions had ended in disaster, the repercussions of which I still lived with. But this wasn't the time or place to examine old scars. 'Or so I've heard, anyway.'

'Do you go around dishing out inexperienced advice?'

I shook my head, unwilling to drag my far from

delightful childhood into this moment. 'We're not talking about me.'

'You're right, we're not. In fact, I'm going to pretend you're not here at all. Feel free to make that a reality,' she suggested, right before she turned on her heel and marched away from me.

And since I was far too intrigued to heed her brush-off... I followed.

If she gave even a hint of needing comfort, I'd offer her a shoulder, and other parts of my body, to cry on.

Bloody hell. I cringed at my own crassness. Then shrugged it off. *I am who I am.* And that person wanted Wren Bingham any way he could get her. Besides that, though, I was here on Mortimer business. Technically.

She ignored me until she reached a bricked pathway. Then she turned and stared at me for several seconds without speaking. For a moment, a deep yearning flitted over her face, then her expression blanked. 'You're really not going to leave me alone, are you?' she murmured.

'Not until you tell me what's wrong.' Before she could reply, I jerked my chin at the hedge. 'What's behind there?'

Her eyes narrowed, her fingers twitching against her thighs. 'Nothing interesting. Just the garden. A pool. Gazebo. The usual.'

She was lying. Or at least holding something back. 'What else?'

'Why do you want to know?' she demanded, then flinched as someone laughed loudly nearby.

'You look like you need a breather. What's out there?'

'A maze,' she confessed with reluctance. 'I go there sometimes…to think.'

Before my brain could growl its warning that this was a bad idea, I stepped closer. 'Show me.'

She tensed. 'Excuse me?'

'I'd like to see this maze. A quick tour. Then, if you still insist, I'll leave.'

Something flickered in her eyes, undercurrents of lust zinging between us. Her gaze dropped to my lips and I almost wanted to crow in triumph. 'Fine. Let's go.'

She wrapped her scarf tighter around her neck and I stopped myself from mourning the loss of the sight of her satiny skin.

Even in the cold, my libido was racing feverishly. I cleared my throat. 'So, what was that with your mother?'

Stubborn fire lit her eyes. 'I'll allow you to stay on condition we don't talk about my mother. Or any member of my family.'

I didn't protest her condition. Families like mine were complicated and she didn't need to vocalise her feelings towards hers for me to get it. Why that little commonality turned me on, I refused to contemplate.

In silence we walked along a dark red-bricked pavement until we reached a tall iron gate set into a walled-off section of the garden. Pushing it open, we followed the path until we reached a tall hedge the size of a barn door that remained full and thick despite the low temperatures. Wren's hand disappeared between the leaves and a section of the hedge sprang open.

With another glance at me, she stepped inside. I followed and stepped onto two diverging paths. She took the left one, her footsteps barely making a sound on the grass as we walked between tall hedgerows. Further chunks had been cut out intermittently and lower hedges transformed into shapes of animals, with a large space transformed into a picnic area with benches and seats.

We went deeper into the maze, her head bent forward as if weighed down by her emotions. I wanted to reach out and cup my hand over her nape, test the suppleness of her skin, feel that electricity between us. Instead, I shoved my hands into my pockets, willed the urge to pass. Jumping her right now would be the wrong move.

Eventually her steps slowed. 'We're almost at the centre,' she said, her voice low, as if she didn't want to speak.

'How big is this place?'

She shrugged. 'Big enough when you're a child seeking adventure. Not big enough when you're a teenager, attempting to flee from your demons.'

I wanted to ask about her demons but her pursed lips suggested she already regretted her revealing statement. I tried a different tack, hoping to take her mind off whatever was bothering her. 'Tell me one good memory you have of your maze.'

She didn't speak for several seconds, and I watched as she trailed her fingers over the tall green foliage. 'That's easy. I had my first kiss in here.'

Envy knotted my stomach. 'It was that good?'

She shook her head. 'It was that bad. It's what happened afterwards that makes it a good memory.'

'Tell me more,' I said, intrigued by the barely there but infinitely more genuine smile tugging up the corners of her full lips.

'I told Winslow Parker I didn't want to be kissed.' She shrugged. 'Call me shallow but I didn't want my first kiss to be from a boy named Winslow with a wet nose and clammy hands. He went ahead and stole a kiss anyway. So I blocked the exit to the maze and left him to freeze his arse off for three hours. When I came back to rescue him, he was crying.'

My lips twitched, a wicked part of me enjoying hearing that her first kiss had been less than memorable. 'So you enjoy making boys cry?'

We reached a dead end and she turned to face me. 'If they deserve it? Absolutely.'

A compulsion I didn't want to fight pulled me closer until I towered over her. Until she had to raise her head to meet my gaze. Despite the darkness around us, every inch of her stunning face and graceful neck was exposed to my keen gaze. 'What else do you enjoy making boys do?'

'I'm not nine years old any more. I'm a grown woman and I prefer grown men to boys now,' she murmured, her gaze fixed boldly on mine. A shiver caught her a second later and I drew closer, locking my fingers in the trellised hedge, caging her in.

'And what do you want this grown man to do for you?' I asked, aware my voice was gruff with the lustful urges running rampant through my bloodstream.

She stared at me for a minute, then cast her gaze around her, looking a little lost for a minute. 'Is it bad to say I don't want to be here? That if I could leave right now, get on a plane and go far away, I would?'

'Because of your mother?'

Her eyes darkened and she didn't repudiate me for ignoring her condition. 'Amongst other things.'

I got it. A long time ago, I'd accepted that it was better my parents lived in another country. Out of sight…out of mind…out of heartache… 'There's absolutely nothing wrong with wishing to be elsewhere.'

'But I can't, can I?'

I didn't answer because there was no right answer to that. I was born into a family where bullshit and dysfunction were the norm but where conversely fierce loyalty and absolute dedication to duty were the cornerstones that held most of us together. I suspected the Binghams were the same.

'Tell me what you want, Wren,' I said instead.

I watched a hot, determined look slowly fill her eyes. She shivered again and my gaze dropped to where her nipples had turned into twin points of succulent torture. Whether her body's reaction was from the cold or the arousal gathering heat in her eyes, I wasn't completely sure. Still, I shrugged off my jacket, draped it over her shoulders, wrapped my hands around her trim waist.

And waited.

Slowly, she slicked her tongue over her bottom lip. I bit back a groan as blood gleefully rushed south.

'Distract me,' she said, a mixture of challenge and pleading in the low, thick words that hardened my rousing cock. 'I don't want to go back to the party. I don't want to make stupid small talk. So just… make me stop thinking about all the crap I have to deal with now that…' She stopped and took a shaky breath.

Despite the flames licking through my veins, I hesitated. 'Are you sure?'

Her gaze grew defiant. 'Are you a boy or a man, Jasper Mortimer?'

I gave a low laugh. 'You don't want to ask me that, even as a challenge.'

'Why not? Will you punish me?' Her voice was breathless, edged with sexual anticipation.

My cock leapt to full attention. Jesus. 'Is that what you really want, Wren? For me to turn you around against this hedge and spank your tight little rump red for daring to question my manhood?'

Her eyes darkened, her mouth parting on a hot little pant. When her hips jerked forward a fraction, I yanked her the rest of the way, until our groins connected. Until she felt the hard, eager rod of my cock against her soft belly.

Hunger exploded over her face, her hands rising to grip my neck. 'Do your worst,' she invited with bite.

I fused my mouth to hers in a rough, carnal kiss powered by every single filthy fantasy I'd had about this woman. And there were hundreds. Thousands.

She opened for me immediately, her tongue gliding against mine in an erotic caress that weakened my knees. I tasted it, sucked on it, bit the tip and felt her shudder. Deepening the kiss, I trailed my hands up her flat belly and midriff to cup her soft, heavy breasts. Another moan escaped her, crushed between our lips as the kiss grew even more frantic.

She tasted intoxicating. Like the shot of adrenaline that brought every sense into vivid focus. I brushed my thumbs over the hard peaks of her nipples, then, giving into the wild clamouring, I nudged her zip halfway down her belly and pushed aside her bra. Before her gasp was fully formed, I swooped down and drew the exposed tip into my mouth. I suckled long and deep, then flicked my tongue rapidly over her burning flesh.

Her fingers bit into my nape. 'God…yes!'

Frantically, I freed the other breast, caught the tip between my fingers and teased. Her fingers gripped my nape, her breathing erratic as she held me to her breasts. After delivering equal amounts of attention to each, I pulled back, again wracked with the need to see her face.

She looked even more spectacular than before. Defiant. Aroused. Wanton.

'You're so fucking gorgeous,' I groaned.

An impatient sound escaped her, intensifying the heat in my veins. Dragging my hands from her breasts, I cupped her bottom, using the firm globes to pull her harder into my erection. She rewarded me by grinding her pelvis against my length, drawing needy sounds from both of us.

'I really, *really* want to fuck you, Wren,' I confessed, my voice a hot mess. 'I've wanted you since you stepped into my boardroom five years ago.'

She gave a cheeky little laugh, her eyes lighting up for the first time tonight. 'You mean when I turned down your internship offer?'

My fingers tightened on her bottom. 'I'll freely admit, I'm still a little salty about that.'

Her smile widened. 'Poor Jasper. Not used to hearing no?'

I smiled in return. 'I'm only sore at losing when what I want goes to a less worthy competitor. We both know why you turned me down.'

She licked her lips, her eyes lingering hungrily on mine. 'Pray, enlighten me.'

I wasn't going to ruin the moment by mentioning our family feud. 'Because neither of us likes to mix business with pleasure,' I said instead, running my thumb over her lower lip. Immediately her teeth nipped at my flesh, drawing a deep groan.

'I'm not going to confirm or deny that assertion.'

'Have it your way. I still want you. Badly.'

Eyes wild with defiance, she nodded eagerly, sucking my thumb into her mouth for a few seconds before she released me. 'Yes. *Now.*'

I planted a long kiss on her mouth as I lowered her zip. Only to groan when shocking reality hit me. For ten long seconds I remained paralysed. 'Shit.'

'What?' Her voice was beautifully slurred, her gaze hazy with arousal as she stared up at me. I wanted more of that look. Wanted to watch her shatter completely. Wanted to feel her pussy grip my cock as waves of ecstasy rolled over her.

'I don't have a condom,' I confessed through gritted teeth.

She stared at me blankly for a few seconds before disappointment drenched her beautiful face. 'Oh.'

I clenched my jaw tighter, unwilling to let go of this unique moment. 'Are you on the Pill?' I asked with more than a little hope. It wasn't my usual practice. I liked to be in complete control of my sexual fate. But just this once I prayed for a *yes*.

'No,' she replied, pained resignation in her voice.

'There are other ways, Wren.' I pulled her closer, trailed my lips over her jaw until I reached her ear. 'Let me make you come with my mouth. I want to taste you on my tongue. Lick you dry. You want to be transported? I can't do it with my cock but I can give you a little relief. Don't you want that?'

For a moment, she wavered, on the verge of calling quits on this madness. Selfishly, I didn't want to let her.

'I will eat you out for as long as you want me to. Think about how much I'll suffer while you do. You get to ride my face while you torture the hell out of me,' I invited.

Her fingers clenched harder into my skin. 'Yes,' she responded breathlessly. 'Please. Yes.'

Satisfied that I had her back in the moment with me, I caught the soft fabric of her jumpsuit between my fingers, careful not to wrinkle the material. Normally I wouldn't care but she had to return to a party filled with gossip-hungry guests and a mother she was clearly locked in tense disagreement with. I didn't want to draw any more attention to what we'd been doing than necessary.

I trailed my lips back to hers and kissed her hard before releasing her. 'Take this thing off for me,' I instructed.

Soft hands drifted down my forearms and wrists and covered mine for a second before she complied. I stepped back, eager for a snapshot of her leaning against her favourite hedge, undressing for me.

When she stepped out of the jumpsuit, I re-draped my jacket over her shoulders to keep her warm.

Call me primitive but the sight of her in my clothing threatened to undo me. With her hair loose and straight and falling around her face, her upper body almost lost in my coat and her lower half almost exposed to the elements, she was breathtaking. Her legs alone were worth an extra minute of worship. But it was cold, and we couldn't stay out here for ever.

With more than a throb of regret, I stepped forward and trailed the backs of my hands up her inner thighs. She gave a soft gasp and quivered. My gaze raced up from her thighs to her face, unwilling to lose a second of her reaction. Her lips were parted, her eyes hooded but not shut. She watched my hand draw closer to where her pussy was hidden behind a layer of sexy black lace.

'Open your legs wider.'

Her gaze rose and caught on mine for a second before she obeyed, widening her stance until I could fit my closed fist at the juncture of her thighs. Slowly I dragged my knuckle lightly against her flesh; from where she was hot and sodden to the swollen nub pushing against the fabric.

She gasped again, thicker, louder, her breath a puff of vapour in the air between us. I repeated the action. She caught her lips between her teeth and moaned.

'You like that?'

She gave a jerky nod, her gaze once again dropping to follow my hand. On the next turn her hips rolled, her body chasing the exquisite sensation. I felt her grow hotter, wetter with need.

'More,' she moaned on the next pass.

'Look at me, Wren.'

Her gaze rose. Defiant fire and deep arousal. God, what a combination. I cupped her chin to hold her gaze, then I slipped my fingers beneath her panty line.

A wet, decadent sound wrapped itself around her gasp as I inserted two fingers inside her. She was hot. And wet. And so damned tight. For the first time in my life I wondered how it would feel to fuck a woman bareback. To replace my fingers with my cock and experience that snug channel sucking me in.

Her hips moved and she gave a greedy little moan. Slowly, I withdrew and pushed back inside her. Her mouth dropped open and her eyes glazed.

'You're gorgeous when you're lost in pleasure. Do you want more, Wren?'

Without replying, she shifted her stance wider, wrapped her hand around my wrist and directed my movements, pressing my fingers inside her.

'I'll take that as a yes?'

Despite the rampant arousal coursing through her, her eyes flashed at me, reminding me that beyond this temporary haven of her maze our families detested each other. That she was using me simply because I was here. That any man who happened to be in her vicinity at the right time would probably have done?

No. Every cell in my body rejected that idea.

'Either you're too turned on to speak or you're

attempting to make this a party for one.' I resisted her when she attempted to hasten my movements. I slowed down, then pressed my thumb against her engorged clit. She shuddered hard, and a hoarse cry broke from her lips. 'Which one is it, Wren?'

'I… I…'

I moved my thumb again and another cry ripped free. 'Do you want me to make you come, baby?'

She hesitated for a mutinous second. Then nodded frantically. *'Yes,'* she hissed.

'Then I want to hear exactly how you want it. And I want you to say my name when you do.' I hoped she wasn't dating anyone, but hell if I was going to be a replacement for some absent arsehole.

I circled my thumb and her head jerked back, pushing into the hedge. 'I want it deeper, Jasper. Faster.'

I smiled in unashamed triumph and increased the tempo. Immediately, she got even wetter…

Bloody hell. Any more and she would blow the top of my head clean off. Or more likely make me blow my load in my pants like a damned schoolboy. But I couldn't stop fucking her with my fingers any more than I could stop breathing. The sounds she was making from both sets of her lips were driving me insane.

'Slide two fingers into your mouth for me, baby. Make them nice and wet.'

Her eyes widened but she obeyed my instruction. The sight of her sliding her digits slowly into her mouth was almost too much to bear. Unable to resist, I swooped down and added my tongue to the play, licking her fingers as she withdrew them. Her pussy clenched around my fingers, a sign that she'd enjoyed that little action. I filed it at the back of my mind for next time as she rested her wet fingers against her lips.

'I have a few ideas of what you can do with those fingers. But I'd love to see you play with your gorgeous nipples.'

Her breath caught then released, and her fingers dropped to one exposed, beaded nipple. Slowly, she circled the bud, gasping as sensation piled high. Then she transferred her attention to the other peak, her breath coming faster as she pleasured herself.

Her pussy began to tighten around my fingers, making pushing inside her both a sizzling thrill and a torture. She wetted two more fingers, then, with both hands, tugged and tortured her nipples as I pumped inside her.

In under a minute, she started to unravel. And it was the most stunning thing I'd ever seen.

'Don't stop. Please… I'm close. So close…' Her hips jerked as she chased her bliss. With a sharp cry, she started to come.

Driven by lust, I dropped to my knees and replaced my thumb with my mouth. Gripping her thighs to hold her open, I sucked her clit hard and long.

A keening cry surged up her throat, the sound

tormenting me as I groaned and sucked her harder. Rolling convulsions slammed into her, fresh wetness dripping over my lips.

'Jasper!'

Frantic fingers gripped my hair and her whole body shook wildly. I cupped her bottom to hold her steady as her knees weakened and her body sagged. I wanted to eat her pussy for ever, but her frantic whimpers turned a little urgent.

The kind that suggested reality was returning.

I stayed an extra minute, licked her clean with gentle laps of my tongue as her trembling quieted and the hold in my hair loosened. And just for the hell of it and because she was too addictive to resist, I shoved my fingers inside her one last time as I kissed my way up her body to her mouth. Our lips fused and our tongues tangled for another minute while I committed her taste to memory before removing my fingers from her.

Still watching her, I brought my hands to my mouth and licked the last of her taste off. When I was done, I readjusted her knickers and helped her redress.

Silence throbbed between us as she furiously avoided my gaze. I suppressed a sigh and shoved my fists into my pocket to stop myself from reaching for her.

'Are you okay?'

She stared at me for a handful of seconds before

she nodded. 'Yes.' Another several seconds drifted by. Then, 'Thank you.'

'My pleasure,' I replied, my voice more than a little gruff.

Her gaze dropped tellingly to the raging hard-on tenting my trousers. I laughed around the agony of my erection. 'Believe it or not, watching you come was a pleasure. Maybe we can—'

The words dried in my throat as her expression altered. Within a blink of an eye she was no longer the sated siren at one with the foliage around her.

She was a cool and collected princess, dispensing rejection. 'This was a one-time thing. Gratefully received but something I intend to forget at the earliest opportunity.'

Disappointment—and, yes, blistering anger because I'd hoped this could be the start of…something—unravelled through me. 'You think I'm that forgettable, sweetheart?' I asked, modulating my voice to that deceptive pitch that always confused my opponents. They weren't sure whether I was pissed off or indulging whatever mood they were in.

Fleeting uncertainty chased across her face before she marshalled it.

'I do.' She handed back my jacket, her lips once again curved in that fake, dismissive smile. 'Because it's already in the past,' she said.

'Like hell it is. We're going to fuck, Wren. I'm going to make you come many, many more times. It's simply a matter of when.'

I gave her props for attempting to fight her excitement. She fussed with her hair, rearranged her scarf and tugged her zip another fraction upwards. And when she achieved that facade of outrage, I allowed it. I intended to disprove it at the very next opportunity.

'I allowed a moment of temporary madness, Jasper. Don't hold your breath that it'll happen again.'

She started to walk away. I shrugged on my jacket and followed. 'Wren.'

She paused without turning.

I stepped around to face her. 'I still want to know where your brother is. This time I'm not taking no for an answer.'

The eyes she lifted to mine were haunted, filled with the tension I'd sensed in her all evening. For a handful of seconds, she pressed her lips together. Then her gaze shifted away from mine. 'I don't know.'

Instinct suggested she wasn't lying. 'When was the last time you heard from him?'

A shaft of pain crossed her flawless features. 'My mother spoke to him a week ago.'

Her mother. Not her. Was that the reason for the tension between them?

'I need to reach him, Wren.'

Her face tightened. 'Is that why you followed me here? To pump me for information?'

I bit back my irritation. 'We both know what just happened has been a long time coming, pun intended. Don't demean it.'

Her eyes flickered and I could've sworn she blushed. Slightly mollified, I trailed my knuckles over her warm cheek. 'Doesn't change the fact that I still need to hear from Perry, though.' I dropped my hand. 'When you do get in touch with him, tell him it's in his interest to contact me, asap.' Knowing I needed to leave before I gave in to the urge to re-enact that heady episode again, I stepped away.

'That sounds like a threat,' she challenged.

I turned back to the woman I intended to have, again and again, in the very near future, and smiled. 'You can see it as such if you want. It's a simple statement that says I'm done playing games. He's fucking around with something important to me. Sooner or later, he's going to have to answer to me. How much mercy I show him is entirely up to him.'

CHAPTER TWO

THE FILES ON the desk in front of me had increased three-fold in the last three weeks. Each one was flagged with a red Post-it note that indicated it required urgent attention.

Except three weeks ago, I'd been in *front* of the desk and Perry behind it. My brother had been the CEO with the full backing of the board of directors at Bingham Industries. Whereas I'd had to fight my way into an *acting* CEO position, even after Perry finally resurfaced a few days ago and accepted that he needed help.

Unfortunately, it'd been too late to stop the tabloids from splashing his alcohol-fuelled downward spiral on the front pages, plunging the company into a stock-market nightmare and me into a fight to protect my own family firm from ruin.

Bitterness soured my mouth as I inched my chair closer to the desk. I'd been here for fifteen minutes and was yet to reach for the first file.

I couldn't. Not because I was scared. Far from it.

I couldn't reach for it because everything in this office reeked of my father. With strong undertones of Perry, the son and heir he'd treasured above everyone else. Including me.

Both hard, intransigent men with firm, ingrained views about a woman's place. Perry had tried to disguise his beneath brotherly concern, but that conceit had been there, inherited from the man he'd looked up to. A man who'd taken reckless risks with the Bingham name and died bitter and broken when those risks had shattered his family.

With hands I refused to let shake, I reached for the phone. My PA answered on the first ring. 'Alana, can you find me a replacement desk asap? Ideally today?'

'I…yes, of course. Right away, Miss Bingham. What do you want done with the old one?'

'Have it couriered to the house in Esher. They can put it in my father's study.'

I set the phone down, took a deep cleansing breath. My position as Acting CEO might well be temporary if I lost my fight against the Big Boys Establishment that were my uncles and cousins. But I intended to do things my way for however long I was here.

And before my stint ends, I'll show them…

That silent vow echoing through me, I picked up the first five files, rose and moved to the chesterfield sofa situated beneath the window. Everything in the office was stuffy and old-school but the chair and coffee table would have to do as a working area until the new desk arrived.

Setting the files down beside me, I opened the first one. Then immediately shut it when the name on the letterhead jumped up at me.

The Mortimer Group

My breath rattled around in my chest, echoing the sensations in my body. Mainly of the hot and bothered kind. Mainly between my legs. All because of Jasper Mortimer and what I'd let happen in the maze a week ago.

I'm done playing games.

The words might have been aimed at my elusive brother, but they resonated deep within me. Probably because Jasper and I had been playing a game for the better part of five years, ever since I walked into the boardroom at the internship fair and first experienced his dynamic magnetism. Heat flared up my body and I fought a squirm as total recall plunged me into that lustful state that never failed to materialise whenever I thought of him.

That searing, dangerous attraction had partly fuelled my decision to decline his internship offer. That and my family's abiding hatred for everything attached to the Mortimer name.

I tossed the file away. I wasn't ready to deal with him. Or the Mortimer Group. Nor did I want to think of how hard he'd made me come. How wanton he'd made me feel.

How much I'd craved a repeat performance ever since...

That madness in the maze was a shameful episode I'd intended to put out of my mind. If only it'd been that simple—

I jumped when the second office phone, positioned conveniently on the coffee table, rang. I didn't want to picture my brother in this chair, drinking himself into a stupor when he should've been safeguarding our family. Unfortunately, so far all evidence pointed that way.

To stop thoughts of the brother I'd never really got on well with, despite my desire to, I snatched up the phone. 'Hello?' I said, then grimaced at the lack of professionalism. Must do better in future.

'Congratulations on your official instatement as Acting CEO.' The deep voice of the last person I wanted to talk to filtered through the handset.

Shock rippled through my body. 'How do you know about that?' The board meeting had only ended at ten. It was barely noon. 'And how did you get my direct number?'

'I have my ways,' Jasper Mortimer said.

'You mean you have a spy in my company,' I deducted.

He chuckled, a rich, indulgent sound that threw me back to the maze. To his very male groans of satisfaction as I lost my mind. 'Let's not start our relationship with accusations.'

'We don't have a relationship.'

'Yet,' he countered smoothly.

'We never will. I suggest you accept that now.'

'Thanks for the suggestion. But how are we going to work together on this Morocco project if we don't have even a basic rapport?'

My gaze flitted to the file I'd flung away. Something inside me shook. 'Why are you calling me?'

'To set up a meeting. The sooner the better.' The lazy indulgence had left his voice to be replaced by a crisp, uncompromising tone. 'Now that you're officially the head of Bingham's, we need to get this deal back on track.'

The ambitious deal that had, by all accounts, driven Perry over the edge. The thought hardened my resolve. 'No.'

'Excuse me?'

'You heard me. The official Bingham position is that we won't be going ahead with the Morocco deal. You'll receive our official statement shortly.' I hung up before he could reply. Then stared at the silent phone, my heart banging against my ribs.

After five minutes without it ringing, my stomach started churning.

Had I been too reckless? The board I'd battled to win over—the same board who'd expressed their wish to remain leaderless until Perry returned from his six-month rehab stint in Arizona—would love to be proven right that I wasn't suitable for this position. Had I, with my very first act as CEO, played right into their hands? Tentatively, I reached out towards the phone. To do what? Admit to Jasper that I'd been too rash? Give him an opening to gloat? I snatched my hand back.

He'd waited for a week. He could wait another day.

Resolute, I opened the second file, putting thoughts of Jasper, his masterful fingers and wicked, orgasm-giving tongue out of my mind.

By five p.m. I'd resolved a third of the issues contained within the various files, and unfortunately received even further insight into Perry's true state of decline— they'd been drastically neglected for months.

My chest tightened the more my thoughts dwelled on my brother. According to the family doctor who'd examined him, he'd been dangerously close to alcohol poisoning, a fact my mother had actively denied even though it'd been an open secret that Perry— like most Bingham men—had harboured a drinking problem for years.

And just like my father, Perry had refused to admit he even had a problem. The board had turned a blind eye to his addiction since he'd managed to keep Bingham Industries above the red line since stepping into Father's shoes seven years ago.

My heart ached as I mourned our deteriorated relationship. Our interaction on the occasions we'd been forced to socialise had been stilted to the point where we'd been relieved to be largely out of each other's orbit for the last three years. Still, his chilled silence when I'd accepted a junior marketing position at another firm had hurt.

Ultimately, he'd been as dismissive of my ambitions as my father had been; he'd fully supported my mother's and aunts' view that I should marry into some wealthy investment family, with guaranteed connections and endless resources, instead of striving to make my own way in the world.

Tears prickled my eyes and I blinked them away.

The bottom line was, Perry was getting the help he needed and I was in charge of steering Bingham's away from bankruptcy.

Frankly, I was surprised the corporate sharks hadn't started circling already.

My gaze dropped to the royal-blue Bingham's logo on the file I held. Once a powerhouse in its field, my family's logistics and hospitality supply reputation had dropped several rungs in the last decade, forcing us to make poorer business choices that'd led to an even steeper decline.

Was that why Perry had joined forces with Jasper Mortimer? Because while Bingham's had faced significant fiscal woes, the Mortimer Group had grown exponentially, expanding its initial construction arm into several other industries at a breakneck rate that I'd watched with secret awe and, admittedly, a little resentment. How could I not, when a part of me wondered if some of that fortune had been achieved at the cost of my family's decline?

I tossed the file away, irritated with myself for my unhelpful thoughts. Whatever the reason for my family's current situation, nothing would be achieved by dwelling on the past. And especially not thinking of the incident in the maze!

My intercom sounded and I pressed the button with guilty relief. 'Yes?'

'I have a message from a Mr Jasper Mortimer for you.'

My pulse leapt. 'Is he on the phone?'

'No, he just wanted me to tell you he'll call again at six. And that you should make sure you're all read up on the project.' The hint of nerves in Alana's voice made me wonder what else he'd said. And why a sensation a lot like disappointment twisted in my stomach that he hadn't asked to speak to me.

'Thanks, Alana. I'll see you tomorrow.'

I hung up, cursing the untrammelled excitement fizzing through me, then my complete inability to slow my heart's crazy racing as the clock approached six.

Wren picked up on the first ring, and even before she spoke my pulse had rocketed to ridiculous levels. Then came her incredible voice.

'I'd appreciate it if you didn't disturb my assistant with unnecessary messages or me with ultimatums.'

'You made going through her necessary by hanging up on me earlier. I simply used her to let you know we'd be skipping the foreplay this time and getting straight to business. Unless, you specifically want the foreplay?'

'I don't want anything from you, Jasper,' she said briskly.

'Are you absolutely sure?'

'Yes, I'm unique like that, you see.'

I laughed a touch incredulously under my breath. 'You think I don't know that? Believe me, Wren, I do.'

I could've sworn I heard her breath catch, but her voice was curt when she replied, 'Trust a man like you to make allusions.'

I laughed harder, knowing it would irk her more. Cool, calm and collected Wren was intriguing, but I'd discovered I preferred the fiery, passionate woman in the maze who'd lost control, if only for a brief time. 'A man like me? And here I thought, like you, that I was one of a kind...'

'Sadly, you're not as rare a specimen as you think you are.'

I gave a dramatic sigh. 'That just makes me want to prove you wrong.'

'You can't. You won't be able to.'

I gripped the phone tighter, felt myself drawn in deeper into the compulsion I couldn't fight. 'Why not? Because every guy you've been with has made you come as hard as I did in that maze?'

'Seeking validity of your male prowess? How predictable. You disappoint me, Jasper,' she said, her voice a touch huskier.

Despite the curious throb in my chest, I smiled. 'I'm wholly satisfied with my strengths, thanks.' *But you weren't always, were you?* I pushed away the taunting voice. 'As for seeking validity, the end result in that maze is all the validity I need where you're concerned.'

'Can we get off that subject, please?' she whispered fiercely. 'I don't have time for personal conversation.'

'Do you despise me as much as you pretend to, or is this you simply toeing the family line?' I taunted, a sudden restlessness prowling inside me.

She inhaled sharply. 'You'll never get the chance to find out. Goodbye, Mr Mortimer.'

'Before you dramatically hang up on me again, let me remind you that your continued failure to engage with me only brings Bingham's closer to being in breach of contract.'

'I've read the file. Nothing in there remotely suggests a breach,' she said tightly, and I got the feeling I'd upset her by that family comment.

Bloody hell.

I tried to get my head back into business mode. 'May I suggest that you read the paperwork again. Carefully.'

Silence greeted me and I imagined her bristling, those eyes flashing with low-burning anger. I wondered what she'd look like in full blaze. God, it'd be glorious.

'I graduated university at the top of my class. You know this because you came sniffing around, trying to headhunt me, remember?'

'I remember you turning me down flat and accepting an internship at a much more inferior company.' That still grated, but it'd been the first inkling for me that, all these decades later, the Binghams were still as bitter about the fallout between our families. Now I knew the depths of my father's ruthlessness, I wasn't surprised. 'Do you regret that decision?'

'Not for a single moment. So I can only conclude you're trying to insult me by insinuating I would've missed something as crucial as a break clause in a contract.'

I took a beat to formulate my reply because this was where it got tricky. Saying anything negative against Perry might backfire. And as much as I liked tussling with Wren, the project I'd worked my arse off for needed to be kept on track. 'No offence intended. But the clause is there, I assure you. I can courier over a copy if you'd like?'

'Now you're implying I'm sloppy with paperwork. And blind, too?'

'You seem hell-bent on taking offence no matter what I say. A meeting will resolve this quickly enough, don't you think? Even if it's so you can put me in my place?'

'Inviting me to prove you wrong won't work, either. I don't need my ego stroked.'

It was time to pull out the big guns. 'I suggest you make time in your schedule. I'm not losing this deal because of some chip you've got on your shoulder. I expect to see you in my office tomorrow.'

'Or what?'

'Or I'll have no choice but to make good on my promise. You're already mired in unwanted publicity. Divorcing yourself from this deal at this late stage is going to bring nothing but unwanted attention to Bingham's.'

'Are you threatening me?'

'I'm laying out the course of action I'll be forced to take if you remain intransigent. The ball is in your court, sweetheart.'

She hung up.

Despite the two-nil score against me, I wasn't overly disgruntled. She hadn't earned her position by being dismissive of a potential lawsuit. Not that it'd come to that. For starters, I wasn't champing at the bit to become *the* Mortimer incapable of closing my division's biggest deal yet. The labels my father had callously and frequently branded into my skin were enough.

No, I was willing to bet my very treasured vintage Aston Martin that Wren would make contact. And if not…

I smiled grimly to myself as I swivelled in my chair to enjoy my multimillion-pound view…

If not, I'd take delight in becoming a very significant pain in her delectable backside.

The break clause wasn't in the contract.

Jasper's insinuation that I'd missed something had spurred a wild need to prove him wrong. After a two-hour search, I'd given up and headed home. Nothing in the electronic or paper files showed Perry had agreed to an early break clause. Sure, there were several clauses—all dishearteningly skewed in favour of the Mortimer Group—peppered within the contract but nothing that stated what would happen if Perry changed his mind about proceeding with the Morocco deal. Because he hadn't planned on it? Like my father, had he gone into this with unshakeable hubris, only to fall?

My heart twisted in dull pain and a little shame for assuming his culpability. He wasn't here to defend himself. And for all I knew, Jasper had twisted his arm into agreeing to this deal. The man was clever enough.

And not just with his words.

My heart skipped a beat and shame deepened, but for a completely different reason. Our heated verbal exchange had sparked something to life inside me. Something that, hours later, made me feel restless. *Needy.* I'd been spoiling for an argument. Then ended up spoiling for something totally different. Something to ease the ache between my thighs.

Like his mouth. His fingers.

His cock.

I pressed my fingers into my eyes, hoping to erase the image of him looking far too handsome for my sanity at the party. But the images simply reeled...of him caging me against the maze hedge. Of him on his knees, enthusiastically bringing me to an insane climax. Hell, even watching him suffer with that incredible hard-on had turned me on. God, what the hell was wrong with me?

You need to get laid.

I dropped my hands in frustration. If only it were that simple. Despite my short, rebellious modelling stint, I was a Bingham, cognisant of my ever-increasing family responsibility. The tabloids would love nothing better than to splash the front pages with details of whatever brief hook-up I indulged in for the sake of getting my rocks off. Especially now I was Acting CEO of a once multimillion-pound company now on the brink of collapse.

While my last two relationships hadn't worked due to lack of chemistry, behind it was the same resentment that had led me into modelling at nineteen. Resentment and rebellion stemming from my mother's attempt to orchestrate those relationships.

Unable to control either my father or Perry, she'd turned her attention to me the moment I reached puberty. Attention I'd mistakenly believed was affection I'd sorely missed in my childhood years when I'd needed her most. Discovering that she was simply using me to while away her time until her husband or son needed her, whereupon she set me back on my isolation shelf, had hurt long before I'd reached maturity. Of course, it didn't stop the foolish hope that sprang inside me whenever she turned her attention on me.

Not until lately. Not until her indifference—identical to Perry's—to my announcement that I'd accepted a marketing position at a different company had forced me to accept that true affection or acknowledgement from her would never happen. I was merely an ornament to be displayed when it suited her.

More fool me…

Exhaling through another tide of hurt, I padded over to the window, while parsing Jasper's parting words. He wanted Bingham's to hold up their end of the deal, agree to a three-year plan to supply the hospitality infrastructure for the four luxury hotels and casinos he was building in Morocco.

On the surface, it sounded like a deal made in heaven, but the reality was that Bingham's would be operating at an eighty per cent loss for the first year with possible gains coming only in the second and third years. Perry had tried to push for a five-year contract. Jasper had refused. Because like a typical Mortimer, he wanted to keep the initial financial gains for himself.

Well, I wasn't going to let the past repeat itself. The maze incident and our phone call tonight had proven two things: this insane attraction between us that made me want to tear off his clothes when he was within touching distance was untenable, and working with Jasper would be a nightmare.

The man was too full of himself. And I was woman enough to recognise that not all battles needed to be fought. Besides, I had several ideas of how to put the resources Perry had earmarked for the Mortimer deal to better use.

Striding over to my phone, I checked my schedule for the next day, then slotted a half-hour to deal with Jasper. It wouldn't take more than that to send the message home.

And if my belly somersaulted and my pulse raced at the thought of tangling with him again...it was only because I looked forward to emerging the victor.

Nothing else.

I strode through the doors of Mortimer Tower after business hours the next day, power-suited and determined not to be impressed with my surroundings. The reminder that all of this had been built by cut-throat Mortimers helped me focus as I entered the executive lift that serviced the upper floors where Jasper's office was located.

A part of me regretted leaving this meeting until last thing on Friday. If I'd tackled it first thing this morning, I'd already be free of this disquieting... *thrumming* in my veins. My brain wouldn't keep flashing scenarios of what could happen when I saw him again. I wouldn't have wasted precious stretches of time replaying his promise that *'We're going to fuck, Wren'* and *'I'm going to make you come many, many more times'*.

I sure as hell wouldn't be riding the empty lift with trembling hands and panties slightly damp from that memory of him going down on me in my family maze.

Enough, already...

The self-admonition worked for the thirty seconds it took for the lift to spit me out into the pristine, ultra-sleek reception area. The whole building had been redecorated recently at huge expense by Bryce Mortimer, the award-winning architect in the Mortimer clan. I might have ignored the impressive atrium downstairs, but I couldn't avoid the burst of bold colours softening the sharply angled steel and dark grey surfaces.

A smartly dressed receptionist smiled as I sucked in a breath and approached her.

'Hi, I have a meeting with Jasper Mortimer. He's expecting me.' Half true. Jasper might have summoned me here today but I hadn't bothered to inform him when I would be making my appearance.

Her smile slipped. 'Is he? Only, he went into a meeting ten minutes ago.'

'We didn't agree on a specific time. Just show me to his office. I'll wait.'

'Of course, Miss Bingham. Right this way.'

The greys were more pronounced than the steel in Jasper's office and the colours came from art rather than flower arrangements, but the effect was the same—sleekly professional, contemporary and elegant. But what made the space different was his lingering scent in the air, coupled with the aura of power I couldn't dismiss as I stared at the immense dark-wood desk and black high-backed chair, and I couldn't help the shiver that coursed down my spine. A throat cleared beside me. Composing myself, I glanced at the receptionist. 'Thank you.'

'Can I get you anything?'

I started to refuse, then changed my mind. 'Coffee with cream, no sugar. Thank you.'

She nodded and glided away. I returned my gaze to my surroundings, noting the absence of files or paperwork. Either Jasper was naturally meticulous in maintaining a paper-free environment or he'd anticipated my arrival. My instinct suggested the latter, eroding a layer of that upper hand I'd hoped to gain by my unexpected arrival.

After the receptionist served my coffee and left, I sat on the wide grey velvet sofa facing the spectacular view of the Thames and attempted to immerse myself in Bingham business. I wasn't sure where the notion of how to handle Jasper came from. All I knew was that it happened somewhere between sipping the excellent java brew—purportedly supplied to every Mortimer establishment by Graciela Mortimer—and when the door suddenly sprang open to reveal Jasper Mortimer in all his breathtaking glory.

Perhaps I sensed the moment I saw his face that

walking away wasn't going to be as easy as I'd convinced myself. Here, in this space, in his *domain*, I realised my first mistake—we should've met on neutral ground.

Because the man striding towards me teemed with quietly ferocious purpose. And yes, regardless of how late it was, he'd *known* I would come. 'Sorry for the wait. I couldn't get out of the meeting as quickly as I wanted. Do you mind?' He pointed to the coffee on the tray.

I shook my head. 'Go ahead.'

He poured himself a cup, added a dash of cream, and took a seat next to me.

Immediately, his dark woodsy smell engulfed me. The strong, visceral urge to breathe him in made me lift my own cup, hoping the coffee smell would dilute the potency of his scent.

That particular quest became redundant because my gaze was on a mission of its own. It took in the strong fingers lifting the cup to his lips for a large gulp, then followed the lines of his throat as he swallowed. The play of his powerful thighs as he crossed his legs and set the cup and saucer on his knee.

'First things first, did you come across the clause we talked about?'

His assumption that I'd gone looking set my teeth on edge. But I answered anyway. 'No, I didn't. We must be looking at different documents because there's nothing in my copy of the contract to support what you're saying.'

Jasper's hazel gaze narrowed on me for a tight, long stretch. Then he set his cup down, rose and crossed to his desk. When he returned with a sleek laptop, my heart lurched, then dropped to my toes as he fired up the machine. A few taps and he turned the screen to face me.

'Perry signed this document down the corridor in my conference room three months ago. It was duly witnessed, and I couriered him a copy for his records. The break clause in question is on page forty-seven.'

With not quite steady hands, I placed my cup on the coffee table and took the laptop. I wanted to blurt out that the presence of the break clause didn't change anything. But I couldn't delude myself. Break clauses were notoriously costly and I suspected Bingham would end up shouldering the burden if I didn't play my cards right.

That outlandish idea that struck me five minutes ago returned, more forcefully, as I read the document. It looked similar to my copy except for the crucial page missing from mine.

'Why is this one different from mine?'

Jasper didn't answer immediately. He drained his coffee before glancing my way. 'Negotiations with your brother weren't…smooth. He insisted on renegotiating several contracts before things were finalised.'

Given Perry's debilitated state, I wasn't surprised. But a question had been gnawing at me since I became aware of this deal. 'Why Bingham's? There are literally thousands of companies out there you could've partnered with. Why us?'

His lips firmed. 'You mean considering our family history?'

He wasn't beating about the bush. I didn't see why I should. 'Yes.'

'Would you believe me if I said that ultimately didn't factor into my decision?'

Who was he kidding? 'No, I wouldn't.'

He sighed. 'Didn't think so. Wren, if you're asking then I'm going to presume Perry didn't tell you.'

'Tell me what?'

Hazel eyes locked on to mine, pinned me in place. 'That he begged me for this deal. He pretty much stalked me for the better part of three months before I even agreed to meet with him. I was all set to go with someone else.'

A flush of shame crept up from my belly and soon engulfed my whole body. I'd seen the books. We were in a precarious financial position. But we weren't crawling-on-our-bellies desperate. Yet. Not enough for Perry to beg for scraps from our sworn enemy. 'I'm not sure why he did that—'

'Aren't you?' Jasper's expression was entirely cynical.

Pride swarmed through me. 'No, we're not destitute. I'm not going to lower myself to prove it to you. You'll have to take my word for it.'

He frowned. 'No need to be so defensive. I'm

simply relating things as they happened. For whatever reason your brother wanted this deal to happen.'

'Then why did he drag his feet?'

Jasper's lips twisted. 'At least you're admitting he did.'

I handed him back his laptop. 'Clearly he wasn't satisfied with something. I've looked at the projections. We supply you with everything from gambling tables and staff to tea towels and garden fertiliser but see very little profit for twelve months? Why the hell should I come on board with something like that?'

His gaze hardened and I caught a glimpse of Hugh Mortimer, the adversary my father had faced—and lost to—decades ago. Was Jasper his father's son in every sense of the word? Whatever. I didn't intend to stick around to find out.

'Because he signed on the dotted line. It's too late to back out now. This project has been delayed by months already. I won't let it suffer another setback,' he said grimly.

I rose from the sofa, gathered my tablet and briefcase as calmly as I could, despite the roiling in my stomach. I'd seen the books. Our company was haemorrhaging money, yes, but we still had substantial assets to hold back the dam for a while. 'I'll look over your papers and get back to you.'

He rose to join me. Despite my above average height, he towered over me, made me feel small and delicate in a way very few people could. And…I didn't exactly hate that feeling. Which was totally absurd. I turned away as he glanced at his watch.

'Let me take you out to dinner. We can discuss this over—'

'No, thanks. I only eat with people I trust.'

His eyes darkened. 'Ouch,' he drawled without a hint of the purported affront. 'You really are determined to make this adversarial, aren't you?'

For some reason, the softly voiced accusation niggled, striking me with a wild urge to apologise. *Stay strong.* 'I'm just looking out for my family's best interests.'

That brought a wry, twisted smile to his lips. 'Can't say I blame you, but I'm really not the enemy here, Wren.'

God, the way he said my name—that name I'd hated for so long—somehow sounded pleasant on his lips. 'If you're not the enemy, then agree to end this amicably,' I replied.

His smile turned edgy, delivering another glimpse of the true man beneath the suave exterior. 'I haven't made it this far by being sentimental over business, Wren. I'm a little disappointed you would play that card. Your brother signed an agreement. I expect you to honour it. Starting on Monday, you'll devote the required time and energy into progressing this deal.'

'Or what?' I dared, even though my stomach dipped wildly. There was something raw and primal in that command, something that incredulously turned my blood hotter, my skin more sensitive. With a compulsion I couldn't deny, my gaze dropped to his lips. Mine tingled, a need to taste him almost overpowering me. It was enough to make me take a step back. But I wasn't totally out of his reach. So when he raised his hand and slowly extended it towards my face, there was absolutely no reason not to take another step away. Out of the path of temptation. Except I didn't.

His knuckles brushed my cheek, slowly caressing down to my jaw. Electricity charged up my thighs, making me bite back a gasp. Why the hell was I getting so wet? *Dear God...*

'You say you're looking out for your family? Then what was that in that maze last week? Was it a touch of much-needed self-indulgence? One you wouldn't be averse to repeating?'

'I...no.'

'Try that once more, with feeling. But before you do, remember my promise. I intend to fuck you, Wren. Very hard and very thoroughly. In every position you desire.'

My clit throbbed and fresh flames shot through me at the thick drawled words. Suddenly, I was very aware of the sofa nearby. That all I had to do was say the word and I'd have him.

But then what? He would be just another temporary act of rebellion that could go nowhere when I should be concentrating on dragging my family's company out of the quagmire. Perry was in rehab. The last thing I should be doing was adding flames to a roaring scandal-hungry fire by embarking on a tryst with the enemy.

'Business,' I insisted, even as a thick coil of regret unravelled inside me, reminding me of how many times I'd denied myself for the sake of family. 'I'm here to discuss business. Nothing else.'

That overconfident smile returned, turning his far too gorgeous face even more spectacular as his hand dropped. 'Good. Then do the right thing. Or you'll leave me no choice but to fight your hot little fire with flames of my own,' he answered, a growl of anticipation in his voice that hastened my heartbeat.

'You don't want to go to war with me, Jasper.'

'To get this deal done, I'll take you however I can get you, sweetheart.'

Much too late, I took that vital step back. Then another. 'Goodnight, Jasper.'

'Would you like me to walk you out?' he asked, right after his hooded gaze circumvented my body, leaving me even hotter than before.

'I can manage on my own, thanks,' I replied, aware my voice was a little hoarse when I needed it snippy.

'Okay. I'll see you on Monday for the phase two meeting at nine a.m. Don't be late.'

I turned and walked away without answering. In the lift, I sagged against one wall, a traitorous little tremble seizing my body as snippets of the conversation scrolled across my brain. Nothing had gone as I'd smugly predicted. If the agreement he'd shown

me was valid—and I didn't see why it would be
fabricated—it meant Perry had agreed to a deal that
would be impossible to walk away from without seriously crippling Bingham's. So why had he signed
it? And why had he left it out of the file?

My phone pinged as the lift reached the ground
floor. I stared at the text, my heartbeat hammering
as I saw the familiar-looking number. Jasper.

I've emailed you a copy of the agreement for your
records.

I checked my email and, sure enough, the agreement was in my inbox. I tapped out a reply as I
walked through his stunning atrium, once again
determined not to admire its grandeur.

Email received. Thanks.

I discovered other hidden bombshells once I was
back home in my maisonette in Fulham, showered
and dressed in my favourite pyjama shorts set. The
glass of red wine was forgotten in my hand as I read
and reread the agreement, tiny waves of shock building into a tsunami as I absorbed just what Perry had
committed Bingham's to.

Besides the supply agreement, which would eat
heavily into our cash reserves, Perry had agreed to
being on hand, day or night, to troubleshoot any
problems that arose either in London or on sites in

Morocco for a minimum of twenty hours per week. To 'help' with that particular clause, Jasper had offered the use of his empty office in London or a suite in the Morocco hotel.

Even before I'd taken up the mantle at Bingham's I was working long hours. Hard work had earned me a fast track from junior to senior executive in my last firm. Adding a few more hours to my workday didn't faze me. What disturbed me was the thought of being that close to Jasper. Because when he'd touched me tonight, every cell in my body had roared to life in a way that shocked me.

I downed the rest of the wine, set the glass down and reclined on my sofa. I had the rest of the weekend to figure a way out of this.

For Perry's sake. For my family's sake, I couldn't fail.

Eyes closed, I tried to work out how to best the man with the wicked tongue and clever fingers.

I'll take you however I can get you...

Why did those words make me so hot? Why the hell couldn't I get his voice out of my head?

I'll take you...

I was flushed and panting as my hand crept down my belly. I bit my lip, hating myself a little for succumbing to the lust trickling through my blood. My nipples beaded as sensation unfurled in my pelvis, heating my pussy and engorging my clit. Uncustomary anticipation fired me up, my fingers tingling as

I spread my legs and slipped my fingers beneath the waistband of my pyjama shorts.

A hot little gasp left my lips when I touched myself, shivering when I noticed how wet and slippery I was.

I'll take you...

Need and lust built. My fingers worked my clit in desperate circles, the realisation that, for once, I didn't need the assistance of my trusted vibrator, ramping up my desire. Working my clit with my thumb, I slipped my middle finger inside my wet heat, finger-fucking myself while I imagined thicker fingers filling me. Or a cock... Jasper Mortimer's cock.

Inside me.

Pounding me.

Making me scream.

My orgasm curled through me, arching my back off the sofa as liquid bliss drowned me from head to toe.

It was as I came down from that intense high, my heartbeat roaring in my ears, that a line from the agreement suddenly flashed across my mind.

I jackknifed off the sofa, almost knocking over the wine glass as I reached for the laptop. And there, on page fifty-one, was my answer, my saviour, in black and white.

I read and reread it for good measure.

The Mortimer Group has the right to terminate this agreement, with due notice, in the

case of non-performance by Bingham Indus-
tries. This includes, but is not limited to, con-
tinued disruption of services…

I smiled.

For now, Jasper Mortimer had the power. I was
going to take it from him by simply doing…nothing.

Even while I blew his mind *out* of the boardroom.

CHAPTER THREE

WREN WAS FORTY-FIVE minutes late. Irritated, I hit my intercom button again.

'Yes, sir?' my PA answered.

'Try her mobile again. If she doesn't answer, call her office. I want to know where she is,' I growled.

'Of course.'

Why I expected Trish to succeed when my own numerous calls had gone straight to voicemail was a mystery but it beat just sitting around fuming because Wren was a no-show. I'd hoped providing her with the valid copy of the agreement would make her see sense but, clearly, I'd overestimated her.

Jaw gritted, I acknowledged that my disappointment in her was more acute than it'd ever been with her brother. Yes, I loved a challenge and I'd known getting involved with Bingham's, all things considered, would be difficult, but I'd convinced myself I could handle it.

Handle *her*.

When the hell was I going to learn my lesson?

Bitterness rose up to fuse with my annoyance. I tamped down both emotions. I wasn't dealing with my father's scathing remarks, disparaging me about wanting peace when we Mortimers were a proudly bloodthirsty lot.

I was dealing with an intelligent, if extremely stubborn, woman. I needed another way to deal with her.

Immediately my mind flew back to the maze, as it had been doing increasingly over the past week or so, but especially since Friday night. It'd taken every ounce of willpower not to kiss her in my office. But I'd needed to prove to her that I wasn't driven by my desire.

Succumbing to the urge to keep touching her, to kiss those luscious lips, would only convince her I was driven by base instincts. Yet I couldn't deny that she only needed to flash those green eyes to trigger a fever in my blood.

I laughed under my breath. I'd had my share of women, some more beautiful than Wren. This rare phenomenon where she was concerned was inexplicable. Why the hell did she trigger this strong reaction in me?

I shook my head, growing more annoyed when I clocked that I'd wasted almost an hour waiting for her. About to open one of the many files that needed my attention, I paused when my intercom buzzed.

'Yes?' I responded, a little too eagerly.

'I'm sorry, Mr Mortimer, I couldn't reach her. Her secretary says she's in a meeting.'

'I know. She's *supposed* to be in a meeting, here, with me.' Aware that I was snapping at my PA, I throttled down my emotions. Christ, she drove me crazy. 'Thanks, Trish.' I collapsed in my seat, forcing calm into my bones.

I'd always been a strategist. A planner. Favouring dialogue over conflict. But I was a Mortimer, as my father had taken delight in reminding me every time I'd displayed what he'd termed my *weakness*. Did Wren really want war with a Mortimer?

Especially when Bingham's, according to trusted sources, was one ill-judged deal away from complete collapse? She couldn't afford to take me on in a corporate battlefield. So why the hell was she trying? Perry had been equally hard-headed but evidently his intransigence had been mostly fuelled by alcohol. Wren was simply stubborn.

And loyal. Perhaps blindly so, but loyal.

It was a stark reminder that my family was acutely different. Mortimers—my father especially—didn't do blind loyalty and, as he'd proven with his callous desertion, wouldn't fight to the death for anyone else but himself.

But wasn't that what had made us who we were today? Successful. Feared. A global powerhouse with immeasurable clout. Sure, we wouldn't win any Family of the Year prizes but there was a lot to be proud of. I wasn't going to let a woman with brains, beauty and fireworks in her green eyes convince me otherwise—

As if I'd conjured her up by my imagination, my door opened and there she stood.

My annoyance didn't recede as I stared at her, but several new sensations crowded in. First, the jolt of electricity just the sight of her rammed through my body. I attempted to control it by taking another deep breath. And failed.

The second was utter shock as I took in the state of her.

She looked as if she'd stumbled in from a night of hard partying. And even harder fucking. Her hair was dishevelled as if some lucky bastard had won the privilege of running his fingers repeatedly through it. Her lips were faintly bruised and smeared as if someone had eaten off her lipstick. Then came her smudged make-up. Dark jealousy spiralled through me as my gaze dropped lower and my gut tightened against the inevitable hard-on heading my way as I took in the rest of her.

Holy hell, she was wearing a trench coat. Not necessarily a fashion *faux pas* considering the time of year, but it was tightly belted at the waist in that highly suggestive *sexual* way that screamed she was wearing very little or nothing at all underneath. Fire lit through my groin as she took a step towards me and justified my suspicions by flashing a bare leg.

Jesus, she wouldn't. Would she?

'Good morning, Jasper.' Whether that husky greeting was deliberately exaggerated or the result of long hours of screaming in ecstasy wasn't something I particularly wanted to dwell on. Either way, it threw another gallon of flammable fuel on my libido. I clenched my gut as I grew even harder.

'You're late,' I bit out, watching her strut across my office in sky-high heels.

With each step, I caught a glimpse of her leg, and nothing else. My nape heated and I desperately scrounged around for every scrap of willpower not to drag my fingers over my jaw and stop myself from salivating like a pathetic dog. I tried to remain pissed off, but my mind fixated on one thing.

Was Wren Bingham totally naked under that coat?

She reached my desk, laid her hands flat on it, and leaned towards me. I kept my eyes on hers, determined not to be drawn into whatever game she was playing.

'Am I? You said the meeting was at ten. It's now…' she paused, glanced around the office before reaching into her pocket for her phone '…nine fifty-nine. Oh, look, I'm a whole minute early.' She waved her phone at me and I caught a glimpse of her home screen.

It featured a picture of her, head thrown back, laughing into the camera. The image only showed her from bare shoulders up but it was again suggestive that she was naked. Arousal attacked my body, leaving me with a serious urge to fidget. I steepled my fingers on my belly, thankful my suit jacket and desk hid my compromised state from her.

'I told you the meeting was at nine o'clock. I've had to put off the Moroccan team twice already.'

'Heavens! In that case I can only apologise. There must have been some sort of mix-up.' She slipped the phone back into her pocket, the movements exaggerated enough to make her coat gape wide. I saw the curve of her breast and swallowed hard.

'What the fuck are you doing?' I bit out.

Her eyes widened. 'I don't know what you mean, Jasper.'

'Do you attend all your meetings dressed like that?'

'You don't like what I'm wearing?'

I gritted my teeth, knowing I was getting close to the danger zone. 'We abide by a dress code here.'

Her smile. 'Ah, but then I don't work for you, do I, Jasper?' she asked softly, but there was a hard glint in her eye, a stubborn flame flaring to life.

Before I could answer, my phone rang. I allowed myself a small smile as I met her gaze. 'You're right. You don't work for me. But we're working together and I expect professionalism, like being on time. I'll let it slide just this once.' I reached for my phone. 'Yes?' My PA relayed the information I wanted to hear, and I hung up. 'Are you ready?'

She tensed. 'Ready for what?'

'I told you I rescheduled the videoconference. The Morocco team is waiting for us in the conference room. Since you made the effort to come all this way despite being late, I'm assuming you'll join me?'

I watched her jaw drop, her whole act vanishing for a second before she composed herself. 'Of course, lead the way. I hope they're just as accommodating as you about my tardiness,' she said, her voice saccharine sweet.

I managed to stop my teeth gritting as I rose, buttoned my jacket and rounded the desk. The last thing I wanted to do was to walk her through my open-plan office floor dressed as she was. Call me a chauvinist but having every guy out there wondering what she was wearing under that coat made my blood boil.

But…business was business. And I wasn't about to let this deal fall apart over yet another hurdle.

I stepped out of my office, keenly aware that she was following, those sky-high heels perfectly displaying her spectacular endless legs with every step. Of course, as I'd feared, seemingly every male in the vicinity suddenly needed to be in the hallway leading to the conference room right at that moment.

Avid eyes gravitated to Wren, her sexily dishevelled state triggering more than one male fantasy. I hurried into the conference room, barely stopping myself from snarling at my own employees as I shut the door behind us.

Strolling to the head of the table, I grabbed the remote and flicked it on. The four women and three men who made up the Moroccan executive team stared back at us. Then, one by one, they switched their attention to Wren. Eyes widened, and wild speculation flickered across their faces.

I cleared my throat, rearranging what I suspected was a scowl into professional neutrality. 'Ladies and gentlemen, my apologies again for the delay. Let me introduce you to Wren Bingham. As of today, she'll be taking over Bingham Industries' side of the project.' I glanced at Wren, who'd taken the seat across from me.

She was staring at the screen with a sultry, faintly challenging smile. As I watched, she swivelled her seat towards the screen, dragging one hand slowly through her long hair before flicking it over one shoulder. With her other hand she waved at the team. 'Hi, it's lovely to meet you all,' she murmured, right before she crossed her mile-long legs.

I didn't need to be on her side of the table to know she was flashing more than a hint of thigh. The expressions on the screen—especially the male ones—telegraphed her effect on them, plain as day. Silence reigned in the room as their gazes flicked between Wren and me.

Bloody hell.

'Wren?' I prompted, aware of the bite in my voice.

She slanted green eyes at me and blinked slowly. 'Yes, Jasper?'

'Are you going to give the Bingham briefing? The team is pretty much on page as to where the Mortimer side of things stand. They need you to confirm the various timetables for delivery of phase two. You did get up to speed on where we are, didn't you?'

Her eyes flashed irritation at me but she maintained her bored expression. 'Oh… Right. Phase two…' She didn't say anything else, just continued to stare at me with those eyes.

'Yep. Phase two. Don't keep us in suspense,' I taunted, ignoring the stares from the screen as our intrigued audience watched our silent battle, suddenly enjoying this tussle with her.

She shrugged, indicating she was going to do just as she pleased. That she was going to enjoy watching me twist in the wind.

After another stretch of mutinous silence, I swivelled my chair towards the screen. 'My apologies, but I didn't quite make a full introduction, did I? I should have mentioned that Wren has a master's degree in Business from Oxford University.'

I felt her gaze sharpen on me. 'She was recently featured in Business Tomorrow's Young CEOs Under Thirty. She's too modest to tell you herself, but she graduated at the top of her class and, according to one of her professors, she has one of the most brilliant business minds of her generation.'

'Stop it,' she hissed under her breath for my ears only.

I ignored her. She wasn't going to win this game. 'I tried to poach her even before she'd finished university but, alas, I lost her to another company. So I guess you can imagine how stoked I am to finally have her on board?' I flicked a mocking smile her way before returning my gaze to the team. 'The reason she doesn't have any files with her this morning is because she doesn't really need them. All the facts and figures she requires are right up there in that exceptional brain of hers. On top of her many accomplishments, she also possesses a photographic memory. I haven't seen it in action myself but I'm dying to. Wren?' I prompted again, finally focusing on her, the gauntlet writhing on the table between us.

Hellfire erupted from her gaze as her hands balled into fists.

I smiled inside, satisfaction eroding my irritation. She'd meant to test me by pretending lack of interest, boredom, even apathy. But the one thing Wren Bingham couldn't do was let our audience walk away with the impression that she was dumb. I suspected, like me, she'd fought too hard for her accomplishments and her true place in her family to let herself be so easily dismissed.

When she swallowed, surreptitiously pulled the lapels of her coat together and slowly uncrossed her legs, I allowed myself an inner fist pump.

Uncurling her hands, she glanced at the screen. 'What do you need to know about phase two?' she asked, the sexy seduction in her voice gone.

At my nod, the team launched into their questions. As I'd suspected, Wren knew the project inside and out. She answered every query concisely, offering alternatives when needed without once requesting information from me or consulting the electronic documents I'd emailed her yesterday.

When the meeting ended and the screen went

blank forty minutes later, she surged to her feet. 'You think you're very clever, don't you?' she snapped.

I reclined in my seat, taunting her with a smile. 'Don't throw a hissy fit just because your little game backfired on you, sweetheart,' I drawled.

Luscious lips pressed together as she raked her fingers through her hair, immediately making my imagination run wild about the array of sexual things I could do with every strand of that hair. 'This isn't going to work.'

I waved a hand at the screen. 'You just proved otherwise. It'll work even better if only you'd stop playing these silly games.'

Her eyes flashed. 'What makes you think I won't just let you list my accomplishments then show you up anyway next time?'

I shrugged. 'I don't. But I can guarantee that I'll keep coming up with different ways to ensure that you don't get away with whatever you have up your sleeve.'

She threw up her hands in exasperation, the closest I'd come to seeing her lose her cool. 'Why don't you do us both a favour and just end this?'

I exhaled slowly. 'I don't get it. Going ahead with this deal will benefit both of us.'

She performed a perfect pirouette and headed for the door. 'Keep telling yourself that,' she threw over her shoulder. 'In the meantime, I'm going to make it my business to make sure that you regret this.' She reached for the door handle. Started to turn it.

Everything inside me clenched tight. 'Wren.'

Fingers frozen, she glared at me over her shoulder. 'Please tell me you're not naked under that coat.'

That slow, cock-stroking smile returned, deadlier than before. 'I'm not naked under this coat, Jasper,' she echoed with a siren voice that transmitted straight to my groin. Then to taunt me further, her fingers dropped to toy with the loops of the belt. 'Would you like me to show you?'

Lust rushed through my blood, making me steel hard in moments. But I remained silent, swallowing down the *yes* that clawed at my throat. Without shifting her gaze from mine, she tugged on the belt. Her coat loosened and gaped. From where I sat, I couldn't see, but anyone who chose to enter in that moment would.

My stomach knotted and I lost the ability to breathe. 'Fucking hell,' I muttered under my breath.

'What was that?' she asked with false, wide-eyed innocence.

'I said keep that damn door closed, Wren.'

'Ah, I could've sworn you said something else.'

'Jesus, what are you doing?' I rasped, forgetting that I was meant to keep my cool.

'I'm going back to my office. I'm assuming we're done here?' she asked, one shapely eyebrow quirked.

My gaze dropped down the coat, fighting the urge to stand, rush over to her to see for myself what she was baring to the door. 'You know what I'm asking.

What are you doing with all that?' I jerked my chin at her attire.

Her smile deepened. 'Why, nothing. Not yet, anyway.'

Her hand dropped from the door. My throat clogged with tension as she slowly retied the belt, cinching it even tighter so her trim waist was fully displayed. My fingers itched with the need to capture that waist. I bunched them to stop myself from acting on the feelings rampaging through me.

'I need you back here tomorrow to discuss the casino outfitting.'

'I have a full day tomorrow.'

'Then we'll meet after you're done,' I countered, and watched her nostrils flare.

'I work pretty long hours. Are you sure you want to wait up for me? I wouldn't want to disturb your beauty sleep.'

'Thanks for your concern, but my beauty won't suffer too badly from a few extra hours of work. And, Wren?'

She cocked an eyebrow at me.

'Don't make me come after you. My patience won't hold out for ever.'

One corner of her lips lifted and she all but vibrated with the *Bring it on* she didn't utter.

I sighed under my breath. This game wasn't over, regardless of my daring her into displaying her intelligence just now. I watched as she opened the door and threw me one last look over her shoulder.

'Until next time, Jasper.'

I collapsed into my seat the moment she left, dragging my fingers through my hair as the rush of adrenaline drained from my body.

Maybe she had a point, damn it. Maybe the Mortimers should avoid the Binghams at all costs. Because even this small taster of what I suspected she had in store for me would wreck my concentration for the rest of the day.

Of course it will. Because you're just that weak, aren't you? Are you going to shy away from another fight, give in that easily? Debate *your way through another fight with an opponent? Maybe you should change your name, then. Because that is certainly not the Mortimer way.*

Arousal receded as my father's pitiless, unwanted voice echoed in my head. My jaw clenched as I fought a different kind of discomfort. But those disparaging words, branded into my soul from childhood, continued to echo through me, followed by bitterness for how long I'd let it rule every corner of my life.

But I'd done something about it…eventually. I'd taken control.

By letting Perry Bingham convince me to allow him to sign on to my deal? Knowing deep down it would probably piss my father off when I proved the generations-long feud meant nothing to me?

I shrugged the suggestion away. Regardless of the reason behind it, I was going to see this thing through. This project was my baby, the biggest deal I'd ever negotiated. I wasn't about to let it fall to pieces now.

Because Hugh Mortimer was still alive and well. Regardless of the fact that he'd removed himself from the immediate sphere of the clan, I knew he kept an eye on what happened within the company. And the last thing I was about to do was to prove him right. Even if I had to fight and wrestle Wren and her whole family under my control, I would bring this deal home.

Just to prove my father wrong about me.

Again.

CHAPTER FOUR

'WHAT KIND OF time do you call this?' I growled at the woman who stood in my doorway, thankfully wearing more clothes than yesterday. That moment of gratitude was fleeting though. On account of her succeeding where I was sure she'd fail at annoying me even more.

She sashayed into my office, looking stunningly immaculate, despite the very late hour, tossed her stylish briefcase on the sofa and shrugged. 'I'm pretty sure I warned you.'

'Working late is one thing. Turning up for a meeting at almost midnight is just taking the piss. How did you get here, anyway?'

'I took a cab. Why, were you worried about my safety?' she asked, one hand braced on her lean, curvy hip as she stopped in front of my desk.

Damn it, yes, I'd been worried. And increasingly vexed about it. I'd succumbed and called her office an hour ago, only to be blocked by her security who rightly wouldn't give out details of their boss's whereabouts. Not knowing whether she was going to turn up or not had kept me rooted in my office, tackling work that could easily have waited till tomorrow with dwindling concentration.

I shook my head as I stalked over to my liquor cabinet, poured myself a stiff Scotch. I toyed with being inhospitable for a few seconds before fixing her the mineral water with lime I'd seen her drinking at her party.

I offered the drink, daring her with my eyes to refuse. She glanced at the glass, a hint of surprise lighting her eyes before, frowning, she accepted it.

'I reread the contract today. The break clause might be skewed in your favour, but you realise I can simply do nothing for six months and watch you crash and burn?'

I tensed at her opening salvo. 'You'd really do that and lose close to half a billion pounds in profits?'

She hesitated for the tiniest revealing moment. 'Yes.'

'Are you sure? Don't you want to run that by your board first?'

Her chin went up and she boldly met my gaze. 'The board will stand behind any decision I make. Perry already had their backing to get out of this deal.'

Shit. That was news to me. 'After going to all that trouble of begging me for the partnership?'

Her lashes swept down and stayed down for a long

time. 'His reasons are none of your business. Same goes for mine.'

'Wrong, sweetheart. They are exactly my business, since we're effectively joined at the hip.'

She shook her head. 'You left him no choice. Not after you bought out the previous company Perry was supposed to partner with.'

I frowned. 'What are you talking about?'

'The Morocco deal. Isn't it true you only intended to go with two hotels?'

'That was the initial plan, yes. But—'

'But then you got greedy and bought up four more adjoining sites? Just because you could?'

'It wasn't a matter of greed, it was a matter of good business. And yes, because I damned well could. I'm failing to see what your point is here, Wren.'

'My point is, Perry came to you only after you became the new owner of the contract he was trying to secure. He didn't want to, but he'd been working on that deal long before you came on board. He...he was forced to come to you.'

My fingers tightened around my glass. 'Unless your family derives some macabre pleasure from hanging on to this shit even after twenty years, he could've walked away. Why didn't he?'

Her gaze rose and I caught a shaft of pain in her eyes. 'Perry hates losing. And some wounds run deep.'

Frustration bit through me. 'What about you? I'm not asking for a family reunion or even a suggestion that we bury the hatchet. All I'm asking for is a business deal where we both stand to profit for a very long time.'

Her lips twisted. 'Money isn't everything.'

I snorted. 'Then what are you doing in that office half a mile away? Running a charity?'

'I meant money isn't everything, *every time*.'

'Maybe not. But is that a strong enough reason to risk everything? For God's sake, who I am shouldn't matter in the grand scheme of things.'

'To my family, it does.'

I approached her until we were a foot apart.

She stayed her ground and that defiant stance made me instantly hard. Surprise, surprise. I leaned forward until her alluring perfume tortured me mercilessly. Until my thoughts began to fracture under the weight of the need to pull her close. Kiss her. Vent my frustration on anywhere she'd let me touch.

Starting with the silky skin of her neck. I'd work my way down, ridding her of that pristine cream shirt, which clung to her body. My gaze dropped to her chest, saw the faintest outline of her nipples. Sweet heaven, what I'd give to suck on those succulent nubs.

My eager mind strayed deeper into erotic realms.

I'd take off every single item of clothing except those red-soled heels, bend her over my desk and ram myself so deep inside her that we'd both see stars. Unlike last time, I had a condom nearby this time. Several, in fact. I'd taken to carrying the things with me wherever I went now. In case Wren Bingham happened to be there and begged me with her alluring mouth and eyes to service her as she had that night in the maze.

I leaned closer. She twitched and shuddered as my mouth brushed her earlobe. I wanted to catch the delicate flesh between my teeth, hear that control-destroying gasp she gave when she was caught in pleasure, but I restrained myself. Barely. 'Then they need to get over themselves, and fast. Because I'm not letting this one go. Now, shall we get on with this meeting? My casino isn't going to fit itself and, I promise, the longer you make me wait, the less reasonable I'll get about accommodating your behaviour.'

She froze, then jerked back a step. Whatever she read in my eyes made hers widen before it narrowed. 'This is your last chance, Jasper,' she said, her voice throbbing with an emotion I didn't want to examine.

'No.'

She stared at me for an age, then nodded. 'Fine. Let's discuss the casino.'

An hour later, I watched her walk out ahead of me—because I wasn't letting her catch a cab home at one o'clock in the morning, despite her protests—her sexy arse and endless legs an erotic sight that made my mouth water.

Just like last time, she'd come fully prepared. I had a set of approved timetables and proposed delivery of top-of-the-line gaming equipment in my briefcase, ready to green light in the morning.

I was buzzing with quiet excitement at her sheer proficiency while she'd grown increasingly despondent as the meeting had progressed. It was clear she wasn't happy about my insistence on our partnership continuing.

She reached the lift and shot me a look filled with venom. And despite a low warning hum at the back of my head suggesting that it wasn't too late to ditch Bingham's, I found myself smiling as I stepped into the lift with her.

I wasn't smiling two weeks later when I slammed my phone down after another failed call to the number that had risen to the top of my speed-dial list.

She didn't answer.

It was time to pull out the big guns.

I typed out a quick text.

I'm calling you in one minute. I suggest you pick up or the next call will be from my lawyers. Trust me, you don't want that.

The speech bubble that said she was answering rippled for several seconds—while I held my stupid breath—before it died. Exactly one minute later, I dialled her number.

'Hello?'

'What the fuck do you think you're doing, Wren?'

'Good afternoon to you, too, Jasper. How's your day going?'

'You know damn well how it's going. You went behind my back and cancelled our meeting with the advertising team. Yesterday you didn't bother to show up for the VIP guest hospitality meeting. The day before that—'

'If you're going to list everything I've done or not done in the last two weeks, do you mind if I pour myself a drink? I have a feeling I'll be thirsty by the time you're finished.'

'This is absurd. You're costing us both a lot of money.'

'Nothing earth-shattering I can't recoup eventually.'

'At the risk of sounding egotistical, I can withstand the losses way longer than you can. Have you thought about that?'

She hesitated for a split second. 'Maybe. But just as you've done your research on me, I've done mine on you. You have a board to answer to. And I dare say not everyone is thrilled about you hanging on to this deal when cutting me loose makes better sense. What do you tell them when they ask, Jasper? That you're holding on, on the off chance you'll get to fuck me as part of the deal?'

My stomach muscles knotted. I wasn't going to deny it. But it wasn't my *entire* reason. 'They trust my judgement, which is more than I'm guessing you can say for your own board.'

'Clearly you don't know as much as you think you do.'

'Enlighten me, then.'

'For starters? My board approved the list of willing partners who have indicated they'd be happy to buy out Bingham Industries' interest in this deal and they know you're refusing to entertain that idea on the basis that you're being a pig-headed—'

'Watch it, Wren. I won't be spoken to like that.'

To her credit, she didn't offer a scathing comeback.

'Has it occurred to you that prolonging this battle leaves you progressively exposed, not to mention in danger of ruining your personal reputation?' I asked.

'What are you talking about?' she replied, her voice tight.

'It's no secret that Bingham's is facing financial issues. Have you wondered why the corporate sharks haven't started circling yet?'

'Because we're not as weak as you think.'

'Bullshit. It's because of your association with the Mortimer Group. For now anyone with a lick of corporate sense knows not to mess with you because you've partnered with me. That protection erodes the second you give the impression we're not on the same page on this.'

'It's not an impression.'

I pinched the bridge of my nose and exhaled loudly. 'Christ, Wren, you're an intelligent woman. Don't let emotion cloud your judgement. I'm reaching the point where I won't feel inclined to keep the wolves from storming your door.'

'I beg your pardon?' she said sharply.

'Frankly, I'd rather have you begging for something else. But more on that in a while. For now, I want you to think hard about what you're doing.'

'I may be wrong, but I swear you just called yourself my saviour.'

'Take the advice or don't. And just so we're clear, the meeting has been rescheduled for tomorrow morning. If you're not in my office at eight a.m., I'll start playing dirty, too.'

I hung up before I lost it. Or let that sexy voice of hers wreak even more havoc on my self-control.

For the third time, I picked up the phone, this time to my assistant. 'Trish, reschedule the meeting with the advertising team for eight a.m. tomorrow and tell them Miss Bingham will attend. Then send her an email to say I want the boutique contracts I sent her last week reviewed and couriered over by close of business today.'

'Right away, Mr Mortimer.'

I replaced the handset and sat back, the throb of anticipation firing higher.

At five past five it'd turned to irritation. By five-thirty, I was pacing my office, my jaw locked in burning annoyance.

Striding to my desk, I hit the number for my assistant. 'Anything?'

'No, sir.'

'The courier is still there?'

'Yes, sir, he's still waiting at the Bingham Industries reception. Should I tell him to leave?'

'No. He stays there until I say otherwise.'

'Okay. Um… Mr Mortimer?'

I paused. 'Yes?'

'Don't forget you have the Art Foundation's Annual Gala at seven-thirty.'

I smothered a curse. I'd forgotten about my next social obligation while indulging in games with Wren. Thankfully, I'd prepared my speech weeks ago. 'Thanks for the reminder.'

'You're welcome. I've sent your new tux up to the penthouse and arranged for the car to be downstairs at seven.'

About to hang up, I tossed in one last question. 'How many more to go until gala season is over?' I asked, praying she'd say this was the last one.

'Another two, and your cousin Graciela sent an email today about the next Mortimer Quarterly launch party.'

'Thanks.'

After hanging up, I took several deep breaths. I was in danger of letting Wren unbalance me. As patron of several art foundations, I had a duty to attend this event. That it'd slipped my mind so completely made me grimace. The grimace intensified when I realised I'd been all set to track Wren down wherever she'd disappeared to instead of tackling the other time-sensitive deals I had piled up on my desk.

She was becoming an obsession.

Becoming?

I smothered the mocking inner voice and resisted the urge to call Trish again and find out whether the contract was on its way back to me. Instead I picked up a random file.

The knock on the door interrupted my focus an hour later. My pulse leapt but it was only Trish poking her head through the door. 'It's six-thirty, sir. And before you ask, no, the courier is still at Bingham's.'

My lips flattened. 'Tell him to leave. I'll deal with Miss Bingham myself.'

Several ways of dealing with her reeled through my head, all of which were most definitely NSFW.

Three hours later, the speeches were done, I'd handed over a very fat cheque and worked the room twice to ensure all present and future donors were appropriately satisfied with my attention.

Then I called the number I'd been hoping not to use any time soon. It was answered on the first ring. 'I need an address,' I said.

'Of course, sir,' my head of security answered.

Twenty minutes later, I leaned on the doorbell of the ground-floor maisonette in Fulham. Enough lights blazed within to make me comfortable she was home. Still, she kept me cooling my heels for a couple of minutes, during which time I wondered whether she was alone. What I'd interrupted.

'Who is it?' she said, her sexy voice coming through the solid wood.

'You know who it is. I just saw you looking through the security glass. At least you're not reckless about your safety.'

'It's almost midnight, Jasper,' she replied after a short pause.

The possibility that I'd caught her off guard pleased me. Which went to show how pathetic I was in gaining this tiny upper hand. 'Isn't that your favourite time of day to talk business? I'm merely obliging you. Open the door, Wren.'

'What could we possibly have to discuss that can't wait?'

Her sheer gumption drew an incredulous laugh from me. I dragged my fingers through my hair. 'I'm going to throw some names at you. Let me know if you're interested in discussing them. Palmer Jones Plc. Winlake Hotel. Morpheus Tech—'

She yanked the door open, her eyes wide with alarm. 'What did you do?'

'Do I have your attention now?'

Her jaw clenched and alarm morphed into a scowl.

'Invite me in, Wren,' I suggested softly.

Her fingers tightened on the door for a few stubborn seconds before she nudged it open.

I entered, walking down polished floorboards and Venetian wallpapered walls into a large sitting room decorated in white with splashes of warm, earthy colours. Exotic artwork featured majorly and I fought the urge to ask about her taste in art. This wasn't a social call.

'I said what did you do?' she repeated.

I turned to face her, noting for the first time what she was wearing. Her black satin, lace-edged top—clearly a nightie set designed to drive men insane—clung to her full breasts. The shorts skimmed her upper thighs, and even in the lamplight I saw enough bare skin to ramp my arousal through the roof. I dragged my gaze up past her face to the hair piled haphazardly atop her head. So far, I'd only seen it down, but she looked even more delectable in that slightly dishevelled, ready-for-bed state.

I tried to reel myself in. What the hell did she just ask me? Oh, yeah… 'So far? Nothing. But I know they're three of your top five clients.'

Her green eyes snapped with fire. 'So what? You've proved you have a spy in my office. Bravo, Jasper. And what exactly are you accusing me of? I sent your boutique contracts back an hour ago. Did you check your email before you came storming over here?'

'Yes, I did. And while I'll forgive the odd typo or two, which wasn't in my version, what the hell do you think you're playing at, allowing your sub-contractors the option to trigger an extended delivery clause?'

She shrugged. 'What can I say? I'm a generous boss. And that option was in exceptional circumstances only.'

'Which every single one of them will take advantage of! Here's a free tip, since you haven't been CEO for long—soft-balling your contracts like that is a sure-fire route to driving Bingham's out of business. Hell, even Perry knew that.' I mentally kicked myself the moment her brother's name fell from my lips.

She sucked in a quick breath and her lips flattened. 'Don't you dare say his name.'

I exhaled slowly. 'I'm done fucking around with you, Wren. This nonsense stops now or, come tomorrow morning, I'm going after your top five clients. You don't need me to tell you that I have enough personal resources to scupper every deal of yours, or, at the very least, stall it as much as you're trying to stall mine.'

Her fists balled. 'Get the hell out of my flat, Jasper.' The words were low but pithy, her eyes burning with anger and pain.

'I will, as soon as you give me your word that these shenanigans are over.'

Her chin went up. 'Agree to a five-year deal instead of three and I'll think about it.'

I considered it for half a second. 'No. As much as you won't like to hear it, it's for your own good as much as mine.'

'How utterly condescending of you,' she tossed back at me.

I didn't realise I'd been walking towards her until I caught the scent of her shampoo. Until I saw the tiny gold flecks in her eyes reflecting the lamplight.

Her head was tilted up and I couldn't help visually devouring the creamy smoothness of her skin.

'I may not deem it good business sense to renegotiate now but I won't deny you the option of doing so at a later date.'

She rolled her eyes. 'Please, stop trying to wrangle yourself into those sheep's clothes when we both know you and your family are wolves.'

Dear God, but she tested me. 'You know something? I regret not giving you that spanking you begged me for that day in the maze.'

She sucked in a quick, betraying breath. I enjoyed watching her nonplussed expression before her features closed. 'Your memory must be faulty. I never begged you for anything.'

'Not with your mouth. But we both know what you wanted that day.'

Her nostrils fluttered delicately, her eyes growing that shade of moss green that betrayed her. 'You have a vivid, and very flawed, imagination, Jasper.'

'I agree with the vivid part. I'm very happy to demonstrate just how flawed you think my memory is. Right now if you want.' I gestured at the wide sofa behind her and for the tiniest moment heat flared in her eyes.

'I don't want, thank you. Not that. Not any of this.' There was a desperate note in her voice. 'When are you going to accept it and end this?'

End our association? Watch her retreat behind that glass building half a mile away from my office that might as well have been a continent away for all the access I'd have to her? Not if I could bloody well help it. 'You know the terms of the deal as well as I do. So far I have zero incentive to give you what you want. Until such time as that changes…' I shrugged '… I want you to accept that and work with me.'

'I won't. And you'll be wise not to push me.'

'Or what?' I challenged.

'Remember those accolades you generously listed for the benefit of your Moroccan team? It's only a matter of time before I succeed.'

And as absurd as the feeling was, a part of me relished that fight with her. Glancing down at her, I drawled, 'It turns you on to fight with me, doesn't it?'

She snorted. 'Now you're just being plain ridiculous.' But her words lacked the punch of conviction.

'Am I?' I murmured. 'Then why are your nipples hard? Why's your skin flushed? I bet you'd be too proud to admit you're hot and wet right now.'

Her nostrils flared. 'Haven't you learned the futility in attempting reverse psychology with me by now?'

I smiled, enjoying myself for the first time today. 'I don't hear a denial, sweetheart.'

'Don't call me that,' she admonished. 'I'm not your sweet anything.'

'You're right. You're like a stiff shot of Scotch whisky, raging and burning all the way down. Problem is, one taste just triggers a need for another. And another…'

She stiffened. 'I wouldn't know. I don't drink.'

The tastelessness of my analogy hit home a second too late. 'Hell. I'm sorry. That wasn't meant—'

'You're still here, Jasper. Why?'

'Because your nipples are still hard. You're breathless and I know it's not because you're offended. Or annoyed with me. You want another taste, too, don't you, Wren?'

She opened her mouth, but I placed a finger on her lips. 'You can take the high road if you want, but I'm not ashamed to admit that I'm dying to kiss you. Can I?'

One perfectly sculpted eyebrow arched, and, God, even that was beyond sexy. 'You didn't bother to ask last time. Why ask now?'

'Last time was…different. Yet you did invite me to do my worst, as you put it. You needed me to take control. You wanted the fastest route out of your head and I provided it.'

She continued to glare at me. 'You think this makes you some kind of noble knight or something?'

I shrugged. 'Or something. So can I kiss you, Wren? Or do you want me to take the decision out of your hands again, give you the chance to tell me off later and claim it was all a mistake?'

The faintest flush of guilt stained her cheeks. 'You think you know me?'

'Not well enough. Not as much as I'd like. But we'll get around to that soon enough. For now…' I inched closer until mere millimetres separated our lips, until her sweet breath washed over my top lip.

Until I craved her so badly it was a physical pain not to just let the lust lashing us take over. But she was right. I wanted her to see me in a better light. Wanted her to want me without the speed bumps of our corporate skirmishes in the way.

Just when I started to give up hope, her beautiful eyes locked on mine. Still challenging. Still vexed. But also aroused. Interested. Hell, even craving.

Her gaze dropped to my mouth. And she swallowed hard. 'For now…you have one minute. Then I'm throwing you out.'

The words were barely out of her mouth before I was on her, intent on not missing a single second. Memories of kissing and touching her in the maze had haunted me for weeks and *finally* I was reliving them. My fingers in her hair held her steady as I stroked her tongue with mine. Yeah, I was a little forceful, but, hell, she'd driven me steadily insane and I wasn't in the mood to play gentleman.

She squirmed, fighting an internal battle, then, with an impatient moan, she gripped my shoulders. She rose on tiptoe, her movements increasingly demanding as she pressed her body against mine and opened wider for me.

Yes! I grabbed one hip, pressed her against me as I walked us back towards her sofa. Seconds later, she was on her back and I was on top of her, devouring her for all I was worth.

Sweet Jesus, she tasted even more sublime. Just as brazen with her needs as in the maze, she spread her thighs, accommodating me as I palmed one breast and toyed with her nipple. Her hips undulating, seeking the iron rod of my cock. We met, strained and groaned at the exquisite intensity of it. In slow, torturous rhythm, we writhed against one another, while the kiss turned hotter, wetter, simulating everything I wanted to do to her, and vice versa.

But through it all, I was keenly aware of the seconds ticking down, aware she could kick me out at any moment.

So I chose to play dirty.

On the next roll of her hips, I pressed hard against her, holding my cock tight against her satin-covered pussy, urging her to feel what I could do for her. What we could do to each other.

I bit back a smile when an involuntary spasm shuddered through her body. 'Let's renegotiate,' I rasped against her lips. 'One minute isn't going to cut it.'

She laughed a little unkindly, even while her fingers dug painfully into my biceps to hold me in place. Why did I love that she wasn't afraid to show me her fire? 'Poor Jasper.'

I growled. 'Give me ten minutes.' It was nowhere near enough for what I craved to do but it was a starting point.

She raised her head a fraction and bit my lower lip, making me shudder. 'No.'

'Christ, Wren. You're a ballbreaker, you know that?'

She stiffened slightly but didn't pull back. 'Five,' she countered after another round of furious kissing.

I yanked down one strap of her nightie top as she eagerly unbuttoned my shirt. Her fingers delved down to caress my chest and abs as I swooped onto one eager nipple. She hissed her appreciation and I feasted, groaning at her silken skin, the mouth-watering taste of her. Her back arched, offering more of herself.

'God, you're beautiful,' I rasped. 'Maddening but breathtaking.'

Against my temple, I felt her faint smile as she raked demanding fingers through my hair. Then, taking my head between her hands, she redirected me to her neglected breast. I teased, tortured and suckled until she was a glorious rose-pink. Only then did I trail one hand down, beneath the elastic of her shorts.

The brazen discovery nearly blew my head clean off. 'You answer your front door not wearing panties, sweetheart?'

'My home, my rules.'

I smiled, deciding to enjoy this particular gift before it was taken away. Spearing her with my gaze, I slid my hand lower, down over that silken strip of hair until I encountered hot, slippery flesh.

'God,' I muttered, a red haze passing over my vision. 'You're so wet.'

Expecting a smart retort, I watched as she sucked in a slow breath, her eyes not leaving mine as she chased my touch. 'Yes, I am. And your five minutes are almost up,' she said a little unsteadily.

'I'm aware, sweetheart.' I pressed my middle finger inside her and her hips jerked, her inner muscles clinging as she whimpered. 'Thing is, do I use that time for you or shall I be selfish and use it all for me?'

Her eyes widened a touch but she remained still, her hands gripping me tight. I was sure she wasn't aware of how her nails dug into me, and I bit back another smile.

Who the hell was I bluffing? I was going to use this for her. When I got around to fucking Wren, I intended to be inside her longer than whatever seconds I had left in this ridiculous game.

Bending low, I flicked my tongue over one ripe nipple as I speared her with my fingers. Her head started to roll, those insane sounds erupting from her throat again. I squeezed my eyes shut to regain some control.

But soon, much too soon, I was at that point of ravening lust, where my mind threatened to cease to function. She did this to me. Every single time. Even before we'd ever had a proper conversation, she'd pulled at me on some level. First with her brilliant mind and now, with her glorious body. The way it softened and moulded beneath my hands, the way she fought the groan tearing through her before finally letting it free to vibrate its feminine power through her body. The way those hips rolled so perfectly into mine.

Every. Single. Time.

But…hold on a sec. How long was I going to keep buckling? Sure, I might have started this, hell, *begged* for this, but she'd ended up dictating the terms anyway.

Because you're weak…

I gritted my teeth against Hugh Mortimer's damning words. Against the growing din of the clock counting down while I was getting lost in my own head. Against the even dirtier game I suspected I had to play if I was going to win this thing. Win her around.

Slowly, I raised my head. 'Wren.'

She ignored me, nibbling on my jaw before sinking her white teeth into my throat. I jerked back before I lost complete control.

'Wren. Stop.'

CHAPTER FIVE

I'VE ALWAYS HATED my name, ever since Perry let slip when I was nine that my father had given it to me as a cruel joke. George Bingham had possessed a rather dark sense of humour. Humour he'd often directed towards me in the rare times I was allowed in his vicinity.

He'd chosen a name with no softness to it, apparently, because he didn't want a soft child. Particularly, he hadn't wanted a daughter. So in his bitter humour and disappointment, he'd named me Wren. Nondescript. Forgettable. All hard angles and far too close to *wrench* for my liking. At school I'd been teased about it. *Wren the Wraith* because of my thinness, my paleness and my height. Coupled with the oppressive cloaks we'd been required to wear at my equally oppressive Hampshire boarding school, the name had fitted all too well.

But now, hearing it groaned from the depths of Jasper's arousal, it sounded…different. Not ordinary. Definitely lusty. Erotic and potent. A name uttered as if he couldn't help himself. As if he had to say it…or die.

Even as I dismissed my thoughts as a stupid flight of fancy, I leaned into him, silently pleading for him to groan it again, to fan the flames of my own arousal to that mindless place he'd taken me that chilly evening in my family's maze.

No, not back to that place.

I wanted a new place. One I could claim wholly for myself, without the spectre of my judgemental family looming over me.

As much as I hadn't wanted to let him into my personal space, now that I had him here, it wasn't so bad. My sofa would be a good starting point. Maybe eventually my bed…if we could drag ourselves there—

Except…he was already pulling away.

Far too quickly, painful reality rushed back in. Dear God, I was literally cavorting with the enemy. And even worse, he was about to leave me hanging moments away from another mind-shambling orgasm. Dazed and more than a little confused, I glanced down at myself, sprawled out with my breasts on display and my shorts pulled up tight enough to frame my crotch, highlighting the need coursing through me.

Somehow my fingers were caught in his and even though he'd rejected me, he still held on to me. Which made my exposed state even more humiliating.

I yanked myself out of his hold, face flaming as I pulled up the straps of my top until my shamefully erect nipples were covered. Jasper was still wedged between my thighs and despite his withdrawal, the outline of his erection pressed behind his fly. The sight of it reminded me of what I'd been grinding up against moments ago. His glorious thickness, the very masculine way he rolled his hips. The promise of how he would feel deep inside me…

Hunger and frustration threatened to overshadow my humiliation. But the very thought that I was considering, even for a millisecond, talking him into finishing what he'd started forced me to locate my elusive outrage.

'Can you get off me, please?'

His lips firmed. 'Wren, we need to—'

'Now, please,' I interjected, infusing my voice with necessary ice.

For several seconds, his hazel eyes narrowed, eyes that seemed to see beneath my skin, examining me intently before, thankfully, he rose from the sofa.

He crossed to the window and stared out onto the street. Whether to give me time to compose myself or because he needed a minute himself, I didn't question as I jumped up. I yanked my passion-tousled hair out of the band securing it, letting the strands fall around my shoulders and partly obscure my face in the vain hope of a shield. I contemplated going to retrieve my dressing gown out of my room and decided against the revealing move. The last thing I wanted was to lose further ground to Jasper Mortimer.

I sucked in a deep breath, exhaling slowly as he turned to face me. His stark hunger was throttled back and the eyes that stared at me held only iron resolution.

'Believe it or not, that wasn't how I wanted this to go,' he rasped.

Something fairly substantial lurched with disappointment inside me. 'And by this you mean what exactly? Storming into my flat or that half-baked seduction on my sofa?'

For some reason, my snippiness amused him. I hated myself a little for liking his smile. 'I didn't storm in and I may have stopped short of the full five minutes but there was nothing half-baked about it, sweetheart.'

Again, something lurched. It was the *sweetheart* I'd outwardly objected to but secretly didn't...hate. While I wasn't about to examine why, I knew it had something to do with the lack of softness and warmth in my life, both in childhood and now. And yes, I feared for my own gullibility at being taken in by a common term of endearment.

I crossed my arms over my chest, stingingly aware my erogenous zones were still on fire and one particular area was announcing it to the world.

'Whatever. You're going to use those extra minutes to leave, aren't you?' I said, striving for boredom.

This time his whole face hardened. 'Not until we've cleared up a few important things.'

'And what would those be?'

'You'll find out in the morning. In the meantime, fix the contract. Bring it with you tomorrow.'

I chose a silent glare as my answer.

He crossed the room to where I stood, gazed down at me long and contemplatively enough to make me tense against the urge to fidget.

'We both know you're better than this, Wren,' he murmured. 'There's absolutely no shame in proving me right. And who knows? You might get a nice surprise when you turn up tomorrow.'

When...not *if.* His confidence would've been insulting had I not spent the last two weeks and most of today confirming what I knew in my gut but hadn't been ready to admit.

I held my breath as he raised his hand, trailed his finger from my jaw to the lower lip that still tingled with the need to repeat that kiss. His eyes burned hot and heavy into mine for another moment before, gritting his teeth, he walked out of my living room.

A moment later, I heard the door close behind him. A breath shuddered out of me. I didn't exactly call it relief because that knot of hunger was still lodged in my belly, intent on reminding me how long it'd been since I'd had good sex. Or any kind of sex, for that matter.

It was only when I realised I was listening out for the sounds of his car leaving my quiet street that I sank onto the sofa. Head buried in my hands, I tried to breathe through confusion and need. Through all the reasons I'd allowed Jasper into my personal sanctuary. I wasn't melodramatic enough to fear that I'd never sit on my sofa without imagining him there wreaking sweet havoc on my body, but I suspected the experience wouldn't be easily dismissed.

Growling with impatience and frustration, I jumped up again, resolutely keeping my gaze averted from the wide expanse of the sofa as I left the room. Half an hour later, I conceded that I wouldn't get to sleep without expelling the sexual energy coursing through my blood.

As I reached for my vibrator, I cursed Jasper Mortimer loudly and succinctly. Then ruthlessly used his image to find a quick, semi-satisfactory but thankfully mind-numbing release.

I stepped out of the cab and paused on the pavement, tilting my head up to stare at the majesty that was Mortimer Towers. During my previous visits I'd used the barrier of righteous indignation to ignore its grandeur and, while I couldn't predict what would happen in the next hour, I instinctively felt today was…different. That it wouldn't be so bad to admit the masterpiece building that had won a clutch of accolades was worthy of them.

Or perhaps it was because I'd accepted on some level that the man I was dealing with was a lot more powerful than I'd given him credit for, and that power could irreversibly impact Bingham's.

Certainly, my visit to my company's archive department yesterday had uncovered the worst of my fears. Perry had been playing fast and loose with several contracts and had 'misplaced' important documents that could have severe repercussions on our business relationships.

That shocking discovery was the reason I'd buried myself in the basement of Bingham's till late last night. I was still staggered by how much Perry had been allowed to get away with by the board.

But truly, when it came right down to it, I wasn't surprised. The board was made up of the extended Bingham relatives and cronies who'd trusted Perry simply because he was male, and a Bingham. There'd been little to zero oversight and no one had dared to question his way of doing business. Just as long as he'd managed to keep the company just above the red and they collected their fat bonuses come Christmas.

Which reminded me…no Christmas bonuses this year.

I sucked in a deep breath, lowering my gaze to the glass doors that led into Jasper's domain. After a restless night that my vibrator had done very little to cure, I'd given up on sleep at five o'clock. The boutique contract was fixed and an email sent to the subcontractors apologising and withdrawing the clause I'd inserted in the last-chance hope that it would frustrate Jasper into releasing me from the contract.

We both know you're better than this...

Perhaps more than anything else that had happened in my flat last night, those words had made the most impact. Because Jasper was right.

Despite my attempts to aggravate him into dropping this deal, a significant part of me had cringed at the depths I was sinking to; the mockery I was making of my own hard-won achievements.

I hadn't quite decided what the new course of action in fighting him would be but I most certainly wasn't going to lie down and let him walk all over me.

Heat caressed my neck and flowed up into my face at the sexual connotation of my thoughts. I'd been more than prepared for him to do exactly that on my sofa last night. Firming my lips, I attempted to push the memory out of my head as I strode towards the lift.

His receptionist greeted me when I stepped out on his floor.

'Good morning, Miss Bingham. Mr Mortimer is waiting for you in conference room six. He says you're to go straight through.'

I told myself my escalating heartbeat was because I was irritated that he'd assumed I would turn up this morning. Not because I wanted to see him again. Not because the smell of his aftershave on my skin and the rasp of his stubble burn on my inner thighs had made me groan into my pillow more than once last night.

And most definitely not because he knew that two of the three company names he'd thrown at me last night were threatening to pull out of their deals with us.

Struggling to empty my mind of the challenges that awaited me back at Bingham Industries, I took a few calming breaths. I'd need optimal mental dexterity to survive this meeting with Jasper.

Running a hand over my stylish skirt suit, I strode down the wide hallway, pinning a cool, professional smile on my face as I passed his executives. I was absolutely not going to wonder how many of them had seen my trench-coat-and-promiscuous-heels performance. I'd been forced into a corner, and doing something was better than doing nothing and letting Jasper win.

What if it was all for nothing?

I mentally shrugged, gritting my teeth when I noticed that conference room six was the last one down a long hallway. Had Jasper orchestrated this walk of shame so his employees would see me? Was he that petty?

A flash of anger whipped through me, threatening to wipe away my smile. I fought to keep it in place as I pushed the door open.

He stood at a long cabinet that bordered the far wall, helping himself to a cup of the same java blend his secretary had offered me that first visit.

As I breathed in that mouth-watering hit of caffeine and watched the ripple of broad shoulder muscles encased in another immaculate suit, I wondered whether I would associate this particular brand of coffee with him for ever.

He turned just then, a small smile playing around his lips as his gaze tracked me from head to toe and back again. As he noted my attire his smile widened, what looked dangerously like triumph gleaming in his eyes.

I forced my gaze away, partly because I didn't want to confirm it and partly because in the morning light, with the sun streaming in, he looked far too delicious for my sanity. Reminded me far too vividly of how thoroughly I'd explored his body last night.

How I craved more?

'Can I get you anything? Coffee? I've had breakfast laid out for us if you're hungry.'

I shook my head. 'I'll take the coffee, but I don't want any breakfast. I've already eaten.' He didn't need to know it had only been a couple of bites of toast, hurriedly wolfed down because I'd got caught up in another woefully mismanaged Bingham file and almost missed leaving on time to get here for his eight o'clock deadline.

He nodded and poured a second cup, then added a dash of cream. When he reached me, he stared at me for a handful of seconds before holding out the cup. 'Good morning, Wren. You ready to begin?'

His voice was a low rumble that travelled through me, reminding me how his lips had felt trailing the sensitive skin of my neck. The sweet abrasion of his stubble against my breast. The filthy decadence of his tongue capturing and swirling around my nipple.

I accepted the cup without answering. Saying yes would be deemed surrender and I couldn't give in, not until I'd exhausted every avenue. Because while I could rightly claim that Perry had been the one to agree to this deal, it wouldn't stop another confrontation with my board, another round of questioning my decision and intentions. Another call from my mother under the guise of checking in on me but really to lament about the path I was taking.

Shaking my head, I approached where the papers were laid out.

'Wren?'

Refocusing on him as he joined me, I glanced at him. His expression was just as resolute as last night, but his eyes held the gentleness that conveyed understanding of my predicament. My guts tightened against the need to sink into that gentle look. It was the opposite of what I needed.

I set down my briefcase and coffee and pulled out a chair. 'I have a long day ahead. Shall we get on with it?' I said crisply.

His gentle expression evaporated, and his face hardened but he joined me at the table, pulling out the chair for himself before settling into it.

'I checked with the subcontractors this morning. Looks like this morning you withdrew your magnanimous offers?'

I wasn't going to give him the satisfaction of admitting my impetuous mistake. 'Is that a question?'

He smiled. 'Just an observation. And an offer of thanks for one less pain in my arse.'

I'd gripped that taut arse last night. Heat tunnelled through me and I moved my gaze to the papers in front of me. 'Sure. Shall we move on to the next item on the agenda?'

He nodded, then took a sip of coffee.

I tried not to let my gaze drop to his lips. I really did. But a mere eight hours ago those lips were devouring mine, and, as much as I hated to concede it, he was one hell of a kisser. Combined with the knowledge of how much sweet havoc he could wreak with those lips between my legs, surely I could forgive myself for five seconds of indulgence?

'Do you need a minute, Wren?' he asked, a thread of amusement in his voice.

My gaze shot up to meet his and he was smiling knowingly. Without breaking eye contact, he nudged the agenda sheet towards me. 'I went to the trouble of printing it out in case you didn't check your emails this morning. So we can be on the same page, as it were,' he added with a definite smirk.

I picked up the paper and quickly scrutinised it. There were twelve items on the list, mostly spelling out in black and white the tasks I was supposed to perform. I already knew the hours I was supposed to devote to the project but one item in particular made me glance up sharply.

'You expect me to go to dinner with you on Wednesday?'

He nodded briskly. 'A tequila producer I've had my eye on for a while is in town this week. He has a new specialised brand coming out around the time we open the first hotel. I want you with me because technically this should have been your job but I'm hoping you'll help me convince him to supply exclusively to us for at least three months before he rolls it out to the general market.'

I frowned. 'I already had a supplier lined up for you.'

'Did you?'

The tight edge to his question made me pause for a second before answering. 'Yes, I did.'

'That's curious. Because I'm sure there's an email in my inbox telling me we'd lost our potential liquor supplier due to non-communication with Bingham Industries.'

The throb of shame was more powerful this time. I tried to hide it by taking a sip of my own coffee. Slightly more composed, I set the cup down. 'I've had lot on my plate, as you know. This project with you isn't the only thing occupying my time.'

He stared at me for another stretch of time before he nodded. 'I'm not too fussed about losing that supplier, to be honest. His product was great but not spectacular. This new one promises to be rather exceptional. That's why I don't want to lose it. So, you'll come with me on Wednesday, yes?' he pressed.

A business dinner with him to secure a supplier wasn't a complete concession. I'd been in this business long enough to know contractors came and went for any number of reasons. Even if Bingham Industries managed to pull out of the contract, I could at least help Jasper secure this small part of his project.

I shrugged. 'Sure, I can do dinner. What time do you want me?'

His eyes darkened. 'I'll pick you up at seven at your place,' he said, his voice deep and raspy.

It would've been far more professional to arrange to meet him at the restaurant. And yet, I found myself answering, 'Okay.'

His smile grew warmer, his gaze several degrees hotter as it dragged over my face to rest on my mouth. Time stretched taut and charged with far too much sexual intensity, before he stared down at the paper. 'What's next?'

We worked through the next few items, and with each one I reassured myself that nothing was set in concrete. Sooner or later, once Jasper realised the futility of a Mortimer-Bingham deal, replacing me would be a simple matter of snapping his fingers.

And if he didn't?

I dismissed the question. Just as I attempted to

suppress the quiet excitement that was building inside me as we went down the list.

My head snapped up as Jasper abruptly rose. 'More coffee?'

A small bolt of surprise went through me as I realised I'd finished mine. I nodded as he walked over to the buffet cabinet, glancing at me over his shoulder. 'Are you sure I can't get you anything?'

I was about to refuse, but my gaze went to the clock and I noticed we'd been working for an hour. As if on cue, my stomach rumbled. It wasn't enough to get his attention but I knew it would eventually if I carried on working without eating.

Setting my pen down, I rose, rounded the conference table and joined him. Trays of warm, mouthwatering pastries were set out next to platters of fruit, juice carafes and assorted condiments.

Jasper grabbed two plates and handed me one.

Our fingers brushed as I took it from him. He heard my sharp intake of breath and stilled, staring down at me.

For several, electrifying seconds, we stayed frozen.

Then, as if pulled by invisible strings, I swayed towards him. At the very last moment, I caught myself, veering away towards the food.

Dear God, what is wrong with me?

He'd gone down on me in the maze and, somehow, I'd managed to work on and off with him for two weeks, but one little tumble on my sofa last night and my concentration was shot to hell?

A little bewildered, I randomly selected food while desperately attempting to downplay how badly Jasper affected me. How badly I wanted to lean into that strong column of his neck, breathe in the after-shave that had so tantalised me last night.

Of course he'd put the brakes on then, though. Which meant, like me, he probably didn't think it was a good idea—

My thoughts stumbled to a halt when he laughed. 'That's the spirit. I love a woman with a healthy appetite.'

I blinked, then glanced down at my plate. My very full, very heaped plate of food. I cringed, aware of the flush creeping up my cheeks.

Then his words registered. Who was the last woman with a good appetite who'd occupied his attention? Did he have a girlfriend? It suddenly struck me that we'd had two sexual encounters without knowing the basics about each other. An uneasy, wholly unwelcome sensation tightened my chest. Surely, he wouldn't do the things he'd done to me if was seeing another woman?

He's a Mortimer, isn't he?

The twisting sensation inside me intensified.

'I guess you were pretty hungry, after all?' Jasper continued.

I dragged my focus from his imaginary harem to the embarrassment of my heaped plate. 'God, there's enough to feed an army here. I don't need all of this. Not really. I was just...'

Just wondering who else you were going down on when you weren't turning me inside out with your tongue...

As I shook my head free of the thought, he stepped closer. 'Here, I'll take a couple of those off your hands if you want.'

I watched, a little annoyed for being so easily distracted by him as he transferred a bagel and croissant from my plate to his. He left far more than I needed on my plate but somehow I didn't protest as his free hand landed in the small of my back, scrambling my brain as he guided me back to the table. 'Come on, let's get back to it,' he said.

In between watching him take healthy bites out of his food and attacking the next item on the agenda, I demolished several pastries, mentally promising myself another twenty minutes on the treadmill at my next gym session.

I didn't object when he returned to the buffet table and brought back a bowl of fruit, only squirmed stealthily in my chair as I watched him toss a grape into his mouth.

God, what the hell was so fascinating about watching this man eat? Whatever it was, I couldn't stop myself from watching him swallow, the movement of his Adam's apple curiously erotic enough to shoot arrows of desire into my pelvis.

'Are we done?' I asked, more out of desperation than anything else.

'More or less,' he replied.

'What else is there?'

For the longest time, he didn't reply. When he reacted, it was to reach into the fruit bowl and pluck out a ripe, juicy strawberry. Then he rolled his chair around the table, breaching the gap between us. 'There's something else I want to talk about.'

Something dark and decadent in his voice made my thighs tingle, my breath rush out in a lustful little pant. 'Oh?'

'I feel the need to apologise for the way I left things last night.'

The reminder reduced the tingles but didn't demolish them altogether. 'You came to deliver a message and I received it loud and clear.'

'I'm not talking about business, and you know it.'

'Do I?'

He leaned forward, held the fruit against my bottom lip then trailed it lazily from side to side. 'I left you hanging,' he murmured throatily. 'I'm not in the habit of doing that.'

Curiously compelled, I licked the fruit before answering, 'I'm a big girl, Jasper. I can take it.'

His nostrils flared in arousal. 'Not if you don't have to.'

I sucked in a breath, the scent of the strawberry and his aftershave a potent mix that rendered me strangely breathless. 'You don't owe me anything…'

'Okay. But you still owe me one minute, possibly two.' He pressed the fruit harder against my mouth. 'Open,' he instructed gruffly.

My lips parted and I took the fruit. His gaze dropped to my mouth as I held it between my lips for a moment then bit into it. Sticky juice trickled down one corner of my mouth. His gaze latched on to it for one tight little second before, groaning, he lunged forward.

He devoured half of the fruit as he sealed his lips to mine.

As if a switch had been thrown, feverish electricity consumed us as we consumed each other. He rose, his urgent hands landing on my waist to yank my body into his. My hands flew up his broad shoulders, explored for mere seconds before spiking into his hair.

Jasper's tongue delved into my mouth, licking away the last of the juices before tangling with mine. Desire shot through me, lifted me onto my tiptoes as I strained against him. Wanting more.

My vibrator last night had come nowhere close to satisfying the need clamouring anew inside me. The thought that Jasper was equally ravenous for me thrilled my blood as he deepened the kiss.

The faint sound of a ringing phone momentarily reminded me of where we were, the possibility that someone could walk in on us at any moment.

With a monumental effort, I broke the kiss and

laid my hand on his chest as I fought to catch my breath. 'Jasper, I...the door...'

Without letting go of me, he walked us a few steps to the middle of the conference table and snatched up a small remote. Aiming it at the door, he clicked a button and I heard the distinct sound of it locking.

Burnished eyes pinned me where I stood. 'No one will disturb or hear us now. The room's sound-proofed.'

My breath shuddered out, my fingers tightening on his nape even as I questioned my sanity. 'Jasper...'

He dropped his lips to my jaw, trailing little erotic bites before he caught my earlobe between his teeth. 'I regret not making you come last night. I sure as hell regret missing the chance to be inside you, even if it was only for one minute.'

My laugh emerged shakily. 'You're assuming I would've let you.'

Just like last night, his lips explored the pulse in my neck. Shivering in delight, I angled my head, granting him access.

'My negotiating skills are exceptional, Wren. I'm sure we would've come to some agreement had I stayed. But no matter. I have a new proposition for you. One I'm sure will satisfy us both.'

My arsenal was depleted. I had very little to fight him with. But he didn't need to know that.

'What is this proposition?' I asked, my in-sides dipping alarmingly at how much I wanted to know. How much I hoped it was something I could agree to.

Yeah, my head definitely needed examining.

He held on to me but eased his torso away from mine. 'You're brilliant and sexy. You've driven me insane thus far but I don't think I've hidden the fact that I want you. Hell, at this point it goes beyond want.' His eyes burned into mine as he inhaled slowly.

My throat dried at the raw, potent need in his voice. A tremble commenced inside my belly as he continued.

'Don't think I haven't noticed you still haven't given me a clear-cut answer as to whether you intend to work with me or not. But I have a way I think we can co-exist for the immediate future. A way that might make working with me a little more bearable?'

I didn't think there was any way forward that wouldn't incite my family's disapproval but I held back from mentioning it. Somehow, discussing family feuds in this moment felt...wrong. 'I'm listening,' I said.

He dropped his forehead to mine. 'You know I'm dying to fuck you. And I know you're not completely immune to reciprocating.'

I couldn't deny it. 'I think you got your answer last night.'

He gave a lopsided smile. 'Even though you also invited me to leave several times?'

I raised an eyebrow. 'You annoyed me. And I'm complicated.'

'Well, maybe this is one thing we can agree on. I'm great at giving you orgasms, despite withholding one last night.'

A husky laugh left my throat. 'Are you seriously tooting your own horn?'

He shrugged, an arrogant gesture that was so completely natural I wouldn't have been surprised if he'd been born with it. One hand trailed up from my waist to rest beneath my chin. His thumb rubbed my lower lip and I felt his erection jerk against my belly. Heat arrowed between my legs, making my core wet and needy as I waited for him to elaborate.

'Okay, here's the deal. For every six hours you devote to this deal, you get an orgasm.'

My mouth sagged open. 'I…what?'

His head dropped and delivered a hard, quick kiss before drawing back. Hazel eyes stayed on mine, his easy manner belied by the fact that every word out of his mouth held fierce determination, a promise to deliver on what he was offering. 'I think it's a better way for us to relieve our frustrations, if you like. Why scream with anger when you can scream with pleasure?'

I refused to examine why I wasn't completely outraged, why, contrary to every scrap of common sense I possessed, I was held rapt and completely aroused by his proposition. 'Let me get this straight. You want to buy my cooperation with orgasms?'

That wicked little smile tilted one corner of his mouth again. 'I want us to make love, not war,' he offered.

I raised an eyebrow. 'Wow, are you sure you're not on some two-for-one deal on clichés?'

His fingers dug into my waist to pull me closer still, ensuring I felt his hard cock against my belly. I shuddered, unable to help but push back, revelling in the power and promise of him. I was racked with mounting need; my gaze darted to the shiny expanse of the conference table.

Jasper followed my gaze and laughed. 'We can christen our new agreement right there, if you want, sweetheart.'

I swallowed, unable to believe that I was contemplating this absurdity. The excuse was that I'd arrived here with very little option but to continue to work with Jasper for the time being. Loyalty to my family dictated that the prize of working with the Mortimer Group was forbidden to me as a personal career choice, but while I was contract-bound to work with him, was it wrong to help myself to the cherry on top when he was freely offering it?

Between the mess Perry had left the company in and pressure from my mother, I didn't plan on dating anyone soon. Jasper's proposition ensured that we could work relatively friction-free, while enjoying a side benefit we both wanted.

The promise of sex lit a fuse in my blood. Before I got completely carried away with it, the question that'd niggled at me for the last hour rose again. 'Is this suggestion of yours inconveniencing anyone else?'

His brow knotted. 'What?'

'Are you dating anyone, Jasper?'

His frown cleared but his eyes remained mildly accusing. 'I'm not sure how to interpret you believing I would give you orgasms while seeing another woman.'

I tried to stop the wild relief flowing through me. 'Is that a no, you're not seeing anyone else?'

'It's a no,' he confirmed with gritted teeth. 'You may not have a very high opinion of me, but I do have some standards, sweetheart.'

His censure shamed me a little, but I brushed it away.

'I'm waiting for an answer, Wren. You want me, I want you. Are we going to do this, or not?' he pressed.

He was still doing that thing with his hips that drove me insane. Just as it had last night. That knot of need I thought I'd dampened with my vibrator came roaring back, stronger than before. The thought of walking out of here nursing that ache suddenly became unthinkable. Unbearable.

Keeping my gaze on his, I reached between us and unbuttoned my jacket. Slowly, I shrugged out of it, then tossed it on the nearest chair.

Jasper followed the action with eyes ablaze.

Next, I reached for his tie, loosening it before snapping it free of his collar. He swallowed, and I smiled.

Leaning forward and trailing my lips up to his throat, I whispered in his ear, 'I accept your proposal, Jasper. And I'd very much like to christen your conference table. Now, please.'

He hoisted me up as if I weighed nothing, and between one frenzied heartbeat and the next I was laid out flat on his conference table and he was staring down at me with eyes that promised mind-altering passion.

CHAPTER SIX

I'D CHOSEN MY attire specially today because I'd needed the confidence boost; and because I'd accepted that the way I'd been handling things the past two weeks needed to change.

And perhaps—okay, extremely possibly—I'd also chosen my underwear because, deep down in a place I didn't want to examine too closely, I'd hoped *this* would happen.

Between frenzied kisses and the need to explore every inch of his sleekly muscled body, I wasn't certain which one of us undid my silk blouse. But I was certain which one stopped in their tracks, mouth hanging open at the sight of the sea-green lace bra I wore beneath it.

I hid a pleased smile as Jasper growled beneath his breath, his eyes rapt on my chest.

My lingerie was the indecently expensive kind, concocted of gossamer-thin scraps of lace, strings and silk, bought on a slightly tipsy whim while late-night online shopping, then shoved deep into the underwear drawer with much chagrin after the hangover wore off and the package arrived on my doorstep.

But in this moment, I patted myself on the back as Jasper's hands hovered reverently over my breasts, as if he wasn't sure whether to worship me or devour me.

'Jesus Christ, Wren. You're exquisite,' he breathed, his eyes darting from my chest to my face and back again.

'Not too exquisite to touch, I hope?'

He started to reach for me, then paused. 'Tell me you weren't wearing this underneath that damned trench coat when you came into my building two weeks ago?'

'Why would I want to stop torturing you by satisfying your curiosity?'

He raised an eyebrow, even while his frantic gaze dropped to latch onto my peaking nipples. 'Because we just agreed to call a truce?'

Trailing my finger down over the firm, tanned skin covering his clavicle, I decided to give a little. 'I wasn't wearing this exact same set, no. Now, are you going to unwrap me or make me wait?' I demanded softly.

With effortless ease, he divested me of my blouse. It landed on the floor, but I didn't care. Because my busy fingers had done some unwrapping of their own, exposing the most perfect set of abs I'd seen outside a magazine. I touched his skin, almost moaned at how warm and firm and utterly delicious he was. About to put my mouth where my hands had been, I whimpered in protest as Jasper pushed me back firmly.

Reading his intent, I relaxed, reclining on the table as he stepped back, took me in, then groaned. 'I'll never be able to take a meeting in this room without picturing you like this.'

'You'll get through it somehow, I'm sure.' I arched my back, the cool surface momentarily chilling my skin; making my nipples harder. He saw the reaction and charged forward with another animalistic snarl.

'I don't like being the only one without a shirt on, Jasper.'

Cracking a taut smile, he jerked off his jacket and tossed it away. A crook of my finger and he was leaning over me. Strong hands framed my hips, trailed up my ribcage as I attacked his remaining shirt buttons. The moment I bared his chiselled torso, I dragged my fingernails over his taut, smooth skin.

'Fuck, that feels good,' he groaned, his gaze latching on to the lace doing a very poor job of hiding my arousal from him. 'As much as I'm dying to get you naked, I don't want to risk ripping anything off… this time. We both need to walk out of here with as many of our clothes intact as possible.' He cupped my lace-clad breasts, squeezing with an urgency that telegraphed his need. 'Help me out?' he requested hoarsely.

I wanted to tell him to rip it off, if only for the

novelty of experiencing such raw passion for the first time in my life. But I bit my tongue. There were other ways to achieve the mindless state his eyes promised. Trailing my fingers back up his torso to his neck, I dropped my other hand to the first strap and slowly lowered it. 'Like this?'

His head jerked in a nod. 'More,' he commanded.

I tugged down the strap another fraction, bearing the top of my breast and exposing the smallest hint of a nipple.

'More, Wren. More. Show me those perfect breasts I tasted last night.'

'Hmm, how do I know you're not going to leave me hanging again?' I teased.

A dash of hectic colour highlighted his cheekbones. He nudged my hips to the edge of the table, until there was no mistaking his hard, potent ridge. 'I promise, this time I'm not stopping until every inch of my cock is buried inside you. Now, please take that damn bra off before I rip it off with my teeth.'

A shiver coursed through me, pooling heat between my thighs. I felt myself getting wetter and sucked in a deep breath to compose my erratic heartbeat. I was dying for him to take me, and, though I suspected this would be more memorable than my previous sexual encounters, I still wanted him to work for it. My instincts warned me that giving in too easily to Jasper Mortimer was the absolute wrong tactic to take.

With a saucy little smile, I abandoned the bra and

reached for the hem of my skirt. He watched me, his face tightening with every passing second as I nudged the material up my thighs until my panties were exposed. A projection in my mind's eyes of how I looked—semi-naked and sprawled out, open to his gaze—sent a hot rush through me, followed swiftly by a pulse of feminine power as I caught his expression. He liked this. Hell, he more than liked it. In a fight where it seemed I was losing at every turn, it felt good to reclaim some ground.

'Take my panties off, Jasper,' I instructed, my voice a husky mess. 'The bra stays on.'

He didn't need a second bidding.

He dragged my panties off with a smooth move that made my heart miss several beats. And in the flip of a switch, I sensed a shift in the power balance. Firm hands grasped my thighs, parted them boldly so he could stare down at my damp flesh. A deep breath expanded his chest as he passed his thumb over my engorged clit. My whole body jerked, a spasm of pleasure rippling through me at that smallest touch.

Lust-dark eyes darted to my face and then back to my core. 'I'm going to enjoy fucking you, Wren,' he declared with gruff anticipation.

His dirty words made me hotter; more impatient. I tried to grasp him with my thighs, nudge him closer, to get this show on the road. Jasper merely smiled, put his thumb to his lips and decadently sucked off my wetness as he looked into my eyes.

'You want it hard or slow?'

Again, I felt my face flaming, even as excitement fluttered in my belly. No other man had ever asked me that. And how pathetic was that? Or had I not been interested enough before to vocalise my own needs?

'Do I have to choose? Can't I have both?'

His smile widened, the confident stamp of a man who knew how to wield his sexual prowess. 'You can have whatever you want, sweetheart.'

I swallowed at his thick promise; watched him reach into his back pocket for his wallet. He plucked out a condom, tore it open and gifted me another erotic sight of watching him slowly lower his zip.

I already knew he was thick and long, but I wasn't quite prepared for the beautiful sculpture of Jasper's cock or the pleasure I took in watching him glide on the condom.

Then he was reaching for my thighs, dragging me even closer to the edge of the table. Breathing harshly, he teased his length over my hot, wet core without entering me, his eyes on my face as he tormented me.

Wrapping his hands around my waist, he tilted his hips in one smooth movement and thrust deep inside me. A curious little sound left my throat, a cross between a muted scream and sheer delight at how deeply, completely he filled me. Then for the longest time he held still, his eyes shut and jaw locked tight.

'Again, please,' I gasped.

Exhaling, he withdrew, slowly…and repeated

the penetration. Fiery desire shot up my spine, my hands scrambling for purchase on the table. 'Oh, God, again. Please,' I begged.

He gave a low, ragged laugh and started to thrust in earnest. My breath shortened, panted as he fell into a steady, mind-bending rhythm. My eyes drifted closed as pleasure collected deep in my pelvis but after a moment, I prised them open, the need to watch Jasper too overwhelming to deny.

And he was a glorious sight. His hooded gaze was rapt on my face, a lock of hair draped over his forehead as he shuttled in and out of me. Dear God, he was beautiful. An animal. One concentrated fully on me. The fierce light in his eyes said he would deliver on every single sexual promise he'd made.

'Tell me more, Wren,' he urged thickly. 'I want to hear everything you're feeling.'

I wasn't sure why that demand rattled something inside me. When was the last time anyone had asked me what I felt? All my life I'd been subjected to what everyone believed was good for me without considering my input. I knew this was just sex, that he'd set himself a goal he was determined to achieve, but something inside me still lurched as I scrambled around for adequate words to describe this unique experience. 'It feels good. So good.'

'What else?' he demanded, a touch harshly.

'The way you're holding me down. I like it.'

His fingers convulsed on my waist, tightening briefly as he pulled me into another thrust. A tiny scream left my throat, the sensation sharper, even more exquisite. 'Yes! More of that. Faster.'

'Fuck yes,' he breathed, as if I'd delivered the very thing he wanted. He dragged me lower until my bottom hung off the edge of the table. Arranging my legs up until they were curled around his neck, he leaned forward, plastered his lips over mine in a dirty, carnal kiss; a brief but frantic duelling of the tongues before he surged back up. His breath emerging in harsh pants, Jasper widened his stance and slammed even harder inside me. A louder scream left my throat, my back arching off the table as sublime sensation curled through me.

'Come for me, sweetheart. I need to feel you come all over my cock.'

Needing somewhere on his body to anchor myself, I wrapped my fingers around his forearms. Moments later, I smashed through the barrier of no return.

'Oh, God, I'm coming,' I whispered, a strange transcendental sensation washing over me as I was thrown headlong into my climax. It arrived as a forceful tsunami, threatening to rip me apart from the inside. My nails dug into his arms when bliss crashed over me, dragging me deep, deeper than I'd ever been before in my life. Longer than I'd ever experienced.

When the storm abated, when I could again prise open eyes I couldn't remember closing, it was to find Jasper propped on his elbows over me, his incisive eyes absorbing my every twitch and gasp.

A half minute passed before I realised he was still hard and solid inside me. Shock must have registered because he gave a tight smile, his face a mask of deep arousal, ruthlessly controlled.

'Did I leave you hanging?' I attempted to tease, although the shifting emotions inside me left me wildly unsettled in the aftermath.

'That one was for you. Watching you come was a pleasure I wasn't about to deny myself.'

'But?'

He didn't answer immediately. His head dropped a few inches, his mouth taking my nipple and sucking hard before, at the sensitive shiver coursing through me, he raised his head.

'But now I get to experience what it feels like to come inside you.' His voice was a raw throb of anticipation that tingled every nerve in my body.

Before I could draw breath, he snatched me off the table. He disengaged long enough to flip me around and repositioned my legs, until my feet met the floor, and then bent me over the conference table.

Then, as if he had all the time in the world, Jasper ran his fingers through my hair, over my neck and down my spine. He unclasped my bra, trailed kisses where his hands had been, and cupped my breasts. As if he knew how sensitive I was, he merely squeezed and fondled them for another minute without teasing my nipples. Then he nudged me upright; my back to his hot, muscled chest, he wrapped one arm around my waist. 'Raise your arms, Wren. Wrap them around my neck,' he whispered in my ear.

Wearing my heels and stockings with my skirt around my waist and my arms angled backwards around his neck, I felt dirty and decadent. Apparently, he thought so too because his breathing grew frantic and rapid. 'You have any idea how long I've imagined you like this?'

I smiled. 'Hmm, roughly about two weeks?'

He laughed. 'Try a whole lot longer, sweetheart.'

With that, he thrust upward inside me.

Every single thought dissolved from my brain as Jasper began to fuck me again.

With his free hand he explored me, from chest to thighs and in between, and when I began to lose my mind again, and his thrusts grew erratic and much deeper than I thought possible, his fingers delved between my folds, expertly strumming my clit in exquisite motions that sent me surging into the stratosphere once again.

His head aligned with mine, I heard his low growls as I started to come. 'Christ, Wren. You feel fucking amazing. So tight and hot and beautiful. *Yes, yes, yes,*' he hissed in sync with his thrusts as we drowned in our mutual orgasm.

Coming down from the second high was just as surreal, and when he pulled out of me and perched me on the table, a twinge of loss staggered me. Watching him stroll to the cabinet, I felt weirdly unmoored, turned inside out as I struggled to get my emotions under control.

None of my previous encounters had affected me this much. But this was still just sex. Great sex. It was the height of stupidity to get emotional or evangelical about it. I repeated those words feverishly to myself as he returned. Striving for composure, I lifted my head, meeting his gaze with a cool smile as he set down the stack of tissues on the table. 'May I?' he asked.

What little poise I'd scrambled together threatened to evaporate at his request.

Stop it. This didn't mean anything. So he cared about my comfort. Big deal. About to tell him I was a grown woman and he didn't need to attend to me, I found myself biting my lip and nodding.

The gleam in his eyes said my answer had pleased him but in the next moment the expression was gone. Surrealness engulfed me again as he cleaned me up, then, plucking my panties off the floor, he sank low and looked up at me. Our gazes connected, I stepped back into my underwear and he pulled it up my legs slowly, his gaze dropping once to rest on my pussy for a long, prolonged moment before sliding the underwear back into place.

Perturbed by how unnerving his aftercare was, how needy it made me feel, I jerked upright and cleared my throat. 'I need to get going.'

Jasper rose calmly, stepped forward and spiked

his fingers through my hair. Tilting my face up, he dropped a soft, brief kiss on my lips.

With every cell in my body, I wanted to prolong the kiss. I sucked in a breath when he stepped away, the loss echoing inside me.

God, what the hell is wrong with me?

A little desperately, I retrieved my bra, slipped it back on before reclaiming my blouse. I kept my back to him as I buttoned it up and slipped on my jacket. On slightly firmer ground, I passed my own fingers through my hair and then gathered my papers off the table.

And turned around to discover Jasper was fully dressed, too. Hell, he was so immaculately put back together, it was as if he'd had way too much experience at this.

Nope. I most definitely wasn't going to think about how often he'd done this. I'd never been possessive or jealous about sexual partners in my life. I wasn't about to start.

'Are we good?' he asked, walking towards me.

My head shot up. 'Of course.'

His gaze raked my face before, nodding, he reached for the control and unlocked the door. 'Good. I'll walk you out.'

I tightened my fingers around my briefcase. This was stupid. I should welcome the chance to escape this room, to regroup. Nevertheless, when his hand arrived in the small of my back, I couldn't help the shiver that coursed through me. I had a long hallway to traverse before I got into the lift; a long hallway where his employees would probably catch a glimpse of my dishevelled state.

'Are you sure everything's okay?' Jasper asked, a frown between his eyebrows.

I started to nod, but then paused.

He leaned down, trailing his lips over my cheek before kissing the corner of my mouth. 'There's a quicker way out of the building if you prefer?'

I looked up, hating myself for the relief bursting through me. Then a thought scythed through the feeling. I glared at him. 'Do you sneak all your lovers through the back door?'

His eyes narrowed. 'Believe it or not, this is the first time I've done it in here. I don't intend it to be the last time though. With you.'

I hated the spurt of excitement that sprang up in my belly. 'The front door will be just fine.'

He smiled, and again I got the funny feeling that I'd pleased him. Mentally, I shook my head. I really needed to get out of here.

Thankfully, the office floor was less busy. And Jasper in calm, professional mode as he walked me to the lift eased my nerves. About to utter a brisk, professional goodbye, I looked up in surprise when he walked into the lift with me. 'What are you doing?'

He didn't answer until the lift doors shut. Then he stepped into my space again, one hand cupping my nape.

'I need one last kiss,' he said gruffly. He sealed

his mouth to mine, tongue curling round mine in a kiss so possessive, so hot and sexy, my toes curled. All too soon, the lift reached the ground floor and the doors parted. With clear reluctance, Jasper released me. But not before he caressed his knuckles down my cheek.

'Have a good day, Wren.' And then, as I shakily stepped out of the lift, he added, 'I'll see you back here tonight at six.'

Before I could ask what he was talking about, the doors slid shut.

A little breathless and a whole lot flustered, I stumbled out of his building then paused on the pavement to check the email that had pinged into my inbox. Jasper.

Six hours until your next orgasm. We can use up three of those hours working tonight. Don't be late.

I tried to summon all the righteous indignation I could think of. But as I hurried to my office, all I could think of was how good he'd felt inside me. How the day was going to absolutely drag until I saw him again. How quickly I could make up the extra three hours I needed.

How much I feared—with addiction stamped into my family's DNA—that I was already way too obsessed with Jasper Mortimer's sexual prowess.

CHAPTER SEVEN

THAT BRACING, TERRIFYING thought turned out to be the impetus I needed to block Jasper from my mind for the better part of the morning, despite my phone pinging intermittently with text messages from him. Even the perfectly valid reasoning that answering his texts could be deemed work and therefore contribute towards my six-hour accumulation terrified me a little when my heart leapt at the idea.

Perhaps fate thought it prudent to deliver me from my increasingly frantic Jasper-induced withdrawal symptoms. Because just before midday, when the door to my office swung open, my heart lurched for one giddy moment at the thought that it was him, before plummeting at the sight of the woman framed in the doorway, dressed from head to toe in designer white, complete with radiant pearls.

I couldn't help but wonder if my mother's inability to feel affection for me was because she resented me for choosing to earn my living rather than marry into it, as she had.

Stifling the bruising thought, I looked past her to a visibly flustered Alana who mouthed *Sorry* before hurriedly closing the door. 'Mother. Did we have an appointment?'

'You're not senile, Wren, you know we don't. Just as you know the reason I don't have an appointment for this meeting is because you've been avoiding my calls. You've left me no choice but to chance this visit. And you know how I feel about impropriety.'

I gritted my teeth, wondered for a wild moment if one of Jasper's texts had included an invitation for a working lunch. And whether I should've accepted it.

No.

If my mother was the frying pan, Jasper was most definitely the fire. Regardless of how pleasurable it'd been to dance in the flames this morning, I needed to pace myself or risk being incinerated. Inhaling calm, I rose from the desk, approached where my mother was pulling off stylish winter gloves to drop them along with her designer handbag on the coffee table. My spirits sank lower at the sign that this wasn't going to be a quick visit.

'I'm sorry, I've been busy. What can I help you with?' I asked, keeping my voice even.

Eyes a shade lighter than mine studied me with cool assessment. 'There's something different about you.'

Oh, Christ.

I sucked in another calming breath and reminded myself I was a grown woman, not a child terrified of chastisement or one desperate for her mother's approval. Or, heaven forbid, her mother's love or whatever dregs remained after she'd already given the lion's share of it to her husband and son. 'I'm not sure I know what you mean, Mother.'

One well-plucked eyebrow rose. 'Don't you? Maybe not. But you were definitely more...flappable the last time I saw you.'

I wasn't going to admit, even to myself, that the skirmish with Jasper had helped me tap into confidence and determination reserves that had been in danger of dwindling recently. Perhaps it wasn't even the sex. Maybe it was accepting that negotiating a better deal with Jasper was better than opposing him and letting Bingham's go down in a fiery blaze. Whatever. For now, I was keeping the wolves away from the company door and I wasn't ashamed about it. 'Perhaps it was because you knew where Perry was and what he was up to but decided not to share it with me?'

My mother was too cultured to roll her eyes but not averse to pursing her lips and delivering a frostier stare. 'Your brother is in Arizona now, getting the help he needs. Let's be thankful for that and not drag him into this, shall we?'

'And what exactly is this?'

She took her time to sit, crossing her long, shapely legs. I thought about offering her tea, then suppressed the urge. Instinct warned me that the reason for her visit wouldn't go down well, tea or no tea. And I wasn't going to prolong it more than necessary. 'You've been seen colluding with that Mortimer boy again, Wren.'

Several protests rushed to the tip of my tongue. Firstly, that Jasper wasn't a boy but very much a man, in every sense of the word. Secondly, that I couldn't wait to *collude* with him again. In various positions I hadn't been able to stop myself from imagining all morning. 'Again?' I echoed, buying myself a little time.

'Anyone with decent eyesight saw you two at the party. And you've been seen at the Mortimer building, too.'

'Because we're partners in a business deal, Mother. A business deal Perry signed with him, which you already know about. Even if you didn't before, I know you have eyes and ears on the board now.'

'And you assured that same board that you would fix any tiny lapses your brother committed while he wasn't quite himself. Or did I get that wrong?'

My heart hammered against my ribs, this time with anger and pain. 'You may not want to hear it, Mother, but the problems Perry left behind are a lot more than *tiny lapses*. I'm just trying to make the best of the situation we now find ourselves in.'

Her face hardened. 'Is that your way of telling me you're about to let this family down? Need I remind you that it's exactly because of *that* family that we find ourselves in this situation in the first place?'

The vise tightened around my heart. 'I'm sorry you think I'm letting you down by doing everything I can to save our company. Would you prefer a complete stranger take over, one without the family's best interests at heart?'

She waved me away with a flick of her wrist. 'Now you're just being overdramatic. If your father or Perry were here—'

'But they're not!' The sharp rebuttal stopped us both in our tracks. A flash of pain crossed her face and I swallowed the sudden lump in my throat. 'They're not, Mother,' I repeated firmly. 'But I am. And I'm doing my best. I promise. Please trust me?'

The plea earned me nothing but a colder stare, which in turn hardened the edges of my pain. 'And I hate to say this, but regarding the feud—are we really blameless?' Was Jasper right? Maybe we needed to lance this boil once and for all, give the wound a chance to heal.

Or maybe not; judging by the paleness of her cheeks and the tightening of her jaw, my mother wasn't of the same mind. 'How dare you?'

I pressed a hand to my eyes. 'How dare I? Maybe I'm tired of fighting, Mother. Maybe I just want to use my energies to save this company rather than perpetuating a ridiculous fight that should've ended decades ago.' I dropped my hand.

She surged to her feet, her eyes flashing disappointment that shouldn't have eviscerated me, but did. 'Your father would be ashamed of you.'

Pain lacerated deeper, enough to drive my fingers into the back of the sofa opposite where she sat. 'Just as you are?'

Her delicate nostrils flared, the exquisite cheekbones standing out in relief as she stared at me. 'Excuse me?'

'Nothing I've ever done has been good enough for you, has it?'

Her mouth worked but no words emerged for several seconds. Then, 'You've known since you were a child what I expected of you—'

'What about what I wanted for myself? Did that count for anything at all?' I blurted, aware my emotions were in danger of running away with me.

'What counts, my dear, is that you seem determined to do the opposite of what's expected of you. I've never understood that about you.'

As usual I was getting nowhere. My mother was entrenched in her thinking where I was concerned. No amount of talking would sway her. So I shook my head. 'I don't want to do this now, Mother.'

'I should think not. I'm not sure what's got into you, but you need to remind yourself where your allegiances lie. Your brother most certainly did.'

For a moment I experienced a resurgence of that searing jealousy I'd tried to suppress for so long. My mother's blind love for my brother and father had made me wonder what I lacked that her love couldn't extend to me. For so long, I'd hated that I couldn't answer the question. In my weakest moments, I still did.

But I'd learned to survive without that emotion in my life, hadn't I? Surely in time I'd learn to do without altogether? The hollow inside me mocked that forlorn hope. If I could live without it, then why had Jasper's gentleness affected me so much? Why did I, even now, yearn for it when the probability of it being ephemeral—like my mother's regard—was the true reality?

Just sex. Given and taken. That was all I had to give Jasper. It was delusional to believe I *could* give anything more when my reservoirs had never been filled.

'Is that all? I have work to do, Mother.'

Her lips pursed, then she snatched her gloves and bag off the table. 'If my feelings and opinion are worth anything to you, Wren, then you'll think harder about distancing yourself from the Mortimer boy. His family have brought us nothing but grief and if they've done it once, they'll do it again. Nothing you say will convince me otherwise.'

She sailed out without deigning to deliver the air-kiss she normally dispensed when we were in public. I told myself I was glad, but the searing realisation that I craved even that small show of false affection made my gut twist in mild sorrow.

God, was I really that needy?

I was still mired in that maelstrom of anguish and anger when my phone rang minutes later. I reached for it without stopping to check the caller. And experienced a different emotion entirely when Jasper's deep, sexy voice flowed into my ear. 'Sushi or Greek food?'

I scrambled to focus. 'Umm…what?'

'Your choice for lunch.'

'Neither.' My appetite was non-existent after dealing with my mother. 'I wasn't planning on eating lunch. I had a very big breakfast,' I replied, then felt heat swelling through me at the double entendre.

The wickedly sexy man on the other end of the phone laughed, sending electrical currents along my nerve endings, making a mockery of my effort to keep him at arm's length. 'Hmm, so you did.'

'Wow, seriously?'

His laughter deepened, surprisingly numbing a layer of my pain. 'Your fault, sweetheart. You teed that up nicely for me.'

I felt a smile playing at my lips and immediately killed it. 'Thanks for the offer of lunch, but no, thanks.'

Jasper went silent for several moments. 'What's wrong?' he asked.

My fingers tightened on my phone. 'What makes you think anything is?'

'Don't play games with me, Wren. We're past that.'

That suggested a new level of relationship I wasn't sure I was ready for, even business-wise. And yet, I found myself answering, 'I had a disagreement with…someone.'

'A board member?' he pressed.

'No.'

'Your mother?'

A gasp left my throat before I could stop it. 'How do you know?'

'Wild guess. With Perry temporarily out of the picture, I'm thinking it could be one of three problems— board, family or lover. And since I'm your lover and I'm being on my best behaviour…'

The remainder of his deductive reasoning melted away, his words eliciting a fizzle of warmth.

Jasper Mortimer. *My lover.*

Lover. Love.

The smile evaporated.

No.

'Wren?'

I snapped back into focus. 'Yes?'

'Tell me what's wrong.'

God, why did that occasional gentleness from Jasper erode every ounce of my resistance? Why did I want to bask in it, roll around in it until I was covered head to toe in warmth?

Because you've never experienced a bona fide version of it. Surplus recycled affection has never been enough for you. Never will be.

But was it wise to accept it from Jasper? Was fate really that twisted as to show me a glimpse of what affection looked like from the very last person I could accept it from? Of course, it was. Because wasn't karma that cruel? I inhaled a settling breath, but he spoke again before I could will common sense into our interaction.

'Before you tell me it's none of my business, know that I've been in your shoes,' he said, again in that calm, even voice. 'More or less.'

Curiosity swallowed me whole. 'How?'

His laugh was a little sharp. A little edgy. 'What's worse than a parent who tells you how to live your life?'

I frowned at the puzzle. 'I'm…not sure how to answer that.'

'Try parents who don't care at all.'

My heart squeezed, this time for the hardened bite of pain he didn't hide. 'I… I'm…' For whatever reason, the *sorry* stuck in my throat. Probably because, freshly bruised from my run-in with my mother, a part of me felt as if it was a betrayal to my family. Or maybe I didn't want even a sliver of softer feelings to slither through my cracks in case the floodgates tore wide open? Either way, bewilderment kept me silent.

'It's cool, Wren. Loyalty is a big deal to me, too, even when the people we're loyal to don't deserve it,' he murmured and, absurdly, tears prickled my eyes.

Jesus, I was pathetic. Determined to wrestle my feelings under control, I cleared my throat. 'Well. This has been fun and all, but I really need to get back to work.'

Expecting him to convince me otherwise, or at the very least remind me I was beholden to him via our contract, I was a little stunned when he said, 'Okay. Bye, Wren.'

Disappointment seared deep as I ended the call and set the phone down. Then spent an absurd amount of time analysing our conversation. What had his parents done to him? As far as I knew, Jasper's parents lived overseas. According to the grapevine, they hardly involved themselves in Mortimer businesses any more. Had their reclusiveness extended to their own children? Did I have more in common with Jasper than I wanted to?

Realising I was spending way more time dwelling on Jasper's phone call than I had my mother's visit, I fought to put both out of my mind. Until a knock on my door revealed yet another surprise, this time a smiling Alana holding a white takeaway box bearing a well-known exclusive Greek restaurant logo.

'This just arrived for you. It smells amazing,' she said, placing the box on my desk before departing.

The giddiness in my heart bloomed as I reached for the note taped to the side of the box. Opening it, I read the bold scrawl.

They may take your good mood, but never let them take your appetite.
Jasper

The note was so absurd I burst out laughing. On wild impulse, I grabbed my phone and sent a two-word message.

Thank you.

The speech bubble started immediately. Breath held, I waited for his reply.

My pleasure. Oh, and just for clarity, not answering my earlier texts doesn't mean it didn't count as work. I make that sixty-five minutes so far. Call me when you're ready to make up some more time.

I knew I should resist, that I was straying far too close to liking our skirmish-banter-tiny-moments-of-emotional-synchronicity, but I couldn't help reaching for my phone again as I opened the box and groaned at the heavenly smelling moussaka, feta cheese salad and tiny bites of grilled lamb. Helping myself to small portions of each dish, I went through his earlier texts, answering each query between bites.

He didn't answer until the last text and email was sent and I was stuffed to the gills after a final sinful bite of baklava.

Mood improved?

Eyeing the half-empty boxes, I smiled and answered.

Much. Thank you.

Any time. See you tonight.

I sailed through the rest of the day, surprisingly focused after my turbulent emotions, and when I arrived at the Mortimer building to find Jasper caught up in another meeting, the idea that had been mushrooming at the back of my mind on my way over sent me wandering into the empty office next to his. He found me there twenty minutes later, with my copies of the Moroccan deal spread out on the desk while I pored over equipment-delivery schedules and personnel management.

'Would it be totally sexist to say you look good behind that desk?' he drawled, leaning casually against the doorjamb.

I bit my inside lip to stop myself from smiling. To stop my insides from melting at the sight of him, tie loosened, hair slightly dishevelled, his long legs and spectacular body framed in a bespoke suit that highlighted his masculine perfection. 'Yes, it totally would.'

Hazel eyes glinted as he rounded the desk I'd appropriated and perched on the edge, his muscled thighs a tantalising touch away. 'You should punish me for my heinous crime, then,' he said in a low purr.

I sat back in my chair, futilely willing my racing heartbeat to slow, while blatantly eyeing him from head to toe. 'Hmm, I think I will. Just give me a few seconds to devise an adequate torture.'

A sexy smile lifted the corners of his mouth and I tightened my gut against the punch of need that threatened to leave me breathless. His eyes left mine to cast a look around the room. 'I take it you've decided to make use of the office?'

I shrugged. 'Since the contract says I need to spend time here, I thought this was best.'

His smile widened. 'I agree,' he said, then those sinful eyes dropped to scrutinise my body just as I did his. He swallowed when his gaze reached the hem of my pencil skirt. Desire spiralling through my veins, I deliberately crossed my legs, allowing the hem to ride higher.

When his eyes met mine again, flames blazed high and dangerous. 'Two hours, forty minutes,' he murmured, reminding me of how much time we'd spent on work so far.

A rush of heated anticipation to my core almost made me groan. Correcting him to say he was off by a vital thirteen minutes felt a little too needy so I let it go. 'I have a bit more to catch up on, so I suggest you leave me alone.'

His gaze dropped to my lips, lingering for an indecently long time. 'Can I get a little bit of that punishment first?' he asked thickly.

No. Say no.

Of course I didn't. Because this morning already felt like a lifetime ago. And damn it, he'd fed me and made me feel better after that argument with my mother. What was wrong with a little give?

Relaxing even further in my chair despite wanting to jump him, I crooked my finger. Hunger deepening in his eyes, he gripped my arm rests, his face hovering over mine. Slowly, I wrapped my fingers around his loose tie and tugged him closer until he was a whisper away. Then I slowly licked my bottom lip.

With a deep groan, Jasper breached that last inch between us, yanked the chair close and fused his lips to mine. Decadent minutes of sliding tongues, playful nips and frantic groping later, I pushed him away.

'I really have work to do, Jasper. And you're wasting my time.' I cringed at the breathless mess of my voice.

He stayed where he was for another handful of seconds, his throat working, his eyes fixated on my kiss-bruised lips, savage hunger and a clear reluctance to end our entanglement pulsing from him.

And yes, it pleased a deeply needy part of me to see him fighting his own need for me. Battling to get himself under control. And when I spotted the thick bulge behind his fly, I fought a hard battle of my own. But ultimately, I knew this was for the best. That I needed this vital distance to control my needs. Before they escalated out of my control.

CHAPTER EIGHT

Two hours, thirty-nine minutes.

That time was emblazoned across my brain as I guided Wren into the exclusive restaurant in Fitzrovia on Wednesday evening to meet the tequila supplier.

The ambient lighting and tropical atmosphere of the Spanish fusion restaurant suited my mood and I watched the lights play on Wren's flawless skin as we approached our table. I'd been unable to take a complete breath since she stepped out of her front door wearing the sleeveless, thigh skimming, butt-hugging moss-green dress. The soft material clung to all the right places and I'd barely been able to keep my eyes on the road on the drive over.

I wasn't entirely sure whether to squander the entire time wining and dining this potential business partner and making her wait as payback for the way she'd tortured me for the last two days, or devote exactly two hours and thirty-eight minutes on Paolo Alonso and spend the last minute locating the nearest flat surface to rip Wren's panties off and drive myself into her snug pussy the way I'd been dying to do ever since the lift doors had shut between us on Monday.

Within fifteen minutes of us being seated, I sensed it would be the former, and not because of the need to torture Wren. Our guest seemed hell-bent on a different type of torturing of his own. Paolo was in no mood to discuss business. The Mexican businessman was only interested in regaling us with tall stories of his journey from simple farmer to multi-millionaire tequila manufacturer.

Every attempt to steer the discussion back to business was merrily lobbed away.

I was hiding gritted teeth behind a sip of wine halfway through the main course when Wren leaned her elbows on the table and smiled at Paolo.

'La Tromba, the name of your tequila brand. That means whirlwind, doesn't it?' she asked.

Paolo grinned. 'It does, *sí*. I named it after my wife,' he mused. 'From the moment I met her until now, she has never stopped making my life…interesting.' A faraway look entered his eyes, private enough that Wren looked away. Straight into my eyes. I stared right back, not bothering to hide the depths of my hunger for her.

Her eyes widened a fraction, but, sweet heaven bless her, she didn't shy away from what I was projecting. Which was that I wanted her more than I'd ever wanted another woman. That I intended to have her the second our six-hour deadline was up.

She matched me look for look, her nostrils flaring slightly as she brazenly acknowledged my intent.

A throat cleared. Paolo. Had he asked a question? Or merely narrated another anecdote? When I looked his way, he raised his glass in a silent salute, which I answered. 'To feisty women and all the exciting ways they keep us on our toes—eh, *amigo*?'

'Sure,' I responded, then grabbed the bull by the horns. 'So, are we doing business, Paolo?'

'It's probably prudent for me to take a day to think on it.'

'But come tomorrow you'll be saying yes, right?' Wren pressed. 'Because otherwise you'd be disappointing me greatly for misjudging you for an astute businessman.'

Shrewd admiration flickered in his eyes. 'Ah, the very fine art of complimenting and challenging that women seemed to have honed over the ages. How can I resist?'

Wren's gaze met mine and we both silently acknowledged that he still hadn't said yes. 'I've sent you all the paperwork. What will it take to convince you tonight?' she asked.

Another flicker of respect, then he set his shot glass down. 'For La Tromba to be the signature drink you serve on the opening night and for the next seven nights. You can throw your vintage champagne and whatever else you like at your guests, but I want my tequila to be the showpiece. Dare I say even base the whole event around it?'

'You aren't trying to hijack my launch by any chance, are you, Paolo?' I asked, my voice firm enough to reflect my seriousness.

He laughed. 'I'm striking a good business deal by getting myself as much of the action as I can. You would do the same, my friend.'

'Seven days is out of the question. But I think we can make something work, can't we, Wren?'

She nodded. 'I'll speak to the event organisers, come up with something to show you by Monday. Provided you give us your agreement tonight,' she said, her eyes steady on his, her smile replaced by steely determination.

Paolo smiled. 'I understand why you brought her along, *amigo*. She drives a hard bargain.'

Wren's challenging gaze slid to mine, and I fought the urge to squirm in my seat. 'You have no idea.'

Paolo grinned and smacked his hand on the table. '*Bueno*, we have a deal.'

Wren smiled in triumph. She looked so stunning in that moment, I wanted to climb over the table and taste the beauty of it. The urge intensified as she snuck a glance at her watch. We'd been here close to two hours but Paolo was only halfway through the extensive tapas he'd ordered. At the very least we were looking at another forty-five minutes until this ordeal was over.

I forced myself to finish my steak and salad, my

temperature skyrocketing with every sultry glance Wren slid my way.

I almost groaned in relief when the waiter arrived to clear away our plates. Only to glare at Wren when she smiled and asked, 'Would you like some coffee, Paolo?'

Before I could utter the strenuous objection firing up my throat, her left hand landed on my knee. Without glancing my way, she toyed with her small diamond pendant with her right hand as her left slowly caressed up my thigh.

Was she really about to stroke me into a frothing frenzy beneath the table? *Fuck yes*, my senses shrieked.

Paolo contemplated the tequila bottle with longing before he shook his head. '*Sí*, I'll take an espresso.'

I watched in frustration as the waiter hurried away to fetch the beverage, then I bit back a tight groan as Wren's clever fingers landed on my steel-hard cock. She stroked me through further small talk as we waited for the espresso, and then under cover of observing the waiter set out the coffee, her fingers slowly lowered my zip, reached inside the opening in my boxers and wrapped her hand around my hot length.

Sweet holy hell.

Stars burst across my vision as she stroked me harder, all the while smiling through another Paolo anecdote. When she toyed with the head of my dripping cock, smoothing the liquid over me in an expert pump, I gripped her wrist, terrified for a second that I would disgrace myself in the restaurant.

'Another nightcap, amigo?' Paolo asked, once he'd finally finished his drink.

'No!' I stopped, cleared my throat. 'I mean, I need to call it a night. I have an early morning meeting.'

He looked from my face to Wren's, a smile twitching at his lips before he nodded. 'You're right, I better get back to my hotel, too.'

As I reached for my wallet, I wrapped my fingers over Wren's, allowing her to stroke me one more soul-searing time before easing her away. And then she threatened to blow my head clean off when, under the guise of fixing her hair, she flicked her tongue over the fingers that were wrapped around me a moment ago.

The knowledge that she was tasting me, right there in front of our guest and restaurant patrons, was so shockingly arousing I knew I'd need five minutes to get myself under control before standing. As if she knew the havoc she'd created, she rose. 'I just need to dash off to the ladies. Shall I meet you at the front entrance, Jasper?'

'Sure,' I croaked.

She smiled, turned to Paolo. 'I'll be in touch in a few days, and I look forward to seeing you in Morocco at the launch.'

'If I didn't think you would do me bodily harm,

my friend, I'd think of poaching that one from you,' Paolo said as Wren walked away.

My grin was all teeth, no humour as I stared him down. 'Yes, I would. So don't even think about it.'

He laughed and rose from the table. Jaw clenched and thankful for the low lights in the restaurant, I joined him as we headed for the door.

Once he left, I eyed the ladies' room, every cell in my body straining to storm through the doors, find the nearest empty stall and fuck Wren into a stupor. And damn the consequences. Before I could give in to the urge, I saw her walking towards me.

Bloody hell, she was gorgeous. I wanted her so badly, everything inside me ached with it. The novelty of it all stunned me for a moment, made me wonder if there wasn't something…*more* to all of this.

Then her perfume was filtering through my senses and I was cheerfully stepping back from examining that peculiar feeling. This was about sex. And business. Nothing more.

Yeah, right… That's why you told her about your rubbish parents. That's why you've been thinking about her non-stop for weeks. That's why something inside you tightened with unfamiliar concern when you heard the pain in her voice on Monday.

I pushed the mocking voice away and held the door open for her. In lust-charged silence we headed for my car, our strides picking up speed. It was past eleven at night and the street was quiet and dim.

Enough for a torrid little quickie. But I didn't want that. Nor did I want to risk someone capturing us on camera. I wanted a feast. I wanted to gorge on Wren until this stark hunger inside me was assuaged. Then I wanted to feast some more.

Nevertheless, for a single moment when we reached my car, we stared at one another across the low hood, her eyes projecting everything we intended to do to each other.

The beeping of her phone wrenched us from the lust trance. When mine pinged five seconds later, the spark in my chest sent fireworks through my blood.

'You set your alarm for the six hours, too?' I asked, inordinately pleased that I wasn't caught in this madness alone.

She shrugged, although a bashful look crossed her face before she composed her expression. 'No need to work overtime if I don't have to.'

'Of course not. You're nothing if not super-efficient, right?' I teased.

The tiniest smile quirked her lips as she slid into the car. I gunned the engine, aiming the car towards the nearest main road when she asked in a low, raspy voice, 'Where are we going?'

My fingers tightened on the wheel. The moment I'd dismissed a quickie on the hood of my car, my mind had zeroed in on the next quickest option. Still, I forced myself to list them all. 'We have three choices. Your place. Mine. Or the penthouse suite at a hotel four minutes away.' My breath locked in my throat, praying she would choose the last option.

'Which hotel?' she asked, her gaze boring into me.

Mentally crossing my fingers, I answered, 'Mortimer Mayfair.'

Perhaps we weren't past the hurdles of our family history but surely she wasn't going to let that get in the way of what we both wanted?

We reached a traffic light and I turned my gaze on her. The look in her eyes was a cross between apprehension and rebellion. It was that same rebellion I'd seen during her interaction with her mother. Wren Bingham wasn't a woman who toed the line. I freely admitted it was partly what drew her to me. Was she going to throw caution to the—?

'Okay.'

Scarily heady sensations rushing through me, I caught her hand and pressed a kiss to her knuckles. 'Excellent choice.'

I shaved half a minute off our journey time. Using the allocated private parking reserved for my family in the underground car park would add at least five minutes to our trip so I pulled up to the front of the hotel, tossing the keys to the valet the moment I stepped out.

A minute later we were in the private lift. To preserve that little bit of my fraying control, I parked myself in the opposite corner from her, but I still couldn't keep my eyes off her.

'You're looking at me with those caveman eyes again, Jasper,' she mused, reaching up to free her bound hair in one sexy little move.

Far from being offended, I laughed, then gripped the railing as her hair tumbled down around her shoulders. 'I can't help it, sweetheart. I'm going insane pondering where to start with you.'

Alluring green eyes on me, she reached into her clutch. I wanted to tell her refreshing her make-up was unnecessary since I intended to besmirch it all in the next five minutes. But she chopped me off at the knees by extracting the tiniest, laciest thong I'd ever seen, dangling it right in front of my face. 'Maybe this will help.'

'Fucking hell, Wren,' I croaked, every drop of blood rushing south until I was terrified I was actually going to pass out. 'You left the ladies' room without panties on?'

She stepped forward, raising the scrap of lace higher. 'I was a little too wet to keep wearing them, you see.'

My jaw dropped as the lift doors parted. I stood frozen as she closed the gap between us and tucked the panties into my handkerchief pocket, then sauntered out of the lift, her mile-long legs making short work of the hallway that led to the suite's double doors. She tossed her clutch on a nearby console table, then, with a saucy look over her shoulder, grasped the handles and pushed the doors open. 'Are you coming, Jasper?'

Sweet Lord in heaven, was I ever? I stumbled after her as she crossed the vast living room to stop in front of the floor-to-ceiling glass window. Below us, London was spread out in a carpet of lights. In the darkened room, all I saw was Wren's stunning silhouette as she braced her hands on the glass.

Before I reached her, I'd wrenched off my jacket containing the panties I was definitely going to keep and unfastened the first few buttons of my shirt.

'I like this view,' she said, casting another wicked look over her shoulder.

'Then stay there. Take it all in,' I suggested, intending to do some sightseeing of my own. I reached her, curled one hand over her plump buttocks as I swept her hair aside and dragged my lips along her elegant neck.

Her shudder and soft moan went straight to my cock. My hand tightened on her soft, rounded arse. 'I should spank this naughty little bottom for walking around with no panties on.'

Her shiver said she liked that idea. Very much. 'Do it,' she muttered, her hands spreading wide on the glass, even as her hips rolled into my groin.

'Fuck, Wren,' I groaned, the indecent thought of reddening her behind punching a fresh bolt of lust through me. With fingers that weren't quite steady, I tugged up her dress as my tongue licked up the side of her neck. The moment she was exposed, I delivered a light slap to her derriere.

A hot little gasp left her lips. 'Oh!'

'You like that?' I growled.

'Yes. Again,' she commanded.

My fingers delved into her hair, gripped her lightly and turned her head to receive my kiss as I spanked her again. I swallowed her next gasp, devouring it the same way I wanted to devour her. Two spanks later and we were both so excited I was in fear of this getting out of hand. Releasing her, I undressed, then reached for the condom. Before me, Wren wriggled out of her dress and bra and tossed them aside, her eyes green flames of need as she watched me.

'Hurry up, Jasper.'

I tugged the condom on, then froze for a moment, arrested by the spectacular sight before me. 'Not yet, baby. I need to look at you.' Despite our previous dalliances, this was the first time I was seeing Wren completely naked. My mouth dried as I took in every inch of her silky smooth skin, the graceful arch of her spine, trailed my fingers from her nape to her tail bone. 'Fuck, you're so beautiful.'

Her head dipped a fraction, another bashful look fleeting across her face before the siren returned, her eyes commanding me to grant her wish. 'I need you inside me, Jasper. Right now.'

And since that was exactly what I wanted, I braced both hands on her hips. 'Open your legs wider for me,' I rasped.

The moment she did, I positioned myself at her heated entrance. Then, volcanic need threatening to rip me to pieces, I thrust inside her. Her scream echoed my gut-deep groan. I lost all sense of time and place, the only sensation the tightness of her sheath as she welcomed me in. 'Fuck, Wren. Fuck!'

'More, Jasper. Give me more.'

I kept thrusting until sweat coated both our bodies, until her final hoarse scream ended in convulsions that milked my own release from me. Bracing one hand on the glass to keep me upright, I planted kisses on her neck and shoulders as we caught our breaths.

Something inside me tightened when she reached back and trailed one hand over my thigh. The idea that she needed to touch me as much as I yearned to caress her kept me at the window far longer than I would've done if she weren't touching me.

I wasn't one for post-coital cuddling, and yet I couldn't find any reason to move away. When my kisses trailed to her jaw and she turned into my kiss, my insides continued to sing and twist and sizzle in a way I wasn't too keen on exploring. And when she gave another soft moan, I knew I was gone.

'We did leave it open-ended as to how many times we fucked once the six hours were up, right?'

Her sultry little laugh went straight to my balls, making me hard all over again. 'I believe we did.'

Bending low, I scooped her up in my arms and strode for the bedroom. 'Wonderful. Let me know when you've had enough.'

* * *

'Let me know when you've had enough.'

Jasper's words reverberated through my mind as I packed for the week-long trip to Morocco a week later. Far from experiencing the emotional apathy I had with my two previous relationships, I felt…alive. Quietly unfettered. As if something inside me were straining to break free.

Perhaps it was all the glorious sex.

Perhaps it was the inroads I'd made into renegotiating the terms Perry had initially tied Bingham's to.

Paolo had signed on the dotted line to be the exclusive tequila supplier for one year in not just the Moroccan resort but in all Mortimer hotels. And as of last night, I'd received a firm *maybe* from Jasper to shorten the one-year profit-margin projections to nine months, a term that I fully intended to reduce to six months before we touched down in Marrakesh.

Success on that front would mean, by summertime, Bingham's could well see a healthy profit from our association with the Mortimer Group. Not that my board was in the mood to heap accolades on my head. Nevertheless, the blatant grumblings had… lessened in the past week. At least from the board members.

My mother on the other hand…

As if summoned by thought, my phone rang. It took a moment to locate it beneath the mountain of clothes I was sorting through, on account of sudden nerves over which clothes Jasper would prefer to see me in.

The thought that I was even remotely interested in pleasing him made me pause for a shocked moment before answering the phone. 'Mother, I'm afraid I can't talk for long—'

'Why? Because you've decided to publicly draw a line in the sand, show me where your true loyalties lie?'

My breath caught at the acid in her voice. 'What are you talking about?'

'You were seen, Wren. Coming out of the hotel with the Mortimer boy last week. And don't bother to convince me it was business.'

My teeth gritted, the urge to demand she stop calling him a boy bubbling up in my throat until I swallowed it down. That insult was minor in the grand scheme of things. As, I was further stunned to realise, was the revelation that I'd been spotted leaving the Mortimer Mayfair. The sharp bite of remorse I expected to feel never arrived. And when I exhaled it was with a certain…pain-edged freedom that made my throat ache when I answered, 'Okay, then, I won't.'

It was her turn to gasp. 'You're not going to bother denying it?'

'Why should I, Mother? It's true. I was in the hotel with Jasper. And it wasn't business. Is that what you called to condemn me about?'

She went silent for a frozen moment. 'Of all

the men in this town, Wren,' she asked bitterly. 'Why him?'

I shut my eyes, a wince catching me hard inside because I'd asked myself the same question at least a half-dozen times since that moment in the maze. And every answer had only deepened my bewilderment. Because not even once had I considered simply...walking away, regardless of the fact that I'd demanded he release me from our business deal. 'No explanation I give is going to satisfy you, so why put ourselves through it?' My question emerged solemn and reserved, directly opposite to the churning in my belly. Something was happening with Jasper. Something I seemed powerless to stop.

'I guess there's nothing more to discuss, then, is there?'

The finality in her tone unnerved me. Enough to make my answer rushed. 'Mother, can you trust me for once? Please? I'm trying to salvage this for all of us.' The worrying thing was, I wasn't sure if the business was the only thing I was attempting to salvage.

'You want me to trust you when you've openly thrown yourself into the enemy's bed? Oh, sweet girl, don't you know this will only have one unfortunate ending for you? Don't you know that's what they live for?'

Jasper's face materialised before my eyes, the ruthless and dogged determination in getting his way. I couldn't deny that so far things had worked in his favour. Mostly. But I planned on changing that.

'It…won't,' I replied, then…stronger when my voice wobbled, 'It won't.'

My mother sighed. 'Your father deluded himself about getting into bed with vipers once upon a time, too.'

Before I could reply the line went dead.

I hung up, hurt and incensed. And when tears filmed my eyes, I dashed them away with an impatient hand. Wasn't there a saying that history repeated itself only if we didn't learn from it? Why was my mother so determined to write me off?

The answer shook through me, terrifying me into blindly throwing random items of clothing into the suitcase. Who the hell cared what Jasper preferred? I would dress for myself and no one else.

Still, my senses jumped into sizzling life when my phone pinged with a message from him.

Be there in ten.

I was waiting by my front door when he pulled up in his Aston Martin. When he started to get out, I waved him away, wheeling my suitcase towards the boot. 'I'm fine. Just pop the boot, please.'

A frown twitched across his face as he flicked the button. I stymied another flare of unease when I saw his suitcase—a top-of-the-range designer exclusive with his name monogrammed in neat letters.

Get a grip, Wren. You're now annoyed because the billionaire you're sleeping with has nice luggage?

'Whoa, did you wake up on the wrong side of the bed, sweetheart?' he enquired dryly when I got into the car.

I shut the door with a tiny slam and yanked on my seat belt. 'What if I did?'

He stared at me for a moment, then nodded. 'Right, you're itching to pick a fight with me. Fine. Go ahead. As long as we get to make up properly afterwards.'

That should've angered me more. Instead, part of me leapt in excitement while the painful knot in my belly expanded. I shook my head, my thoughts bewildered. 'Can we just go, please?'

He set the car in motion and stayed silent for the first few miles.

Far from the silence easing my churning emotions, I grew even more unsettled.

After another few minutes, he sighed. 'Can I take a wild guess at what's eating you up? You're raging at fate for matters that aren't in your control? That had nothing to do with you but in which you're fully embroiled somehow? And the more you think about it, the more it pisses you off, and the more ridiculous guilt eats you up?'

I shifted in my seat, a little riled and lot bewildered by his acuity. 'Don't shrink me, Jasper.'

A wry, cynical smile curved his lips. 'I'm not. But have you considered that I'm stuck in the same situation? My nightmare of a father did something to yours and now the sins of our fathers are being visited upon us.'

'Don't you mean the sins of *your* father?' I snapped.

He flinched. 'Since we're talking about Hugh Mortimer, renowned bastard and destroyer of lives, then yes, maybe I am willing to take full responsibility on his behalf.'

A touch mollified, if a little unjustly since I suspected my father also bore some of the responsibility, I breathed through the easing of the knots inside me. 'Careful there or I'll take you up on that *mea culpa* you're bandying about.'

He shrugged. 'Take it, sweetheart. It's all yours.'

The peculiar thickness in his voice made that curious little hook catch once more in my midriff. Only this time it was positioned higher, dangerously close to where my heart hammered an erratic tattoo. He switched lanes in a suave move, increasing our speed. He said nothing more after that and I gladly welcomed the silence, a chance to contemplate how best to deal with my mother.

When we pulled into the private-jet section of the airport just outside London forty minutes later, it was with the acceptance that it would be better to let things play out, show her the proof of my success when I accomplished what I meant to. Anything else would be akin to banging my head against a stone wall.

What if it's not enough?

That bleak little question echoed through me, threatening to dull my enjoyment of my surroundings long after I'd boarded the seriously opulent Mortimer jet.

But with the even bleaker thought that this was a cycle I'd found myself repeating with my mother, and that, like before, I needed to snap out of it, I forced myself to look around. To steep myself back into the present as the plane taxied down the runway and rose into the sky with a smooth take-off.

The inside of the 747 private jet was worthy of its own spread in a premium airline magazine. I'd flown in enough such jets in my modelling days to recall that the general layout meant the bedroom suites were located at the back.

Back then, I'd done nothing more than sleep to mitigate jet lag, but I grew hot and needy at the thought of changing that on this trip. The flight to Morocco would take a little over four hours. The possibility of stepping off the plane as a member of the mile-high club made me tingle.

On the tail of that thought, Jasper stepped out of the cockpit where he'd gone after take-off. And just like that, my breathing bottomed out.

In my unsettled mood, I'd failed to clock what he was wearing and as he strolled down the aisle towards me it struck me that I was seeing him in less formal clothes for the first time. Then came the more potent acceptance of how devastatingly handsome he looked in whatever attire he wore. Today's selection of white polo shirt with raised collar, coupled with khaki chinos that hugged lean hips and hard, muscled thighs, lent him a charming swagger and assured sophistication that made my mouth dry and my chest palpitate like a hormonal schoolgirl the closer he got.

And when he was close enough to touch, those distinctive eyes piercing mine, it was all I could do not to launch myself at him. Because being in Jasper's arms was a guarantee that every other thought would be pushed out. That I would only be consumed by him. Which was a scary thought in itself…

Don't you know this will only have one unfortunate ending? Don't you know that's what they live for?

'You still have war and pain in your eyes,' Jasper murmured, a thoughtful observation forged with a little steel and a lot of contemplation. 'Will you permit me to find a way of combating that?' he asked.

The shiver that went through me was a warning against embracing that offer. It was strong enough to make me shake my head. 'I'll pass, thanks.'

If my answer displeased him, he hid it well. In a blink, the steel was gone from his eyes and he was taking the seat next to mine. 'Something else, then? Champagne? Or shall I order us something to eat?'

With my mother's warning still echoing through me, I lifted a leather briefcase from where I'd dropped it next to my seat.

'I'm not hungry. And the champagne can wait for a while.'

I pulled out the newest version of the contract and

placed it in front of him. We'd been dancing around with a parry and thrust that was frankly a little too thrilling. But the bottom line was that I had to secure Bingham's business interests regardless of whether I shared Jasper's bed or not.

'You said you'd consider a nine-month profit-sharing clause. I've changed my mind. I think a six-month contract is a more viable option.'

He remained silent for almost a minute. Then his shrewd gaze flicked over my face. 'Convince me.'

'Hobbling Bingham's into working with one hand behind our backs stymies your productivity, too. We need money to make more money. With an earlier profit-sharing contract, you make half a per cent more than you would in the next six months. I've done the figures.' I rose from the chair. 'I'll go and freshen up while you look it over.'

Instead of concentrating on the file I'd placed before him, his eyes travelled over my body. 'Or we can look it over together and I'll help you freshen up when I'm done?'

I smiled even while my pulse leapt wildly. 'No can do. I wouldn't want to ruin your concentration.'

'Too late for that,' he responded, his voice hoarse with arousal.

I leaned over and tapped a finger on the file. 'Deal with this, Jasper. It's important to me that we're on the same page by the time we land.'

While we'd been embroiled in enough sexual tension to break a few records, business had never been muddied by sex. This deal, for better or worse, meant too much to both of us to allow that so I was confident, once I left the room, he'd give it his full attention. Still, I basked in the sizzling heat of his regard as I headed for the rear of the plane. When the stewardess directed me to the bathroom, I thanked her, then, unable to resist, glanced over my shoulder.

As I suspected, Jasper was engrossed in the file, eyes slightly narrowed as he digested the facts and figures I'd painstakingly put together.

I took my time in the well-appointed bathroom, splashing cool water over my wrists and touching up the very light make-up I'd worn. My unbound hair didn't need much attention, but I ran a brush through it all the same. Then, with nothing more to do, I left the suite.

To discover Jasper had moved from the living area into the business area and spread out more papers on the desk. He looked up as I entered.

'I've read your contract. There are a couple of issues that need ironing out.'

'Oh?' It wasn't a flat refusal. I could work with that.

'I think you're underutilising manpower on the ground. At least three per cent of the staff members can double up on other tasks without affecting quality or productivity. Here, take a look.'

I joined him at the table and within ten minutes I was admitting the sheer genius of Jasper's input.

'Give me an hour and I'm sure I can find other areas to increase productivity,' I countered.

He gave an appreciative smile. 'Do that and we have a new deal.'

My breath caught. 'Really?'

'Really. And once we're done with that, we can get down to what's bothering you and the reason why you haven't kissed me since I picked you up.'

CHAPTER NINE

HER FEATURES TIGHTENED and I knew she was about to shut me down. 'I don't need you to fix my problems, Jasper.'

An expected response. One I fully intended to smash through. 'When that problem directly impacts me, I think I'm entitled to a basic understanding of what's going on.'

Her eyes flashed with annoyance. And I admitted quietly to myself that it was way better than the bitter, silent pain I'd seen there before. That kind of pain was acidic, had a tendency to eat away inside you until only a husk remained. The last thing I wanted to see was the woman I was growing increasingly attached to stripped of her vibrancy. Of the passion that blazed through everything she did.

'Impacts you in what way?' she challenged.

I raised my eyebrow and let her read the answer on my face.

'You mean sex?' There was a tight edge to the question that made me wonder if the surface answer wasn't what she wanted. And fuck if that didn't thrill me. I wasn't sure how much of myself I could give but if she wanted more, I would oblige. Up to a point. Because I was a Mortimer, after all. And we were renowned for the amount of dysfunctional baggage we tended to lug around.

'Not necessarily. But I expected the trip thus far to be a little more…stimulating.'

She stiffened, her back going ramrod straight. 'I didn't throw myself into your arms like an overeager teenager when you rocked up in your fancy car, so I must be defective somehow?'

'Stop. You're deflecting.' I hardened my voice.

She opened her mouth, about to snap my head off, but then swallowed and looked away. The weight of that action sat uncomfortably in my gut. Wren never shied away from confronting me. Added to that weight was the realisation that I would fix it, regardless of what it was. Regardless of my suspicion that this would hit close to my own parental issues. Issues I'd happily placed in a vault my whole life.

I cupped her chin and redirected her gaze towards me. 'Tell me what's bothering you, Wren. I may not have crystal-clear answers for you but, much like this contract here, we can figure our way through it, even if it requires several iterations before we're satisfied with it.'

Her eyes grew suspiciously filmy, then she blinked them clear. 'It'll take much longer than a few weeks of hard negotiations to unravel a lifelong conundrum.'

Her voice was solemn, much more subdued than I'd ever heard it, and that unnerving weight in my gut grew.

I rubbed my thumb over the smooth-as-silk skin of her jaw, felt her pulse leap beneath my touch. 'I get that. But conundrums remain that way if you leave them alone. Shove them into the light. Show them to me, Wren. I want to see.'

'Why?' she asked, her voice a little bewildered.

Why indeed? I could've given her the flippant answer, told her I was a ruthlessly determined Mortimer who despised secrets and wanted full disclosure for the sake of our business dealings. But since I hid fat, ugly secrets of my own...

I shrugged. 'I've seen you in business mode and I've seen you content with a well-put-together meal. I've watched you wow a room full of corporate sharks and had you aggravate me with a trench coat I'm still determined to burn the first chance I get. Your many facets fascinate me. This sad version of you irks me. If helping you work through your pain is the only way for you to free yourself of it, then it's a task I'm volunteering to undertake. No strings attached.' Yeah, that last bit was a white lie. I wanted a few strings. The kind of strings that made me want to feed her when she was hungry. Tear a few arseholes to shreds when they upset her. Bask in her smile when she was happy.

She swallowed, and I caught another sheen of tears in her eyes. Then, determinedly, she dragged her chin from my loose grip. 'I won't be deemed weak by divulging things that trouble me, Jasper,' she said, her voice low but stern, her warning clear.

'Believe me, Wren, you're the last person I'd consider weak.'

Green eyes locked on mine, probing for several moments before, satisfied by whatever she was looking for, she nodded. 'Let me get this business out of the way. Then I'll let you feed me champagne and whatever delights your chef has in store for us.' Her gaze flicked past me to the double doors that led to the master suite. 'I might even let you experience that other facet of me you enjoy so much. Then…maybe I might tell you a thing or two about…stuff. Agreed?'

The weight shrank in direct proportion to my expanding relief. 'Agreed, but with one tiny addendum.'

One perfect eyebrow rose. 'Yes?'

'Since you'll be working full-time on Mortimer business, shall we dispense with the six hours nonsense?'

Her smile slowly grew, banishing a few shadows in her eyes. And the reappearance of my vibrant, gorgeous Wren made something unnervingly vital shake loose and free inside me. Instinct warned me that it might be irretrievable. For the moment, I didn't scramble to chase after it. Because her smile was knocking me for six and I wanted to bask in it until I passed out.

'You have yourself another deal, Jasper Mortimer.'

It was a good and bad thing that Wren was a meticulous businesswoman. It meant that she came up with the goods eventually. But it also meant that we were left with only forty minutes to eat and fuck by the time she presented me with the promised solution. I happily signed on the dotted line of the new contract while the stewardess poured the celebratory champagne. The moment she left us alone, we wolfed down the succulent array of canapés and finger food the chef had prepared before we stumbled into the master suite.

'Bloody hell, we only have thirty minutes,' I grumbled against her lush lip as my fingers dived beneath the light pink cashmere sweater she'd worn to combat the cool English weather.

Her laughter was sultry and musical, her earlier mood finally evaporated as she tackled the zip to one ankle-high boot. 'I'm confident you can make me come at least…twice before we land.' She drew back, teasing in her eyes. 'I'm not overestimating your prowess, am I, Mr Mortimer?'

I chased after her cheeky mouth, playfully biting her lower lip before I growled against it. 'Challenge fucking accepted.'

We tumbled into bed in a tangle of half-undressed frenzy, laughing and growling our frustration until, gloriously, she was naked, her sinuous body warm and welcoming beneath my eager caress.

Knowing I had to wait a few hours more to discover what was bothering her threatened a return of that unease, but then she was rising above me, a siren with her willing captive, the look on her face ethereal and breathtaking as she sank down, taking me inside her tight, hot channel. Then she rolled her hips in a sensual claiming that had my breath hissing out.

'I love it when you do that.'

Hands on my chest, she smiled wider until I was certain I would get lost in it. I didn't give one little damn. Instead I focused on rising to her sensual challenge, my own smug smile appearing when she threw her head back and screamed her first orgasm. Then a second. And just for the hell of it—and probably irritating the hell out of my pilot for ignoring his announcement to return to our seats and fasten our seat belts—a third.

She was locked in my arms, light shudders wracking her beautiful body, as the wheels touched down in a smooth landing in Marrakesh.

From the many hours of work I'd poured into the project, I knew the resort was situated on the outskirts of Marrakesh, midpoint between Essaouira and Agadir. What I hadn't known was that we would be travelling there by helicopter after disembarking Jasper's plane.

A further surprise arrived when he slid behind the

controls of the sleek and powerful-looking aircraft with discreet lettering announcing it as a property of the Mortimer Marrakesh Resort.

'You're piloting this thing?' I asked when he donned the headgear and passed me a smaller set.

His teeth flashed in a boyish grin that tunnelled straight into my chest. 'Don't worry, sweetheart, I've had a pilot's licence since I was twenty-one. I think it'll come in handy when I have to step in to ferry VIP guests to the resort. And who knows? It might even knock a quarter per cent off your staffing streamlining.'

Two things struck me just then, the first being that Jasper would most likely spend a great deal of his time here to ensure the resort got off to the good start the projections predicted. And secondly that his absence would…devastate me.

Because…*because*…

My mind seized up, unable to grapple with the emotions mushrooming inside me.

'Wren?'

I heard the frown in his voice but couldn't summon the nerve to look him in the eye. In case he read the very thing I was unable to accept myself? Still feeling tasered by emotions I wasn't ready to deal with, I answered, 'Yeah, sure, I think we can manage that.' Aware that my answer was spacey at best, I forced myself to rally and smile his way as I slid on my head gear and buckled up.

Hazel eyes bored into mine for an extra few seconds before his large hand squeezed my bare thigh. 'You good?'

Perhaps because he was inside me less than twenty minutes ago, or because I was really losing my mind, I dropped my hand on top of his. 'Yes. I am.'

His answering smile hit me square in the solar plexus but even though I was braced for it, it still took my breath away. As did the arid but incredibly stunning landscape as we took off and headed west.

I basked in the beauty of Morocco, happy to play tourist as Jasper pointed out various landmarks. But the most breathtaking of all was the distant but majestic vista of the endless, snow-capped Atlas Mountains, a watchful range of giants dominating the horizon.

'The resort is coming up now, on your right,' Jasper said after fifteen minutes, his voice intimate through the headphones.

Sliding up sunglasses I'd worn to protect against the mid-afternoon sunlight as he went low enough for a close view, I was awed all over again at my first sight of the hillside resort.

Rather than one giant building, it was a sprawling collection of sand-coloured mini castles, joined together by long interconnecting walkways, which would offer spectacular views of landscaped gardens and the Atlas Mountains on either side through elegant Moorish archways.

After landing and an introduction to the general

manager in the cool, marble-floored interior of the staggering beautiful reception, I discovered on the tour that followed that those archways had been painstakingly hand-painted in swirls of gold and bronze and turquoise.

Each mini castle contained four luxury *riad* penthouses, complete with private pools, hammam suites and endless sources of pampering and relaxation facilities, a true desert oasis unlike any other.

While I'd seen it all laid out in one report or another in the past few weeks, experiencing it in person was a thrill that drew increasingly loud gasps from me as we toured the extensive grounds. At my latest one, Jasper turned to me, a wide grin splitting his exceedingly handsome face.

'Am I blowing your mind a little bit, sweetheart?' he drawled, assured in that fact even before I answered.

'You're blowing my mind a lot,' I replied. And not just with the architecture. More and more, it seemed as if getting on the plane and leaving England behind had lifted a layer of tension off us despite our little charged conversation.

His smile widened, then slowly morphed with sexual heat, increasing in temperature until that space between my heart and stomach tightened with a new kind of tension. The one that warned the addiction I'd feared I was succumbing to had probably passed the point of no return.

When he caught my hand in his and brushed

his lips across my knuckles, I experienced an even harder kick. And when he kept hold of my hand for the remainder of the tour that once again led us outside, I let him, that fiercely intimate connection of palms gliding together a sensation I suddenly didn't want to do without.

Outside, a long rectangular pool was banked by a palm grove, offering the perfect balance of sun and shade that meant guests could linger for hours, the inviting water sparkling in the sunlight.

A little further on, amongst fig and citrus trees that sweetly scented the air, giant awnings resembling the wings of a Bedouin tent offered more stations of shade, with plump cushions and beaten leather pouffes laid out on Persian carpets. It was a seductive and decadent invitation to lounge and indulge, to free up one's senses to the pleasures the resort provided.

I felt the last of the tension leave my body as we meandered back into the resort.

'Ready for the *pièce de résistance*?'

'There's more?'

His hand tightened around mine. 'The jewel in the crown. You'll like it, I think.' He stopped to order a tray of mint tea and refreshments at the concierge desk before ushering me into a discreetly tucked away lift that didn't jar with the blend of traditional and contemporary gold and turquoise decor. Pressing a button that only had a star next to it, he pulled me into his arms as the lift doors shut, content to simply hold me as we were whisked seven floors up.

We stepped into the foyer of what was clearly the largest of the mini castles. A discreet plaque announced it as the Tower Suite and I soon discovered why when, after a jaw-dropping tour of the decadent master suite housing the largest four-poster bed I'd ever seen, I stepped out onto an equally vast terrace. No, to call it a terrace was a gross understatement.

The tennis-court-sized space came complete with turrets, parapet and three-hundred-and-sixty-degree views, the interior accommodations perfectly centred and smaller versions of the whole resort repeated in the vast space.

'Oh, my God, this is incredible! You can experience everything the resort has to offer without leaving the tower if you don't want to.'

He nodded. 'That was the general idea. Even the desert sand can be brought to you if you wish it.'

Stopping at the rectangular bathing pool fashioned from the same coloured turquoise tiles accenting the decor, I trailed my fingers through the cool water. 'I've never felt the need to be clean the way I do right now.'

Strong arms wrapped around my waist, his voice a husky rasp in my ear, 'Hmm, I can't wait to watch you bathing under the stars, with just moonlight covering your skin. Well…moonlight and me.'

My laugh felt as unfettered as the contentment seeping into my bones. Then, his words sinking in,

I turned within the confines of his arms. 'Wait, I don't get my own suite?'

He looked a little startled, then mutinous before he quirked one brow at me. 'Do you want your own suite? I'm sure I can organise one for you if that's what you want?' His tone said he would do so reluctantly.

But it was a moot point anyway because it wasn't what I wanted. I yearned to spend every spare moment with him. 'No. I'd love to share this suite with you.' Why not go all out and embrace this temporary insanity?

The shadows left his eyes, that almost conceited confidence drenching his smile. 'Brilliant answer.'

The wind-chime doorbell went and Jasper excused himself to answer it. A sharply dressed waiter wheeled out a silver trolley, positioning it under one of the four awnings where a traditional floor seating of rugs and cushions was laid out.

'Thank you, Azmir. I'll take care of the rest,' Jasper said.

The waiter left with a huge tip and a wide smile and when Jasper held out his hand, I joined him, happily kicking off my platform shoes that went with the orange and white polka-dot sundress I'd hurriedly changed into before disembarking the plane.

Reclining against one thick cushion, I accepted a plate of sandwiches, which I finished in record time. With my second cup of mint tea, I sighed my pleasure at my surroundings.

Everything I'd experienced so far impressed a bone-deep belief that I was doing the right thing by not walking away from this deal, regardless of what my mother wanted. It had every promise of becoming the kind of exclusive, six-star resort reserved for the elite. Even without the Mortimer name attached to it. And with Jasper fronting it, I wouldn't be surprised if there was already a mile-long waiting list.

No wonder Perry had bent over backwards to grab a piece of this.

Thoughts of my brother made my mind veer down a different path.

'Hey, why the frown?' Jasper asked.

About to give an evasive answer, I surprised myself by blurting out the truth. 'I was thinking about Perry. I'm wondering whether he'd think I've stolen this project from him. It was his baby, after all.'

It was a testament to the kind of family we both came from that he didn't think the question absurd considering Perry and I were siblings, supposedly working for the same team.

'Have you heard from him?'

I shook my head, a wave of concern and sadness washing over me. 'I don't expect to even if places like that allowed contact with family. Things weren't that great between us even before all of this.' I waved my hand at the resort.

Jasper nodded. 'You think he'll be angry because he'll believe he teed it up for you to hit the winning shot?'

I frowned, knowing he was making a point. 'You don't think he did.'

He snorted. 'Absolutely not. And I'll be happy to set him straight on that score. Sure, you and I have had a few ups and downs but think of the progress we've made in the last three weeks. It sure beat the months I was chasing him around to stop this project from suffering a catastrophic and costly setback.'

The praise was welcome but the hollow feeling inside remained. 'Telling him is one thing. Getting him to accept it might be something else.'

'And you believe it's that something else that might drive a deeper wedge between you?'

Feeling a mournful little lump climbing into my throat, I took a hasty sip of tea. 'I don't know. On the one hand it seems inevitable that he'll resent the progress I've made. On the other, I'm hoping I get lucky and he comes out of rehab, all goodness and mercy, champing at the bit to end our…estrangement.'

Jasper only frowned deeper. 'Were things really that bad?'

My lips twisted, my inner voice mocking the hope of my latter statement. 'You sound surprised. I got the impression your family wasn't sweetness and light, either.'

His lips twitched sardonically. 'We aren't but our dysfunction is curiously programmed to infect the parent-child bond rather than the sibling one. Don't get me wrong, Damian only recently emerged from some self-imposed secondment in New York and Gem is busy with her own family.' He shrugged. 'I don't see much of them, anyway.'

'And let me guess, you prefer it that way?'

The flash of disconcertion on his face told me I'd hit the nail on the head. For some reason, that deepened the chasm yawing inside me.

Before I could ask him more questions about his family—mainly to deflect from answering painful ones about my own—his eyes speared me again. 'Was that what was bothering you this morning? The friction between you and Perry?'

Staring into the leafy green depths of my tea, I answered, 'No, it was the parent-child part. I'm lucky enough to have it from both sides.'

'Tell me,' he encouraged, much as he had on the plane this morning.

'My mother saw me leaving your hotel last week. Amongst my many other failings, that apparently makes me an irredeemable traitor to my family.'

His jaw clenched tight, his face a gathering thunderstorm. 'Wren—'

'Which is rich, considering they barely acknowledge my existence ninety-nine per cent of the time. I've been barely a Bingham since before my father died.'

This time my voice did break the smallest fraction. He heard it. Abandoning his tea, he slid his fingers over my nape and pulled me into a tight embrace. Unfortunately, that only reminded me of every other embrace I'd been deprived of for as far back as I could remember. I dissolved into Jasper's arms, tears I seemed to have battled all day resurging, this time spilling down my cheeks as I buried my face in his chest.

I felt…cherished. Protected in a way I'd never done before in my life. As unwise as everything indicated, I wanted to hang on to it. Absorb it into myself until it became a part of my soul. Until I could look back on it some time in the dismal future and bask in its afterglow.

'I'd love to say fuck them all but it's not as simple as that, is it?' he rasped, a deep understanding in his voice that spoke of his own demons.

Tears welled faster. 'No, it's not.'

His chest heaved in a long sigh, then I felt his lips brush the top of my head. 'Our inability to kick them permanently out of our lives doesn't mean they get to control us, though, correct? Only you have the power over you. No one else.'

The depths of bitter conviction in his voice said this was as much about him as it was about me. I looked up and his jaw was set in iron, his gaze on a faraway point I suspected didn't involve me. And yet, I still felt…wanted.

The earlier need to probe his own family situation rose again but I was a little terrified and a lot selfish to lose the warmth and security of his arms. So I bit my tongue, closed my eyes and breathed him in.

After an eternity, I felt his gaze on my face. 'Are

you glad you came? And don't say yes because this is work,' he tagged on gruffly.

Raising my gaze, I met his. 'Yes, I'm glad I came,' I replied, my voice a husky mess. We were crossing an invisible but dangerous line and yet, I was…exhausted with resisting its magnetic pull.

Jasper dropped his head slowly, and I held my breath until his lips sealed over mine. We kissed with slow languor, allowing the heat to build between us until we were both breathless.

He raised his head in torturous increments and when he spoke, his lips still brushed mine. 'The sunsets here are quite spectacular. Want to experience the outdoor bath tonight?'

I shook my head. 'Too tired to appreciate it,' I replied, just as a yawn caught me unawares.

He stood and held out his hand. 'I think an early night is on the cards. We have a full day tomorrow.'

I frowned, trying to remember the itinerary and realising…there was none. 'What exactly is happening tomorrow?'

That boyish grin, totally lethal to my state of mind, flashed into life as I let him help me up. 'Everything.'

With that ominous declaration, he tugged me back into the *riad*, to the master suite. Then, catching my hem, he freed me of my dress and panties, and nudged me into the bathroom. Bypassing the Jacuzzi bath, he switched on the jets in the shower, then made short work of undressing himself. All the while watching me with an expression that made my breath catch and my heart squeeze.

To mitigate the erratic mess that was my pulse and my emotions, I reached for an apple-shaped bottle with an exquisitely carved stopper top in the shape of the M'Goun Valley rose, the national flower of Morocco.

Jasper stopped me with a soft grip. 'No, let me.' He took the bottle, uncapped it, poured a decent measure into his palm, then motioned for me to come closer. I watched him rub his hands together, that simple act so intensely erotic, my nipples beaded and my thighs clenched hard with desperate need. 'I've dreamed of at least two dozen ways to do this.'

Swaying towards him, I lifted eyelids that were curiously heavy to meet his gaze. 'We've showered together before.'

'Hmm, but always when one of us had to rush off somewhere. Or when one of us needed to fuck the other super urgently.'

Heat rose up my body. Yes, so I'd attacked him the last time we'd been in the shower together. 'No need to rub it in my face.'

'Oh, I intend to rub it in all right. All over your body.'

Laughter caught me completely unawares, a peculiar strain of joy fizzing through me. It died in a sigh as Jasper's hands proceeded to wreak exquisite magic on my body. I didn't bother to hold back my moans of pleasure because it felt disingenuous in this place. Instead, I closed my eyes and gave my-self over to him. And by the time he swung me into his arms and carried me to the four-poster, I was a boneless, mindless creature, ready to receive every-thing he had to give.

Like the kiss before, the lovemaking was indul-gent, decadent and slow, tapping into the rhythm of the land.

And just like before, I blinked back tears when it was over. Then gasped with a different sort of pleasure when, with a touch of a remote, the doors slid back to reveal the insanely gorgeous sunset he'd promised.

From the perfect vantage point of our bed, it felt as if we were being treated to the creation of an extraordinary oil painting. The world itself seemed ablaze, streaked with the richest scarlet, vibrant or-ange and saffron yellow.

'My God, that's beautiful,' I whispered.

Jasper pulled me tighter against him. 'Yes. And just in case I didn't mention it before, I'm glad you came, too.'

Later, when it all went wrong, I would remember this moment.

The moment that last sane string unmoored me from reality as I knew it and gaily wove its way through the air into the hands of the last man I should've trusted it to.

The next day, rested and sated from glorious early-morning sex, we set off on dune buggies to a desert encampment half a mile away that formed part of the resort. The objective of the visit was to judge the experience as a possible business retreat and relaxation exercise. The twelve Bedouin tents were each large enough to host up to thirty guests and, as evidenced by the signals from our laptops as we got down to work, the business facilities were more than adequate.

By lunchtime we'd pronounced it a success and moved on to the next item on the agenda. Thrilled at the rate we were checking things off our extensive to-do list, we didn't stop until after the sun had gone down.

Dinner was an exquisite lamb and vegetable couscous cooked in an authentic tagine, followed by a creamy locally made dessert of sugared almonds and crushed dates served over a baked yoghurt. Over rich, cream-laced coffee, Jasper regarded me with heavy-lidded eyes. 'I'm getting you in that bath tonight.'

Since the stars were shining bright and I'd had exactly the same idea, I smiled. 'You have my full cooperation.'

With a heart-stopping smile, he reached for the tablet next to his coffee cup. I'd discovered to my delight that most amenities within each suite could be operated digitally and when I heard the sudden rush of water hitting the cavernous bath, my temperature rose. I set my coffee down as Jasper reclined back in his seat, his eyes promising everything he intended to do to me. But I intended to flip the script on him tonight.

'How long do we have until it's ready?'

'About eight minutes.'

I smiled. 'Hmm, that's long enough.'

Telltale heat scored his cheekbones. 'For?'

'For me to drive you a lot crazy.' I crooked a finger at him. He rose, prowling over to me in a way that made every cell in my body sing. When I made space between my knees, he stepped into them, hands hanging loose at his sides.

Slowly, teasingly, I placed my hands on his calves, then dragged them up. Arousal darkened his eyes as I explored muscular thighs for several seconds before heading north. He hissed out a breath when I brushed my knuckles over his very prominent erection. Keeping my eyes glued on his, I unbuttoned his chinos and drew down the zip. Another slow but firm tug freed his beautiful, engorged cock.

I gripped him, revelling in the hot smoothness of him, while attempting to contain the wildfire hunger rushing through me.

Still keeping my gaze on him, I pumped my hand once…twice. 'Would you like me to taste you, Jasper?'

His fists clenched convulsively. 'Holy hell, yes,' he rasped.

Moaning in anticipation, I leaned in close and wrapped my mouth over his broad head. A thick groan left his throat and I felt a light tremor wash through him. Ravenous, I took more of him in my mouth, my tongue shamelessly circling and licking as pleasure swelled through me.

'Ah, that's so good, Wren.'

I explored his cock from root to tip, licked and sucked and teased until he was panting, one hand firmly lodged in my hair as he fucked my mouth. I was so absorbed by the filthy and beautiful act, I protested when he started to draw away.

'I'd love to come in that gorgeous mouth of yours, sweetheart, but the bath's waiting.'

The bath I'd forgotten about. A little drunk on him, I watched him tear off the rest of his clothes, then tackled mine. Together we stumbled to the immense rectangular bath that could easily have accommodated a dozen.

Jasper paused long enough to tug on a condom before stepping into the warm water and helping me in. Dropping down onto the last step, he stared up at me, his eyes blazing. 'Do it, Wren.'

With a needy moan, I braced my hands on his shoulders. Then slowly, my eyes locked on his, I sank down, taking him deep inside me. Shudders of bliss wracked us both as I fucked Jasper into a panting frenzy. Lips bruised, nails raking over flesh as our simultaneous orgasms swept us under.

And when it was all over, he carried me deeper into the water, making space for me between his thighs so I could recline against him. Soft lingering caresses followed, my dreamy gaze on the stars above our heads as minutes drifted by.

Perhaps it was that sense of being untouchable by life's cruelty in that special moment that made me speak up just then. 'Can I ask you a question?'

His answer was a contented rumble, his lips trailing kisses against my bare shoulder. 'Sure.'

'Your father. You called him a destroyer of lives. Why?'

Jasper stiffened behind me, the hand caressing my thigh freezing. 'Bloody hell, Wren,' he replied. 'I have the most beautiful woman in the world bathing under moonlight with me. The last thing I want to talk about is my father.'

I said nothing, leaving him with the option to answer or not.

Another minute drifted by. 'Fine. Yes, he was.'

'Why?'

Another long pause. 'He called me weak for trying to be the peacemaker of the family. For as long as I could remember, he butted heads with Damian. Even Gem, to some extent. But I was the boy who wouldn't fight the bullies in school; the one who happily gave away his pocket money to the poor kid I felt needed it more.' Bitterness coated the laughter that punctuated his words. 'He particularly hated that when my teachers mentioned it to him, thinking they were doing me a favour and praising me for it. What they didn't know was that Hugh Mortimer was all for anarchy in the name of dividing and conquering.'

It was my turn to stiffen, the evidence of his father's ruthlessness the very thing that had created
our feud in the first place. But as I heard his clear
opposition my soft heart felt for him.

'He would've been prouder of me if I'd thumped
everyone who eyed me the wrong way. And he didn't
pull his punches by keeping that shit to himself.'

I twisted in his arms, my shocked gaze searching
his. 'He hit you?'

Relief poured through me when he shook his
head. 'No. Weirdly enough, he had a line he wouldn't
cross. Apparently. But he wasn't shy about delivering emotional bruises.' He laughed again.

I cupped one taut cheek. 'Jasper, I didn't mean to
bring it all up—'

'It's fine. He's no longer in my life. And I may
be many things now but weak I'm definitely not.'
The harsh proclamation sent a cold shiver over me.

No, Jasper Mortimer wasn't weak. I knew that
first-hand.

And when he dragged his lips over my jaw and
unerringly claimed my mouth again in a ruthless
kiss, I wondered whether there was a warning in
there for me, too.

CHAPTER TEN

'MORNING, SLEEPYHEAD.'

The miniature roller coaster that had taken residence inside me over the last three days since our arrival in Marrakesh performed a deep spiral at the sound of the sexy voice in my ear. Despite the sensation, I grinned, rolling over to find Jasper perched on the side of the bed, completely naked and looking gloriously virile in the morning light.

'Sleep well?'

I nodded, sighing at the memory of what felt like the best three days and nights of my life. Days filled with work that didn't feel like work at all and nights of transcendental sex.

'Good.'

Hoping I'd get a good-morning kiss, I silently grumbled when he turned away and reached for something on the bedside table. 'Pick one.'

I glanced down at the two envelopes stamped with the Mortimer logo in one corner. The wicked gleam in his eyes made me glance suspiciously at the mysterious offering. 'I don't think…'

'Do you trust me?' he murmured.

The right answer was…no. Perhaps love and affection were conditional but I'd discovered that even after jumping through hoops the way I'd done for my family for most of my life, they'd still let me down. And while cloud nine felt like pure heaven, my instincts shrieked for me to beware. Or, at the very least, take it down a notch the way I'd been utterly unable to since we arrived.

'Don't overthink this, Wren,' he said, his voice a low rumble. 'It's all good, I promise.'

Stupid tears clogging my throat, I plucked the nearest envelope and tore it open to distract myself before I blubbered in front of this man. Again. The words blurred for a minute. When I blinked and they came into focus, my stomach dropped to my toes.

'No way. I want the other one.' I lunged for it.

He held it out of reach, his hazel eyes dancing with humour. 'No, you picked that one, so we're doing that. Unless you're afraid of heights?'

'I never agreed to abide by your rules. And no, I'm not.'

A glimpse of steely ruthlessness surfaced in his eyes. 'So are you going to back out or are you going to trust me?'

Like before, I felt as if he was testing me, weighing me up for something more profound than…sweet heaven…*paragliding* in the desert. Again, the urge to say no pummelled me. Again, I held it at bay. Then I responded with a compulsion pulled from deep within me. 'Okay, fine. I'm going to trust you. This once,' I added, drawn by a desperate need to protect myself, emotionally and otherwise, despite the growing suspicion that it might already be too late.

An hour later, after a succulent Moroccan breakfast of yoghurt, dates, rich coffee and muesli, we left the resort.

I was pleasantly surprised when we arrived at the adventure camp set several hundred metres high up in the High Atlas Mountains. The makeshift camp I'd expected turned out to be a first-class, well-run outfit, with different groups for different levels that put me slightly at ease. The safety lesson further eased my nerves, enough to spark excitement. But not enough to fly solo when given the option.

The smouldering looks Jasper sent me as we suited up said he was pleased I'd chosen to double up with him; the intimacy of being strapped in tight against him only underlined that fact.

Regardless of all of that, my nerves nearly gave out as we stepped closer to the cliff edge.

'Jasper…wait, I don't think I want to do this—'

'One small step, Wren. That's all it takes,' he whispered in my ear. 'One small step and the belief that you're not alone. That I won't let anything happen to you.'

Dear God, what was he doing to me? I glanced back at him, saw the unshakeable promise in his eyes, and just like last night I wanted to open myself up and fill my soul with it. For however long it lasted.

With that assurance cloaking me, I swallowed, stepped forward into nothingness and felt my belly drop away from my body.

For the first five seconds, sheer terror gripped me, my scream searing my throat. But over the strong rush of air, Jasper spoke again. 'Sweetheart, open your eyes. See what your bravery has earned you.'

Reluctantly obeying, my jaw dropped as the beauty of my surroundings slowly engulfed me.

Now that we were in the air, it was as if I were sitting on a soft, swaying cushion. And below us, the majesty of the mountains and trails gave a true bird's eye view. 'This is…incredible,' I murmured, delight replacing terror.

'Told you,' Jasper said smugly.

I glanced up, saw his smile and the easy confidence with which he operated the glider and ventured a smile of my own.

'Want to go higher?'

At my nod, he sent us soaring higher, then, before I could catch my breath, his lips pressed close to my ears. 'Look to your left.'

I looked and gasped out loud. 'Oh, my God.'

A flock of grey-winged geese on their migration path flew in perfect V-formation about fifty metres away. Caught on a warm thermal, their wings barely moved, the only movement the graceful undulation of their necks. Totally entranced, I stared until my eyes watered, until my smile threatened to split my face.

When Jasper alerted me that he was changing direction, I felt a moment's sadness, then intense joy that I'd experienced this once-in-a-lifetime moment. My heart slamming against my chest, I wondered if that was a harbinger of my relationship with Jasper. Was he destined to blaze through my life like a comet, then fade away once this trip was over? Because really, once the last few teething issues in our contract were ironed out, there would be no need for further day-to-day contact.

And as we glided towards our designated landing spot, the ground rushing up at us, my breath was snatched from my lungs. Because I knew the seventy-minute flight would've been right up there with the most intensely exhilarating thing I'd ever done had I not felt another thunderbolt of emotion the moment we stepped back onto *terra firma*.

Despite suspecting this was coming, I stood shell-shocked and completely willing for Jasper to believe, as he laughingly loosened my harness and pulled it off, that it was the flight that held me tongue-tied. While all the time, the sonic boom of revelation ripped my life apart.

I was in love with Jasper Mortimer.

I struggled to hold myself together as he trailed a finger down my cheek, his eyes caressing my face. 'You should feel this free every day, Wren. Let the baggage go. It suits you.'

I must have given a satisfactory response, because

his teeth flashed in another devastating smile before he took my hand and walked me back to our SUV.

In the car, I grabbed my laptop and attempted to make notes about the experience, even though my focus was shot to pieces. Thankfully, it kept Jasper from engaging me in conversation, gave me the reprieve to contain the uncontainable.

My heart had handed itself over to my family's worst enemy and I knew deep in my bones that it was irretrievable. Did I even want it back? In a different world, had there been a chance with Jasper, would I have taken it? While my soul wanted to scream *yes*, my head forced me to face reality.

We'd gone from regular sex sessions for the sake of peaceful contract negotiations to a week in a desert paradise already counting down to its conclusion.

None of it reeked of permanence or commitment. And even if it did, did either of us have the tools to sustain it in the long term?

Shaken by the glimpse of the desolate future that awaited me, I was relieved when, on arriving at the resort, Jasper was handed a note that made him frown.

'I need to make a call to London.'

The tightness in his voice temporarily prised me from my inner turmoil. 'Is everything all right?'

His lips firmed. 'It's Gemma. She's been trying to reach me. So has my aunt.' He anticipated my next question with a shake of his head. 'I can't tell you why because I have no idea.' When he raised his gaze from the note, I caught a glimpse of apprehension.

'Go deal with it. I'll be fine.'

He gave a brisk nod and strode away, tension vibrating off him.

As quickly as my relief arrived, it evaporated. I was in love with Jasper. And whatever permutation I came up with showed our liaison as heart-wrenchingly temporary. My mother's stark condemnation and Perry's possible reaction aside, Jasper had initiated this thing between us out of frustration over my reluctance to sign on to his deal. Would we even be together otherwise?

If you want to know, ask him.

For the first time in my life, I shied away from my rational inner voice. Every inch of my soul recoiled against receiving another rejection. And yet, when the voice retreated under the relentless force of the shower I took when I returned to the suite, I mourned its silence.

My senses were still in turmoil when Jasper stalked into the *riad* half an hour later. His hair stood in haphazard spikes, as if he'd repeatedly run his fingers through it.

'Is everything okay?'

'No,' he growled. 'I need to head back to London.'

My heart lurched. Was this over already?

Dear God, I'm not ready!

The need to stop the damning words from spilling out kept my lips firmly shut as he paced to the liquor cabinet. His jaw remained set as he splashed a finger of cognac into a glass, then glanced over at me, one eyebrow raised. When I refused the silent offer of a drink, he picked his up and swallowed it in one gulp. Setting it down with suppressed force, he faced me.

'There's a board meeting tomorrow morning that requires my presence.'

I frowned. 'You didn't know it was happening?'

Granite-jawed, he answered, 'Hell, no. But I have no intention of missing it.'

Questions crowded my brain but his forbidding demeanour dried them all up. And really, wasn't this short, sharp shock of a break exactly what I needed?

No, my senses screamed. *Take whatever you can get.*

And then what? My chest squeezed painfully as desolation took hold. When Jasper crossed over to me, slid his hands into my hair, it was all I could do not to melt against him as he fused his lips to mine. To do everything my instinct warned me would only intensify the impending anguish.

'I'm sorry, sweetheart, but this is unavoidable.'

I forced a nod. 'It's fine. But I think I'll stay, make sure everything is in place before I leave.'

He took a long moment to reply and when he did it was with a curt nod. 'Okay. I'll send the plane back for you in a couple of days. And I'll take you out to dinner when you get back to London.'

One small step, Wren. That's all it takes.

The words that fell from my lips seared my insides raw and bloody. 'No. I don't think that's a great idea.'

A frown clenched his forehead. 'Why not?' he growled.

'What are we doing, Jasper?' I blurted before I could stop myself.

To his credit he didn't give me a flippant answer. And even when his hands dropped, his gaze remained fixed on mine. 'Do we need to label it? As long as it feels good, why question it?'

'But that's the problem. How long would it feel good for?'

I was aware I was worsening the mood when his eyes shadowed. 'Wren—'

'That ride this morning? It felt exhilarating. But it ended.'

He shrugged. 'So we'll choose the next adventure. And the one after that.'

'That's all life is to you? A series of thrilling rides?' If so, how long before I was a stale experience he needed to replace with a more stimulating one?

He paced away from me. 'This is so not the time to be dealing with this, Wren.'

A part of me felt sympathy for him. Whatever reason had triggered the unscheduled board meeting, it'd rattled him. But the grounded part of me stressed this was exactly the moment to end this, before I lost even more of myself. 'Is there ever a right time?'

His eyes narrowed, my answer obviously incensing him. 'Nice try, sweetheart, attempting to slot me into some ordinary box you usually reserve for past lovers.' His phone beeped and his jaw gritted after a furious glance at it. 'I need to leave for the airport. But trust me on this…this isn't over.'

'Isn't it?'

With strides powered by frustration, he returned to me, dragged me against his body and stole another hard, tongue-stroking kiss. 'Fuck no, it isn't.'

Self-preservation insisted I didn't prolong this moment, so I pursed my lips, remained in the living room as he stalked to the bedroom. Five minutes later, his suitcase was at the door. Another kiss and he was gone.

And for the next twenty-four hours, I remained in suspended animation of heartache, anguish and mind-shredding debate as to whether I'd done the right thing.

Then it all ceased to matter as all hell broke loose.

'Let me get this straight. You called a board meeting to get us to vote for you to stage a hostile takeover of Bingham Industries?'

I stared at the man who'd had the audacity to claim a seat at the head of the conference table. The years had turned his hair white and his face weathered. But those piercing eyes and that cruel mouth were the same.

The roar in my ears was nothing compared to the tight vise around my chest. Wren would never forgive me for this. I'd left things in a precarious enough state in my rush to return to London. And taking her to Morocco would be seen by her as the perfect opportunity to get her out of the way in order for my family to stage this ambush. Hell, I'd feel the same in her shoes. Which was why I needed to end this debacle asap.

'You have balls of steel, I'll give you that,' Damian murmured from his place two seats over. Next to me, my cousin Gideon snorted and reclined deeper in his seat, his expression reeking of boredom. I knew it was deceptive because he wouldn't have attended this meeting at all if he were uninterested. But he knew what the instigator of this meeting had done to me. To my siblings. Just as I knew he was here to support me. Hell, maybe my family wasn't so dysfunctional after all.

'Big, fat ones. Trouble with big balls is, expose them like this and they're stupidly easy targets,' I tossed in.

Hugh Mortimer's gaze turned to ice, his gaze tracking his eldest son's, then Gideon's before meeting mine. With me, he lingered, as if trying to spot the weakness he'd condemned me for all those years ago.

I stared him down. *Look all you like, old man. I'm immune to you now.*

He blinked first, his gaze shifting to take in the other Mortimer board members. 'Have you all gone soft in my absence? Bingham is ripe for the plucking.'

'Along with a hundred or so other struggling companies. Why this one in particular?' I taunted.

'Because it's the lowest hanging fruit, that's why,' he answered, his voice booming across the room.

'So much hot temper, Hugh. Calm yourself before you suffer a stroke.' This from Aunt Flo, whose gaze threatened to turn my father into icicles.

To my left, my cousin Bryce sniggered. 'This is way more fun than the reality TV shows Savvie's addicted to,' he murmured.

I allowed searing jealousy to consume me for a moment before I shrugged it off. If I let my guard down, I'd walk away with nothing. Destroy for ever the possibility of having what Gideon, Damian and Bryce had with their new but thriving relationships. Hell, even my wild-child cousin, Graciela, had settled down and was insanely happy with her new man.

'I don't have time to sit around all day debating this. This company isn't in the habit of staging hostile takeovers. I, for one, don't intend to start now.' I glanced at Uncle Conrad, chairman of the board. 'Shall we put it to a vote?'

He glanced at my father, his expression apprehensive. 'Um…'

'I vote nay,' I snarled.

Gideon's hand barely left the armrest. 'It's a *fuck, nay* from me.'

'And from me,' Damian growled, his eyes shooting daggers at the man who'd sired us.

I lost interest after Aunt Flo, Bryce, Gem and Graciela also sided with me. Even if the remaining board members voted against me, I'd still win.

The second the votes were counted and confirmed as fourteen to six, I rose from the table.

All my calls to Wren so far had gone to voicemail. The moment I'd discovered what my father was up to, I'd tried reaching her in Marrakesh, only to discover she'd packed her bags and left without waiting for my plane. She was probably still in the air. Or blocking my calls.

Stomach hollow at the strong possibility it was the latter, I reached for my phone again. It would be easy to check which flights had left Marrakesh—

'Jasper, a word.'

I stiffened at my father's voice. Damian's eyes narrowed. But when his gaze flicked to me, I nodded. Ten seconds later, I was alone with my father for the first time in years.

He sauntered away from me, hands deep in his pockets as he looked out of the window for a full minute before turning to face me. 'I expected you to be the loudest dissenting voice and you didn't disappoint. Still grappling with that bleeding heart, son?' he sneered.

The bite of his condemnation was less...sharp than I'd expected. 'You say bleeding heart, I call it exercising good business sense. You still know what that is, don't you? Or are you so locked on this trifling obsession you can't see straight?'

He inhaled sharply. 'What did you say?'

'You heard me. When are you going to let this go?'

'Not for as long as I draw breath, that's for sure.'

I studied him for a handful of seconds. 'There's more to this than just business, isn't there? What really happened between you and Bingham?'

I didn't expect him to answer but, surprisingly, he responded. 'The upstart had the nerve to try to steal your mother from me.'

Shocked laughter barked from my throat. 'All of this because some guy made a pass at your wife?'

Volcanic rage built in his eyes. 'He disrespected me. No one disrespects me, boy. No one.'

My humour evaporated. 'I'm not a boy. And in case you haven't heard, George Bingham is dead. Don't you have better things to do than to wrestle with a ghost?'

His nostrils flared but the hard rejoinder I expected didn't arrive. Eyes eerily similar to mine considered me for several seconds, before a hard smile twisted his lips. 'I heard you were sleeping with her…the Bingham girl. I didn't think you would be so dense. Obviously, I was wrong.'

'I'd seriously watch it, old man.'

The flicker in his eyes said my warning had got through. 'Answer me this, son. Would you let it go if someone made advances on what you considered yours?'

He clearly knew which buttons to press because the answer was *hell, no.* Wren was mine. She'd been mine long before that first sizzling episode in her maze. But scent-marking her was one thing. Destroying countless lives over an overblown feud was another. 'No, I won't,' I answered my father. 'But neither would I use a bulldozer to squash a gnat.'

'Ah, ever the peacemaker, eh, son?'

A flash of pain and anger twisted inside me. Then curiously the ache eased, leaving in its place a feeling of…acceptance. Calm. Some things just weren't meant to be. 'You keep calling me son, and I really wish you'd stop.'

His eyes narrowed. 'Excuse me?'

'No, you're not excused. Stop calling me son because you haven't earned the right. You were simply a biological ingredient that helped form my existence. You made it clear your children were simply a means to an end. So do us all a favour, *Hugh*, and go back to wherever the hell you came from.'

I headed for the door, the urgency to get to Wren a nuclear force inside me.

'Come back here, Jasper. We're not done.'

I delivered the same corrosive smile his genes had helped me perfect and had the satisfaction of watching his eyes widen. 'Oh, yes, we are.' I turned away from him, then veered back to make the final, vital point. 'Stay away from Bingham's, too. Or so help me, I'll devote every single penny of my many billions to crushing you.'

Every second of my trip to Wren's house four harrowing days later felt like a light year. Unsurprisingly, Hugh hadn't heeded my warning. And even without the weight of the Mortimer board behind him, he managed to cause an uproar that gripped the city. Every photo I saw of Wren looking anguished as the tabloids hounded her intensified my fury. Staying away from her until I resolved this disaster had felt like death by a million cuts.

My mouth dried as I turned into her street. While my trusted spies had confirmed she was home, gaining entry was another matter.

But I couldn't give up now. Striding to her front door, I leaned on the doorbell. My heart leapt as I heard faint steps and her voice ending a phone call.

Then, 'Fuck off, Jasper.'

'No, sweetheart. I'm not leaving.'

The door burst open. 'Who the hell do you think you are, coming here like this?'

'Let me in, Wren. Please.'

'Are you deaf? I said fuck off.'

God, she looked glorious. Fierce pride elevated her chin even as pain clouded her beautiful eyes. Unable to heed her request, I simply shook my head. 'No.'

Her face twisted as she tried to hang on to her composure. 'You cut me off. Wouldn't even take my calls. Now, my lawyers tell me I'm all out of options and I have forty-eight hours to accept your terms. So, I guess you've come to gloat?'

'No, I haven't. And I'm not the one threatening you. It's my father.'

She paled, her hand dropping from the door. 'What?'

'Let me in and I'll explain.'

Numbly, she stepped back, then flinched from me as I turned to her.

Gritting my teeth, I went down the hallway into her living room, relieved when she followed. Since there was no point beating about the bush, I launched into explanation. 'I didn't answer you because I was dealing with my father. The board backed me against him, Wren. Our contract is airtight. As for that farce of a takeover, it'll happen over my dead body.'

Her jaw sagged open. 'What are you saying?'

'I'm saying that before end of business today, the threat to your company will be over. And before I'm finished with him, Hugh will know that his lastborn son isn't weak. That like I've always done, I'll fight for those who matter to me. To the death if I have to.'

Her eyes grew into alluring saucers and I wanted to grab her, wrap her tight in my arms and never let go. But we'd been through the mill the last few days. I knew it would take more than a few declarations to make things right. Plus I had a feeling that, while I might have won this skirmish with my father, he would continue to be a nuisance for a while.

As those thoughts flashed through my head, the light died from her eyes. 'It's too late, Jasper. The Bingham board are seriously thinking of selling—'

'Fuck that. You won't be selling Bingham's. Not to someone who'll break it into little pieces and sell it, and certainly not to my father.'

Her chin went higher. 'It's not up to you, though, is it?'

I tried a different tack. 'Did I tell you Damian is married now?'

She frowned. 'What?'

I shook my head, the very thought still bewildering in the extreme. 'My hard-hearted, closed-off brother, whose only friend in the world is my certifiably psychotic cousin Gideon, is in love. With an actual red-blooded woman. Who apparently loves him back.'

Her confusion grew. 'Why are you telling me this?'

'Because he's proof that the unthinkable can happen. And they're not just in love, they're also in business together.'

'That's great, but were they locked in a family feud before they got together?'

'No, but fuck that, too,' I snarled. 'Tell me you don't want this to end, once and for all, Wren. That we haven't paid enough for the wrong decisions our parents made?'

She swallowed and that small hesitation sparked hope in my chest. Her gaze flicked to the phone she'd tossed onto the coffee table, and my instinct latched on to it.

'Who were you talking to just now?'

Her lips pursed for a second. 'Perry. Apparently he's allowed phone calls after the first four weeks.'

'What did you talk about?' I pushed, that blind hope still building.

She slicked her tongue over her bottom lip. 'He said he didn't hate me for sealing the deal with you. Or…for going out with you.' The relief in her voice was palpable.

'Good. What else?'

'He said he would support me in whatever decision I make about the company. And…'

'And what?'

'He knows he was the favourite child, that I got a raw deal when it came to our parents' love. He wants me to forgive him for taking advantage of it.'

'As he should.' I paused for a heartbeat before speaking the words that blazed from my soul. 'While you're giving your brother a chance, would you consider giving me one, too?'

Panic flared over her face before her gaze swept away. 'I told you, I'm not some lost cause you need to save. You can go ahead and bid for Bingham's if you want but I—'

'I love you. Does that count?'

Her jaw dropped and a visible tremble shook her body. 'What?'

'I love you, Wren. And you're far, far from a lost cause. You're fit to command armies and your indomitable spirit makes me fall harder for you every passing second.'

She inhaled. Right before her eyes narrowed into accusing slits. 'You refused to take my calls. You left me floundering in the dark for days, Jasper!'

'Because I was scrambling to stop Hugh from getting his hands on Bingham's. Between Gideon, Damian and I, we've been up round the clock for days, blocking every conceivable avenue Hugh might exploit.'

Several layers of anger drained away. 'You... have?'

'If it was just a question of money, it would've been easy. Between the three of us, we have enough to stop Hugh financially. But before you got your lawyers to implement the freeze on the votes, he was busy trying to buy off your board members. And I was busy trying to put this together.'

Her gaze dropped to the document I held out. 'What is that?'

'A solution I'd love for you to consider when we're done taking care of what's more important. I love you, Wren,' I reiterated. Because I needed her to hear it. To know that the powerful emotion that had taken root inside me when I wasn't looking and fused itself to my very soul wasn't going away. 'I think I fell in love with you five years ago, at the intern's seminar.'

Green eyes grew shiny and I dared to go closer, to hope for an echo of what I felt. 'I don't... I can't...'

'Sweetheart, be brave. One last time. Let's defy the odds and shove our happiness in the faces of our doubters.'

A shocked gasp left her lips. 'Perry said something just like that.'

'And I'd kick his arse for stealing my thunder if I didn't wish with every fibre in my being that you would consider it.' Unable to bear being apart from her, I stepped closer, cupped her chin and nudged her gaze to mine. 'Please, Wren. You mean everything to me. I want to build a life with you. I want to see that smile every day, wait with bated breath for you to blow me away with your brilliant mind. And, sweet heaven, I want the privilege of fucking you every chance I get, even if some of those include you and a certain trench coat I've decided can stay. For now.'

Her laugh was music to my ears and manna to my soul. Too soon, it died away. 'Are you sure, Jasper? This upheaval…it feels like a lot.'

I nodded. 'I get it, and there will probably be a few more to come. But would you rather face it alone or with a seriously handsome dude who worships you?'

Again that smile threatened to make an appearance.

'Take the step,' I pleaded.

Her breath caught and her hand rose as if to touch me. I held my own breath until she did. Then I tugged her into my arms, groaning as my lips found hers. But far too soon, she pulled away.

'Wait. Tell me you didn't know what was happening when you left Morocco.'

I grimaced. 'All Gemma would tell me was that I was needed at the board meeting. I think she suspected I wouldn't attend if she told me Hugh was the one behind it. I didn't know, sweetheart. It killed me the way you found out. But hopefully, I can make it up to you.'

She glanced at the document, then her gaze returned to mine. 'I was terrified you'd betrayed me, Jasper.'

'Never. For as long as I live, I'll never let you down that way. Or in any other way. You're mine. I fight for what's mine. And you are right at the top of that list.'

Tears filled her eyes and neither of us cared when they drenched her cheeks. Because she was smiling through them, her arms encircling my neck. After another long, soul-stirring kiss, she whispered in my ear, 'Do you want to know when I fell in love with you?'

The electric shock that went through me held me rigid. Then, pure happiness blazing through me, I said, 'Yes, I do.'

'When you took me into the sky with the promise to be the wind beneath my wings and laid the world at my feet.'

A knot in my throat hoarsened my words. 'You have my promise that I will do that for you every day, Wren.'

Fresh tears filled her eyes but she looked more beautiful than ever. 'Only if you let me do the same for you.'

'Deal.'

We kissed, long and deep and soul-sealing. 'I love you, Jasper.'

'My heart and soul and trust and body are yours. And if you can squeeze in a wedding before the launch, I swear to you that I'll find another fraction of love for you.'

Her laughter branded my soul and I vowed to wear it with pride. Because I was Wren's and she was mine.

'Challenge accepted.'

EPILOGUE

THERE WERE MOMENTS in the past three months when I was a little bit ashamed of the precious time I'd wasted fighting this feeling even though I recognised things had played out the way they were supposed to.

That pain and desolation made this all-encompassing bliss suffusing me now even more precious.

'You're smiling again, Wren. I swear if you don't get your act together, you'll blow this for me.'

'Sorry.' I laughed at my almost sister-in-law's mournful voice. 'I can't help it.'

Gemma Mortimer approached, tweaking the veil she'd tweaked a dozen times already. 'I know, but maybe just…pretend for five seconds? I really want to see Jasper's face.'

'Why?'

Gemma shrugged. 'Just…a little payback for all the tricks he pulled on me when we were kids.'

The woman who was fast becoming as precious to me as her brother stared at me with pleading eyes.

Damn, those irresistible hazel Mortimer eyes. 'Three seconds, that's all I can give you.'

Gemma whooped. 'I knew you were awesome when you chose me as your maid of honour.'

My smile widened, my heart swelling at the closeness between the siblings these past few months. But my heart was even more grateful for the transformation within my own family.

As if summoned by my thoughts, my mother walked in as Gemma retreated.

Agnes wore a burnished orange lace dress that perfectly complemented the tan she'd cultivated in the pre-wedding week we'd been in Morocco. But her attire wasn't what interested me. The tentative smile that grew at my silent welcome was what touched my soul, the light kiss she dropped on my cheek before stepping back what drew tears to my eyes.

An open conversation with her on my return to London, and then with Perry after his successful stretch at rehab, had stopped the rot of our relationship. Full recovery was a long way off, but my mother's raw admission that she didn't want to lose her daughter, that she'd taken a wrong stance in order to please my father, had helped.

'You look beautiful, Wren.'

'Thank you, Mother.'

She stepped closer. 'I hope this doesn't make you cry and ruin your make-up, but thank you for healing our family.'

Swivelling to face her, I felt a small sob burst out of me. 'Oh, Mum!'

Her own eyes watered. 'You've never called me that before. I... I like it.'

I gripped her hand as she sniffed. Then after touching up my make-up, she looked into my eyes. 'Your brother is ready to walk you down the aisle. Are you ready, Wren?'

'The love of my life is waiting for me, Mum. I'm ready.'

I watched the woman twirling expertly on the dance floor, drawing smiles and laughter from family and guests alike. Silently I shook my head in wonder as she caught my gaze and blew me a kiss.

My wife. Wren Mortimer-Bingham was my wife.

'Jesus, don't let her catch you with that idiotic smile on your face, Jasper. She'll own you for life.'

'Don't listen to Gideon,' came the rejoinder from Damian. 'I catch him staring at Leonie like that at least a dozen times a minute.'

I mourned the disruption of my adoration and turned as Bryce joined us. 'Yeah, I say don't watch her like that because it creeps the rest of us out.'

I couldn't help the laughter that barked out of me or the now familiar warmth that infused me. I'd come to recognise it as a different kind of love. The sustaining kind that was always there but buried beneath the clutter of other emotions.

All it'd needed was the right woman to help us

236 ENEMIES WITH BENEFITS

all buff off the hardened edges to rediscover the diamond-strong connection beneath.

And, sweet heaven, the shine of their love was blinding. For a silent moment we watched the women in our lives—Wren, Leonie, Neve and Savvie—dance some more.

'Are you ready to talk business or shall we wait for this sappiness to pass?' Damian muttered.

My gaze flicked from my brother to his wife, Neve, who looked up just then and sent him a secret smile. Then I gazed at my own wife. 'Don't hold your breath, Damian. This is a lifelong thing,' I replied.

He turned and watched me for a second. Then slapped me on the back. 'I'm proud of you, brother.'

The lump was still in my throat when I wove through the guests to my wife's side. Wrapped my arms around her, held her tight and just breathed her in as she threw her arms around my neck.

'I missed you,' I confessed. 'And I love you like mad, even though I still owe you big time letting Gem pull that prank at the wedding.'

Gemma had suddenly frozen halfway down the aisle, stared at me and mouthed *Sorry*. A heartless trick that'd nearly killed me until Wren stepped into view on her brother's arm, her smile incandescent.

Wren threw back her head and laughed now, and I shamelessly buried my face in her neck, basked in her joy and beauty.

'And how are you going to punish the love of your life?'

I kissed her long and deep, uncaring of who saw us. 'I'll come up with something, I'm sure. Right now, I'm a little stumped since you've blown me away with the success of this launch and I'm scrambling to see past your genius.' All around us, A-listers enjoyed the buzz and celebration of the opening of Mortimer Marrakesh. And according to the data, we were fully booked for several months.

Wren's fingers brushed my cheek, her eyes shining with love. 'You're the genius. For urging me to take this wild ride with you. I love you, Jasper. So much.'

'Are you glad we joined forces?' The document I'd brought to her flat had been a merger proposal between Bingham and the Mortimer Group. Her agreement had stopped Hugh in his tracks. He'd left London soon after and I didn't miss him one little bit.

'Absolutely ecstatic. I couldn't be happier. With you. With our life. With our partnership.'

'Hmm, but I bet I could make you a tiny bit happier…'

Her eyes sparkled. 'Let me guess. Are you going to take me flying again?'

'Any time you want. But for now…' I looked over her shoulder, spotted a darkened doorway that led to a secret place '… I promise a different, way better type of flying. Come with me?'

Her smile threatened to burst my heart wide open. 'To the ends of for ever.'

* * * * *

THE PRINCE'S
STOLEN VIRGIN

MAISEY YATES

For my mum and dad, who read to me always and made me fall in love with books – most especially fairy tales – from the beginning.

My favourite stories always ended with 'they lived happily ever after.' And they still do.

CHAPTER ONE

Once upon a time...

BRIAR HARCOURT MOVED quickly down the street, wrapping her long wool coat more tightly around her as the autumn breeze blew down Madison Avenue and seemed to whip straight on through to her bones.

It was an unseasonably cold fall, not that she minded. She loved the city this time of year. But there was always a strange sense of loss and nostalgia that mixed with the crisp air, and it was difficult for her to figure out what it was.

It would hover there, on the edges of her consciousness, for just a moment. Then it would slip away, like a leaf on the wind.

It was something to do with her life before she'd come to New York; she knew that. But she'd only been three when she'd been adopted by her parents, and she didn't remember her life before them. Not really. It was all impressions. Smells. Feelings. And a strange ache that settled low in her stomach.

Strange, because she loved her parents. And she loved her city. There shouldn't be an ache. You couldn't miss something you didn't even remember.

And yet, sometimes, she did.

Briar paused for a moment, a strange prickling sensation crawling up the back of her neck. It wasn't the cold. She was wearing a scarf. And anyway, it felt different. Different than anything she had ever experienced before.

She paused then turned around. The crowd behind her parted for a moment and she saw a man standing there. She knew, immediately, that he was the reason for the prickling sensation. He was looking at her. And when he saw that she was looking back, a slow smile spread over his face.

And it was like the sun had come out from behind the clouds.

He was beautiful. She could see that from here. Dark hair pushed back from his forehead, making him look carelessly windswept. There was dark stubble on his jaw, and something in his expression, in his eyes, that suggested he was privy to a host of secrets she could never hope to uncover.

He was… Well, he was a man. Nothing like the boys that she had been exposed to either at school or at various functions put on by her parents. Christmas parties at their town house, summer gatherings in the Hamptons.

He wouldn't stumble around, bragging about conquests or his beer pong score. No, never. Of course, she also wouldn't be allowed to talk to him.

To say that Dr. Robert Harcourt and his wife, Nell, were old-fashioned was an understatement. But then, she was their only child, and she had come to them late in life. Not only were they part of a different generation than many of her friends' parents, they had always made it very clear that she was precious to them. An unexpected gift they had never hoped to receive.

That always made her smile. It made the ache go away.

It didn't feel like a chore to do the best she could for them. To do her best to be a testament to all they'd put into raising her. She had always done her very best to make sure they were happy they'd made that decision. She'd tried—so very hard—to be the best she could be. To be perfect.

She had done her deportment lessons and her etiquette. Had done the debutante balls—even though it hadn't appealed to her at all. She had gone to school close to home, had spent every weekend back with her parents so they wouldn't worry. She'd never even considered rebelling. How could you rebel against people who had chosen you?

Except, right now, she felt a little bit like disregarding their concern. Like moving toward that man, who was still looking at her with those wicked eyes.

She blinked, and just as suddenly as he had appeared he was gone. Melted back into the crowd of black and gray coats. She felt an unaccountable sense of loss. A feeling that she had just missed something important. Something extraordinary.

You wouldn't know if it could have been extraordinary. You've never even kissed a man.

No. A side effect of that overprotectiveness. But then, she had no desire to kiss Tommy Beer Pong or his league of idiot friends.

Tall, sophisticated-looking men on bustling streets were another matter. Apparently.

She blinked then turned back around, heading back in the direction she had originally been going. Not that she was in a hurry. She was on break from school, and spending the days wandering her parents' town house wasn't terribly appealing. So she had decided she was going to go to the Met today, because she never got tired of wandering those halls.

But suddenly, the Met, and all the art inside, seemed lackluster. At least, in view of the man she had just seen.

Ridiculous.

She shook her head and pressed on.

"Are you running away from me?"

She stopped, her heart slamming against her breastbone. Then she whirled around and nearly ran into the object of her thwarted feelings. "No," she said, the word coming out on a breath.

"You seemed to be walking quickly, and with great purpose."

Oh, his *voice*. He had an accent. Spanish, or something. Sexy and like the sort of thing her brain would weave out of thin air late at night when she was trying to sleep, concocting herself the perfect mystery dream date that she would likely never find.

He was even better-looking up close. Stunning, even. He smiled, revealing perfect teeth. And then, he relaxed his mouth. There was something even more compelling about that. About being able to examine the shape of his lips.

"I wasn't," she said. "I just…" Somebody bumped into her as they walked by quickly. "Well, I didn't want to be in the way," she said, gesturing after the person, as if to prove her point.

"Because you had stopped," he pressed. "To look at me?"

"You were looking at *me*."

"Surely you must be used to that."

Hardly. At least, not in the way that he meant. Nobody likes to be different, and she was different in a great many ways. She was tall, first of all. Which was one refreshing thing about him. He was at least five inches taller than her height of five eleven, which was a rare and difficult thing to come across.

But yes, that was her. Tall. Skinny. All limbs. Plus, her hair was never going to fall in the effortless, silken waves most of her friends possessed. It took serious salon treatments to get it straight and she often questioned if it was worth it. Though, her mother insisted it was.

She was the opposite of the typical blonde beauty queen in her sorority or at any of the private schools she had attended growing up.

She stood out. And when you were a teenager, it was the last thing you wanted.

Though, now that she was in her early twenties, she was beginning to come to terms with herself. Her first instinct still wasn't to assume someone was staring because they liked what they saw. No, she always assumed they were staring because she was out of place.

"Not especially," she said, because it was honest.

"I don't believe that," he said. "You're far too beautiful to walk around not having men snap their necks trying to get a look."

Her face grew warm, her heart beginning to beat faster, harder. "I'm not really… I'm not supposed to talk to strangers."

That earned her a chuckle. "Then perhaps we should make sure to become something other than strangers."

She hesitated. "Briar. My name is Briar."

A strange expression crosssed his face, though it was fleeting. "A nice name. Different."

"I suppose it is." She knew it was. Yet another thing that made her feel like she stood out.

"José," he said, extending his hand.

She simply stared at it for a moment, as if she wasn't quite sure what he intended her to do. But of course she did know. He wanted to shake her hand. That wasn't weird. It was what people did when they met. She sucked in a sharp breath and allowed her fingers to meet his.

It was like she'd been hit by lightning. The electricity was so acute, so startling, that she immediately dropped his hand, taking a step back. She had never felt anything like that before in her life. And she didn't know if she wanted to feel it again.

"I have to go."

"No, you don't," he said, insistent.

"Yes. I do. I was on my way to… I was just going to… to a hair appointment." A lie easily thought of because she'd just been pondering her hair. But she could hardly tell him she was going to the museum. He might offer to walk with her. Though she supposed he could offer to take her to a salon, too.

"Is that so?"

"Yes. I have to go." She turned away, walking away from him quickly.

"Wait! I don't even know how to get in touch with you. At least give me your phone number."

"I can't." For a whole variety of reasons, but mostly because of the tingling sensation that still lingered on her hand.

She turned again, taking too-long strides away from him.

"Wait!"

She didn't. She kept on walking. And the last thing she saw was a bright yellow taxi barreling down on her.

* * *

Warmth flooded her. The strangest sensation assaulted her. Like she was being filled with oxygen, her extremities beginning to tingle. She felt disembodied, like she was floating in a dark space.

Except then it wasn't so dark. There was light. Marble walls. White. With ornate golden details. It was so clear. A place she'd never seen before, and yet…she must have.

Slowly, ever so slowly, she felt like she was being brought back to herself.

First, she could wiggle her fingertips. And then, she became aware of other things. Of the source of the warmth.

Lips against hers. She was being kissed.

Her eyes fluttered open, and in that instant she recognized the dark head bent over hers.

The man from the street.

The street. She had been crossing the street.

Was she in the street still? She couldn't remember leaving it. But she felt… Tied down.

She opened her eyes wider, looking around. There was a bright, fluorescent light directly above her, monitors all to her side. And she was tethered to something.

She curled her fingers into a fist and felt a sharp, stinging sensation.

She looked down at her arm and saw an IV.

And then, all her focus went straight back to the fact that she was still being kissed. In a hospital bed, presumably.

She put her hand up, her fingers brushing against his cheek, and then he pulled away.

"*Querida,* you're awake." He looked so relieved. Not

like a stranger at all. But then, he was kissing her, which was also unlike a stranger.

"Yes. How long was I...? How long was I asleep?" She posed the question to the nurse that she noticed standing just behind him. It was weird that he had kissed her. And she was going to get to that in a moment. But first she was trying to get a handle on how disoriented she felt.

"You were unconscious. Only for an hour or so."

"Oh." She pushed down on the mattress, trying to sit up.

"Now be careful," he said. "You might have a concussion."

"What happened?"

"You crossed the street right in front of a taxi. I was unable to stop you."

She vaguely remembered him calling after her, and her continuing to walk on. Feeling slightly frantic as she did. Logically, she knew that her parents were overprotective. She knew that they had been hypervigilant in instilling the concept of stranger danger to her, but she had taken it on board, even knowing that it was a little bit over the top.

They had told her that she had to be particularly careful because Robert was a high-profile physician who often worked with politicians and helped write legislation pertaining to the healthcare system, and that made him something of a target. She had to be extra vigilant because of that, and because of the fact that they were wealthy.

It had made her see the bogeyman in any overly friendly stranger on the street as a child, but she supposed it had kept her safe. Until she had met *him* and run out in front of a car.

Her parents. She wondered if anyone had called them. They wouldn't be expecting her home until evening.

"Excuse me..." But the nurse had rushed out of the room, presumably to get a doctor? She didn't know why the woman hadn't stopped to check her vitals.

"My father is a doctor," she said, looking back up at José. That was his name. That was what he had said his name was.

"That is good to know," he said, a slight edge in his voice that she hadn't heard earlier.

"If he hasn't been called already, somebody should get in touch with him. He's going to want input on my treatment."

"I'm sorry," José said, straightening.

Suddenly, his face looked different to her. Sharper, harder. Her heart thundered dully, a strange lick of fear moving through her body.

"You're sorry about what?"

"It isn't going to be possible for your father to have input on your treatment. Because you're going to be moved."

"I am?"

"Yes. It seems to me that you are stable, and that has been confirmed by my nurse."

"Your nurse?"

He sighed heavily, lifting his hand and checking his watch. Then he adjusted the cuff on his jacket, the mannerism curt and officious. "Yes. My nurse," he said, sounding exasperated as though he was explaining something to a small child. "You do not have to worry. You will be treated by my doctor once we arrive in Santa Milagro."

"Where is that? I don't understand."

"You don't know where Santa Milagro is? I do question the American school system in that case. It is truly a shame that you had to be brought up here, Talia."

Something niggled at her, something strange and steep. As deep as those wistful feelings she often felt when the air began to cool. "My name isn't Talia."

"Right. Briar." His smile took on a sardonic twist. "My mistake."

"The fact that I don't know where Santa Milagro is is not the biggest issue we have. The biggest issue is that I'm not going to see your doctor. You're just a crazy man that I met on the street. For all I know you stole that coat—it is a really nice coat—and you're actually an insane vagrant."

"A vagrant? No. Insane? Well. That matter is fully up for debate. I won't lie."

"José—"

"My name isn't José. I'm Prince Felipe Carrión de la Viña Cortez. And you, my dear Briar, are mine by rights. I have spent a great many years looking for you, and now I have finally found you. And you're coming with me."

CHAPTER TWO

PRINCE FELIPE CARRIÓN DE LA VIÑA CORTEZ had yet to lose sleep over any of his actions. As long as he steered clear of covert murders to further his political status, he was better than his father.

A low bar, certainly. But Felipe liked a low bar. They were so much easier to step over.

And while this might be the lowest he'd stooped, it was also going very well. Surely if he wasn't supposed to have Princess Talia she wouldn't have delivered herself quite so beautifully to him.

Well, the part where she was hit by a taxi was perhaps not ideal, but it had certainly made the second half of his scheme easier. Because she was now confined to a hospital bed, being wheeled through an empty corridor—something he was pleased he'd arranged, because she was yelling for help, and it was much nicer to not have to deal with anyone trying to come to her aid—and he was going to have her undergo a quick check by a privately hired physician before having her loaded onto the plane.

He was covering all his bases, and truly, being quite generous.

Though he supposed the kiss hadn't been wholly necessary. But remembering the way she had jolted when she'd seen him on the street, he had wondered. Wondered if there was enough electricity between them to shock her awake.

It had worked, apparently.

Other men might feel some guilt over kissing an unconscious woman. Not this man.

Not with this woman.

She was owed to him. Owed to Santa Milagro. She should be thankful that he was the one who had found her. Had it been his father...

Well. Yet more reasons Felipe would be losing no sleep over this. Life with him would be a kindness by comparison.

Though it was clear to him that his princess did not see it now.

"Are you insane?" She was still shouting, and he was becoming bored with it.

"As previously mentioned, it is entirely possible that I'm crazy. However, hurling it around like an epithet is hardly going to help."

She looked up at him, her dark eyes blazing, the confusion from earlier cleared from them. Even now—in a hospital gown—she was beautiful. Though her rich skin tone would be better served in golds, colors like gems. Not the sallow, white and blue cloth her slight curves were currently covered by.

No, he would see her dressed like a queen, which she soon would be. His queen. Once his father died and Felipe assumed the throne.

He had a feeling his father would be distinctly unhappy to know that Felipe had managed to track down the quarry his father had spent so many years searching for. Good thing the old bastard was bound to his bed.

Though, even if he was not, Felipe had the support of the people, and at this point, the support of the military. He supposed considering treason in the form of dispatching his own father was probably not the best course of action.

Though, if the old man was healthier, the likelihood of him considering it would be much higher.

There would be no need to do that. No. Instead, he would bring Talia back to the palace, and he would parade her before his father like a cat might deliver a bird to its master. Except the old king was not Felipe's master. Not anymore.

He passed the nurse a large stack of US dollars after she helped load the princess into the back of the van he had hired. He would not be paying anyone with anything traceable. No. He wanted all of this to go off without a ripple in the media.

Until he decided to make the tidal wave.

This would be one of his grandest illusions, and he was a master of them. Sleight of hand and other trickery so that he would be consistently underestimated on the world stage. Because it suited him. It suited him endlessly.

Well, that wasn't true. The end was coming.

Talia was a means to it.

"To the airport," he said to his driver as the van was secured.

"The airport?" She was sounding quite shrill now.

"Well, we aren't swimming to Santa Milagro. Not in your condition, anyway."

"I am not going with you."

"You are. Though I appreciate your spirit. It's admirable. Particularly given that you're currently in a hospital bed. I will have you undergo a preliminary examination before we get on the plane."

The physician he'd hired moved from his seat over to where Talia was. He proceeded to examine her, taking her blood pressure, looking at her eyes. "You may want to order a CT scan once you get back to your country," the older man said. If he was feeling any compunction about being involved in this kidnapping, he was hiding it well.

But, considering the amount of money that Felipe was throwing at him, he should hide it well.

"Thank you. I will make sure she has follow-up appointments. I do not want her broken, after all."

She did not look relieved by that news, though in his opinion she should.

"If you have any integrity at all," she said, reaching out and grabbing the doctor by the arm, "then you'll tell somebody where I am. Who I'm with."

The older man looked away from her, clearly uncomfortable, and withdrew his arm.

"Talia," Felipe said, "he has been paid too well to offer you any help."

"You keep calling me Talia. And I'm not Talia. I don't know who Talia is."

Well, that was certainly an interesting development. "Whether or not you know who Talia is—and that I question—you are her."

"I think maybe you're the one who hit your head," she said.

"Again, sadly for you, I did not. While I may not be of sound mind, I certainly know my own mind. This... Well, this has been planned for a very long time. You think it accidental that I encountered you on a busy street in New York City? Of course not. The most random of encounters are always carefully orchestrated."

"By some sort of higher power?" she asked, her tone wry.

"Yes. Me."

"I have no idea who you are. I have never heard of you, I have never heard of your country, so I can only imagine that it is the size of a grain of rice on a world map. While we're talking size, I can only assume that plays a factor in a great many things, since you seem to be compensating."

He chuckled. "If I were not so secure I might be offended by that, *querida*. Anyway, while I am a believer in the idea that size matters in some arenas, when it comes to world events, often the size of the country is not the biggest issue. It is the motion of the… Well, of the cash flow. The natural resources. And that, my country has in abundance. However, we are going through a few structural changes. You are part of those changes."

"How can I be part of those changes? I'm a doctor's daughter. I'm a university student. I don't have a place on the world stage."

"And that is where you're wrong. But we're not going to finish having this discussion here."

He had paid the good doctor for his silence, that much was true, but he did not trust anything when a larger payday had the potential to come into play. And when news of Briar Harcourt going missing hit the media, there was a chance that the man would go forward with his story.

That meant that the details revealed in the van needed to be limited. Soon, however, they arrived at the airport, and the vehicle pulled up directly to Felipe's private plane.

"Don't we have to go through customs? I don't have... Well, I don't have a passport."

"Darling. You're traveling with me now. I am your passport. Does she need the IV any longer?" He posed that question to the doctor.

"She shouldn't," came the grave reply.

"Then remove it," Felipe commanded.

The doctor did so, carefully and judiciously, putting a Band-Aid over where the needle had been.

"She is not hooked up to anything else?"

"No," the doctor replied.

"Excellent." Felipe reached down, wrapping his arms around Talia and hoisting her up out of the bed. "Good help is all very well and good, but in the end it's always better to do things yourself."

She clung to him for a moment, clearly afraid of falling out of his arms and getting another head injury, and continued to hold on to him while he got out of the van and began to stride across the tarmac toward the plane.

And then she began to struggle.

"Please do not make this difficult," he said, tightening his hold on her, not finding this difficult at all, though he would rather not end up with a bruise if it could be helped. If he was going to be marred, he preferred for it to happen in the bedroom. At least then, there would be a reward for his suffering.

Hell, sometimes the suffering was just part of the reward.

"The point is to make this difficult!"

"I have never had a woman resist getting on my private plane quite so much."

"But you've had them resist. That says nothing good about you."

He sighed heavily, taking them both up the steps and into the aircraft. His flight crew immediately mobilized, closing the door and beginning the process of readying for takeoff. As they had been instructed prior to his and the princess's boarding.

"You say that as though it should bother me," he said, setting her down in one of the plush leather chairs on the plane before sitting down in the chair across from her. "Don't bother to try and get up and unlock the door. It can only be unlocked from the cockpit now. I made arrangements for some high-security additions to be added to the plane before coming to get you."

"That seems stupid," she said. "What if we need to get out and the pilots can't let us out?"

He chuckled, reluctantly enjoying the fact that she seemed so comfortable running her mouth even though she had absolutely no power in the situation. "Well, I can actually control it from my phone, as well. But don't get any ideas about trying to do it yourself. It requires fingerprint and retina recognition."

"Fine. But if the plane catches fire and we need to get out and somehow your fingerprints have melted off and you can't open your eyes and we die a painful death because of your security measures…"

"Well," he said. "In such a case I will feel terribly guilty. And, I imagine continue the burning in hell."

"That's a given."

"Are you concerned for the state of my eternal soul?"

"Not at all. I'm concerned for the state of my present body." She looked around, and he could tell the exact moment she realized she had nothing. That she was wearing a hospital gown, that she had no identification, no money and no phone.

"I do not intend to harm you," he said, reaching down and straightening his cuffs. "In fact, that runs counter to my objective."

"Your objective is to…improve my health?"

"Does it need improving? Because if it does, I most certainly will."

"No," she laid her head back, grimacing suddenly. "Okay. Well, right now it needs slight improvement because I feel like I was hit by a taxi." She sat upright, slamming her hands down on either side of her, her palms striking the leather hard, the sound echoing in the cabin. "Oh, yes! Because I was hit by a taxi!"

"Regrettable. While I orchestrated a great many things, that was not one of them. I would never take such a risk with you."

"Maybe now is a good time for you to explain yourself. Since we've established I'm not going anywhere. And I assume that Santa Milagro is not a quick and easy flight. I suppose we have the time."

"In a moment." The engines fired up on the plane, and they began to move slowly. "I like a little atmosphere. And I don't want to be interrupted by takeoff."

The aircraft began to move faster and he reached across to the table beside him, opening the top and pressing a button. An interior motor raised a shelf inside, delivering a bottle of scotch, along with a tumbler.

As the plane began to ascend he opened the bottle and poured himself a generous measure of the amber liquid. He did not spill a drop. That would be a mistake. And he did not make mistakes.

Unless he made them on purpose.

"And now?" she pressed.

"Do you want to change first?" He took a sip of his drink. "Not that the hospital gown isn't lovely."

Her face contorted with rage. "I don't care what I'm wearing. And I really don't care what you think of it."

"That will change. I guarantee it."

"You don't know very much about women, do you?"

He set his glass down on the table. "I know a great deal about women. Arguably more than you do."

"You don't know anything about this woman. I don't know what kind of simpering idiots you normally capture and drag onto your plane, but I'm not impressed by your wells, by your title, by your power. My father did not raise a simpering, weak-willed idiot. And my mother did not raise a fool."

"No, indeed. However, they were raising a princess."

"I'm not a princess."

"You are. The Princess of Verloren. Long-lost. Naturally."

"That is… That is ridiculous."

"It is the subject of a great many stories, a great many films… Wouldn't you think that something like that, a story so often told, might have its roots in reality?"

"Except this isn't *The Princess Diaries* and you are not Julie Andrews."

He chuckled. "No, indeed." He took another sip of his scotch. Funny, alcohol didn't even burn anymore. Sometimes he missed it. Sometimes he simply assumed it was a metaphor for his conscience and found amusement in it. "A cursory internet search would corroborate what I'm telling you. King Behrendt and Queen Amaani lost their only daughter years ago. Presumed dead. The entire nation mourned her passing. However, in Santa

Milagro it was often suspected the princess had been sent into hiding."

"Why would I be sent into hiding?"

"Because of an agreement. An agreement that your father made with mine. You see, sometime after the death of his first wife, the king fell on hard times. His own personal mourning affected the country and led the nation to near financial ruin. And so he borrowed heavily from my father. He also promised that he would repay my father in any manner he deemed acceptable. He more than promised. It is in writing." Felipe lifted a shoulder then continued, "Of course, at the time King Behrendt felt like he had nothing to lose. His wife was dead. His heir and spare nearly grown. Then he met a model. Very famous. Originally from Somalia. Their romance stunned all of Europe for a great many reasons, the age gap between them being one of them."

"I know this story," she said, her voice hushed. "I mean, I have heard of them."

"Naturally. As they are one of the most photographed royal couples in the world. What began as a rather shocking coupling has become one of the world's favorites."

"You're trying to tell me that they are my parents."

"I'm not *trying* to tell you that. I *am* telling you that. Because when it came time to collect on the king's debt… My father demanded you."

"He did?"

"Oh, yes. Verloren, and indeed the world, was captivated by your birth. And when you finally arrived, a great party was given. Many gifts were brought from rulers all over the world. And my father—not in attendance because he was any great friend of yours, but because your father was obligated—came, but it was not with a gift. It was a promise. That when you were of age he would come for you. And that you would be his wife."

Her skin dulled, her lips turning a dusky blue. "Are you… Are you taking me to your father? Is that what this is?"

He shook his head. "No. I am not delivering you to my father. For that, you should be thankful. You will not be his wife."

"No," she said firmly. "I will not be."

He looked up at her then, his eyes meeting hers. She looked fiery, determined. Anger glittered in those ebony depths, and perversely he ached to explore that rage. Sadly, it would have to wait.

"You will not be my father's wife," he repeated, pausing for just a moment. "You will be mine."

CHAPTER THREE

SHE LOST CONSCIOUSNESS after that. And really, she was somewhat grateful for that. Less so when she woke up feeling disoriented, cocooned in a bed of soft blankets in completely unfamiliar surroundings.

At least when she woke up this time it wasn't because he had kissed her.

Though, he was standing on the far side of the room, his arms crossed over his broad chest, his expression one of dark concern. Perhaps that was an odd characteristic to assign to concern, but she had a feeling the concern wasn't born out of any kind of goodness of his heart, rather over the potential thwarting of his schemes.

His schemes to make her his wife. She remembered that with a sudden jolt.

She sat up quickly, and her head began to throb.

"Be careful, Princess," came a slow, calming voice. "You do not have a concussion, but you have certainly been through quite a lot in the past twenty-four hours."

She became aware that a woman was standing to the left of her bed. A woman who had that kind of matter-of-fact bedside demeanor she typically assigned to physicians.

"Are you a doctor?" she asked.

"Yes. When you lost consciousness on the flight, Prince Felipe called and demanded that I make myself available to him as soon as the plane landed. I told him it was likely stress and a bit of dehydration that caused the event." She sent him a look that carried not a small amount of steel.

"I have indeed been placed under stress," Briar said. "Since he kidnapped me."

The woman looked like she was about to have an apoplexy. "Kidnapped. Lovely."

"Did you have a criticism, Dr. Estrada?" Felipe asked, his tone soft but infinitely deadly.

"Never, Your Majesty."

"I thought not."

"Perhaps you ought to criticize him," Briar said.

"Not if she would like to retain her license to practice medicine here in Santa Milagro. Also, not as long as she would like to stay out of the dungeon."

"He would not throw me in the dungeon," Dr. Estrada said, her tone hard. "However, I do believe he might strip me of my license."

"Do not think me so different from my father," he said, his tone taking on a warning quality. "I will have to assume control of the country soon, and I will do whatever I must to make sure that transition goes as smoothly as possible. I would like to give you all that I have promised," he said, directing those words to the doctor, "but I cannot if you don't help me in this. I am not evil like my father, but I am entirely focused on my goals. I will let nothing stand in my way." He rolled his shoulders backward, grabbed the edge of his shirtsleeve and pulled it down hard. "I am hardly a villain, but I am…morally flexible. You would both do well to remember that."

"You can't exactly issue threats to me," Briar said, "as I've already been kidnapped."

"Things can definitely get worse," Felipe said, a sharp grin crossing his lips. "I'm quite creative."

A shiver ran down her back and she thought wildly about what she could do. There was no hope of running, obviously. She wasn't feeling her best, even if she didn't have a concussion. She was also stranded in a foreign country with no ID, no money, nothing but a hospital gown.

"Help me," she said to Dr. Estrada, because she had no idea what else she could do.

"I'm afraid I can't," the woman said. "Except when it comes to your medical well-being. You can take a couple of these pain pills if you need them." She set the bottle on the nightstand.

"I might take the whole thing," Briar responded.

"I will not tolerate petulant displays of insincere overdoses." Felipe walked across the room, curling his fingers around the pill bottle and picking it up. "If you need something I am more than happy to dispense it. Or rather, I will entrust a servant to do so."

He was appalling. It was difficult to form an honest opinion on his personality, given that he had kidnapped her and all. That was the dominant thing she was focused on at the moment. But even without the kidnap, he was kind of terrible.

"That will be all, Dr. Estrada," he said, effectively dismissing what might have been Briar's only possible ally. "She would not have helped you," Felipe said, as if reading her mind. "She can't. You see, my father has had this country under a pall for generations. People like Dr. Estrada want to make a difference once the old king is dead—and he is closer and closer to being dead with each passing moment we spend talking. I would prefer that he live for our marriage announcement, however. Still, if he does not, I won't lose any sleep over it. The sooner he dies, the better. The sooner he dies, the sooner I assume the throne. And change can begin coming to the country."

"There's nothing you can do until some old, incapacitated king dies?"

He waved a hand. "Of course there is. If there was nothing that could be done, Dr. Estrada wouldn't have been here at all. In fact, she's somebody that I've been meeting with for the past couple of years, getting a healthcare system in place, ready to launch the moment I assume power. I have pieces in a great many strategic places on this chessboard, Princess. And you were the last one. My queen."

"I don't understand."

"Of course you don't. But you will. Ultimately, this will benefit your country. Your parents."

"My parents live in New York," she said, gritting her teeth. "I don't care about anybody else."

He made a tsking sound. "That's quite heartless. Especially considering the king and queen assumed great personal cost to send you to safety."

"I might feel something more if I knew them," she said, ignoring the slight twinge of guilt in her chest. "As it is, I'm concerned that the mother and father I know are going to be frantic, looking for me."

"Likely they will be. But soon, very soon, I will be ready to announce to the world that we are engaged."

"And what's to keep me from flinging myself in front of the camera and letting everybody know that I'm not

your fiancée, I'm a kidnap victim? And you are dangerously delusional."

"Oh," he said, "you've got me there. Something I
didn't think of. I've only been planning exactly how my
ascendance to the throne would go for the past two decades. But here, you have completely stumped me with
only a few moments of thinking." He laughed, the sound
derisive. "Your country, your father's country, owes mine
an astronomical amount. I could destroy them. Bankrupt
them. The entire populace would spend the remainder
of their days in abject poverty. A once great nation top-
pled completely. I, and I alone, have been the only thing
standing in the gap between my father and his revenge
on Verloren. My own had to go neglected so that I could
protect yours. I spent every favor on that. Used every
ounce of diplomacy to convince him that it was not the
time to move on Verloren. I placated him with ideas that
I had gotten leads on your whereabouts." He shook his
head. "I did a great deal to clinch this. If you think you're
going to thwart me with a temper tantrum then you are
truly delusional."

"Well, I was hit by a taxi."

He laughed again. "True. I should have given the
driver a tip. He made this all that much easier. Anyway,
you will be well taken care of here."

"I just have to marry a monster."

"There is that," he said, looking completely unfazed
by the insult. "What sort of monster do you suppose I
am, Princess?"

She couldn't tell if he was asking the question with
sincerity. She wasn't sure she cared. But as she looked
at him, a picture began to form in her mind. His eyes
were gold, glinting with heat and the possibility of a kind

of cruelty she didn't want to test. There was something sharp about him, whip-smart and deadly.

"A dragon. Clearly," she said, not entirely sure why she had provided him with the answer.

"I suppose that makes you the damsel in distress," he said.

"I'd like to think it makes me the knight."

"Sorry, darling," he said. "I kissed you awake not eight hours ago. That makes you the damsel."

"If we're going off fairy tales then that should make you Prince Charming, not the dragon."

He chuckled. "Sadly, this is real life, not a fairy tale. And very often the prince can be both."

"Then I suppose a princess can also be a knight. In which case, I would be careful, because when you go to kiss me again I might stab you clean through."

He lifted one dark brow. "Then the same goes for you. Because the next time I go to kiss you, I might decide to swallow you whole instead."

There was something darkly sexual about those words, and she resented the responses created in her body. No matter that he was... Well, insane almost by his own admission, he was still absurdly beautiful.

And that, she supposed, was ultimately what he meant about the dragon and the prince being one and the same. On the outside, he was every inch Prince Charming. From his perfectly tailored jacket and dark pants, to his classically handsome face and picture of exquisite masculinity that was his body.

But underneath, he breathed fire.

"I am announcing our engagement tomorrow. And you will not go against me."

"How do you know?"

"Because I'm going to allow you to call your parents tonight. At least, the people you know as your parents."

"They'll send someone for me. They'll contact that... They'll contact the president if they have to."

"They won't," he said, his voice holding an air of finality. "And you know why? Because they do know the whole story of how you came to be theirs. They know exactly who you are, and they know why they cannot interfere in this. They were charged with keeping you safe from me, and they failed. Now, there is nothing that can be done. Once you have passed into the possession of the dragon... Well. It is too late. Tell them everything that I told you. And they will confirm what I've said. You don't have a choice. Not if you want to keep your homeland from crumbling. Not if you ever hope to see things actually fixed. This is bigger than you. When you speak to them, you'll know that's the truth."

Then he turned, leaving her alone with nothing but a sense of quiet dread.

"I will be having an engagement party in the next week or so," Felipe said, staring fixedly out the window at the view of the mountains.

"That seems sudden," his friend Adam said on the other end of the phone.

Adam was recently married to his wife, Belle, after years of isolating himself on his island country, lost in grief after the death of his first wife, and hiding the terrible scars he had received from the accident that had made him a widower. But now things had changed. Since he had met Belle, he had come back into the public eye, and he seemed to have no issue with public appearances.

All the better as far as Felipe was concerned, because he wanted to have as much public support as possible.

"It isn't," Felipe said. "Believe me."

"Why do I get the feeling this is the sort of thing I don't want to know the details about?" his other friend Rafe said, his tone hard.

"You likely don't," Felipe said. "But I would happily give them to you. You know I have no shame."

He didn't. Though he was hardly going to engage in unbridled honesty and a heart-to-heart with his friends about the current situation. That wasn't how he worked. It wasn't the function he fulfilled in the group.

He'd cultivated the Prince Charming exterior long ago. Out of necessity. For survival. Image had been everything to his father, and the older man had always threatened Felipe and his mother with dire consequences if Felipe were to reveal the state of their lives in the palace.

The consequences of behaving otherwise were dire, and he had discovered that the hard way.

So he had learned, very early on, not to betray himself. Ever. He kept everything close to his chest, while appearing to give the whole world away.

"I would like details," Adam said, "before I know what sort of circus I'm bringing my pregnant wife to."

"Congratulations," Felipe said. "Please make the announcement before you come to my party. I don't want the impending arrival of your heir to overshadow my engagement."

"I suppose that's about all the sincerity I can expect out of you," Adam said, his tone dry.

"Probably. But you see, I have found a long-lost—presumed dead—princess. And, I'm making her my wife. This is good for me for more than one reason. All political things, I won't bore you with them. Suffice it to say, this party is going to be quite the affair."

"I see. And how exactly did you find this princess?"

"Well, there's an app. I just opened it up and trapped her inside a little ball."

Adam snorted. "I wish that were true, Felipe. But I have a feeling that a lot more skullduggery was involved."

"There was skullduggery. I cannot deny the existence of skullduggery. Ultimately, I consider that a good thing since skullduggery is a sadly underused word."

"I do not need details," Rafe said. "But is my support of you going to damage the value of the stock in my company? That, I do need to know."

"And I need to know if she is the princess of any country possessing nuclear weapons. Because again, my support cannot endanger my people," Adam added.

"If the actual details of how I came in to possession of the princess were released, it might in fact cause you both trouble. But they won't. First of all, her parents owe an astronomical amount of money to my country. As much as they might want to contest the marriage, they won't be able to. And, once she is more familiar with the situation, she will feel the same way."

"So, you're forcing her into marriage?" Adam asked.

"Do I detect a hint of judgment in your voice?" Felipe returned. "Because if I remember correctly you came into possession of your wife when you took her prisoner."

"That was different."

"How?"

"Because *I* did it," Adam said. "Plus, I wouldn't do it now."

"Because love has changed you and softened you. I understand. Sadly, I'm not looking for love." The very idea almost made him laugh. "No chance of softening. But I do believe that in the end this is going to be the best thing for Santa Milagro. If it isn't the best thing for one woman, when all of my people could be benefited, I have to say I'm going to side with my people."

"So," Rafe said, slowly. "You are asking us to attend your engagement party, where you will announce your intention to marry a woman that you kidnapped, who doesn't want to marry you, but who will have to pretend as though she does so that you don't bring terrible consequences down on her mother and father, and her entire country."

"Yes," Felipe said.

"That sounds about right," Rafe responded.

"My wife will be...unhappy," Adam said.

"Then don't tell her. Or, tell her that's how all the girls meet their husbands these days. Stockholm syndrome."

Adam growled. "I'm not going to keep it from her."

"Fine. But I do expect that she fall in line," Felipe said, having not considered that his friend's potential loose cannon of a spouse might be an issue. Who knew what Belle might say to the press?

"Belle does not *fall in line*," Adam said. "It isn't in her nature. However, I will explain the sensitive political situation. I know she would not wish to cause harm. And while I don't trust that you won't cause any harm, Felipe, I do trust you're trying to prevent greater harm."

"Of course. Because I'm an altruist like that. Details will be forthcoming, but of course I had to call and give you the good news myself."

"Because you're such a good friend," Rafe said, the words rife with insincerity.

No, the truth was, they were friends. True friends, the

kind that Felipe had never expected to have. The kind that, he imagined, had prevented him from becoming something entirely soulless.

They had some idea about his upbringing. About the way that he was. But mostly, he showed them the face he showed the world. Prince Charming, as he had just discussed with Talia.

The dragon, he kept to himself.

Usually.

CHAPTER FOUR

BRIAR WAS ABOUT to give in to despair when there was a knock on the door. She knew immediately that it wasn't Prince Felipe, as she had a feeling he didn't knock. Ever.

She was proven correct when a servant came through the door after she told her to come in.

"This phone is programmed so that you may call your parents," the woman said. "I will give you some privacy."

She turned and swept out of the room, leaving Briar there with the phone. The first thing she tried to do was call 911, which was stupid, because she knew that it wasn't an emergency number in Santa Milagro. The phone wasn't connected to the internet, so she couldn't search any other numbers, but she had a feeling that even if she could it was programmed to only connect to one other number.

She should dial them immediately. After all, except for when she was at school, this was the longest she'd gone without contact with them. And even when she'd been at university it had been...different. She'd been in an approved location, doing exactly what they'd asked her to do.

Right now she was...well, somehow rootless, even as she learned the truth of where she'd come from. On her own, in a way she never had been before, even while she was being held captive.

For one moment, she thought about not calling. It was a strange, breathless moment, followed by her stomach plummeting all the way to her toes, even as she couldn't believe she had—for one moment—considered something so selfish.

They were probably sick with worry. And it was her fault, after all. She was the one who had approached Felipe. She was the one who had opened herself up to this. She had failed them. After trying so hard for so much of her life to make sure she could be the daughter they deserved to have, now they were going through this.

With shaking fingers, she dialed her parents. And she waited.

It was her father who answered, his tone breathless in rush. "Yes?"

"It's me," she said.

"Briar! Thank God. Where are you? Are you okay? We've been searching. We called the police. We've called every hospital."

"I know," she said. "I mean, I knew you would have. But this is the first chance I've had to call. I wasn't...I've been kidnapped," she said. As much as she didn't want to cause her parents any alarm, kidnapped was what she was; there was no sugarcoating it.

Her father swore violently, and a moment later she heard the other line pick up. "Briar?" It was her mother.

"I'm okay. I mean, I'm unharmed. But I'm in..."

"Santa Milagro," her father said, his tone flat.

The world felt like it tilted to the side. "You know? How do you know?" He had told her they would. But she realized that up until that moment she truly hadn't believed him.

"Perhaps it was a mistake," her father said slowly, "to keep so much from you. But we saw no other way for you to have a normal, happy life. It wasn't our intention to keep your identity from you, not really. But we didn't know what kind of life you would have if you knew that you were a princess that couldn't live in a palace. If you knew that you had parents who had given birth to you across the world, who didn't want to give you up but had felt forced into it."

"It was selfish maybe," her mother said, her tone muted. "But your mother and father did agree. They agreed that it would be best if you knew only us. They agreed it would be best if you didn't feel split in your identity. But we all knew it couldn't go on forever. We simply hoped this wouldn't be the reason."

Briar felt dizzy. "Am I Talia? Princess Talia. That's what he keeps calling me. Is that true?"

"It is true." Her father said it with the tone of finality.

"How? How can everybody just keep something like this from me? This is my life! And yeah, you were always overprotective and everything, but I didn't realize it was because I was in danger of actually being kidnapped by some crazy prince from half a world away." She took a deep breath. "I didn't realize it was because I was…a princess."

It felt absurd to even think, let alone say.

"It lasted longer than we thought it would," her mother said, her voice soft. "And I can't say that I've been unhappy about it. You're all we have, Briar. And to us, that's who you are. Our daughter. We wanted so badly to protect you." She heard the other woman's voice get thick with tears. "We failed at that."

Briar felt…awash in guilt. A strange kind. They were distressed because of her. Because they had been embroiled in this and probably hadn't a clue what the best way to handle it was. Of course there wasn't exactly a parenting book called *So You Have to Keep an Endangered Princess Safe While Raising Her as Your Own*. It might hurt, to find all this out now, but she certainly couldn't blame them.

"He says I have to marry him," she said, her voice hushed.

"The king?"

"Prince Felipe," she said.

The sound of relief on the other end of the phone was audible. "At least he's not… His father is a devil," her father said. "That was why your birth parents, the king and queen, sent you away from your country. Because they knew a life with him would destroy you."

"I don't want to marry Felipe, either, though," she said. "I don't want to be a princess. I just want to go back home."

There was a pause. A silence that seemed to stretch all the way through her.

"I'm afraid that's impossible. Now that he has you… It would be catastrophic to your birth parents…if any of this were to get out. The money that was borrowed by Verloren. Because any business done with King Domenico would be considered a blight on your mother and father. They would never recover from it. And the consequences to the country would be severe if Santa Milagro decided that the terms of the deal had been violated. The national treasury would be drained. People would have nothing. No food, no housing. No healthcare."

As he spoke those words, she felt weight settling on her shoulders. A new one added with each thing he listed would be denied to the citizens of her home country—a home country she couldn't even find on a map—if she chose not to comply.

"So I have to… I have to marry him?"

"Unless you can convince them there is some other alternative," her father said. "I'm not sure what else can be done. You are beyond our reach. This is something we never wanted for you."

Fury filled her anew. "But you knew it could happen. You knew all along, and I didn't."

"We never wanted you to be afraid of your own shadow," her mother said.

"Well, I don't want to be afraid of my own shadow. But I should have been warned to be afraid of charming Spanish men who tried to talk me up on the street." She hung up, and as soon as she did the door swung open. And there was Felipe.

Immediately, she was filled with regret.

He crossed the room, taking the phone from her hand. Why had she hung up? Who knew how long it would be before she was able to speak to her parents again.

"I assume everything that I said would be confirmed was?" he asked.

"I assume you were listening in, based on your perfect timing."

He smiled. "You know me so well already. We're going to be the perfect married couple."

"I don't understand. Marry somebody else. Why does it have to be me?"

He reached out then, grabbing hold of her hand and tugging her up out of bed. She was still wearing nothing more than the hospital gown, and she felt a breeze at her backside. She gasped, realizing that there was nothing but a thin pair of white cotton panties separating her from being bare back there.

His golden eyes were blazing then, blazing with that kind of fire and intensity she had sensed was inside him. And more than that. Fire, and brimstone. She had the sudden sense that there was hell contained inside this man. And whether it was just the shock wearing off, or a sudden connection with the reality she found herself in, for the first time she was afraid of him. Really afraid.

She found herself being dragged over to a window. Heavy drapes obscured the view, and he flung them back, roughly maneuvering her so that she was facing the vista before them. A large, sprawling city, nothing overly modern. Villas with red clay roofs, churches with tall steeples and iron bells hanging in the towers. And beyond that, the mountains.

"Do you see this?" he asked. "This is my country. For decades it has been ruled by a madman. A madman more concerned by power—by shoring up all of the money, all of the means through which he could blackmail—than caring for the people that live down there. And in that time I have spent decades doing what I can do in order to change things once I assume the throne. Working toward having the military on my side. Toward earning as much money as I could personally to make a difference the minute I had control. I have been making contacts and arrangements behind the scenes so that the moment my father's body is put into the dirt a new dawn will rise on this country. I never wanted to take it by civil war.

No, not when the cost would be so dear in terms of life. At least, I didn't want to take it in an open civil war. But that is exactly what I have been fighting for years. Playing the part of debauched playboy while I maneuvered in the background. You are part of that plan. And I will be damned if I allow you to do anything to mess it up. There is no amount of compassion that could move me at this point, Princess. Nothing that will stir me to change my path. I will be the King of Santa Milagro. And you... You can be the queen. You can help fix all the evil that has befallen my people, and you can improve the lives of yours, as well. Or you can go back to life as a bored sorority girl in the city. I'm sure that's an existence, as well. And all of these people... Well, they can slide into the sea."

She had to smooth her fingers over her eyebrows to make sure they hadn't been singed off during that fiery tirade. "Am I really so important to your plans?"

"Everybody knew that you were supposed to marry my father. And the things he would have done to you... But if you marry me, and you do so willingly...it will mend the fences between Santa Milagro and Verloren. It will do much to fix the image of my country—and me— in the media. I need everything in my power. Absolutely everything. All the pieces that I have set out to collect. I will let nothing fall by the wayside. Including you."

"And if I don't?"

"I didn't think I could possibly make that more clear. If you don't there will be destruction. For everyone. Everyone you love. Everyone you will love."

She blinked. "Are you going to have people killed?"

"No. I'll only make them wish they were dead."

"And how will that help your *improve your image* attempt?" she asked with a boldness she didn't feel.

"I'm not so stupid that I would go about it in the public view. But your New York parents…they are vulnerable. And suitably low visibility. Nonetheless, I can ruin them financially. He works with American politicians. And believe me, if I offer the right incentives, I can decimate his patient base, his reputation. Because far better to have an alliance with a prince than continue to support a specific physician."

Ice settled in her stomach. She believed him. Believed he would do that. Harm her parents. And if she allowed that…what sort of daughter would she be? They had protected her all her life. The least she could do was protect them in kind.

He smiled, and something in that smile made it impossible for her to doubt him. And then his expression shifted, and he returned to being that charming-looking man she had seen on the street in New York. "Now, you can't possibly meet my people in that hospital gown. Rest for tonight. Tomorrow… Tomorrow we shall set about fashioning you into a queen."

Felipe walked into his father's room. It was dark, the curtains drawn, none of the lights on.

"Good evening, Father," he said, sweeping toward the bed.

"Your jacket is crooked," his father said by way of greeting.

Felipe lifted his arm, tugging his sleeves down, hating the reflex. "It is not," he returned. "And you're very nearly blind, so even if it was, there would be no way for you to tell."

It was a strange thing, seeing this man in this state. He had always been fearful to Felipe when he'd been a child. And now, here he was, drained, shrunken. And still, something twisted with something sour whenever he looked at him.

This man, who had abused and tortured him and his mother for years. A slap across her face when Felipe was "in disarray."

He could remember well his mother being hit so hard it left an instant bruise beneath her eye. And then her makeup artist had been charged with making it invisible before they went to present themselves in the ballroom as the perfect royal family.

A facade of perfection. Something his father excelled at. He had convinced his country of the perfection of his family and the perfection of his rule. The citizens of Santa Milagro slowly and effectively stripped of their freedom. Of art, education and hope.

All things Felipe would see restored. Though he would never be able to fix what had become of his mother, at least he could restore Santa Milagro itself.

There had always been the temptation to try and claim the country by force, but that would only entail more loss of life.

There was enough blood shed already. Blood that felt as if it stained his hands.

"Is that any way to talk to your dying father?"

"Probably not. But since when have I cared? I only wanted you to know something."

"What is that?"

"I found her. The princess."

His father stirred. "My princess?"

A smile curved Felipe's lips. "No. She's mine now. I'm

going to make her my wife. There is nothing you can do about it. Not from your deathbed."

"You're a bastard," his father said, his voice thin, reedy and as full of venom as it had ever been. But he had no power now.

"Don't I wish that were true," Felipe said, twisting his voice into the cruelest version of itself he could manage. Projecting the sort of cruelty that he had learned from the man lying before him. "If only I were a bastard, rather than your flesh and blood. You have no idea how much I would pay to make that so."

"The feeling," his father said, the words broken by a ragged cough, "is mutual." He wiped a shaking hand over his brow. "I never was able to break you."

"Not for lack of trying," Felipe said. "But I do hope that I will go down in history as one of your greatest failures. The only truly sad thing is that you will not be here to see it."

He turned to leave his father's room. Then paused. "However, if you're still alive by the time the wedding rolls around I will be sure to send you an invitation. I'll understand that you won't be feeling up to attending."

He continued out of his father's room then, striding down the hall and on to the opposite wing of the palace where his rooms were. It was only then that he acknowledged the slight tremor in his own hand.

He flung open the doors to his chamber, crossing the length of the space, and took a large bottle of whiskey from the bar that was installed at the back wall. He looked at the glass that he kept positioned there—always, for easy access—and decided it was not needed. He took the cap off the bottle and lifted it to his lips, tilting it back and trying to focus on the burn as the alcohol slid down his throat.

It took so much more for him to feel it now. So much more for him to feel anything.

He slammed the bottle back down onto the bar. And he waited. Waited for something to make that feeling of being tainted go away. It was because he had gone into his father's room. Or maybe it was because of the princess who resided down the hall against her will.

Or maybe it was just because his father's blood ran through his veins.

Felipe roared, turning toward the wall and striking it with his forearm, his fist closed. He repeated the motion. Over and over and over again as pain shot up to his shoulder, and all the way down to his tightly closed fingers.

Then he lowered his arm, shaking it out. He took a deep breath, the silence in the room settling over him. He looked down, and he noticed a trail of blood leaking out from beneath his now crooked shirtsleeves.

He frowned. Then reached down and grabbed hold of the fabric, straightening his cuffs. And took another drink.

When Briar awoke the next morning she was greeted by three stylists. A man dressed in a shocking green coat, wielding a pair of golden scissors. A woman in a skin-tight fuchsia dress, and another wearing a pale blue top and a navy-colored skirt.

"The prince has ordered that we help prepare you for your public debut," the woman in pink said, her features seeming to grow sharper as she examined Briar.

"I don't normally wear hospital gowns," she said, her

voice stiff. "But I kind of left home without a chance to gather any of my clothes."

The woman waved a hand, the shocking neon fingernails a blur against her brown skin. "None of them would have been acceptable anyway. I'm confident in that fact."

After that, she found herself being plucked from bed and herded into the bathroom where she was instructed to get into the shower, where she would find acceptable soaps. She bristled at the idea that somehow what she had used before wasn't acceptable, but gladly walked into the massive tiled facility and stood beneath the hot spray for longer than was strictly necessary.

Then she began to scrub her skin with the toiletries provided and had to concede the fact that it was essentially like cleansing herself with silk. Perhaps, she also had to concede that as nice as the items in her childhood home were, they weren't palace material.

Then she got defensive again when she was seated in front of a vanity and that man with the golden scissors began to paw at her hair.

"Don't cut too much off," she all but snarled.

"I'm sorry," he said, "where did you go to school for hair?"

"I didn't. But it's grown out of my head for the past twenty-two years, so I have to say I'm pretty well educated on that situation."

He appraised her reflection in the mirror, squinting his eyes. "No. Not more than I am. You should not have straight hair."

"Well, clearly I disagree with you," she said, feeling defensive.

"Your bone structure agrees with me."

There was no argument after that. And she had to

admit that when he was finished she appreciated the curls in her hair in a way she didn't normally. He had managed to find a nice middle ground between the tightly wound natural curl and the board-straight style she normally aimed for. The fact that she didn't hate it was a little bit annoying.

She had a similar interaction with the stylist who was intent on choosing silhouettes that Briar normally avoided. She was averse to things that clung too tightly to her curves, but the woman in bright pink seemed to think that Briar needed to show off a bit more.

The makeup artist didn't believe in subtlety, either, and by the end of it Briar barely recognized the woman in the mirror. Or rather, she almost did. Because the tall, slim creature with her eye-catching curls and slim figure wrapped tightly in a blaze-orange dress, bright pink blush on her cheeks and gold on her lips, looked more like Queen Amaani than she did herself.

It was becoming more and more difficult to deny the reality of the situation.

Although, resemblance didn't confirm genetics, but her parents had told her it was true. And even if they hadn't…it would be very difficult to push it aside now.

"Beautiful," the man in green said.

She felt complimented, but at the same time didn't really want the compliment as she was being made beautiful for a man she didn't really want to feel beautiful for.

She said nothing, but her beauty team didn't seem to care. Instead, they packed up their things and left as quickly and efficiently as they had arrived.

Briar wobbled on the high heels she was wearing then sat quickly on the edge of the bed. She put her hand to her chest and looked at the mirror that hung across the room, looked at the wide-eyed, undeniably beautiful woman staring back at her.

She was a princess. Really and truly. And she was supposed to marry a prince who was quite possibly the maddest bastard on the planet.

The door to her room opened again and a man she hadn't seen before appeared. "His Majesty would appreciate it if you would join him for breakfast. Provided you are dressed suitably."

"Does that mean he didn't want me to show up in a hospital gown?"

The servant didn't react, his expression carefully blank. "He did not specify."

"Well, I imagine I'm suitable." She stood, following him out of her bedroom. She had been tempted, if only for a moment, to deem herself unsuitable and stay in her bedroom. But she had been in there for two days and eventually she was going to have to face her adversary. Face the man who claimed he was going to marry her whether she wanted him to or not.

And she was going to have to try to get out of it.

She walked silently with the servant, the only sound in the corridor the clicking of her high heels on the flagstone. The man opened the door to what she presumed was the dining room and stood to the side. "This way."

He didn't enter with her. Instead, she heard the doors close firmly behind her and found herself standing alone in a cavernous room with Prince Felipe. He was seated at the opposite end of the table from her, a newspaper to his left, a cup of coffee to his right.

"Good morning," he said.

Then, from behind the paper, he produced a velvet

ring box. He set it firmly in front of him then said nothing more about it. "Have a seat," he said.

"As you wish," she returned, taking her seat in the farthest possible place from him, nearest the door.

"That is not what I meant," he said.

"But it is what you said."

He chuckled and folded the paper then retrieved the ring box and picked up his cup. He stood then, and she was reminded of how tall he was. How imposing. He walked across the room and sat down next to her. If he was fazed at all, he didn't show it.

"You seem to have woken up in a good mood, Briar."

"That's the first time you've called me that," she said. "Apart from when you were pretending to be José."

"I suppose it doesn't benefit me to be at odds with you," he said, tilting his head to the side, a dent appearing between his brows. As though he was truly considering this for the first time. "If you are more comfortable being called Briar in conversation, then I will call you that. However, in public I will refer to you by your given name."

"A given name I don't remember being given."

"Do any of us really remember being given our names? I know I certainly don't." He placed his index finger firmly against the top of the ring box and slid it toward her. "See if this is to your satisfaction."

"It won't be," she said, not making any move toward the box.

"I doubt that. The diamond is practically large enough to eradicate world hunger."

"Then eradicate world hunger. Don't put it on my finger."

"I will make a donation to charity that matches the value. Put it on your finger."

"No," she responded. "I have been given no real compelling reason why I have to actually marry you. It's only because you're choosing to consider me payment for a debt, which I think we can both agree is a bit archaic. You say that your father is a monster, so I don't understand why you want to be monstrous, as well."

"Because I will be a better monster," he said. "Anyway, I have explained my terms, and they will not change."

"Well I don't—"

"Do you want to meet your parents? King Behrendt and Queen Amaani?"

A strange, yawning void opened up inside her chest. One that she hadn't realized was there until that moment. And she flashed back to earlier when she had seen her reflection in the mirror and realized how much she favored the queen. Realized that there was most certainly truth in the stories she had been told about her lineage.

She loved the mother and father she knew, and nothing could ever replace them. But she had other parents. Parents who hadn't actually wanted to give her up. Parents who had done it for her protection.

A king and queen who had lived halfway across the world from her for almost her entire life. A king and queen that she could meet.

That longing was an ache, so acute, so intense, that it stole her breath.

But she refused to respond to him. Apparently, she didn't need to, because only a moment later it became clear that her longing must have been written across her features.

"Excellent," he said. "If you ever want to meet your

parents, if you want to see the palace again… We can always attend the annual ball they throw every year in October. I hear you loved it when you were a little girl. There is always spiced cider, which I'm told was your favorite."

It hit her in the chest with the force of a brick. That feeling. That nostalgia. That hook she felt in her gut whenever the air began to chill and the leaves started to fall.

It was what she remembered. Oh, she didn't remember it in pictures. Didn't remember it as an actual event. But it lived somewhere inside her. Resided in her bones. It transcended specific moments and images and existed in the realm of feeling. Deep and powerful. It was a root; she couldn't deny it. It always had been. A part of her that connected her to the earth, that ran beneath the surface of all that she was. That had formed her into who she was now.

She wanted to see it. She wanted to connect that with something real. With something more than a feeling.

"You remember," he said, the amusement in his voice almost enraging. "And you do want it. More than anything. You have very expressive eyes, *querida*. All the better for me."

All the better for him to manipulate her, he meant. And he was doing it. Doing it with all the skill of a master. She suddenly felt like a puppet whose strings had been cut. Like someone who had been restrained all her life, who was left standing there with an endless array of choice.

Her parents weren't here. She didn't like Felipe, and he needed her. Which meant she was under no pressure at all to behave a certain way. As long as she was here, she was doing his bidding and he couldn't—and wouldn't—

lash out at her so long as she didn't bring her behavior into the public eye.

She didn't have to behave. She didn't have to do anything for anyone.

She didn't have to be perfect.

"Of course I want to meet my parents," she said, not bothering to soften her tone. "Who wouldn't want to understand where they came from?"

"It will be impossible for you to meet your family, of course, should you fail them in the way that you are suggesting you might."

"They sent me across the world, pretended I was dead, in order to avoid this fate for me."

"No, they wished for you to avoid my father. However, a marriage of convenience is not uncommon between royals. And I am not my father. Believe me. It matters. That is not just an incidental. Had the marriage been set between you and I from the moment you were born…they would have happily handed you over. What I can offer them, what I can offer your country, and what yours can offer mine, is no small thing. Conversely, what I can do if you disappoint me on this score is no small thing. Do you honestly think that your mother and father would be content to allow you to marry a doctor on the Upper East Side?"

"They sent me to be raised by one. I'm not entirely certain why one wouldn't be good enough for me to marry."

"But you were never intended to live there forever. You were always meant to come back and assume your place. Tell me… What did you expect to do with your life?"

"I was an art major."

He made a dismissive sound. "So you're poised to become an incredibly useful member of society. I'm terribly sad to have interrupted that trajectory."

Anger fired through her veins, and since she wasn't worried about making friends with him, she let it show. "Art is important."

"Of course. It's the thing that people worry about after all of their necessities are met."

"It's one of the things that makes the world beautiful. It gives people hope. It's part of moving from surviving to living."

A smile curved his lips. "I seem to have found a bit of passion in you. That is encouraging. I would put you in charge of the art program. For all the schools in my country. You will have the opportunity to change the face of education in this country. My father has kept things quite austere, it may not surprise you to learn. When I say he has been something of an evil dictator I am not exaggerating. That is not the kind of job offer you're going to get in Manhattan. What else are you going to do with that degree? You going to marry someone successful and plan all his parties for him? I grant you that often princesses can be quite decorative, but my queen will not be. I will use you in whatever capacity you see fit, whatever way you can find to improve my country."

He spoke with…well, sincerity, which was the most surprising thing. That he seemed to so easily hand this to her. The chance to reconnect with her parents, with her heritage, and the chance to make a difference. All by using the subject that she was most passionate about.

"And you should see the art collection we have in the palace. Just sitting in the basement waiting to be curated. Our museums need to be opened. We have been in the dark ages. It is time that we come into the light. And if— as you say—art is a part of living and not surviving, then help my people live."

It was strange, because she could actually see that he cared about this. About his country. That of all the things in the entire world, this might be the only thing that mattered to him. She might be at a disadvantage here, but so was he. Because he cared about this. And he needed her. Needed her to cooperate. Needed her to help insulate his image.

"And if I get up in front of the entire world when you try to announce our engagement and tell them that you kidnapped me?" She had to ask.

"If I go down, Princess, we are going down in flames together. I promise you that. I'm not a man to make idle threats. I have been lying in wait for years, waiting for the moment when I might liberate my kingdom, when I might save my people. Believe me when I tell you I will not be stopped now. I would not say that I am a man consumed with serving the greater good. I don't really care about whether it's good or not. I care about serving my goal. My goal is to make this country great. My goal is to liberate the people in it. Whatever I have to do."

He slid the ring closer to her again. "Now. Put it on."

She hesitated for a moment before reaching out and curling her fingers around the box. Then she opened it slowly. Her breath caught in her throat. It truly was beautiful. A stunning diamond set into an ornate platinum setting. Definitely designed to tempt a woman on the fence about accepting a marriage proposal.

If it was a show of love it would be personal.

It hit her then, with the speed and impact of a freight

train, what it would mean to marry him. It would mean never having a real boyfriend. It would mean never falling in love. And it would mean...

She looked up at him, her heart slamming against her breastbone. Images flashed through her mind. Him touching her. Kissing her. She had never kissed a man before, unless you counted that time he had kissed her when she was unconscious. And she didn't really. Except, it was difficult not to. Because it had most certainly been the first time another person's lips had touched hers. And thinking of it now made them burn.

"Did you have questions?" he asked.

"I don't have another choice. Do I?"

"We always have choices. It's just that the results of those choices are going to be better or worse. You have one choice that doesn't ruin a great many lives. That isn't having no choices."

"One requires me to be completely selfish, though." And if she decided to walk away from him, she supposed that she could go back to life as she had always known it. She would simply ruin an entire nation that she hadn't known much about until this week. Would never meet her parents. But she could go back to how things were. Could pretend that none of this had happened.

"And if I were you, that is perhaps the choice I would make."

His dark eyes glittered, and she had a feeling that his comment had been calculated. Because the moment he had said that, she had known that her decision was made. She wasn't him. She wasn't, and she never would be. Her parents had always instilled in her the fact that having money as they did didn't make her better, didn't make them better. That she had been given a great many advantages and was responsible for making the best of those advantages.

She had been intent on doing that. As soon as she had finished school she had planned on getting involved in inner-city art programs, in establishing funds and foundations. She was being given the opportunity to do that here. And more.

The influence she would have as a queen was inestimable.

She wrapped her hand around the ring box. "Okay. I'll do it."

He didn't smile. Didn't gloat. No, he reacted in a completely different way to what she had imagined he might do. His handsome face set an expression of grim determination. "Good. And it is done. The announcement will be made tomorrow. And we are going to have a ball celebrating our engagement. I have already sent out invitations."

"Ahead of my acceptance?"

"I never doubted you."

The words hit her strangely, bounced around inside her chest, ricocheting off her heart. They made her angry, but they made her feel something else, too. Something she couldn't quite put a finger on. Something she didn't want to put a finger—or anything else—on.

"Perhaps you should. Someday I might surprise you."

He shook his head. "Good people are rarely surprising, Briar. It's bad people you have to watch out for." He stood then. "You should order yourself a coffee." He turned to walk out of the room.

"Are you a bad person?"

His expression turned grave, deadly serious, which

was strange. "I am… Whatever I am, I am beyond help. If I were you, I wouldn't try."

Then he left, leaving her alone with her fear, her doubt and a diamond.

CHAPTER FIVE

IT WAS THE headline the next morning. That Prince Felipe Carrión de la Viña Cortez was engaged to the long-lost Princess of Verloren. He assumed it was not the best way for the king and queen to discover that he had found their daughter, but he was going to send them an invitation to the engagement party so they could hardly be too upset.

Though he didn't think they would come. No, they would assume that it was some kind of trap, of course. It would take time. It would take time for anybody to trust that he wasn't as conniving as his father.

Starting with the kidnapping of a princess was perhaps not the best opening move, all things considered. But that was one thing that he and Briar were going to have to discuss.

He flung the doors to her bedchamber open, unfazed by the gasp and eruption of movement that resulted. He saw nothing but a flash of curl and a blur of brown skin as she dashed behind a changing screen.

"I'm not dressed!"

"And I'm your fiancé," he said. "Which is exactly what I came to speak to you about. You cannot behave this way in my presence. I cannot have the world thinking that I forced you into this."

She poked her head out from the side of the divider. "But you did."

"Sure. But we're not going to advertise that, are we? It undermines my aim for building bridges between nations."

"Well, God forbid you could build an actual bridge," she said, disappearing behind the divider again. He heard the rustle of clothes.

"Don't dress on my account."

She made an exasperated sound then appeared a moment later wearing a black pencil skirt and a bright green crop top. She was stunning. She had been from the beginning, but the new wardrobe, the makeover, provided to her by his staff, had truly brought out the uncommonness of her beauty. It had elevated her from mere beauty to someone who would turn heads everywhere she went.

Exactly what he wanted in a queen.

He enjoyed her ability to stand up to him, as well. Had she no spine at all he would have kept her, certainly, but it would have been a much greater trial. It would have made him think too much of his mother.

And he knew where that ended.

"I'm not going to stand in front of you in my underwear."

"You will eventually."

She paled slightly. "Well. We'll cross that bridge when we come to it."

"The bridge you just accused me of not building?"

"It's a different bridge, obviously."

"Just clarifying. I wish to give you a tour of the castle."

She looked startled by that. "Why?"

"Because you live here. And you will live here for the foreseeable future. Don't you want a tour of your home?"

"I guess it's practical. But I don't know why you're giving it to me."

"I am going to be your husband. And we are going to be required to make a great many public appearances together. You will have to learn to act as though my presence doesn't disgust you."

"I was never a very good liar," she said, looking at him with those fathomless dark eyes, her expression almost comically serene.

"Well, get better at it." He extended his arm. "Shall we?"

She accepted the offered arm slowly, curving her fingers around him as though she thought he was a poisonous serpent. Something about that light, tentative touch sent a shock of heat through his body.

That electricity that had been there from the moment he had seen her pulsed through him with renewed strength. She had been quite pitiful after her accident, and that—along with the logistics of convincing her to marry him—had pushed some of that attraction onto the back burner. But he was reminded now. With ferocity. He was also reminded that it had been a very long time since he'd had a woman in his bed. He had been too focused on getting all the pieces in play to see to the typical pleasures he filled his time with.

"You've seen the dining room already," he said, indicating the room to their left. "My chambers are that way. My father is kept in another wing entirely, and you have no reason to ever set foot in that part of the palace." The old man might be incapacitated, but he still didn't want Briar anywhere near his father.

The shock of protectiveness that slammed into his chest surprised him. Briar—as far as he was concerned—

was a means to an end. He did not have particularly strong feelings about her. But he did have particularly strong feelings about his father and the sort of influence he wielded over women. He didn't want that old man to put one drop of poison into Briar's ear. Not when he knew full well that it was the sort of poison that could be fatal.

"I don't think I want to, all things considered." She hesitated for a moment. "He's really dying?"

"Any day now, truly. His body has been failing him for quite some time. There is no hope left. Nothing to be done. Just waiting for him to choke on his spite and bile."

"You don't sound…sad at all."

"I'm not. I thought I had made that perfectly clear. I hate my father. I'm not simply ambivalent toward him. I loathe him. My legacy shall be upending his."

She said nothing to that, though she shifted to the side of him, the soft swell of her breast brushing up against his biceps. A simple touch, one that would have barely registered had it been any other woman. At any other moment. But he was going to marry this woman.

For the first time, that part of the plan truly settled in his mind. She would be the mother of his children. And he would need her to be…happy. That had not been part of the plan when he had first conceived it. He had not considered her happiness—her feelings of any sort—when he had decided that he needed to bring her here and make her his. Why would he? Considering that would run counter to his objective. He didn't like anything getting in the way of his objective.

And considering it now had nothing to do with the goodness of his heart. If he possessed a heart he very much doubted it had any goodness in it. But she would give birth to his children, and she would need to be there for them. He knew too well the alternative.

Suddenly, the promise of art programs was much more than simple bribery. "I meant what I said," he said. "About the art collection. About the programs. You will be in charge of those. You can appoint an entire team to help you with teaching, with organization. I will give you a very generous budget. The country has fallen on difficult financial times under my father's rule, but I have made billions on my own. And I have kept it all out of the country, tightly under my control so my father couldn't get his hands on any of it. But that will change once he's gone."

She stopped walking, looking at him, her expression full of confusion. "Why are you giving me this? It's for your country, right? It isn't for me."

"My aim is not for you to be miserable."

"Why do you care?"

"Because I know what it's like to exist beneath the rule of a totalitarian regime. My father was a dictator to the country, but he was even worse to those who lived under his roof. It will not be so, not in my house. I will not subject my wife or my children to such things."

Her mouth dropped open. "Children."

"Of course we will have children. The single most important act for a ruler is to produce an heir, is it not?"

"I...I suppose. I hadn't really thought about it."

"Of course you haven't. You were raised as a commoner. But it is a requirement. I have to carry on my line."

She frowned. "But I... But we..."

"Do you not want children?"

She frowned. "I...I do. I... Things are different now,

because I'm going to meet my parents. My biological parents. But I always wanted someone in my life that I shared a genetic bond with. Which is silly. It doesn't matter. Blood doesn't matter. All that matters is that somebody loves you. And my parents—the ones that raised me—they love me. But still."

"You don't have to explain yourself to me," he said. "I'm a man entirely driven by the need for vengeance. I'm hardly going to call your motives into question."

"Yes, I want children. But I didn't anticipate having them… Now. Or with…" She was blushing. Her cheeks turning a dusky rose.

"With me?" He finished for her.

"Well. Yes. You're a stranger."

"I won't be. By that point." They wandered down the long hall, and all the way to a pair of blue, gilded double doors that were firmly closed. "This is where we will hold the ball where we celebrate our upcoming nuptials." He flung them open then reached out for her this time. "Come with me, Princess."

She took his hand reluctantly, but eventually curved her delicate fingers around his. He smiled. He knew full well how to put people at ease, but he hadn't done the best job with her since that first day. Since that first moment.

He would do well to charm her. She would certainly be happier. And he knew how to charm women. He had been told a great many times that he was very good at it. And, if the notches on his bedpost were any indicator, it was the truth. It would not cost him to turn on that part of himself for this woman.

Now that he had her, now the she had agreed…

"Do you know how to dance?"

She laughed. "Of course I do. I had an entire…coming out."

"A debutante?"

"Yes."

"You really are excellent. And your parents did a wonderful job raising you. Because they knew that this would ultimately be where you'd land."

She frowned. "Well. If what you say is true, then they hoped I would end up back in my country and not in yours at all."

"Perhaps." He shifted their positions, keeping hold of her hand, then he wrapped his arm around her waist and pulled her up against him. "Would you care to practice?"

Her dark eyes widened, her full lips falling open. "I don't need to practice."

"The world will be watching when we take our first dance as a couple. It is not enough to simply know how to dance. You have to know how to move with me." And with that, with no music playing and no sound in the room but their feet moving over the glossy marble, he swept her into the first step of a waltz.

She followed beautifully, her movements graceful, but her expression spoke far too readily of her feelings.

He leaned in slightly. "You must work at looking as though my touch doesn't disgust you."

As he spoke the words, he realized that he must work at making sure his touch didn't disgust her. Yes, the relationship had started with force, but there was no reason it could not be mutually satisfying. Oh, there would never be any love, nothing like that. He didn't believe in the emotion. Even if he did, he wasn't capable of feeling it. But they could have a reasonable amount of companionship.

They could certainly have more than violence and death. Than aching loss. Yes, they could have more than that.

He moved his hand slowly down the curve of her waist, settling it more firmly on her hip. She looked up at him, her dark gaze meeting his, the confusion there evident. He knew why she was confused. She didn't find his touch repellent at all. And she couldn't figure out why.

"Don't feel bad," he said, keeping his voice soft. "I'm very experienced at this. I promise you I could take you from shouting at me in anger to screaming my name in pleasure in only a few moments."

Color suffused her cheeks and she tried to pull away from him. He held her firmly. Didn't let her leave. Kept on dancing. "You're ashamed of that. Of the fact that you enjoy me touching you." He was fascinated by that. That somebody would waste one moment being ashamed of something that brought them pleasure. He'd had very little of it in his childhood, and he could admit that he had possibly gone overboard with it once he had gotten out from beneath his father's roof. Once he had discovered women. Once he had discovered that, as profoundly terrible as his father could make him feel, a woman's hands on his skin, a soft touch, could make him feel that much better.

But whether or not it had been too much, he didn't regret it. No. He never let himself regret feeling good.

"I don't understand," she said, her voice flat, not bothering to deny the accusation.

"There's very little to understand with chemistry, *querida*. And there is very little point in fighting ours. We are to be married, after all." Her flush deepened and she looked away from him. "Did you imagine that you would be a martyr in my bed? I promise you, you could start out as serene and filled with sacrifices as Joan of Arc, but in the end, when I made you burn, it would not be in the way you're thinking."

"You're so arrogant," she said, her voice vibrating with some strong emotion he couldn't place. "Assuming that I'm not comfortable with this because I feel shame. It didn't occur to you that maybe—just maybe—I'm not feeling exactly what you think?"

"Sorry," he said, knowing he didn't sound apologetic in the least. "But you're a little too late in your denial. And even if your words haven't already betrayed you, your body betrays you, Princess. Your eyes…" He lifted his hand, tracing a line just beneath her left eye. "They've gotten darker looking at me, your pupils expanding. This speaks of arousal, did you know?"

She swallowed visibly. "My eyes are dark. I sincerely doubt you noticed anything of the kind."

"All right. Then let's move on. There is color in your cheeks. You're blushing."

"Perhaps I'm angry. Maybe that's why."

"I suspect you're angry, as well. More at yourself than at me." He moved his thumb down the curve of her cheek, to her lower lip, sliding it slowly over that soft, lush skin. "You're trembling here. And your breathing… It has grown very shallow. Quick."

"And that," she said, her voice unsteady now, "could be fear."

"Yes. But you don't strike me as the kind of woman who scares easily."

"I don't suppose being hit by a taxi and kidnapped, then taken half a world away, scaring me, would qualify as *scaring easily.*"

He laughed. "No. I don't suppose it would. Still…"
He moved his thumb even slower across her lower lip. "I
don't think you're afraid of me. I think you're afraid of
what you might do." He moved in slowly and she sucked
in a sharp breath, drawing backward. "Yes. You're afraid
of what you might want. That's the scary thing, isn't it?
Knowing that I'm not Prince Charming. Knowing that
I am the monster. And wanting me anyway. That does
make you unique. Most women only know the surface.
Most of them have not had the pleasure of being kidnapped by me. They want the facade. You know what's
underneath and you want me still. I wonder…"

A strange sense of disquiet filled his chest and he did
his best to ignore it. He couldn't afford to be growing a
conscience now. Couldn't afford to be concerned with her
or her feelings. He needed to seduce her. She was supposed to be his wife, after all. He was hardly going to
live in a sexless marriage. Then again, he wasn't entirely
sure he was going to remain faithful during the course
of their marriage. That would depend. On a great many
factors. Namely what would keep the peace in the palace. It was entirely possible that she would not want all
of his attentions focused on her.

But as he had realized only a few minutes ago, her
happiness was going to have to come into consideration.
Something new, and strange. Needing to care about the
emotions of another person. If only to keep her from…
Well. He had no desire to repeat the sins of his father.
That was as far as he would go with that line of thinking today.

"What do you wonder?" she asked. It was strange that
she seemed to be asking the question genuinely. That
she did not seem to be teasing or testing him. He had

a very limited amount of experience with people who were genuine in any fashion. But Briar seemed genuine. She was sharp, and she possessed a rather whip-smart wit. But even so, there was something…well, something untested about her. Young. Innocent. In his circle, in his world, there were very few innocent people. Everyone was guilty of something.

He supposed eventually he would find out what she was guilty of. Because there was no way she was everything she seemed on the surface. Nobody was.

Still. The way she asked the question…

"I wonder if it would be the same for anyone," he said, his voice hard. "Perhaps you're not unique. Perhaps any woman, faced with the possibility of marrying a prince who was set to become a king, given the chance to be a queen, would overlook the fact that I'm a bit…beastly."

"I'm not looking anything over," she pointed out. "You're holding quite a few things hostage—including me—in order to get me to agree to the marriage."

He found himself oddly relieved by that, and he didn't know why. "That is true."

He was still touching her lower lip, and the color in her cheeks was only growing more intense. "You can stop that now," she said.

"I'm not sure that I want to."

"Well, I want you to."

He dropped his hand down to his side. And he was gratified when she let out a long, slow breath that he was certain spoke of disappointment. She wished that he would push harder. She did. Whether she admitted it or not, she did.

"It must be nice," he said, releasing his hold on her

and stepping back from her. "Releasing all responsibility in a situation."

"What are you talking about?"

"I'm a kidnapper. A kidnapper, a blackmailer... Well, it's not a long list, but it is a fairly damning one. You, on the other hand... What are you? Victimized, I suppose. You have no other option but to marry me. And certainly, it benefits you in a great many ways, but you're able to claim that you're not actually swayed by the title, by the money...when in fact, you might be."

"Stop it," she said. "You're twisting the situation. It's bad enough without you adding gaslight."

He drew back, feeling as though she had slapped him. He *was* manipulating the situation, and he found that it was something of an impulse on his end. Which ran counter to the fact that he had just realized he needed to do something to make her happy. But he didn't know how to...have a real conversation. He didn't know how to do anything other than poke and prod, and attempt to make himself come out with the advantage.

He didn't know how to connect.

She seemed to. She had asked a question. And it had been genuine. Part of his answer had been, as well.

"Very well," he said, moving away from her. "We can finish for the day."

"What else am I supposed to do with my time?"

"Anything you like. Except for returning to New York. But I have informed my staff of the position that you will be filling after our marriage, and it's possible that you can begin organizing the art collection right away."

She looked shocked. "I can?"

He waved a hand. "Yes. Why would I prevent you

from doing that? It was one of the things I used to bribe you with."

She blinked. "I suppose so."

"I don't want you to be miserable. Sure, the foundation for the marriage might be kidnapping and blackmail, but I don't see why you can't enjoy yourself."

"You know I think that might be the most honest thing you said since we met."

"What?"

"That you don't understand why I can't enjoy myself even though I've been blackmailed and kidnapped."

"The situation is what it is. Make of it what you will. I suppose I will see you again for our engagement party."

She looked relieved. Relieved that she wouldn't be seeing him for a while. Well, that was going to have to pass. But there was time.

He turned and walked away from his fiancée, the woman who was wearing his ring, who didn't even want to be in the same room with him. And he ignored the tightening in his gut and below his belt as he did. She was beautiful, but she wasn't special.

No woman was. No one person was. He wasn't sentimental; he didn't believe in that sort of thing.

But as he walked down the corridor toward his office he had to make a concerted effort to banish the image in his mind of that wide-eyed, genuine look that had been written on her face when she had asked him what he wondered. With nothing but curiosity. Nothing but honesty.

And as he sat down at his desk he did his best to banish the grim thought that her honesty wouldn't last long. Not with him. That kind of openness, the little bit of innocence that she possessed, would be snuffed out by the darkness inside him.

It was as inevitable as her becoming his queen. And as necessary, as well.

There was nothing that could be done. And he would waste no time feeling guilty about it.

Guilt was for men who could afford to have consciences. He was not one of those men.

CHAPTER SIX

THE ENGAGEMENT PARTY came more quickly than Briar was prepared for. The moment when Felipe was going to present her for the entire world to see as his fiancée. Yes, the world at large knew, but this was different. This was the first time she was actually going to make an appearance. The first time she was going to have to contend with it.

She had been presented with two couture gowns to try on for the event. And her stylists were currently in a heated debate as to whether or not she should choose the pink or the blue.

Both were cut dramatically, designed to show off her figure, and billowed around her feet. Ultimately, she went with the blue. Because when she twirled, it moved effortlessly with her body. That, and it had a little bit more give around the hips. She had a feeling that she was going to need it. She was naturally thin, much to the chagrin of most of her friends at university, but even she felt a little bit constrained by a gown after a long evening of standing around eating. And the delicacies here at the palace really were amazing.

She supposed if one had to get kidnapped, getting kidnapped by a prince really was the way to go. Good food, good lodgings. And really amazing clothes.

As she was zipped into the beautiful blue gown, she looked down at the ring sparkling on her left hand. Right. There was that. The fact that her particular kidnapping had come with a fiancé. But also with a royal title. Of course, she supposed she had that title on her own.

Her stomach lurched a little bit when she remembered that her parents—her birth parents—had been invited to tonight's event. Would they come? Would this be the first night she saw them since she was a little girl? And what would she do? She had a feeling that she would crumble. Break down completely, which she hadn't done once since she had been kidnapped from her home in New York. That was strange, she realized then. That she hadn't cried yet.

She supposed part of it came down to the fact that she was afraid if she shed even one tear she would shed endless tears, and then they might never stop.

She sucked in a deep, shuddering breath and looked at her reflection. At the woman staring back at her who was less a stranger now than she had been a week ago. With the expertly applied makeup and the beautifully styled curls.

Panic fluttered in her breast, and she had to look away.

This wasn't the time to have a meltdown. She was going to have to save it for later. She would pencil it into her brand-new schedule. A gift from Prince Felipe. At least, she had been told. True to his word, she hadn't seen him between that moment in the ballroom and today.

There was a very large part of herself that was grateful for that. What had happened was…confusing. The fact that he had made her feel things. The kinds of things she had felt that first moment when she had seen him standing there on the street.

And she kept turning over what he had said to her. About what it meant that she liked him even knowing he was a monster. Well, like maybe wasn't the word for it. That she was attracted to him.

That she *wanted* him.

She turned away from her reflection, pressing her hand against her stomach.

"You will be fine, Princess," the stylist said, reading her nerves incorrectly. That was fine. She didn't care if he thought she was nervous about going to the ball. Well, she was. But it had to do with her parents. And it had to do with him. The man that she should be disgusted by. The man that she should hate.

The man that made her feel things no other man ever had.

She was herded down the hall, to an antechamber that was seemingly outside a private entrance to the ballroom. She knew that guests had already arrived. She also knew that she was going to be presented, along with the prince, in a formal way.

She understood all of that. She hadn't grown up as traditional royalty, but growing up as she had, with her father occupying a very prominent position in high places, she had been American royalty in some regards.

Ceremony was part of that upbringing. She supposed that was helpful. Of all the things that she did have to worry about at least she didn't have to learn this entirely new language of formality.

She didn't know what she expected. Didn't know who she had expected to guide her into the ballroom. But she hadn't expected Felipe. Or maybe she had, and there was simply no way for her to prepare herself for the sight of him.

He was… Well, it simply wasn't fair how good he looked in a suit. He really should look monstrous. Because she knew that he was one. That he was selfish. That he was willing to do anything to meet his ends, no matter who he heard. It didn't matter. It didn't diminish the intensity of his masculine beauty.

The perfection of those broad shoulders, the exquisitely sculpted face that was a work of art all on its own.

"You look beautiful," he said as though he had pulled the word she was thinking right out of her head. Except, she had been thinking that he was beautiful. And she would rather die than confess that. Still, she had a feeling that he knew. It seemed evident in the glint in those dark eyes, in the slight quirk of his full mouth.

He certainly wasn't a man who possessed humility. Why was that appealing? Why was anything about him appealing?

You're going to marry him. You're going to marry him and sleep with him.

Her entire body went hot. She shouldn't be thinking about this. Not now.

Really, she was going to have to put off thinking about it for as long as possible. And then when she did, she was going to have to wait until she was alone. Until he wasn't standing right in front of her acting like a visual reference for what was going to happen. So that she wasn't tempted to imagine what he might look like without those layers of fabric over that masculine physique.

She should be appalled by him. If there was any justice, if there was any logic involved in hormones, she should be appalled.

She had always thought herself above this kind of

ridiculousness. Apparently, she had just been waiting for the right kind of wrong man to get hot and bothered over.

"Are my parents in there?" That was the one thing she had to know.

"You're welcome," he said, his tone dry. And it took her a moment to remember that he had just called her beautiful. Well, she wasn't going to thank him for that. Mostly because she wanted to keep her interactions with him anything but cordial. For now. She supposed, since she had agreed to marry the man, she had to relax that eventually.

Maybe around the time that she let herself think about being intimate with him.

Maybe.

"Are they in there or not?"

"They are," he said. "And they have requested a private audience with you, which I will grant them after we've been formally introduced."

Suddenly, she felt dizzy, but rather than reaching out to steady herself against the wall, she found herself pitching forward. She stretched her hand out, her fingertips coming into contact with his chest. Then she swayed. And he caught her around the waist, pulling her up against his body. "Are you okay?"

She looked up at him, or rather, at his Adam's apple, at the sharp line of his jaw, and then the wicked curve of his lips. She could feel his heart raging beneath her palm. And she wondered if his heart always beat so hard, if it always beat so fast. "No," she said, her tone hushed. "How can I be okay? I always knew that I was adopted. I always knew that I had birth parents out there somewhere. But I never expected to meet them. I certainly didn't expect them to be a king and queen. And I didn't expect them to have given me up reluctantly. To have given me up to protect me."

She found herself blinking back tears and wondering if her mascara was waterproof.

And he looked... Well, for the first time since she had met him Felipe looked afraid. As if her tears terrified him.

"I'm sure it will be fine," he said, his tone stiff suddenly.

"How can it be fine?"

"I only had one set of parents, and they were never particularly useful to me. Neither were they particularly loving. You seem to have two sets of parents who were quite fond of you. How can it not be fine?"

There was something strange about the way he said that, but then, there was something strange about the way he talked about emotion in general. The way he talked about connections with people, or the lack of them. She had noticed that the day they danced in the ballroom. It made her sad. Almost.

"I don't know how to face this. I don't know how to handle any of this. A week ago I was just Briar Harcourt. And now I'm...I guess I'm a long-lost princess."

"You were found," he said. "You are not lost anymore."

She didn't say, as she took hold of his arm and allowed him to lead her toward the double doors of the ballroom, that she felt more lost now than she ever had. No, she kept that observation to herself. And then the doors opened, and they walked out to the top of the stairway, where they were announced as Prince Felipe and Princess Talia. It was strange, and it felt somewhat detached, since the name still didn't feel like her own. But as they descended the stairs the sense of fantasy faded. And she felt the moment as sharp and real as anything had ever been.

Strange, because this was something out of a movie. Strange, that it was the first moment that felt truly real in the past week. Or maybe it was just the events catching up to her. The undeniable reality of the whole thing. The fact that if it was a dream she would have woken up by now, and she could no longer pretend that she might.

Then she saw them. Well, she saw Queen Amaani. A near mirror image of herself. A beautiful, dark-skinned woman standing there holding her husband, King Behrendt's, arm. She had a heavy golden crown on her dark hair, signifying her ranking.

The king himself had piercing blue eyes, a strong nose and neatly kept gray hair and beard. Clearly much older than his wife, he was still a handsome man, his presence announcing his status more clearly than a crown ever could.

Briar found herself clutching Felipe's arm as though without him she would collapse completely. It was a perverse thing, that she found herself leaning on his strength in this moment. She should push him away. She should push him away and run to her parents. But she was afraid that if she let go of him she would crumble to the floor.

The people in the ballroom blurred into indistinct shapes, the men a wave of black, the women a watercolor rainbow. All she could see was her mother and father. And Felipe. She could still see him. She could feel his warmth. Could feel his strength.

She swallowed hard as she approached the king and queen.

"Let us step out onto the balcony," Felipe said, leading the way, holding on to her as he led her through the crowd and out toward a large balcony that overlooked the gardens.

Nobody followed them, and then she realized that there were guards preventing anyone from leaving the ballroom and interrupting the reunion.

Suddenly, Briar found herself enveloped in her parents' arms. And that was when she lost hold of everything. Of her emotions. Of her control. And she let the tears fall.

There was nothing to say. Because it transcended words. She supposed that there would be time to ask about what had happened in the years since they had seen each other. Though she gathered quickly that they knew things like what she had majored in, and that they had been sent photographs all through her growing up. She was the one with the real deficit. The one who knew nothing of her past, the one who knew nothing of her family. Of her country, of the palace that she had once called home, of her half brothers and their wives and children.

But there would be time for all of that later. Because for now, there was nothing but this. But this deep, happy, devastatingly sad reunion that she had been waiting for all her life without even realizing it.

She looked up and saw Felipe studying them as though he was looking at something he simply couldn't understand. She shouldn't be looking at him now. Except, he had been instrumental in this reunion. But without his father she wouldn't have been given up in the first place. But then, she wouldn't have known the parents that she loved so dearly, the mother and father who had raised her. Everything was mixed up in her head and she didn't know how she felt anymore. Didn't know if she was happy, didn't know if she was sad. Didn't know if she was angry at that devastatingly handsome man standing apart from them, or if she felt sorry for him.

If she wanted to run from him, or if she wanted to draw closer to him.

"Sadly," he said finally, "we cannot stand out here all night."

King Behrendt looked up at Felipe, his expression stern. "Haven't you and your people robbed us of enough time already?"

"It is unfortunate," Felipe returned. "However, in the future you will have endless time to spend together. I do not intend to keep her from you. In fact, I intend to ensure that we have brilliant relations between our two countries. This is a reunion. Not simply for our families, but for the goodwill between Verloren and Santa Milagro. I understand that you might not appreciate the tactics. But Briar has agreed to marry me. I'm sorry, Princess Talia has agreed to marry me."

Queen Amaani looked stricken by the use of her other name. But she stepped forward. "Which name do you prefer?" she asked Briar, her voice soft.

"I don't know that I prefer either one," she said. "I'm just getting used to everything."

"We've always known what they called you," she said. "If that's what you want to be called, if you want to be Briar, you can be."

"I'll be Talia," she said, not sure if she meant it or not. But she didn't want to cause these people any more pain. Not after all they had been through.

"We can find another way," her father said, his expression hard as he looked at Felipe.

Briar shook her head, because she knew they couldn't. It was just that her father was too proud to acknowledge anything else. "You don't have to. I've been away for a long time. I haven't had the chance to be part of this. To be part of royal life. To serve my country in any way. This is how I can do it." She realized, as she spoke the words, that she meant them.

Her parents gave her one last lingering hug before they headed back into the ballroom, with promises to have her travel to Verloren as soon as possible, and promises to visit the palace in Santa Milagro often.

"I think," said Felipe, walking up slowly behind her, pressing his hand against her lower back, "that I will call you Briar."

It sent a strange, electric jolt through her. To have him touch her. To have him say that. She didn't know why that affected her. The thought that he would call her Briar.

"You don't have to," she said.

"I'm going to."

She stopped walking and turned to face him. He kept his hand planted firmly on her lower back. "And if I don't want you to?"

"I still will."

She frowned. "Why?"

He examined her closely, something in his dark eyes sharper, clearer than usual. It was then that she realized that lazy, indolent manner he sometimes threw over himself like a cloak was exactly that. Just something he put on.

She wondered about the real man. The one who wasn't a monster or Prince Charming. The man beneath all of that. Then, just as quickly as she wondered about that, she wondered if he even existed anymore. Or if he had been buried underneath a rock wall that he had carefully constructed around any and all authenticity.

"Because I should think you would like it if your entire past wasn't erased."

"It might be less painful." To just pretend that her childhood in New York, her family, her friends, didn't exist anymore. To pretend that Briar didn't exist anymore. That thought made her feel hollow.

"Life is painful," he said. "Loss is painful."

"You're acknowledging that I'm experiencing loss at your hand?"

"Circumstances are what they are. It doesn't have to be a loss. Unless... Did you have a lover back home?"

She shook her head. "If I did I never would have talked to you on the street in the first place." Maybe she should have lied. Maybe that would have been better. To make him think that she had another man in her life. But he would find out soon enough that it wasn't true. If he hadn't figured it out already. If this question wasn't just another piece of bait.

Because he seemed to know what she was feeling before she did. Seemed to understand what was happening in her body even when it mystified her.

"Because you felt it, too," he said, his voice like a touch, skimming over her entire body. Touching her in places no one ever had before.

She wanted to deny it. Wanted to pretend she had no idea what he was talking about. And she really didn't want to question what he meant when he said that she had felt it, too. As if he had felt something. Something other than the thrill of a hunter spotting his quarry.

She didn't want to get drawn into this. Didn't want to get drawn into looking at him and searching for humanity. It was much better if she only looked at the facade. If she only looked at the monster. Much better if she never tried to search behind that rock wall.

And yet she felt the pull, the tug toward him. The undeniable need to understand him. Maybe that wasn't so bad. Maybe it wasn't so dangerous. To try and understand the man she would supposedly spend the rest of her life with.

"What did you feel?" she asked. "When you saw me."

"You were beautiful. I responded to that. I'm a man, after all."

"There are a lot of beautiful women."

"Yes. But there are very few women who represent payment for an outstanding debt owed to my country." Something shifted in his expression. He was so difficult to read. His moods seeming to shift like sand without giving any warning. "Did you know my father had renounced marriage at the point when he announced he would claim you? He did not intend to take you as a wife. He intended to make you a mistress. On your sixteenth birthday."

Horror pierced through her. "He did?" She blinked rapidly. "But what about your...? What about your mother?"

"At that point she was dead. And anyway he never cared about her. He had mistresses all through their marriage. He paraded them about the palace whenever he saw fit. Women who were younger, women who weren't made weary by a lifetime of abuses and indignities. And he made sure that my mother knew they were infinitely more desirable than she would ever be. He made sure to let her know that she was a failure. For a great many reasons, though I was one of them. She never could keep me in line. Never could keep me in my place. My father demanded that one small thing from her, and she couldn't do that, either. And so he made her life hell. In part because he enjoyed doing it. In part because of me."

"He...he showed you that sort of thing was normal," she said, wondering how he'd ever had a hope of developing a conscience.

"Yes. But I knew they weren't. I knew that intending to take a woman some forty years younger than him—not a woman, a girl!—and make her his plaything was wrong. I never intended to use women that way. I never intended to use you that way. But I did recognize that you would be useful. That your symbolism could be changed."

"How very strange. Because I have never felt like a symbol. I've only ever felt like a girl."

"I'm well aware that you're neither of those things. You are not a symbol." He moved nearer to her, brushing the backs of his knuckles over her face. "You're far too warm. You're too alive. But also... You're not a girl. You're a woman."

For the first time, she felt like one. With his finger slowly drifting over her skin, those dark eyes pinning her into place, she didn't feel like a tall, awkward girl who was hopelessly different than everyone around her. Didn't feel like a simple curiosity. Didn't feel like a child in sophisticated clothes playing at something she was not.

No, in this moment, rooted to the spot, she felt every inch a woman. And she wanted to find out why that was. Wanted to respond to everything that was male in him and explore what it all meant. But it was all tangled up. Jumbled together with the reality of the situation. And then weighted down completely by the diamond on her finger, as if it were a millstone.

Perhaps she was simply succumbing to the insanity of the situation. Perhaps she had lost her mind completely.

Did it matter? That was the real question.

He let his fingertips drift down to the edge of her jaw then traced the line to the center of her chin. He tilted her face upward, his mouth a breath away from hers. She felt like she was being lifted off the ground. Her lungs, her body, filled completely. Expanding until she felt like she might burst with whatever feeling was taking her over. It was strange, and it was foreign. She wasn't entirely sure she liked it. Wasn't entirely sure she didn't.

"Your Majesty," a voice came from behind them.

Felipe dropped his hand and took a step back. "What is it?" he asked without ever taking his eyes off her.

"Prince Felipe. It's your father."

At that, Felipe turned and faced the man who had joined them on the terrace. "What is it?"

"The king is dead."

Something went horribly blank, flat in Felipe's eyes. She could feel ice radiating from his skin. He said nothing for a moment. And then, he tilted his face upward, his expression one of schooled arrogance, overlaid with a breathless lack of remorse.

Then he finally spoke, a strange smile curving his lips. "Long live the king."

CHAPTER SEVEN

"I SUPPOSE WE will be making more than one announcement tonight," Felipe said, his tone hard.

Then he straightened the cuffs on his jacket and walked back into the ballroom. Leaving Briar standing there by herself feeling utterly helpless. His reaction was frightening, and she didn't know what to do with it. Didn't know why she cared. Didn't know why it hit her quite so squarely in the chest and made it so hard for her to breathe.

Then she saw people begin pouring out of the ballroom. Heading back up the stairs, leaving the party much sooner than she was sure they had been planning. She lifted the front of her gown and hurried inside. She could hear Felipe shouting, but didn't understand what he was saying as he was speaking in Spanish.

Then he switched to English. "The party is over," he said. "My father is dead. I will be assuming the throne now. But we will not dance anymore tonight. Go home. Everybody get out."

And his word was obeyed for, after all, he was the king.

The only people who hesitated were her parents. She looked between Felipe and her mother and father, then she went to the king and queen. "You should go," she said, reaching out and placing her hand over her mother's.

"Are you certain you'll be all right?" the other woman asked.

She looked back at Felipe, who was standing there perfectly smooth and unruffled. She knew it was a lie. She just did. Whether or not it made any sense, she knew. This was another of his games. Another of his facades.

"Yes," she said. "I'll be fine. Leave me with him."

That left her in the ballroom, empty all except for herself and Felipe. And she realized that it had not been the moment she had accepted his proposal, not the moment he had placed the ring on her finger, that she had truly chosen this, chosen him. It was now.

She wasn't sure she would ever be able to explain why. Only that he needed her. He needed someone. She didn't know who else it would be.

The tables were still laden with food, and there was music being piped in over the speakers. But no one else was there. Not a single guest, not a single servant. With the chandelier glittering above and all the lights lit, casting the golden room in a fierce glow, it all seemed rather eerie. Particularly with the deep emotion radiating from the man who stood before her.

Apparently, she was with him. She had a feeling that she had been from the moment she'd first set eyes on him. Her world had shifted then. Regardless of what had happened since, in that moment…she had connected with him.

"Are you all right?"

He looked at her, the expression on his face indicating that he was surprised to find her still there. "Of course I am. Why wouldn't I be?" He straightened his sleeves, then his hands moved to the knot on his tie, and he straightened that, too, even though it hadn't been askew at all.

"Your father is dead."

"Yes. And I am now the king. And everything that I have wanted to do for the past two decades can now come to fruition. I'm more than all right."

He didn't look it. He didn't sound it.

"Felipe," she said, taking a step toward him.

He turned abruptly, gripping the edge of one of the tables that was laden with food, and he turned it over. She gasped and took a step back as glass shattered on the marble floor, champagne running through the tiles like a river.

"I feel better," he said. "Yes. I feel better."

"That was a waste of food."

"I'll make a donation. Around the time I make a donation that matches the cost of your ring. Do you find that acceptable?"

"I wasn't... I was just..."

"My father had not one quality to redeem him, Briar," Felipe said. "Not one. He victimized every person who walked through his life. And this—" he swept his hand to the side, indicating the mess he had just made "—would have appalled him. He could not abide disorder. Could not abide disorder while he created chaos inside everyone who lived underneath his roof. I always found that the greatest irony. He claimed he wanted everything to run smoothly while he ruined my mother from the inside out. Tell me, does that make any sense?"

She shook her head. "No."

"No. It doesn't. I will not make you miserable. I promise you." He began to pace, his movements agitated. He gripped the edge of his sleeve with his thumb and fore-finger and straightened it again. Then he repeated the action again. "Because it makes no sense. I'm not a soft man. I don't believe in love. I don't believe in romance. But I can certainly accomplish the amazing feat of not being a cruel bastard."

She stood where she was for a moment, not moving away from him, but not moving forward, either. She wasn't sure if another explosion of violence was going to come. She wouldn't be surprised if it did. He was all barely leashed energy and a strange kind of manic emotion that she had never seen before.

It turned out, she didn't have to move toward him at all. Because a moment later he was closing the distance between them. His dark eyes blazing into hers. And then, those eyes were all she saw. All she saw as he wrapped his arm around her waist and drew her hard up against his body.

She couldn't breathe. She didn't even have a moment to react. Because then, his mouth was crashing down on hers, his lips taking hers, consuming her. She had never been kissed before, so she didn't know what she had expected. But it hadn't been this. No, she never could have anticipated this, not in her wildest fantasies.

Because in her imagination a kiss had always been a sweet thing, romantic thing. In her fantasies, a kiss was meant to be shared with someone you loved, or at the very least someone you cared about. She couldn't claim that she cared about Felipe at all.

But that didn't seem to matter. Because while there wasn't…caring, there was something else. Something hot and reckless that burned through her like wildfire. And whatever he had been before, whatever she thought about him, was consumed by it, leaving behind nothing but ash. Making it impossible for her to remember how she had gotten here, and who she was. If she was Princess Talia, or Briar Harcourt. If she was a prisoner, a forced bride, or if she was kissing this man simply because he was the only man she had ever wanted.

For a moment she simply stood there, stood and marveled at the kiss. As his tongue slid over the seam of her lips, requesting entry. She didn't know what to do. Didn't know what she wanted. Her heart was thundering so hard she was certain that he could hear it. Certain that he could feel it butting up against his own chest as close as he was holding her.

Her arms were pinned to her sides, her hands curled into fists.

But then, his hold on her changed. He shifted, spreading his fingers, holding on to her in a way that was firm, sure and comforting in the oddest way. Then with his other hand he cupped the back of her head, tilting his head and granting himself access to her mouth, tasting her deeply.

After that she was lost. Completely and utterly. In the sensations that were pouring through her body like a liquid flame, in his heat, his presence, the strength of his body. And in the need that she hadn't realized her body was capable of feeling.

She had always thought she was somewhat dispassionate. After all, she had never even been tempted by the boys she had gone to university with. But that was the problem. The problem, which she had realized that first moment she had laid eyes on Felipe. They were boys. They were nothing but boys, and he was a man. A man who called to everything woman inside her. The man who made her realize that she was a woman.

The man who made her realize what a wonderful thing that was.

Her breasts ached, and he tightened his hold on her, crushing her up against that hard, muscular wall of his chest. She wanted him to touch her. Wanted his hands on her, not just this kind of passive contact that teased her with what she wanted without actually giving it.

As if he read her mind, he shifted, and instead of putting his hands on her he simply let her feel what she did to him. Let her feel the evidence of his own arousal, pressed up against her belly like an iron rod.

She had never been close enough to a man to experience anything like this. And she... She loved it. She was glorying in it. In the effect that she had on him. She didn't feel awkward. She didn't feel different. She felt *singular*. She felt *beautiful*. That she had the power to affect this man—this glorious, intoxicating man—in the way that she was... How could she feel anything but wholly, purely *desired*?

Except that he was the man who had kidnapped her. The man who had forced her into this engagement. Those thoughts swirled around in her mind along with the fog of arousal. She knew that she should grasp on to those little bits of sanity. But she didn't want to. She didn't want sanity. Not now. She just wanted this. This kind of reckless madness that she was certain would be her undoing.

But she was undone already, wasn't she? She had been cautioned all her life, told to be careful, and it was all because she was running from this man. But here she was, she was in his palace, she was in his arms, and he was consuming her. It was too late. She had been taken by the dragon, and she might as well give in to this, as well. There was nothing else that could be done. And in this moment, it seemed the most logical thing of all to give him this, too.

He growled, reversing their positions and pressing her back up against the wall. Against the windows that overlooked the garden outside. She knew that—despite the fact it seemed they were in isolation—there were still hundreds of people milling around the palace. She didn't care. She didn't care about anything. Nothing but this.

He moved his hands, dragging them down so that he was gripping her hips, his blunt fingertips digging into her skin. But she liked it. Loved that feeling of him anchoring her to the earth, because she still felt like she was in danger of floating away.

Then his hands moved upward, and he gripped the neckline on her dress, tearing the delicate fabric, exposing her breasts to his hungry gaze. She gasped, wrenching her mouth away from his, the breath dragged from her lungs in long, unsteady pulls.

"Felipe," she said, gasping his name, but he didn't seem to listen. Didn't seem to hear. He was like a man possessed—his dark eyes wild, desperation pouring from him in waves. This was the real man. It was, and she knew it. Shaken, unhinged, broken. Needing something that she wasn't certain she knew how to give. Something she wasn't sure she wanted to give.

She had only known him a week. And in that time she had pledged her life to him. But she had not fully known what it might mean to pledge her body to him, as well. She still didn't. But then he lowered his dark head, sucking one tightened bud deep into his mouth, groaning harshly as he did.

She lifted her hands, not sure if she was moving to hold him to her or push him away. Instead, she ended up threading her fingers through his dark hair, resting them there as he continued to lavish attention on her breasts. And she wondered, just for a moment, what sort of woman she was. She flashed back to those words he had spoken to her. Knowing that he was a monster, she still wanted him.

And seeing him like this now, she wanted him even more. She liked this man better than the playboy she had met the first day. Liked him more than the twisted, cynical prince who always seemed intent on scoring points off her. She liked him sharp, liked him dangerous, with rough edges that could easily cut her all the way down to the bone.

Or perhaps *like* wasn't the word. Perhaps it was something deeper than that. Something that cut through the loneliness of that careful childhood she'd led. That strange sense of isolation, of feeling wrong, feeling different, that had always followed her wherever she went.

No, *like* was not the correct word. She wasn't sure that she *liked* any of this. But it was driving her, creating a need inside her as quickly as it satisfied it.

She had spent her entire life fully in control. Of her actions, of her desires, of everything around her. Being so entirely without it was terrifying. Liberating. She should tell him to stop. She should want him to stop. She wasn't going to. She didn't want to.

She had a feeling she knew where this was going. She might be inexperienced, but she wasn't innocent of the way things went between men and women. Though she wasn't sure she had any way of knowing how she would withstand it. What the consequences might be for her. It was like helplessly clinging to a speeding train, unsure of whether she should ride it out or jump off. Unsure of which might do more damage.

"I have to," he said, his voice sounding frayed, tortured, as he tilted his head to the side, sliding his tongue down the column of her neck, all the way down to her collarbone and down farther still, tracing the outline of one tightened nipple. "I have to," he repeated again, tearing her bodice completely so that the whole front of her gown was gaping wide.

She clung to his shoulders, the glass against her back warm now from her body being pressed against it for the past few minutes. She looked beyond him, at the empty ballroom, still all lit up as though it was expecting a crowd. But it was just the two of them now. Just the two of them and the broken glass on the floor and whatever ghosts Felipe was contending with.

He took hold of the flimsy skirt of her gown, curling his fingers around it and tugging it upward, past her hips. Then he pressed one hand between her thighs, bold fingers moving beneath the waistband of her panties, and then on through her slick folds. She was wet for him. There was no hiding it. Not from him, not from herself.

What does that say about you, I wonder?

Those words rolled to her head again, and she pushed them away. It didn't matter what it said about her. She didn't care. She had always cared. Had always tried to be the perfect daughter. To do exactly what her parents had told her to do. To earn her position in their household. No, they had never acted as though she had to do that, but it didn't matter. She had put that weight there. Had done her best to follow their rules, had done her very best to succeed, to be a monument to all that they had poured into her.

This stood in antithesis to that.

This served her. The immediate. The moment. The physical, yawning need inside her. And whatever the consequences might be after, she couldn't bring herself to think of them now. Couldn't bring herself to care.

He pressed one finger inside her then drew it back out again, rubbing it over the sensitized bundle of nerves at the apex of her thighs. She gasped, letting her head fall back, and he took advantage of that vulnerable position, pressing a hot, openmouthed kiss to the tender skin on her neck.

And all the while he created wicked magic between her legs with his fingers. Made her feel things that she had never imagined possible. Things that she had certainly never managed to make herself feel, no matter how hard she'd tried on long, lonely nights in her bedroom. This was different. This was different because it was him. Because she had no control over what he might do next. Over how hard or soft he might touch her, how quickly he might stroke her, or when he would pull away again.

Then he growled, removing his hand and gripping her hips again, pressing her more firmly against the window. He took hold of one wrist and raised it up over her head, before going to collect the other, pinning that one down, as well, holding her fast with one hand.

He tried to hold her skirt in place with his free hand, but quickly became frustrated and wrenched the skirt to the side, rendering it nothing more than an expensive strip of silk. Her panties suffered the same fate. And she realized she was standing there wearing nothing but the facsimile of a dress in front of this man who might as well be a stranger.

But could he really be considered a stranger now? Now that he had touched her in the most intimate place on her body? Not when she had let him. Surely, they were more than strangers now.

He kissed her then, deep and hard, and she could feel him shifting against her, but it didn't click exactly what was happening until she felt something hot, blunt and hard pressing up against the entrance of her body. Her stomach went into a freefall, nerves assaulting her. Of course she had known where this was going.

She felt a shock of nerves, but then he was kissing her so long and deep, and her head felt dizzy with desire and pleasure. And nerves didn't matter anymore. Only how much she wanted him.

He flexed his hips upward, breaching the barrier there, a sharp, tearing sensation assaulting her, making her feel as though she couldn't breathe. He was too much. Too big. She was too full and it didn't feel good. She wiggled her hips, trying to get away from him, but she was trapped completely between the hard, uncompromising window, and the hard uncompromising man. And he was too far gone to realize that she was in distress.

He only gripped her harder, retreating from her body before he thrust back inside her again. Only this time, it didn't hurt quite so bad. This time, a part of her welcomed the feeling of fullness. He retreated again then returned to her. And with each thrust pleasure began to edge out pain. Desire consuming fear.

And then she gave herself up to it, to him. Opened herself to him, rolled her hips in rhythm with his movements. There was nothing gentle about it. Just like her first kiss—which had happened an astonishingly short time ago—this was void of the kind of sweetness and gauzy romance she had always imagined the act would contain.

But she didn't mourn it. Because she had never wanted anyone else. She wanted him. So how could it be anything other than perfect?

It was a messy kind of perfect. A broken kind of perfect. But as the pleasure built, deep and intense inside her, she realized she didn't care. He rolled his hips up against hers, and bliss broke over her like a wave on the rocks.

She just shook and rode it out. As she shuddered out her pleasure, turning her face into the curve of his neck, doing her best to hold back the tears that began to push against her eyes, pressure building to almost unbearable levels.

He tightened his hold on her, his thumb and fingers digging so hard into her wrists she was certain it would leave a bruise. And then, he let out a harsh, feral growl as he found his own release. He released his hold on her, burying his fingers into her massive curly hair and claiming her mouth in a kiss that mimicked the act they had just finished.

This was no sweet, silent afterglow. It was a conflagration that still raged on in spite of their release.

And when it was done, he took a step away from her, regarding her with wild, dark eyes. "You will spend the night in my bed tonight," he said, the words a command and not a request.

And then, he turned away from her, striding away from her, not offering her so much as a comforting touch.

In spite of the heat that was still coursing through her body, she shivered.

CHAPTER EIGHT

SHE HAD BEEN a virgin. And he had taken her against a wall—no, a window—with absolutely no finesse.

Then he had left her standing there in a tattered dress, the bright streaks of blue a shocking contrast to that smooth, brown skin. Her small, high breasts and that dark thatch of curls at the apex of her thighs exposed, her hair a dark halo around her face.

Had left her standing there with the command that she join him in his bed tonight, when the fact of the matter was no one should come anywhere near him tonight. And he shouldn't inflict himself on anyone.

What had been in his mind? Sending everyone away as he had? He had come into the ballroom, waiting for the surge of triumph to flood his veins. Waiting for a sense of completion. Waiting for his lips to form the words to an eloquent speech.

About dark ages rolling forward into the light. But instead he had cleared the room.

Instead, he had done what he seemed compelled to do from some dark place inside him that had purchase on his soul, that he seemed to have no control over, and that was to sabotage the moment. To break. To destroy.

And he still felt no relief. No sense of completion.

Nothing but an end. A dark, blank end that offered him nothing but more emptiness. Like a chasm had opened inside him, one that had always been there, but one he now had to admit might always be.

His father was dead. That was supposed to be the key.

But now he couldn't yell at the old man. Couldn't scream at him and demand answers. Could never shout at him about the fact it was his fault Felipe's mother was dead. How it was all his fault.

Felipe swallowed hard, trying to get a handle on himself, on his control. This control he had long prized so much. He should not have Briar come to his room. He should deal with his demons alone.

But he would have her again. Because there was no other choice. Because the hollow feeling inside him was threatening to consume him, and the only moment of peace he'd had since his father's aide had come and announced the old man's death had been when he was buried in Briar's tight, welcoming heat.

It occurred to him as he flung open the doors to his chamber that she might not come. That she might go back to her room. Might hide from him.

She should. There was no question about that.

But if she did he would go after her.

There was also no question about that.

With shaking hands, he poured himself a glass of whiskey then stared down at the amber liquid. He was dangerous enough as it was. Unsteady, unstable. Disorderly. There was no greater sin in his father's eyes and there never had been.

The thought made a smile curve his lips. He might have wasted some opportunities tonight, but he had rebelled in a rather spectacular fashion. His father had prized all that surface order. Never mind if beneath the surface everything was jagged and destroyed.

Destroying the ballroom appealed to that part of him that wanted to wound the old man still. That hoped his ghost had watched the whole thing.

He looked down at the glass. As on edge as he was he wasn't entirely certain he should add alcohol to the equation. For Briar's sake and for no other reason. And so, he tilted the glass to the side before cocking his arm back and flinging it against the wall.

"I imagine that's a bit too disorderly for you as well, Father," he said.

There was every chance the old man could hear him. That he was now haunting the halls like the malevolent spirit he had always been. It would be fitting. This palace was full of ghosts; Felipe had never thought differently, no matter that his father had tried to tell him otherwise.

He was failing again. Which seemed to be what he did. Failing at not being a horror to the woman he was intent on taking as his wife. But then, he wasn't sure he was capable of being anything other than this. Anything other than the creature his father had set out to create.

He gripped the edge of the bar, lowering his head. He had to be different. He had to. If for no other reason than for Santa Milagro. His people had lived in darkness long enough.

Of course, he had no idea how he was supposed to remedy that when he feared he had no light inside him.

Then the door to his bedchamber opened and he lifted his head, turning it to look behind him. It was Briar. She was no longer wearing the shredded ball gown that he had left her in downstairs. She had changed into a long, flowing robe in a luminous pink that contrasted beautifully with her smooth, dark skin. She had washed her makeup off, leaving her looking young and freshly scrubbed. He had to wonder if she had been so eager to wash his touch from her body.

But she was here. And he felt almost certain she had brought some light in with her. Perhaps that was the key. Perhaps she was the key to more than he had originally imagined.

He ignored the slight twisting feeling in his chest that questioned this reasoning. That forced images of his mother to swim before his mind's eye.

"You came," he said.

"Yes," she said, scanning the room slowly, her eyes falling to the broken glass and spilled alcohol on the floor. "Clearly you can't be trusted around food at the moment."

"I can't be trusted around you, either," he said, his tone hard. "And yet, here you are."

She clasped her hands in front of her, wringing her fingers. "You asked me to come."

"I confess, I thought I might have to go retrieve you from the depths of your room. I thought I might have frightened you."

She lifted one elegant shoulder. "I'm not frightened of you."

He narrowed his eyes. "Truthfully?"

She released her hold on her hands, one fluttering slightly as she made a dismissive gesture. "Well. I suppose I am afraid of you. But not enough to hide from you."

"Is that because you've accepted your fate or because you find yourself fascinated by me?" The answer was important.

She frowned, a small dent growing between her eyebrows. "I think it took you stealing me away from the city for me to think I could do anything other than accept my fate, actually. And when I say that, it isn't because my life was terrible. I don't mean it in that way. It's just that it seemed predetermined. Like the path had been set since the beginning of my life. And then you showed me that I had no idea. None at all. I didn't know where I had started, and I had no idea what was out there, what was hunting me—so to speak. I would say that never in my life have I been at a point where I was more likely to accept the way things are than I am right now. And yet, here I am."

Something shifted inside him, a rumble of satisfaction beginning in his chest, growing. "Perhaps because I was your first man?"

Color tinged her cheeks. "You could tell?"

"Yes."

"And you did it anyway?" She tilted her head to the side, a strange expression on her face.

"It wasn't forefront in my mind. It was afterward. If I had stopped and thought about it while it was happening, I would have realized. As it was, I didn't put everything together until it was too late."

She looked somewhat appeased by that. "Okay."

"Does it matter to you?"

"I don't know if it matters. Well, yes, it does. I wouldn't like to think that it meant nothing to you. I have never wanted a man before. I wasn't a virgin because I was waiting for anything. I mean, nothing moral. I wasn't waiting for you, or some other mythological husband. I was just waiting for somebody that I wanted. I was waiting for the moment I didn't want to say no. And that happened downstairs with you. I don't know why.

I just know that it was different. That it changed something in me. So yes, if it meant nothing to you I would find that painful."

He felt a smile touch the corner of his lips. He walked toward her, closing the distance between them. Then he reached out, pressing his thumb against the center of her lower lip. "You want to be special to me, *querida*?"

She trembled beneath his touch, her dark eyes questioning. Searching. She wouldn't find anything. Not in him. Nothing but more darkness. That endless, blank pit that existed in his chest. Selfishly, he wanted her answer to be yes. And yet, he knew that he should want nothing from her. And he should rejoice if she wanted nothing from him.

Still, he waited. And he hoped. A strange, costly thing for a man like himself. To reach for a flame, wondering if it was going to warm him, or if the action would simply snuff it out.

"That's not so shocking, is it?" she asked, her voice hushed. "We… We were intimate with each other. Of course I want it to matter."

"Intimate?" He could honestly say he had never considered sex intimate. It was a release. It was bodies, only bodies. And long ago he had determined to detach himself from his body when he needed it to be so. To be able to make it so he felt no pain while undergoing excruciating torture.

To feel nothing but pleasure when he was in the arms of a woman—no matter what he might feel inside.

A body was simply that. Fallible, temporary. Losing himself in someone else's had never felt like anything more than pleasure.

And yet she called it intimacy. She had never wanted

another man. Had never allowed another man to touch her. He was not sure if he knew how to make someone special to him, but it seemed that he might be special to her.

He was equally at a loss as to what he was supposed to do with that.

But it satisfied him. Satisfied something inside him he had not known existed until that very moment. It was the deepest kind of satisfaction, satiating him in a way his orgasm hadn't even managed to.

"Yes," she said, her voice soft. She lifted her hand, pressed it flat against his chest. "What we did was intimate. Something that you don't share with just anyone." She frowned. "Or do you?"

"I have," he said, with no shame at all. "Desire exists to be satisfied."

"I don't think that's true. I think what makes desire matter is that it can't be satisfied in any time. What makes it so deep is that it's reserved only for certain people. For certain moments."

He wrapped his fingers around her wrist, held her hand more firmly against his chest. "As the woman who just confessed to having never felt it before? You say that, but what if it were another man to fire these feelings inside you? If it were to happen again, would you simply accept his advances as you did mine?" The thought was like acid, eating through his mind and sliding on down to his chest where it began to burn around the edges of the blackness there.

She shook her head. "No."

"So that makes me important?" He tightened his hold on her. "That means I'm important to you."

He never had been. Not to anyone. Not to his cruel,

sadistic father or his broken, fragile mother. He wanted it. More desperately than he had ever wanted anything, and he didn't care what that meant. Because he only understood want in a very singular way. Wanting was having as far as he was concerned. So he would have this. And he would feel no compunction about it.

"I said I would marry you," she said, looking away from him. "But you never answered if I was important to you."

"I said I would marry you," he said, parroting her words back to her. "Do you see any other women around here wearing my ring?"

She shook her head.

"There's your answer," he said. And then, the phone in his pocket vibrated. He said a curse then took it out, looking at the screen.

It was Rafe. The bastard really did have lousy timing. Why had he decided to have friends?

"We didn't get a chance to speak tonight," his friend said. "You threw everyone out of the palace."

"I'm surprised you left without being forced," he said to his friend, all the while keeping his eyes on Briar.

"Oh, Adam and I were forced," Rafe returned. "Though Adam was forced by his bride, who felt that your wishes should be respected. Because she simply doesn't know you well enough to know when you should be ignored."

"And what's your excuse?"

"I didn't suppose, given the disadvantage of my lack of sight, that I should engage your royal guards in a fight."

Felipe laughed. "Please. We both know you still had the advantage in the fight, Rafe."

"True enough."

"I assume that Adam was involved in this goodwill mission. You checking on my mental well-being." He took that moment to look at Briar more fully, to allow his gaze to travel over her beautiful curves. To truly relish just how flimsy that nightgown she was wearing was. He needed this phone call to be short.

"Your father has passed away. It isn't a small thing."

"It's better that he's dead. It was a cruelty of fate that he drew breath for as long as he did. There are a very great number of people who die far too young and don't deserve it."

"They say the good die young," Rafe pointed out.

"Then you and I are both safe."

"We are that," Rafe said, his tone hardening slightly. "We are that. I should be dead already. And likely would be if I were worthy of life."

Rafe's cynicism was one of the many reasons Felipe counted him a friend, when in general he found friendship to be pointless.

"Right now I'm grateful to be alive. I outlived that old bastard—" his gaze returned to Briar "—and I have a promising evening before me."

"You're with your fiancée, I assume," Rafe said.

"Yes. So you'll understand that I have to cut this call short."

"A word of caution," Rafe said. "This woman you have... I did a bit of research. And Adam described her to me. She is too soft for you, my friend. Far too young."

"Very much," Felipe returned, his eyes never leaving Briar, who was blushing beneath his frank appraisal. "She's too innocent for me, as well."

Her gaze sharpened, her mouth dropping open as she

realized she was the topic of discussion. She, and her virginity.

"That's even worse," Rafe said. "You have to be careful with women like that."

Felipe laughed. "Please. I spent my entire childhood at the mercy of a sadistic old man. I'm not in any danger."

"That makes it even clearer to me that you might be. Men like you and me... We can't be broken by the hard things. It's the soft things. Believe me. I know of what I speak."

Rafe had never given the details of how he lost his eyesight. All he and Adam knew was that there had been an accident. But Felipe had long suspected a woman had been involved in some capacity. This... This confirmed it. Except, Felipe had a difficult time imagining his friend falling prey to a woman, no matter how soft or beautiful she was.

"I'll keep that in mind." He hung up then. He wouldn't be keeping it in mind. Not tonight. Tonight he wanted only one thing. And as he advanced on his beautiful fiancée, he could think only that she had much more to be afraid of than he did.

"You were talking about me," she accused.

"Yes."

"Who was it?"

"A friend."

"You have friends?" Her eyes widened. If it wasn't objectively such a surprising thing that he had friends, even to him, he might have been offended. Instead, he found himself amused.

"I do. Two of them. And to answer your question, yes, they have myriad issues. Definitely not normal."

"I suppose I'm not normal, either."

He wrapped his arm around her waist, drew her up against his chest. "I don't need you to be normal. I need you to be mine."

She looked at him, marveled at him as though he were some kind of curiosity. Something she had never seen before, and was trying to figure out. Then she lifted her hand, drawing her fingertips lightly across his cheek.

He growled, taking hold of her wrist again and holding her steady as he brought his lips down to hers. As he claimed a kiss that he needed more than his next breath.

And then, Rafe didn't matter at all. Neither did the ghosts of his past. The ghost of his father that was likely rattling chains and wandering restlessly down the halls even now.

Nothing mattered but this. But her. But her beauty, her delicacy. The fact that he should stay away from her, because she would be so easily bruised, crushed like a delicate rose.

Perversely, he wanted it. Wanted to see the effect that he had on her. Wanted to ruin her. To make her his. Like he had wanted to ruin everything in this whole damn palace from the moment he had found out his father was dead. Disorder. That was what he wanted. Utter chaos. And he would be the king of it.

That drove him on. Spurred him to deepen the kiss. To crush his mouth against hers, to swallow the sounds she made, whether they were of pleasure or protestation, he wasn't entirely sure. But he was consumed by this. Consumed by his need for her.

He knew nothing else, and that was a blessed relief. He opened his eyes, looked at his own hands, holding on to her face, at his sleeves. Those damn sleeves. He released his hold on her, wrenching his jacket off, then working at the buttons of his shirt before he cast it to the ground, as well.

He hadn't been naked the last time they had been together. Hadn't felt those soft, sweet hands pressed up against his skin. Well, he needed it now. Needed it more than he needed his next breath. And as much as he wanted her to be marked by him, he wanted the same in return.

"Touch me," he demanded, his voice rough, a stranger's voice. He had learned to conduct himself with the manner of a gentleman. Had learned how to be suave, how to be smooth. How to cover up the monster inside by pretending to be a man of impeccable manners.

That was gone now. Cast to the ground with his clothes. Shattered like the glass he had broken against the wall. She already knew. She knew he wasn't that. That he never could be. Because he had shown her the truth. And she was still here. Said that she still wanted him. That she wanted to mean something to him.

Foolish girl. Inexperienced *girl*. She was everything that Rafe had said. Too soft. Too innocent. Too young.

But he was his father's son.

He pushed that thought to the side. He didn't want to examine it, not now. Couldn't. There was no possibility of thought, not now.

His father was dead anyway. And all the duplicity he had lived under, the extreme control, the calculated air of not caring at all…it was dead with him.

He didn't need it anymore.

He was king now. And he would do as he wished.

Inexperienced fingers brushed against his throat, moved down his chest. "Like you mean it," he growled, his lips against hers as he issued the rough command.

Her touch grew firmer, a bit more confident, and she dragged her fingertips down his washboard-flat stomach, to the waistband of his pants. "Yes," he said, the word rough and encouraging. "Like that."

She fumbled with his belt, and he clung to her as she pushed his pants down his thighs, taking his underwear with it. Leaving him completely naked standing in front of her. He watched her expression closely, tried to read her thoughts. It seemed as though she didn't know where to look, her dark eyes darting every which way as she examined his body.

"Have you never seen a naked man before?" Oh, he liked that. Liked this far too much. That he was corrupting her. That he was altering her in ways that were irreparable.

She shook her head. "I mean, in pictures."

"You've never undressed anyone. Never touched them. Never watched a man get hard because of you."

"No," she said. "Until you I had never been kissed."

Without being conscious of making the decision to do so, he found himself closing the distance between them. Growling as he took her into his arms and kissed her with all the uncivilized ferocity inside him.

She whimpered, her hands trapped between them, her palms resting on his chest. He was hard, throbbing and insistent against her body, and he knew that she could feel it. That she could feel just how affected he was by her. Just how much he wanted her. There was nothing civilized about this. But perhaps, just maybe, it was intimate. Because this was beyond him in a way that sexual desire had never been before.

This seemed to be tangled up in emotions in a way

that the need for release never had been. And it had been so from the moment he had taken her downstairs. When he had turned that table over, ripping the mask of the civilized prince off and letting the monster free. He had done that. In front of her. For her. Almost because of her. It was as though she reduced his control in ways that he could scarcely understand. Ways he certainly had not given permission for.

But strangely, she didn't seem to fear him. Didn't seem to fear that at all.

None of it made sense. That she would be the one to see that side of him, and yet not be afraid. That he would be the one to make her desire for the first time, when he was little more than a villain to her. The man who had ripped her from her life and dragged her into this. Into his domain.

But he didn't need sense. Not now.

"Now," he said, the words pulled from him, "you have been kissed."

She nodded, her kiss-swollen mouth soft, completely irresistible. And he leaned in to devour her again. It made no sense. That she was so receptive to this. To him. She should be disgusted by him. By the beast he had transformed into from the moment he had brought her back here to the palace. Or rather, from the moment he had revealed to her his intentions to take her back to his country.

But then he supposed that he should be disgusted by those things, as well. He wasn't.

He needed her. Needed her to rule his country in the best way. And more than that, now he wanted her. Wanted her in his life, in his bed. Wanted to be inside her. He would not deny himself.

And so, he could feel no guilt.

"Shall I teach you something?"

She looked up at him, her dark eyes luminous. Then she licked her full lips. "Yes. Teach me."

CHAPTER NINE

HIS HEART THUNDERED HARD, the blood firing through his veins hot and fast. He drew himself away from her. "Get down on your knees for me."

"The floor is hard," she said, her expression blank.

"That is true," he said, sweeping her up into his arms and crossing into his bedchamber. "We shall make it a bit more comfortable for you." He set her down in front of his bed, on the plush rug there. "Will this be a little more gentle on your royal knees?"

She blinked. "I..."

He cupped her chin, gazed into her eyes. "Kneel for me."

She complied, and he had to close his eyes, grit his teeth tight, to keep from coming then and there. She hadn't even touched him, but that simple act of compliance did more for him, did more to him, than a thousand illicit acts before had ever done.

"Take off that gown," he said, indicating the belt that held her robe closed. "I need to see you."

With shaking fingers, she undid the knot, let the silken fabric slide down her shoulders. And there she was, naked before him on her knees, her black hair tumbled over her shoulders, her sleek curves so enticing it took all his control to keep himself from lifting her back up into his arms and tumbling her onto the bed. To keep himself from burying himself inside her body again, and forgetting these little power games.

It occurred to him then, that if she was a virgin it was entirely possible she wasn't on any sort of birth control. He had taken her earlier without a condom, and he had no intention of using one this time, either. The idea of her pregnant, growing round with his child, only sent another shock of satisfaction through him. Then she would truly be bound to him. Forever.

She would not be able to leave. At least, not easily.

Ah, yes, your father's son.

He pushed the thought away again as he tangled his fingers in her hair and drew her toward his body. "Take me in your mouth," he said.

She looked up at him, uncertainty on her face. Perhaps she would reject him now. And perhaps, that was what he had been pushing her toward the entire time. Maybe that was what he wanted. To find her breaking point. To find the point at which she would become disgusted with him. For it had to exist. The fact that she had wanted him up until this point made no sense to him.

But, she did not pull away. Instead, she adjusted her position, lifting her hand and curling her fingers tentatively around his length. Then she leaned forward, her slick tongue darting out over the head of his arousal before she slowly took him inside her mouth.

And then, whatever he had imagined might happen, whatever guidance he thought he might give, was lost completely. There was nothing. His mind was blank and his body was on fire. She had absolutely no skill, was clearly not a woman who had ever touched a man before, and yet, it was the most erotic experience of his life.

Because it was just for him. As she had said. It was an intimacy. It was special. And that mattered. It mattered to a man who had never had such a thing before. A man who had never even known to hope for such a thing. She wanted him. She wanted him when she had wanted no other man before him.

She gave to him, generously. Gave him far more than he deserved. Those inexpert hands moving in rhythm with her lips and tongue as she lavished pleasure on him. Like a woman would do for her beloved, not for her kidnapper.

Not for a man who had commanded she get down on her knees and give him pleasure as though it was his due.

And then, he was no longer able to control himself. He tightened his fingers in her hair, pulled her head back. "Not like this," he said.

She rocked back on her heels, wobbling, and he caught her by the wrist, drawing her up against his body and claiming her mouth in a searing kiss.

He tumbled her backward onto the bed, groaning loudly as every inch of her naked body pressed against every inch of his. She was impossibly soft. Refined. Delicate. Lovely beyond measure.

Not for him.

And he felt… He felt like a criminal, getting away with the perfect crime. Which was—he discovered in that moment—an intensely satisfying feeling. To be in possession of something far too lovely, far too fine, for a man such as himself.

Perhaps other men might feel guilt.

He was not other men.

He was a monster. And she knew it. She wanted him still.

He groaned, lowering his head, taking one tightened nipple between his lips and sucking hard. She arched beneath him, a raw sound on her lips.

"Why do you want me?" he asked, the question surprising even himself, the words broken, torn from a part deep inside himself he had not known existed.

She looked at him, her dark eyes glazed, her expression full of confusion. "What?"

"You're too good. You're too soft. Why do you want me? It doesn't make any sense. You should be disgusted by me. Don't you understand that? I'm not a good man. You are a good girl. A very good girl. Soft and fragile. Protected. Protected from monsters like me. And yet, here you are, flinging yourself at me. It makes no sense."

"You asked for me," she said simply. "That's hardly me flinging myself at you."

He growled, taking her other nipple into his mouth and sucking on her until she gasped, until she arched against him again. And then, he released her. "There you are. Flinging yourself at me. And I need to know why."

"Did it ever occur to you that it's because you're everything I don't have? You're hard, where I'm soft. Dangerous. And I've been so protected, just like you said. And you are... Well, you're a bit bad, aren't you?"

She lifted her hand, touched the side of his face, and he turned, grazing her fingertip with his teeth. "Just a bit."

"Maybe I've been just a little bit too good, then. Maybe people need both, and I don't have any of my own. So, I need some of yours."

He rolled his hips against hers, felt slick, receptive

flesh beneath his unyielding hardness. "You need my darkness," he said.

She gasped, grabbing hold of his shoulders. "Yes."

He needed her light. Dammit, but he needed it. He wouldn't say it, not now. Couldn't say it. Because he was too consumed by the need to be inside her.

He pressed the head of his arousal against her entrance, slid inside inch by excruciating inch, torturing them both with that slow penetration. Belatedly, he was concerned that she might be sore. But he banished those concerns quickly enough. They paled in comparison to his need. His need to have her. To consume her in the way she was consuming him.

To have her light.

Darkness had been his constant companion, but right now he felt like he was standing on the edge of an abyss that was something beyond darkness. And only she was keeping him from falling completely.

He lost himself in her, burying his head against her neck as he chased that white-hot flame of release that he could only find in her. She grabbed hold of him, her fingernails digging into his skin, sounds of pleasure escaping her lips as she met his every thrust with one of her own.

Then she grabbed hold of his arms, a raw scream on her lips as she found her own release, her fingernails scraping a long trail down his forearms, all the way to the backs of his hands.

Marks from their encounter he wouldn't be able to hide. Disorder. Beautiful chaos. Found within his princess.

No. His queen.

And as she convulsed around him, he gave in to his

own release, flinging himself into the darkness. Because he knew that her light would be there when he reached the bottom.

The next few days passed in a flurry of activity. Briar scarcely saw Felipe in the light of day. But at night... Yes, she saw him at night. It didn't matter if she retreated to her own room, in that case, he would come and find her. He would find her, and he would make love to her for hours. Tapping into parts of herself she hadn't known existed.

But in the morning he was always gone. She had a suspicion that he never fell asleep with her. But rather, waited for her to drift off before succumbing himself.

It was times like this she felt her isolation keenly. The separation from her mother. If she was back in New York she could talk to Nell about this. Well, in some vague terms. She wouldn't go talking about everything they'd done in detail.

Her cheeks heated.

She wasn't quite sure how she had found herself in this situation. Bonding—physically at least—with the one man she should be most distant from.

When she tried to think of her life before Felipe, before coming here, it all seemed hazy. She supposed that wasn't a good sign. That for some reason these past weeks in Santa Milagro seemed bolder, more colorful, than the life before she had arrived here ever had.

She wondered if it was a trick, too. Some magical spell that Felipe had over her, even though she didn't believe in magic. Or rather, she hadn't before discovering she was a princess, and being spirited away to a foreign country by a prince that was far too handsome and far too wicked for anyone's good.

The very strange thing, though, was the fact that even though she had stepped into this life that was entirely unknown to her, had stepped into a role she had never imagined she might fulfill, she felt more herself than she ever had.

And it wasn't just because she had been happily creating art programs, working out grants and funding for various schools and cataloging the artwork long forgotten in the years since King Domenico had shuttered the museums.

Art had always made her feel alive, it was true, but it was more than that. Perhaps it was because Felipe seemed to require nothing from her other than that she stand by his side, and that she make herself available to him when he had need of her body.

Otherwise, he didn't want a particular sort of behavior from her. At least, not that he'd said. There was no pressure to present herself as something perfect or demure, not when she was in his presence. He liked to push her, and he seemed to enjoy when she provided him with a spirited response.

He certainly seemed to enjoy that in the bedroom. Thinking of it even now made her cheeks heat. She pressed the back of her hand against the side of her face, cool skin pressing against hot, making her shiver.

She was currently digging through a room in the back of the palace that seemed to have been abandoned. There were a great many artifacts that she wanted cataloged for the museums, and she was doing her best to sort through what she might have different appraisers come and have a look at, and what probably didn't have any value beyond the sentimental.

She had been doing a lot of historical research on her adopted country, trying to give context to all the various pieces she was discovering. It seemed that the poor nation had only experienced pockets of peace and prosperity, while mostly enduring long stretches of time with kings who were tyrants.

But the people had created beautiful things, even during their oppression. Almost most especially during their oppression.

In the palace she had mostly found personal collections. Portraits of past rulers and their relatives, pieces of the crown jewels, which had been stowed in a very secure vault. She would prefer they be on display than sitting in the back growing tarnished. Felipe seemed to have no opinion on the matter, so she was proceeding.

But in the rooms she had discovered only yesterday, it was different. The jewelry was not cataloged. It was not organized at all. And yet, it seemed to be of amazing quality. Millions of dollars in gems hidden in drawers. Beautiful paintings—still life and portraiture—hidden behind canvas. Hand-carved furniture beneath tarps.

She let out a long, slow breath and dragged one large tarp off a piece that sat against the back wall. Her eyes widened as she looked over the beautiful chest of drawers. Different pieces of wood were inlaid to create a representation of the mountainous skyline visible from the windows here in the tower.

Thin strips of gold separated the different pieces of wood, and she had a feeling it was real precious metal. She brushed her fingertips over the mountain peaks, over the sun, positioned in the upper left-hand corner of the bureau.

There was so much hidden beauty here. She couldn't help but think it might be a metaphor for the man she was going to marry. She paused for a moment, Felipe's handsome face swimming before her mind's eye.

He was such a puzzle. Charming and smooth one moment, then rough and out of control the next. He seemed to crave order, his appearance never anything but perfectly polished. And yet, the night his father had died he had laid everything in his wake to ruin, including her.

She felt her cheeks grow even hotter.

What a ruin it had been.

She took a fortifying breath and turned away from the chest of drawers, making her way across the room to a shapeless mass covered by canvas that she assumed was more framed paintings of various sizes. She dragged the canvas down and was rewarded with exactly that.

Landscapes in gilt-edged frames, a painting of fruit on a table. She enjoyed looking at this sort of thing. Because it proved that people had always been people. Compelled to capture the things around them. Compelled to take some kind of snapshot of their dinner for the world to see.

She carefully moved the first couple of paintings to the side and paused when she saw a portrait of a woman she had never seen before.

She was beautiful. Her black hair was swept up into an elegant bun, a golden crown on her head. Her crimson lips were curved into a half smile, one that seemed to contain wicked secrets. It reminded her of… Well, it reminded her of Felipe.

"What are you doing?"

She jumped, turning at the sound of Felipe's voice.

"Just exploring the rooms. I'm handling the art, as we discussed. Getting everything ready for the museums."

"That isn't art," he said, his voice taking on a strange tone.

She frowned. "It is a painting."

"It's my mother," he said, swift and hard.

She looked between him and the painting, speechless for a moment. "I…I can see it, actually."

He laughed. "Can you? I had thought that she and I bore no resemblance at all."

"You do," she said softly, not sure if it was the right thing to say. She couldn't read his mood. But then, she so rarely could. Trying to grasp Felipe's motivations or feelings was a lot like grabbing hold of a handful of sand. You could wrap your fingers around it for a moment, but then it all slid away into nothing.

"I would prefer if her things stayed here," he said.

"I didn't realize these were your mother's things."

He nodded once. "Yes. I think they have been in here untouched since the day she died."

"How old were you when she died?"

"Seven," he said, his tone detached now.

He crossed the room, making his way over to the window. It had bars over it, she had noticed earlier. She had thought very little of it then, because often windows that were so high up had a precaution of some kind in place so that no accidents happened. But for some reason, when he made his way there, when he pressed his fingers against the pane of glass, she wondered about them.

"She died here," he said, the words conversational.

"Was she… Was she ill?"

"In a manner of speaking. She was not well, that's certain."

She didn't say anything. If there was one thing she had learned about Felipe—and she had actually learned several—it was that if he wanted to say something he would eventually. And if he didn't, there was no amount of pushing that would get him to speak. There were other ways of dealing with him that were much more effective.

She took a moment to think about those ways, curling her fingers into fists as she imagined running her palms over his face. It would be rough now, because it was late in the day and dark stubble covered his jaw. She liked that. Liked when he was a bit unshaven. A bit feral.

She liked herself that way, too. Which was surprising, she had to admit.

He pressed his palms flat against the window, and she noticed his gaze dropped to his shirtsleeves. But she didn't speak then, either. She was collecting bits of information about him. Had been from the moment she had first laid eyes on him. He fascinated her. He called to something deep inside her that she couldn't explain, not really. Except that… He seemed to need her. And in every other situation in her life, she had needed those around her.

It wasn't a bad thing. It was just that she'd had to make sure she behaved, make sure she was good so that she could somehow make her presence worthwhile.

He had needed her so badly he had kidnapped her. And perhaps there was some kind of twisted logic trying to make that a good thing, but then again, maybe there was no logic at all.

Maybe it was all just a feeling, and that was okay, too.

"My cuffs weren't straight," he said.

She looked down at them now, saw deep scratches

extending from them now, lending him a look that was much less than civilized. Marks she'd left on him.

Marring his perfection. Making a mockery of hers.

She felt her face heat.

"What?" She found herself taking a step toward him.

"That was the start of it. I was never quite so orderly as my father would have me be. And he took it out on my mother. He demanded perfection that could never be achieved, particularly when he himself was creating chaos beneath the surface." Felipe tapped the glass then turned to face her. "I did not have a nanny. My father demanded that my mother care for me. Otherwise, what was her use?"

"How did you... How did you know about all of this? It doesn't seem right that a little boy should have heard all this going on between his parents."

He flashed that wicked smile, but there was no joy behind it. "That was never a concern. In fact, my father demanded I bear witness to all manner of indecency he subjected my mother to. If I misbehaved and she had to be slapped across the face, he wanted me to see it. And vice versa. He much preferred punishing her for my sins and me for hers. You see, it's so much more painful to watch your mother be struck because you spoke at a moment when you should not have than it is to be hit yourself." He looked back at the window. "She was always quite delicate. Like a bird. She escaped him. She flew away."

"She left him?" Briar asked, searching for clarity.

"She jumped out the window." He wrapped his knuckle against the glass. "That's why there are bars. I suppose my father didn't want to lose another family member in the same way. It would begin to reflect poorly on him."

He said the words so dispassionately, and Briar found

herself unable to breathe through the grief that exploded in her chest like a bomb. For his mother. For him. It seemed unfathomable that a small boy should lose his mother that way.

It seemed equally unfathomable that the woman in that portrait, the woman who had most certainly started out with as much spark in life as Felipe himself had, could have been reduced, tormented, until she felt that was her only escape.

"Felipe… I'm so sorry. I don't understand how he got away with that. With tormenting you both. What did the public think?"

"That it was an unfortunate accident. And of course, my father controlled the press. And no one would ever question what he had decreed."

"So no one knew. No one has ever known."

"No," he said, his tone hard. "We had to perform. For the nation, for the world, pretend that everything was okay when we were…when we were dying."

"What does that have to do with your cuffs?" she asked, her eyes falling to his sleeves. It was one of his many obsessive-looking mannerisms. He straightened his jacket and dress shirt constantly. She had seen him do it frequently from that first meeting.

"There was a state dinner. And my father chose to make that the issue of the day. My jacket sleeve was rolled up, or it was ill fitting, something." A crease appeared between his brows, and there was a measure of confusion in his dark gaze. She had a feeling that he remembered all of it. But that he preferred not to. That he preferred not to show himself and get all of the details right, because the details were so horrifying. "She tried to protect me. She brought me up here. And then my father followed us. And he poured all of his rage out on to her. He struck her. Again, and again. And then she… She went to the window. Then she was gone." He frowned. "I thought about following her. But I thought…I thought it could not be safe. And yet if my mother had just jumped out the window how could it be dangerous?"

His expression went blank. "All of that was answered for me later."

Her throat worked, but she could force no words to her lips.

Felipe regarded her closely. "Have I shocked you?"

She pressed her hand to her breast. "Of course you have. It's a terrible story. It should be shocking. You saw her… You saw your mother…"

"Yes," he said, that same detached tone she had heard from him many times prevalent now. "You can see now why I hate him so much. My father. There was nothing good about him, Briar. Nothing at all."

She nodded silently, swallowing hard.

She looked around the room, surprised that he was standing there. That he was standing so near that window. Had she endured something like that she doubted she would ever have been able to set foot in that room again.

"You're wondering how I'm in here," he said. "It's okay. I understand that it must seem strange to you. That it would seem strange to a great many people. People with a heart. But I cut mine out a long time ago, Briar. Because so long as you care it is dangerous. So long as you care you can be broken. My father tried to break me. He made me come in here. Told me that he would not allow for me to become softer, weak, would not allow me to build a shrine to a dead woman. So I learned." He looked around the space. "There is no real power in this room, anyway.

The real power was in plotting my father's downfall. The real power is in the fact that I now have control of this nation, and that I will right the wrongs that have been perpetuated against the people here. That I will write the history books and I will make sure my father's name is nothing but dirt. These are just four walls and a window. And anyway, the memories are with me wherever I go. I don't have to be here."

For the first time she truly believed he had a monster inside him. One made of memories; one comprised of the past horror he had lived through. And it most certainly drove his actions now. But it wasn't him. It wasn't. All she could do was picture a small boy who had been abandoned. Who had seen something no one should ever see.

Who had thought—naively—that he could perhaps fly out that same window to be with her, because in spite of all the indignity, in spite of all the abuse he had suffered, there was still trust inside him.

Trust that, she had no doubt, had been broken that day.

"You have a heart, Felipe," she said, the words strangled.

He frowned. "I don't. And why would I want one?"

She couldn't answer that. Except, she wanted him to understand that he wasn't broken. That his father didn't have the power to keep him in that blank, emotionless state he had been forced to assume to protect himself. The old man was dead, and he had no power. Not now. She wanted him to know that. Wanted him to understand.

Why? For you? Because you wish it were true?

She took a step back, those thoughts halting her words. Maybe. Maybe it was about her. And about what she wanted him to need from her. She swallowed hard, trying to catch her breath.

She shook her head. "I don't know."

She knew why she wanted him to have one. She wished that she didn't. She wished that she could ignore those thoughts. That she could deny the feelings rushing through her like a wave.

They shouldn't be possible. She should hate him. It shouldn't matter how terrible his childhood was; it shouldn't matter that he was broken, that there was no way he could possibly know how he was supposed to treat another person. He had kidnapped her. Was forcing her into marriage, or as good as forcing her, and she needed to remember that.

The trouble was that she did remember it. All too clearly.

And still...

Still, he made her body tremble. Still, he made her heart ache.

"I know what I need to do. For my country. I don't need a heart to accomplish those things." He closed the distance between them, brushing his knuckles over her cheekbone. "And have I not been kind to you?"

"You kidnapped me."

He waved his hand. "Have I not given you pleasure, *querida*? I believe that I have."

Pleasure isn't love. But she didn't say that. "Yes."

"I don't need a heart for such things. I only need this." He took hold of her hand and pressed it against the front of his slacks, over his hardening arousal.

She couldn't even be angry with him. That was the problem with Felipe.

"You're a very bad man," she said, no censure in her voice. "Do you know that?"

"Yes," he responded flippantly.

Then he kissed her as if to prove that didn't matter, either. And he proved it quite effectively.

Warmth flooded her body, flooded her heart. And there was simply no denying the truth. She loved him. She loved him and it mattered whether or not he had a heart because she needed him to have one so he could love her, too.

Later she might try and figure out if all of this was crazy. Might try and figure out why she felt this way. Right now she just clung to him. And felt a kind of certainty she had never experienced before. She didn't feel different. She didn't feel wrong. Like a misshapen piece shoved into the only available space.

But she wanted—so very much—to be all he needed, and she hoped that she could be. That she could be enough. That she could be...

This was her place. Here with him. Felipe was king, and in order to rule he would need a heart. Whether he believed it or not.

So she was determined to give it back to him.

CHAPTER TEN

FELIPE HADN'T INTENDED to confess all of that to Briar earlier. There was something about her. Something that got beneath his skin, got beneath his defenses. Well, he imagined it was the same thing that got beneath his pants. And frequently. Nothing to be too concerned about.

Neither were the headlines currently calling into question whether or not he was a sociopath. Considering he had broken with tradition and declined to give his father a funeral.

He didn't know why he would make a show of burying a dictator, and he had said as much to the media. Implications had been made—more than implications—that he was no different than the old man. That his lack of compassion—whether or not his father had deserved it—was indicative of a flaw in him, as well.

He could not be certain that wasn't the case. Nobody could be.

He strode out of the media room, tearing at the lapel mic he had been wearing. He was done giving interviews for the time being.

Another error, and he was damned if he could figure out what the hell was driving him. He'd spent years married to a facade, and he couldn't seem to find it now. He was damaging that which he sought to build with his inability to simply play the part he ought to.

Though he didn't know why he was surprised.

He destroyed. It was what he did. No matter whether he wanted to or not.

He was surprised to see Briar walking toward him, dressed as though she was prepared for an evening out. She was wearing a green silk dress that conformed to her curves, with a hemline that fell well above the knee, showing off those endless legs he was so fond of. Of course, he preferred it when they were wrapped around him.

He had half a mind to grab her and drag her to his room now. Whatever plans she had. She was his, after all. His queen. To do with as he pleased. If he wanted her, then she would have to cancel her plans and see to him. He paused, frowning. He wondered if that was the sort of thing his father thought about his mother. About anyone in his life. They were his. His to use as he pleased.

"I was looking for you," she said, her bright smile at odds with the thoughts currently chasing around his head.

"Were you?"

"Yes. I thought we might go out for dinner."

"If you haven't seen the headlines today I have created something of a scandal. Perhaps it would be best if we stayed in."

She looked stubborn. Mutinous. She was quite difficult to argue within that state, he had learned. "I have seen the headlines. People are calling your character into question, and it isn't fair. Of course you shouldn't have thrown a large public funeral for your father. It would have been a farce. I understand that. And that's the entire point of the two of us going out. You want me because you needed my help in softening your image. Well, let me do that."

"I'm not sure I understand."

"We will ostentatiously make an appearance together going for dinner. The entire nation will see that whatever the press says I'm on your side. Whatever anyone says, I stand with you."

Her words rang with the kind of conviction he didn't deserve.

"I'm not certain it will accomplish anything."

Her dark brows lowered. "I am," she said, her tone every inch that of a queen.

"You've grown very comfortable with your new role."

She tossed her head back, her curls bouncing with the movement. "Would you prefer that I remain uncomfortable with it? I think it would be much more effective for both of us if I were comfortable. And I think it would be best for you if you complied with my plan."

"Answer me this, my queen. Are you kidnapping me?"

A smile curved her lips. "Yes."

"Then I suppose I have no option but to comply."

The press was waiting outside the gates to the palace, and when the limousine he and Briar were riding in exited the gates they were nearly mobbed. Briar held on tightly to his arm, glaring out the window. "I would have us present a united front," she said, her tone stiff. "Because I believe that what you did was right. You did it for you, and for your mother. And whether or not anyone else ever understands the full circumstances... I do."

Those simple words caused a strange shift in his chest, and he didn't pause to examine them. Her soft fingertips were drifting down past his arm, over his thigh.

"Careful," he said, his tone full of warning. "The flash photography may make it so they can get shots through the window."

He didn't know how effective the tinted glass would be against those high-powered bulbs.

"I don't care," she said. "Like I said. Let them see that I stand with you. That you're mine."

"I'm going to have the car drop us off a little way from our destination." She tapped on the glass, and the driver lowered the divider. "Leave us just near the university," she commanded.

He quite liked seeing her like this. So at ease with her position. So perfectly at ease in his life. It made him feel much less like questioning himself. Much less like he might be the villain, as he was worried he might have been a few moments earlier.

"There are no restaurants over by the university," he said, reaching out and brushing some of her hair from her face. "Unless you intend to have us eat fast food."

"I'm not opposed to a French fry, Felipe. But that isn't what I have in mind for us tonight. I have a plan. But we need to make sure we're seen a little bit more before we get down to it."

He wrapped his arm around her, burying his face in her hair, his lips touching the shell of her ear. "I'm more than happy to get down to it. We don't even need to have dinner."

"Later," she said, her dark eyes burning with promise. "I promise later."

For some reason, those words caught hold of something in his chest. Sparked a memory. A feeling. One of loss. The kind of loss he hadn't truly allowed himself to feel since he was seven years old.

He caught hold of her chin, held her face steady. "Is that a promise? A real promise? One you won't break."

"Have I ever denied you my body?"

She had not. And still, he couldn't quite credit why that was. "No."

"Then trust me."

He couldn't remember the last time someone had asked him to trust them. Moreover, he couldn't remember the last time he had actually trusted someone. He wanted to. He found that he very much wanted to.

"I will hold that in reserve," he said finally.

The car pulled up to the university, and he and Briar got out, Briar taking hold of his hand as though it was the most natural thing on earth. He couldn't remember the last time anyone had asked him to trust them, and he couldn't remember the last time he had held a woman's hand, either. Had he ever? He had lovers from time to time, fairly frequently, in truth. But their interaction was confined to the bedroom. That meant there was no reason for them to ever walk around with their fingers laced together.

This touch was not... Well, it wasn't sexual. And in his life that meant it was pointless. Except it didn't feel pointless. It felt very much like something essential. Felt very much like air. He couldn't explain it even if he wanted to. He found he didn't. He found he just wanted to enjoy the feeling of her soft skin against his.

It only took him a moment to realize she was taking him to the museum.

"Are you subjecting me to a gala?" He looked at her sideways. "Because I must warn you I am not in the temperament required for a gala."

She narrowed her eyes. "What temperament is required for a gala?"

"Something much more docile than I'm capable of."

She made a dismissive sound. "You don't need to be docile." She tugged on his hand, drawing him toward the entrance. "Of course, this is our own private gala. And our own private dinner."

"I thought the point of coming out was to be seen?"

She pushed open the museum door. "It is. Well, it was. But we were seen as much as I intend for us to be tonight."

She looked at him, her expression slightly mischievous. It made his heart beat faster, made his groin tighten. She grabbed hold of the door and pulled it shut, and impish grin tugging at the corners of her mouth.

"If I didn't know any better I would say you had lured me here to seduce me," he said. He disliked his own tone. It was far too dry, far too insincere, when there was absolutely nothing insincere about Briar. Or this act. He closed some of the distance between them, pressing his hand to her cheek. "That was not a complaint, mind you."

She lifted her own hand, covered his with it. "I didn't take it as one."

"You set dinner out for us?" he asked, doing his best to keep himself from poking at her. From twisting the conversation into something overly light and familiar.

"Well, people who work for you set dinner out for us. I don't know how to cook." She cleared her throat. "But I didn't bring you here to try and impress you with the food."

She turned the lights on, and the entire antechamber lit up, the antique chandelier that hung in the entry blazing into glory. Everything was clean. A statue placed just at the foot of the staircase well lit, showcasing the marble, and the incredible skill of the artist.

"It's nearly ready," she said, nearly bursting with excitement. "I wanted you to see this. I wanted you to see what you have made it possible for your people to have." She turned a circle, her arms spread wide. "All of this history. All of this beauty. It's part of the fabric of this country and it's been hidden from them for so long. But now it won't be. Now everyone can come and see this. Everyone can experience this."

He was humbled. Not so much by the art, not even by the work she had put in here. But by her exuberance for it. The happiness that she felt. Why should she be happy? Why should she be happy here with him? And excited for this task he had assigned to her as something she should be grateful for when he had uprooted her from her home? He didn't understand it. He didn't understand her.

And he didn't understand the kind of unfettered joy she seemed to radiate.

Moreover, he didn't understand the passion that she had for art. For something that seemed to exist for no other reason other than to be beautiful. For no other reason than to be looked at. It was a frivolous beauty, and he had never found much beauty in life at all. But she seemed to relish it. Seemed to worship it almost.

He wondered what it must be like to care like that. To feel like that. To live for something beyond the grim march to a goal.

"Come this way," she said. "They've set a table for us in my favorite wing."

"What is your favorite wing?" he asked, finding that he was unable to wait for the answer to that question to be revealed naturally.

She paused. "Impressionists." She smiled, her expression pretty, clearly pleased with the fact that he had asked.

"Why?" he persisted as he followed her down a long corridor, and into a large, open showroom with paintings mounted on each wall. A table was set in the middle with plates covered by trays. There were no candles, and he found that didn't surprise him.

She wouldn't expose her beloved art to anything that might burn it.

She was clearly puzzled by his question. "I don't know. I mean, I do know. But it's hard to put into words. It speaks to my soul in a way that…resonates beyond language."

Those words put him in the mind of something that resonated in him. It brought to mind images of his hands on her skin. The contrast of his fingers gliding over her dark beauty, an erotic kick to the gut that shocked him every time. The feel of her…of being over her, in her… there was nothing on earth like it.

He'd had sex more times than he could count, with more women than he cared to count. This reached beyond that. He imagined she would not enjoy him comparing their physical relationship to the art she loved so much. But he had no other frame of reference.

"It's not as detailed as some styles," she continued. "It's not perfect. There's something almost…messy about it when you look up close. Chaotic. And yet, when you stand back and you look at the whole picture it creates something beautiful."

"Why does that appeal to you so? You seem like nothing more than perfection to me, Princess."

She tilted her head to the side, her expression full of speculation. "I suppose it's because I like to think that…

if someday I should ever become…something other than what I have tried to be, then somebody would look at me and try to see the beauty. That somebody would step back and see who I am as a whole. And find me lovely."

"You could never be anything less than beautiful," he said, his voice rough. "It would be impossible."

"You're talking about physical appearance. And it isn't that I don't appreciate that," she said, looking down. "It's just that… That isn't all there is. And it isn't really my primary concern. But I always felt that…my parents—the parents I was raised with, not the king and queen—were older when they took me in. And they loved me. They have always behaved as though I was their own. But they never had any children before me. I was the first. And I could tell that though I brought them joy I brought them an equal measure of anxiety. And I did my very best to transcend that. To make up for it. To be worth the sacrifice. Because before I came into their lives they had so much less responsibility. So much less worry. I always felt like I had to do something to offset that. To be the girl that was worth that sacrifice."

"That is quite the feat. For a young girl to attempt to be perfect. To try and justify your existence. A child should never have to do that." His existence had always had purpose, for he was his father's heir. And then in end, his purpose—no matter that it had been a secret one—had been to right the wrongs his father had committed against his people.

But she had wondered. Had wondered what she should do to make herself worthwhile, when she should have known all along she had a kingdom depending on her. When she should have known she had parents in the US and in Verloren who cared for her.

She had not. It had all been hidden from her.

He despised his role in that. The role his family had played in that. His father. But then, that was nothing new. His father ruining lives. Him ruining lives.

"I can't remember any different," she said, her tone soft. "It has always been that way for me. For as long as I can remember."

"Except, you *can* imagine different. If not, you wouldn't like these paintings quite so much."

"Perhaps not."

She stopped talking then, directing him toward the table that was set for two, any staff who might have placed the settings now conspicuously absent.

"If I didn't know any better I would think you were trying to seduce me," he said.

She smiled, her earlier sadness vanishing. "I am," she said, her tone light, cheerful, as she picked up a glass of wine and lifted it to her lips.

"You should know that you don't need to go to so much effort. In fact, you don't need to go to any effort at all. Showing up is about all it takes."

Her expression changed, and suddenly, she looked slightly wistful. "Is that true of me? Or is it true of all women that you...that you do this with?"

"I have never done this with another woman. Oh, of course I have had lovers, Briar. But I have never...I have never *associated* with a woman outside the bedroom."

"Never?"

He shrugged. "You have never had a relationship, either. Why is it so alarming that I haven't?"

"Well, I had never had a sexual relationship with anyone, either. It seems like one should...lead to the other. So yes, *alarming* is the word I would use. That you've been physically intimate with someone and never..."

"You use the word *intimate* to describe sex often, but to me seeking physical release with someone was nothing." He could see by her expression that those words had hurt her. "In the past," he said, softening his tone, not quite sure why he felt the impulse to do so, only knowing that he did not like that he had been responsible for putting that desolate expression on her beautiful face.

"So I'm different?" She sounded so hopeful, and he wondered why on earth she would waste her hope on him.

"It is so important to you to be different." Suddenly the words that she had spoken when they had walked in and spoken of the Impressionists clicked together with these. And he understood. More than that, he cared. Whatever that meant.

"It is not so unusual that a woman would want to be special to her lover." She slid her wineglass back and forth, her focus on the dark liquid.

"Yes, but that is the thing." He pressed his hand over hers, stopping the nervous movement. "You are more than my lover. You are to be my wife. You have more power, more position, in my life than any woman ever has."

She smiled, clearly pleased by that. And he was happy that he had made her smile. He couldn't recall ever taking such pleasure in someone else's happiness before. Except... Dimly, in the recesses of his mind he could remember trying to make his mother happy when his father had just been being an ogre. Could remember trying to make her smile in spite of the abuses they had both suffered.

As if the antics of a little boy could heal the actions of a madman.

They hadn't. Clearly. If they could have, his mother would still be here. She wouldn't have leaped out a window rather than continue to suffer at the hands of his father. Rather than continue to try to deal with a little boy who would always make that situation untenable. Order. His father had wanted order and he hadn't been able to give her that much. Hadn't realized that if he'd simply…

He tugged on his cuffs.

No, he had never been enough. Not when it counted.

Much like then, that smile on Briar's face probably didn't extend as far down as it needed to go. Much like then, he imagined he would be found wanting. But Briar would be queen. And she would have her art. She would have this place. And they had their passion. He would be faithful to her. He remembered then that he had never told her so.

"I will not repeat the sins of my father," he said.

"Which sins?"

"I will be faithful to you."

She blinked. "I didn't realize that was ever up for debate," she said.

"I had not promised you fidelity."

She frowned. "I thought that was a given with marriage. Unless you're an awful person. Like your father."

"I kidnapped you," he said simply. "At what point did you begin thinking I was a decent man?"

"You've never hurt me. I understand why you did what you did," she said, looking down at where his hand was still pressed over the top of hers. "I understand why you need my help. And I'm honestly happy to give it."

Suddenly, he didn't like that. Didn't like that she was offering him help. That she was putting herself forward as another mark of her perfection. He didn't want that.

Perversely, he wanted her to be with him because she wanted to be.

There was no logic in that. To want that from the woman he had forced to accept his proposal.

Offer her freedom. See what she does.

No. He could not do that. She couldn't have her freedom. She could not be given that opportunity. Because he needed her. He did. Whatever he wanted, he would have to be content with what they had.

There was no reason he should not be. He had everything he wanted.

He would not be everything she wanted, that was inescapable. For this was not the life she had chosen for herself. And why did he care about that at all? Only a few weeks ago he would not have. He had not. He had kidnapped her from a hospital for God's sake.

And now, sitting here in this quiet museum with her, his hand pressed over the top of her knuckles, he burned. Ached. Wanted more than he should. Wanted things that conflicted with his goals.

"If you're offering martyrdom to me—the kind of martyrdom that you gave your parents—then I will state for the record that I don't want it."

"You want me to help with your cause. To comply with your wishes. You never cared why I was giving it before. You threatened me, in fact, if I didn't give it. How can it not be martyrdom?"

"You're offering me your help, saying that you understand, looking at me with those angelic eyes of yours... Pity. You look at me like I'm a dog you *pity*. I may have taken that from my queen, but not from my lover."

"I'm trying to help. I'm trying to do what's expected of me. I'm trying to find my place here. This is for me as much as it is for you. I never knew where I fit. All my life I didn't know. I felt wrong. I knew I had come from somewhere else. I knew that. There were people all around me who can trace their lineage back to the May-flower and I couldn't trace mine back to my parents. I couldn't remember the first four years of my life. Well, apparently, I was born to be royalty. So here I am. And I'm trying my very best. To make this mine. To make a place for myself. And you're accusing me of playing at empty perfection."

He didn't know why he was pressing this. Didn't know why he cared at all. Mostly, he didn't know why there was a howling, wrenching pain in his chest when he thought of her simply lying back and doing her duty for him.

He wanted to mess her up. Mess them both up.

"I have pushed you every step of the way," he said. "And you... You seem completely and utterly compelled to prove your worth. Why should I think it's anything different?"

She stood, pushing her chair back, her dark gaze level with his. "What do you need? You need some sort of sym-bol that I'm here on my own? That I'm making choices? That this isn't about me simply complying quietly?"

She reached behind her back, and he heard the soft sound of a zipper. Then she stepped out of her dress. The shimmering fabric fell to her hips, and she pushed it down all the way to the floor.

"When have I ever complied quietly when it comes to you, Felipe?" She unhooked her bra, pushed it down her arms and then sent her panties along the same path, until she was standing naked before him wearing noth-ing more than a pair of high heels that made her impos-sibly long legs seem all that much longer. "I screamed and shouted at you as you kidnapped me from the hospital. I refused you until…"

"Perhaps only until you found that there was enough here to make compliance worth it." He was pushing. Pushing hard. And he wanted to see how hard she would push back.

She moved to him, and he stayed seated in his chair, allowed her to curl her fingers around the back of it, to lean over him, her breasts hovering temptingly close to his lips. "Do you think I'm weak? Do you think I'm frightened of you?"

"I think you should be." He lifted his hand and touched her chin. "I ruin people." Then he tilted his face up and scraped his teeth along the underside of her chin. "If you think that by playing perfect you can somehow outrun that fate, then I have news for you."

"Perhaps you should ruin me. Perhaps…we all need to be a little bit ruined. Like one of my paintings."

It so closely echoed his earlier thoughts that it blanked his mind for a moment. But she seemed to be able to read him. That she seemed to…understand him. And that she had not run in the other direction.

He placed his hands on her shoulder blades then slid his fingertips down the elegant line of her spine, to the perfect curve of her ass. He was already so hard he hurt, his arousal pressing against the front of his slacks.

He reached up then, forking his fingers in her hair, curling his fingers around the massive curls and tugging her head back as he pulled her more firmly onto his lap, rolling his hips upward, well aware that he was rubbing his hardness against that place she was already wet and needy for him. She was undoing him, he couldn't deny it. But he would see her undone, as well.

If he was going to break, she would break along with him. They would break together.

He leaned forward, pressing a kiss to the pounding pulse at the base of her neck, then tracing a trail up to her jaw with the tip of his tongue, along upward to her lips, where he claimed her fiercely, with no delicacy at all.

She gasped, her fingers working clumsily on the front of his shirt, tearing at his tie, at the buttons there. And then she gave up, hands moving to his belt buckle, tugging at the fabric until she freed his erection. She curled her delicate fingers around him, her hand small and dark, soft, over that rock-hard arousal, the contrast an aphrodisiac that nearly sent him over the edge.

"Show me," he said, planting his hands on her hips, holding her steady over him. "Show me how much you want me."

Keeping her hand on him, she tilted her hips forward and guided him toward her slick entrance, placing him there, slowly lowering herself onto him. His breath hissed through his teeth and he let his head fall back, let himself get lost in all that tight, glorious heat.

It was tempting to close his eyes, to shut everything out except for that sensation. But he forced himself to keep them open, so that he could look at her. So that he could watch the glorious bounce of her breasts as she rocked herself up and down over him.

He looked beyond her shoulders, at all the art that was mounted on the walls. She rivaled all of it. Made these masterworks as finger paintings in his eyes. He slipped his hands up to her narrow waist, holding her hard as she moved.

Then he leaned forward, capturing one of her nipples with his mouth, sucking it in deep. She let out a low, hoarse sound and her pleasure exploded all around him. She didn't close her eyes; instead, she looked deep into his, her expression one of fierce intensity and concentration.

This was just for him. She had never even kissed another man before him. She had certainly never come for another man. And here he was, buried deep inside her, wringing out every last bit of her pleasure, taking it on as his own. He didn't deserve it. Didn't deserve her. And yet, he couldn't stop. Couldn't fathom not taking this. Not taking her.

She tossed her head back at the last moment, planting her hands on his shoulders as she ground her hips against his, extracting each and every possible wave of pleasure from him, her climax a fierce and wild thing he didn't deserve in the least.

When she righted herself, when she looked at him again, he was the one who had to look away. He was undone by that emotion in her eyes. A vulnerability that ran beneath the strength he had just seen. The kind of vulnerability a man like him could exploit. A softness he could so easily destroy.

The sort of thing he would do well to be gentle with. And yet he found himself tightening his hold on her. Driving himself up inside her as he chased his own release. As he allowed that white-hot wave to wash over him, to steal every thought, every doubt, from his mind. At the moment he was inside Briar. And she was all around him. Her soft skin, her delicate scent, everything that she was filling him, consuming him.

A soft smile curved her lips, an expression of wonder on her face. She cupped his head in her hands, sliding her thumbs along the line of his jaw as she gazed down at him. No one had ever looked at him like this before. As if he were a thing they had never before seen. As if he were something magic.

He should explain to her that he was not magic. He was not unique. And he would only destroy her.

Instead, he found himself reaching up, wrapping his hands around her wrists, pulling her more firmly against him, forcing her to wrap her arms around his neck. His lips pressed against hers, and when he spoke it was nearly a growl. "We will be married next week. Then you will truly be mine."

Her lashes fluttered, a slight hint of shock visible in those dark eyes. But then she smiled. "I'm glad."

She shouldn't be. And he had a feeling in time she wouldn't be. But self-sacrifice was for another man, a better man. And if he was a man capable of those things, perhaps he would be worthy of her.

And so it was an impossible situation. For *her*.

As for him, he would have what he wanted.

The dragon inside him was content. And the man... Well, the man wanted her already, all over again. As though she had opened up a need inside him that he'd never before known existed. One he was afraid would never entirely be satisfied again.

Good thing they would have a lifetime for him to try and exhaust it.

Then she did something he could not have anticipated. She leaned forward, kissing him softly, sweetly. And then she spoke.

"I love you."

CHAPTER ELEVEN

SHE HADN'T INTENDED to say that out loud. But now that she had she couldn't regret it. Wouldn't regret it. How could she? She had fallen in love, for the first time in her life. With this wild, untamable man who had suffered unimaginable loss. Who had endured unimaginable pain. And she just wanted to give to him. She wanted him to feel everything that she did. This bright, intense emotion in her chest that made it difficult for her to breathe, that made her want to cry and laugh and shout all at the same time.

She felt brave, and she felt frightened. She felt more than she had ever felt in her life. And she felt everything. How could she not share it?

"I wasn't looking for that," he said, his voice flat. Hands planted on her hips, he removed her from his lap, and she felt the loss of him keenly, leaving her body and her heart feeling cold. She wrapped her arms around herself, raised goose bumps covering her arms.

"That's all right. I offered it anyway."

"Why? Because it makes you feel better about accepting my proposal? Make no mistake, Princess. It is not a proposal, but a demand. You do not have to offer anything in return. Unless it's simply to salve your own conscience." He narrowed his dark eyes. "Is that the issue? You're disturbed by the fact that you enjoy the body of a man you don't love? So you had to manufacture emotions in order to justify your orgasm?"

Heat seared her cheeks, wiping out the cold sensation that had rocked her only moments earlier. "I don't feel the need to justify any orgasm I've had with you," she said, not quite sure where her boldness was coming from. "I wanted you, and I was never ashamed of that, regardless of the emotions involved. I had never wanted a man before, and I can't think of a better reason to be with someone and wanting them the way that I wanted you. That isn't why I love you."

A cold, cruel smile quirked the side of his mouth. "Go on, then. Enumerate the reasons you find me emotionally irresistible. I can provide you with several reasons why you find me physically irresistible, as I'm not a modest man, neither am I unaware of the charms that I present to women. So if any of it has to do with my body I shall have to sadly inform you that your reasoning is neither original nor rooted in finer feelings. That is lust, my darling, and nothing more."

She recognized this. This kind of bitter banter that played at being light but was designed to cut and wound, was designed to keep the target at a distance. He had done it from the beginning, and only recently had he made an effort to connect with her in ways that went deeper than this. But he was retreating.

He was also misjudging her. Sadly for him, she did know him. More than just his body, and she saw this for exactly what it was.

She wanted to fix it. Wanted to find a way to be what he needed. To be…

She wanted so much to keep him. To have his heart and not just his body. To be the wife he didn't know he wanted.

She wanted to be perfect for him.

"You are strong," she said. "Determined. You believe in doing what's right, even if you have to do the wrong things to accomplish it. Your moral code might not be the same as what the rest of the world would call good, but you have one. And it is strong."

He laughed. "Yes. So very strong. In that I do everything within my power to establish myself as a better ruler than my father, to ensure that my place in the history books is superior to his. To create a country richer in resources and wealth, to forge better alliances with neighboring nations. If you imagine me to be altruistic, I will have to disappoint you on that score. I'm simply much less base than my father was, much smarter about how I might wield my power."

"It suits you to say that, and I can guess at why that might be. But that isn't the beginning and end of it. I know it, whether you do or not."

"You suppose that you know my motivations better than I do?"

"Yes. Because I think you're hiding from your motivations. I think you hide from a great many things, and I can't blame you. You were forced into hiding as a child because of the way that your father treated you."

He laughed, hard and flat. "Oh, no, Princess, do not make the mistake of imagining that I am some little boy trapped inside a man's body, still cowering in fear. That little boy was obliterated long ago. I did learn how to survive, and it was by hardening myself. I might not have thrown myself out the window that day, but my mother took a piece of me with her, and I gladly surrendered it. Love. I am not capable of it, not anymore. And I don't want to be. So whatever you say, whatever you feel you must force yourself to feel for me… Understand that I cannot return it. I will gladly take your body, Briar, for I am not a good man, and I'm not a soft man. All that I can give you in return is pleasure."

Once again, she found herself standing before him naked while he was clothed. Vulnerable while he seemed impenetrable. But she knew that wasn't the case. Knew that it was all an illusion. She was naked because she was strong. It takes a great amount of strength to stand before somebody without any covering, not on her body, not on her soul.

He, on the other hand, was desperately concealing all that he was. Was trying so hard to protect himself with that barrier that he had placed between them. And she could understand it in a great many ways. Sometimes she wondered if she had held herself apart from friends, from men, if she had set about to working so hard on this idea of perfection and earning her place because she was afraid of loss. Because even though she couldn't remember her life before going to live with her parents in New York, that feeling, that emptiness, lived inside her. A memory that didn't reside in her brain, but in her heart.

"I don't believe that," she said, her tone muted. "I don't believe that it's all you have inside you. Maybe it's all you feel you can give right now, but I don't think it's all we'll have forever. And I can wait. I can wait until you love me."

"I won't," he said, the words clipped, hard. "I cannot."

Her throat tightened, tears stinging her eyes. "Then I suppose I'll have to love you enough for both of us."

"You're still going to marry me?"

She nodded. "Of course I am. We didn't start here because of love. Why should it end because of a lack of it?"

It was easy to say, but she felt...devastated. A part of her destroyed that she would have said didn't exist. Because how could she hope for Felipe to love her? How had they gotten here? It still mystified her in some ways.

That she had gone from being terrified of him, from hating him, to needing him more than she needed her next breath. But he was... He was the most extraordinary man. So strong. And most definitely not loved enough.

Right then she felt a surge of anger—not at his father, but at his mother. For leaving him. How dared she? Why couldn't she have stayed for him? Shouldn't love have been enough to make her stay and protect that little boy? Or try to find a way to escape, but with him?

She would stay. No matter what he said he could give. Because she did believe that in the end he would find more for her. That they would have more. No one had stayed for him; no one had ever truly demonstrated their love for him. Well, she would be the first one. Even if it hurt.

She would be what he needed, because it was what she needed.

"Very pragmatic," he said, his tone as opaque as his expression.

"It's not, actually," she said. "It's just... Perhaps a bit blindly hopeful. But I feel like one of us needs to be, Felipe. You want your country to have beauty. You want it to be filled with the kind of light it's been missing... Well, I think one of us needs to believe in it in order for that to be accomplished, don't you?"

He reached out, gripping the back of her neck, drawing her to him, kissing her fiercely. "You're welcome to hope for that, Briar. You're welcome to believe in it. But don't be surprised when all you're met with is darkness."

She had difficulty talking to Felipe over the next few days. But at night he remained as passionate as ever. He announced the wedding to the media that very next day, and Briar's head was spinning with how quickly an elaborate event could come together when you had unlimited wealth and power.

She had a wedding dress fitted to her in record time, the design altered so that it was unique only to her. A menu had been planned, elaborate cakes conceptualized. Somehow, a massive guest list had been amassed, with RSVPs coming in fast. If anyone had something else to do, they had certainly rearranged their schedules quickly enough.

The wedding of Prince Felipe Carrión de la Viña Cortez to the long-lost Princess Talia was definitely a worldwide curiosity. The kind of event that everyone wanted to be included in.

For her part, Briar felt numb. Her parents—both sets—had been invited to the wedding and she felt strange and had trepidations about seeing both of them. Mostly because she had a feeling they would all try to talk her into calling it off. Even though everyone involved knew that was something that couldn't be afforded. Plus, at this point, she didn't want it called off.

Regardless of what he had said to her the other day, she still loved him. In fact, watching him put this wedding together, watching him contend with matters of the state, with his new position, only made her love him more.

The morning of the wedding dawned bright and clear,

the preparations being made about the palace awe-inspiring as far as Briar was concerned. But she didn't have a chance to observe the decorating process to the degree that she wanted to, because she was accosted by her stylists early in the day and subjected to a beauty regimen that left her feeling like she had run a marathon.

She was scraped, scrubbed, plucked and waxed, left so that she was glowing to an almost supernatural degree. Her hair was tamed into an elaborate up-do, some kind of powder that left her glowing brushed over her face, her lips done in a deep cherry color, her fingernails painted to match.

Large gold earrings with matching gems weighed down her ears, and a crown was placed on top of her head, heavy and unfamiliar.

The gown had a fitted bodice, the skirt voluminous, great folds of white, heavy satin fashioned into pleats, falling all the way to the ground, and trailing behind her in a dramatic train.

She had to admit, she certainly looked like a princess bride. She only hoped that she would be the bride of Felipe's dreams. She clasped her hands in front of her, twisting her fingers. Maybe she was foolish; he certainly thought that she was. To hope that this could ever be more than a bloodless transaction, necessary for him to gain the sort of reputation in the world that he coveted.

But she had to believe it. Someone had to believe in them. Believe in him. She did. And she would do it until... Until he left her no other choice.

She was supposed to marry him, after all. For better or worse. Until death did them part.

Nerves twisted low in her belly and she pressed her

palm up against herself, taking a long, slow breath out, hoping that she would find some sense of calm. Of peace.

Then the door to her bedchamber opened, and her eyes clashed with Felipe's. There was no calm to be had there. Just a sort of dark excitement that hit her all at once like a freight train. There was nothing that could prepare her for the impact, not even after weeks of being his lover.

She wondered if he would ever become commonplace, this man who had the face of a fallen angel and the body of a Greek god, and a soul that had every dark thing imaginable crammed into it, until that gorgeous, mortal frame—for however perfectly he was formed, he was mortal—seemed as though it might crack from the force of it.

How could a man such as that ever be common? How could he ever fail to make her feel things? Everything.

How could she ever give up on him? It was inconceivable. Unfathomable.

"You're not supposed to see me before the wedding," she said.

He laughed, flinging himself down onto an armchair. "Because the beginning of our relationship was so auspicious and traditional you're going to concern yourself with superstition now?"

She lifted a bare shoulder. "I suppose at this point we are somewhat bulletproof."

His expression turned dark. "Nothing is. Are you prepared for this?"

"I don't know. Can anyone really prepare for something they've never done before? Lifelong commitment and all of that."

"And if you marry me," he said, his tone uncompromising, "it will be a lifelong commitment."

She couldn't quite place the thread running underneath those words, hard and angry-sounding though they were. There was something else. But with Felipe there was always something else. There had been from the first moment she had met him. He covered it all up with that world-weary cynicism of his, with that brittle banter designed to make the recipient die of a thousand small cuts.

But there was more. He was just so very desperate to hide it. She wanted to uncover it. But that probably would be bad luck before their wedding. If she did that, he could well and truly crack. Spilling all the dark things out into the room. She wasn't afraid of that. She knew the day would come eventually.

She just thought that maybe…just maybe…it wouldn't happen right before they took their vows. Anyway, while she wasn't afraid of it, she had a feeling that he might be.

"I know that, Felipe. If you recall, I love you, so it isn't really going to be a great burden for me to bind myself to you for the rest of my life. Actually, when you love someone you consider that something of a goal."

He flinched when she spoke those words, as though she had struck him. "So you say," he responded.

"Did you want me to throw myself on the ground and scream about how I shan't marry you, because you're a brute and I cannot possibly fathom a future with you? It would be both embarrassing and disingenuous. Plus, I would mess up my hair."

"It would make more sense than this," he said, standing, waving his arm at her standing there in her wedding gown. "You are far too serene. Far too accepting of your fate."

"You say fate, I say destiny."

"They end in the same place, Princess," he said, his

tone brittle. "Either way, I expected a bit more in the way of hysterics on this day of days."

"Why? Haven't I demonstrated to you over the past weeks that I'm here with you? You threw everyone out of that ballroom, Felipe. You told everyone to leave, and yet I remained. You told me about your mother, we stood together. I showed you my artwork. I gave you my body. I have continued to do so every night in the days since, and I will do it every night after. You're the only one who seems to be perturbed by the impending wedding. The one that you literally crossed the world and committed a crime to make happen."

He scowled, his dark mood rolling off him in waves. "I am not. What surprises me is your lack of emotion." He prowled across the room, stopping in front of her. "You should feel something. You should do something."

"I professed my love. It's really not my fault you don't acknowledge that as an emotion, Felipe. But there are other emotions beyond rage. Beyond grief. Beyond hatred. They are no less valid."

"Yes, you seem overjoyed."

She blinked, the corners of her lips tugging down. "I'm not sure that I am overjoyed," she said honestly. "I'm slightly afraid. Of how it will be between us. Of what might happen along the way. Of the ways in which you might hurt me. But I love you. And I've made my decision. I'm not going to pretend. I'm not going to paste a smile onto my face when my feelings are more complicated than that."

That seemed to light a match on the gasoline of his anger. "So you admit you are not thrilled to marry me. All your posturing about love and forever was simply that. Why don't you fight against it? Why don't you do something other than stand there grimly prepared to do your duty? Lying to both of us about how you feel so you can try to justify what's about to occur? Why do you have to be so damned perfect all the time?" He wrapped his arm around her waist, pulling her hard against his chest.

"I'm not," she said, her voice strangled. "I'm not. And I don't know what I have to do to show you that that isn't what this is. Stripping naked in a museum wasn't enough? Telling you about how hard I worked all that time to earn love... That wasn't enough?"

"No," he said, his voice rough, "it's not enough. You're here because you want access to your family. Because now you're afraid to leave, because you're afraid of the state you believe the nation in. You're a martyr," he said, spitting those words, "and what you do is for your own conscience. So that you can feel important. So you can feel special. And if you have to call it love in order to make yourself feel better then you will. But that's not going to insulate you against a lifetime with me, Princess."

He said those words as though they were intended to push her away, and yet he tightened his hold on her as they escaped his lips. And she was not such a fool.

She reached up, grabbing hold of his tie. "I don't need insulation. Don't you dare accuse me of being weak. Don't you dare accuse me of lying to myself, or to you, about my feelings. I spent my life trying to simply get through and make no waves. Trying to be worthy of the sacrifice my birth parents had made for me, and of the upending of the lives of my parents who raised me. You're right. I did spend my life trying to be perfect. Trying to do the right thing. The best thing. Trying to do my best to make sure nobody regretted taking me on. But that's not what I'm doing with you. I'm not afraid of you. I'm not afraid to fight against you. I'm not afraid to push you. Do not mistake me, King Felipe. When I say I am prepared to stand as your queen it is not so that I can be an accessory to you. Not so I can stand demurely at your side. I intend to make a difference. I intend to make a difference not just in this country but in your life. If I have to push you then I will do so. If I have to fight you, I will do that, too. You will never become your father, Felipe, because I will not allow it. Because I see more in you, and I see bettering you. You might not know it's there, but I do. *I do.*"

He wrapped his fingers around her wrist, pulled her arm back, prying her fingers off his tie. "Do you think my mother thought she would be crushed beneath the boot heel of my father? I highly doubt that was her goal. And yet... And *yet.*"

"I'm not your mother," she said, brushing her fingertips over his lips, satisfied when he jerked beneath the touch. "And you're not your father."

"Such confidence in me," he said, parting his lips, scraping his teeth over her fingers, leaving a slight stinging sensation behind. "For what? And why?"

"Love, Felipe. The very thing you keep dismissing as a lie. As an incidental. It's not. It's everything. It's what will keep you grounded. It's what keeps me here with you. I want to be here with you. I want to be what you need. I want to be perfect for you."

Her words echoed between them, and they made her stomach sink.

It was all so circular.

She had been consumed with being perfect for her mother and father, and then she'd come here and found a freedom in her lack of caring. But now she did care. Now she loved him. And she was back to trying to be whatever she had to be.

She could see the moment he heard it, too. The moment he realized what it meant.

"Was it love that saw my mother jumping from a window, Briar?" he asked, his voice rough. "Because that's the only love I've ever known," he said, his voice rough, harsh. "It's soft and weak. It can be used against you. Used to destroy you."

"You think you'll destroy me, Felipe? And you're angry at me for believing differently? Is that what's happening here?" Nerves ate at her as her own words began to fray. Would he destroy her? He had the power to do so now. Now that she cared.

"Why should you believe in me at all?" he asked, his tone harsh. "There is nothing good in that. Nothing good that could possibly result from it."

"What do you want? You want to drag me kicking and screaming down the aisle so that you can be thought of as a villain by your people? That isn't true, because you care about your reputation. So I can only imagine it's yourself you're playing the villain for. But I can't for the life of me figure out why."

"You're trying to figure me out as if I am a puzzle, *querida*. But you assume there are pieces for you to assemble. I am broken beyond repair. I told you already, my mother took her last leap with my heart, and there is no fixing that. But more important, I don't want it fixed."

"Stop trying to be so damned messed up all the time," she said, shooting his words back at him. "Don't commit yourself to this. You accuse me of being a martyr, but what are you, Felipe? You're determined to atone for your father's sins, but must you punish yourself for them, as well?"

"Someone has to," he said. "The old man is dead, and for all that I hope he's burning in hell, the only assurance I have that things will ever be right is what I fix in this life."

"But you can't have anything good while you work at that?"

"I can't…" He closed his mouth, a muscle working in his jaw. "I cannot afford distraction."

She knew that wasn't what he'd been about to say. That there was something else. But she also knew he wasn't going to let his guard down enough to actually speak with any honesty. There was something about this—whether it was the wedding, the sight of her, or the declaration of love—that unnerved him. That…that scared him. And no matter how deep he might deny it, she could see it.

If she could just make him see. She needed him to see. She had to make him understand that she could be what he needed. That she could fix this. That…

It hit her again, what was happening now.

She had convinced herself that if she behaved in a certain way she could earn his love. Could make him see that she wasn't a burden. That she was everything he needed. That in the end, he would be happier for having her in his life, if she would only just…find the perfect way to be.

She couldn't step back into that. She couldn't do that to herself. Mostly, she could not be the woman he needed her to be if she did. He was so afraid of breaking her. And if she didn't learn how to stand on her own, he might, and it wouldn't even be his fault. She couldn't force him to change. No amount of smiling prettily and inviting him into her bed could do that. He was going to have to love her.

She was going to have to demand that. Not sit around and wait for it.

She was going to have to make waves. There was no other option. She was going to have to take a risk that in the end she wouldn't be worth it. It was the one thing she had always feared most. That ultimately, she would be far too much of an inconvenience for her parents if she stepped out of line. That everyone would find her to be too much trouble to care about. Unless she acted just so. Unless she contributed just enough.

She had stopped. She had to stop or it would go on forever. And it could not.

She took a deep breath and looked up at him, trembling from the inside out. "I love you, Felipe," she said, the words steady.

"So you have said."

"Do you love me?"

"I already gave you my answer."

"I know. But I have to ask again. Because I have to be absolutely certain."

"I cannot," he said, his voice rough. "It is not in me."

She nodded slowly. "I understand. And I need you to understand this. I can't marry you. Not without your love."

"Oh, so suddenly now you require love. Before you said this was never about love, and it wouldn't change."

"Well… I changed."

"What do you want from me? You want me to lie to you, say the words and they will somehow have the magic power to force you to walk down the aisle?"

Her throat started to close up, her hands shaking, misery threatening to overwhelm her. She wanted—with almost everything she had, everything she was—to throw herself on the ground in front of him and tell him she didn't mean it. That she would marry him no matter what. That she would stay with him forever and just hope that everything worked out okay.

And she would grow dimmer and dimmer. And he would consume her. In the end, it would sign both of their death warrants. For their happiness, at least.

"No," she said, forcing the word through her tightened throat. "I would know. If you turned around and said it to me now I would know that you didn't mean it."

"And so you have forced me into an impossible situation."

"You forced us into an impossible situation, Felipe. Because you are not the monster that you seem to think you are, not the monster that you wish you were. You kidnapped me, you dragged me here. And if you had been truly awful it would have been easy for me to resist you. But the fact is you aren't. You're simply broken. And whatever you say, you're more that little boy who lost his mother all those years ago than you are a dragon. But I can't fix it for you. I've tried. And I will break myself in the process. You're right. I can't martyr myself to this cause. You asked me to reconsider. That's what you came here for. To push me away. To make it so that I would leave." She blinked hard, tears threatening to fall. But she wouldn't let them. "Congratulations. You've won."

"There is an entire room full of guests waiting for us to say our vows, Princess. You would disappoint them?"

"I would disappoint them now rather than devastate myself later. It has to be done. I have to go. And if, when I am gone you are able to look inside yourself and find that heart you seem to think doesn't exist... Then you can come and find me."

"And if you leave," he said, his lip curling up into a sneer, "you know that I will make things very difficult for your mother and father."

She nodded slowly; this time a tear did track down her cheek. "I know."

"And you will have failed everyone," he said, the words hard, cruel. "You will have failed me, you will have failed Santa Milagro, you will have failed your adoptive parents, the king and queen, and Verloren herself. Is that what you want?"

She shook her head. "No. It isn't what I want. It's the last thing I want. But sadly, I could never be Princess Talia. I could never be the person I was born to be. I've only ever been able to be Briar Harcourt. She doesn't want any of those things. But she does want to be loved. And at the end of the day, I think she deserves it." She shook her head, battling with the ridiculousness of speaking about herself in the third person. But it was so hard to say what she knew she needed to say. "I deserve to be loved. I deserve it. I don't need to earn it. I shouldn't have to. Someday, Felipe, I'm going to find a man who wants me. One who didn't track me down to the ends of the earth simply because I presented a political advantage to him. But a man who would track me down to the end of the world if I could offer him nothing but a kiss. If I came with no title. If I was only me. I have...I have never been able to say that I thought I deserved such a thing. That I've possessed enough value to be worthy of it. But now I do."

She looked down at the ring, sparkling on her finger. A ring that represented a promise that would now not be fulfilled. She slipped it off, held it out to him. "I suppose I'm the monster now," she said softly, dropping the gem into his open palm. "But I'm a monster that you created. You made me more myself than I have ever been. But I fear that if I stay here it won't last. It will only fade away as I try everything in my power to please you, to make you love me the way that I love you. We both deserve more than that. Because it will only be a self-fulfilling prophecy, don't you see? I will begin to feel I don't deserve love, as I cannot earn it. And you will become the monster you were always afraid you were while you break me slowly into tiny pieces. I won't do that to you. I won't do it to me."

She stood, and she waited. Because whatever she had said if he was to fling himself at her feet, if he was to grab her and pull her into his arms and confess his undying love, she would surely stay. Even if it was a lie. It would take nothing. A half a beat of his heart, a flutter of his eyelash, an upward curve to his lip. Just a sign. A small one, and she would crumble completely, all her good intentions reduced to ash.

"Get out," he said, his voice hard.

"What?"

"You heard me. Get out of my sight. Get out of my palace." He cocked his arm back, threw her ring across the room with a ferocity that shocked her. It was a gem of near inestimable value and he had cast it aside as though it was garbage.

Still, she didn't obey him. She simply stood, shocked, unable to move.

"Get out!" He shouted now then turned to the side and grabbed hold of her vanity, tipping it over onto its face, the glass shattering from the mirror, small bottles of perfume smashing on the tile and sending heavy, drugging scents into the air.

She jumped backward, pressing her palm against her chest, her heart fluttering in her breasts. But still she felt rooted to the spot.

He advanced on her, radiating fury, his eyes a black flame. "Do you think I'm joking? Do you think I am anything less than the product of my father's genetics and upbringing? Do you think I am anything less than a monster? Get out of my sight. Pray that I never see you again, Princess, because if I do I cannot promise you I will not make you my prisoner again. But this time, it will be far less pleasurable for you, I can assure you."

"Felipe…"

He reached out, gripping her chin, the hold hard and nearly painful. "I do not love you. I do not possess the capacity. But oh, how I can hate. You do not want to test the limits of that."

He turned and walked away from her then, and perversely she missed his touch. Even though it had hurt. Because this was worse. This total separation from him. This finality. It was for the best, and she knew it. By doing this she had revealed his true colors. Had uncovered the truth as it was in his heart. If he could not love her to keep her with him, then he never would.

"You had best not be here when I return," he said finally before he walked out the double doors to her room, closing them behind him with a finality that reverberated through her entire frame.

She looked around the room, panic clawing at her. She didn't know what to do, didn't know where to go.

She took a breath and tried to keep calm. She had just done what needed to be done. But she felt terrible. She didn't feel better at all, and she had a feeling it would be a long time before she did. She waited a few moments. Waited until she was certain Felipe wouldn't be standing out there in the hall.

And then she flung the doors open, picked up the front of her dress and ran through the empty corridor. She ran until her lungs burned. Until she reached the front of the palace, going straight out the doors and across the courtyard. There were steps that led up to an exit point that she knew would be less watched, and she tried to scramble up them, taking them two at a time. And then she slipped and fell, her knees hitting the edge of the stones, her dress trailing behind her. She just lay there for a moment, feeling like this was a perfectly fitting moment for how she felt inside.

But then she pushed up, getting back to her feet. Because there was nothing else to be done. She had made the decision. And there was no going back. She had decided that she was worthy of love. No matter what she submitted herself to, or refused to submit herself to. She should be more than payment for her father's debt.

She should be more than Felipe's humanizing face that was presented to the people. More than a perfect daughter.

She was Briar. No matter who she had been born as. That was who she had become. And she needed to keep on becoming that. Because it was ongoing. Because she wasn't finished. And if she stayed here and allowed her desire to please him to become all that she was…

She couldn't. No matter how badly it hurt to leave. She would only hurt them both if she stayed.

CHAPTER TWELVE

FELIPE HAD CERTAINLY created headlines on his wedding day, but they were not the headlines he had hoped they might be. No, rather than photographs of the happy couple, the news media was filled with photographs of him storming into the chapel and demanding everybody leave. A repeat of the night his father had passed away, and proof that he was no more stable than the previous ruler, at least, so said a great many of the papers.

His lungs were burning as he walked up the stairs to the tower. He didn't know why he was going to the tower. One of the things his father had done early on—shortly after his mother had killed herself—was drag Felipe back up to the tower. He had demanded that he stand there. Demanded that he look out the window and see that there was no longer anything there.

"There is nothing," his father had said. "No ghosts. No bodies. She is gone. And she isn't coming back. This place holds no power. Emotion has no place here. And it certainly shouldn't sway you as a ruler."

Felipe laughed cynically as he remembered that. Of course his father would say that emotion had no power. But he didn't mean anger. He didn't mean rage.

It struck him then, with clarity—a disturbing clarity—that he held a similar worldview. That love didn't count. That happiness was something that could easily be destroyed. Those were the emotions he had banished from himself. All while retaining the kind of toxicity his father had carried around with him.

He walked across the room, making his way over to the window. He wrapped his fingers around the bars. Briar had left him, and it was for the best that she had done so by going out the front door and not flinging herself from a tower.

He also despised that she had taken his words and thrown them back at him. That she had done exactly what he had been trying to get her to do. He had wanted her to leave, in the end. But he had thought that...

Perversely, he had hoped that in the end that love, that he felt was such a folly, that he considered a weakness, would prove to be the thing that was strong enough to hold her to him. It was wrong, particularly when his aim had been to get her to call the wedding off, and yet, part of him had hoped.

He had goaded her. He had pushed her. And in the end she had made the right decision; he knew it because he didn't possess the kind of softness in him that she deserved. He knew only how to break things. How to break people.

Pushing his hand through the bars, he rested his palm on the window. "I am sorry, Mama. I truly am." And then he pounded his fist against the glass, watching it crack, splinters embedding in his skin. He relished that pain. As he had done earlier. As he had done for a great many years. Punishing himself because his father was no longer able to do it.

And, oh, how he loved to break things. Because the old man wanted order. And Felipe wanted to defy that.

And then you straighten your shirtsleeves like a naughty boy.

He pounded his forehead with his bleeding fist then lowered his hand slowly, his heart threatening to rage right out of his chest.

For the first time he wondered if he was not like his father. He wondered if he was merely controlled by him. If he had allowed the old man to gain access to him. No. He was going to make his country better. He was going to atone.

And yet you let him steal your ability to love, with all that fear he gave you. You let him cost you Briar.

He gritted his teeth. No, letting Briar go had been a kindness. Because as she had said to him it would only damage them both in the end if the two of them were to be together.

He thought of her, of everything she had told him about the way she had grown up. So afraid that she would be found unworthy. So desperate to prove her value.

All she had to do for him was simply breathe.

The thought of her... Well, it created a pain in his chest that was so severe it blotted out the pain in his hand.

What was it? All of this pain. He wasn't supposed to be able to feel anything. He had made sure. He had promised himself.

He curled his fingers around the window bars again.

He had promised her.

He hadn't been brave enough to follow her. And so he had done what he thought was best. He had sent the most vital part of himself with her. Had consigned it to the grave. Because he had failed her. In the end, it had been his fault.

He clutched his chest, unable to breathe. His heart. His *heart*. Of course, he knew that his heart was there physically. It was the metaphorical heart he had long since surrendered. But if so then why did it hurt so badly now? Why did it feel as though he was going to suffer cardiac arrest because he didn't have Briar with him? Why did standing here in this room, the room where he had witnessed his mother's death, feel like he was submerged under water and he couldn't breathe? Like his chest was going to explode. If you didn't have a heart…then why the hell was it breaking?

Why was he standing here imagining days filled with darkness? Days without her soft hands touching his skin. Without her looking at him as though he was a person of value. Without her telling him that he mattered? Why was he imagining those things and not the loss of all his political alliances? Because that was all she should mean. It was all she should have ever meant. He should be mounting an attack. Plotting revenge against her for taking herself away from him and ruining his plans. He did not allow such things. He never had.

But the problem was, she was already perfect for him. She didn't even have to try. And without her…without her he was nothing.

He reached into his pocket and pulled out his phone, and without thinking, he dialed Adam's number. Felipe was not the kind of man who depended on the kindness of friends or strangers. Indeed, he had done his very best to never need anyone's kindness. Mostly because he had grown up with none, and had never assumed it would be there when he needed it.

But he needed something now. And he didn't know where else to turn.

"Adam," he said.

"I'm surprised it took you this long to call. Considering your wedding was just dramatically called off."

"Yes. Well. I didn't think I needed anything to deal with that. She's gone. What's done is done. There's nothing I can do to fight that. Nor do I want to. At least, I didn't think so."

"I see. It turns out you're not so happy to have lost your fiancée?"

Felipe felt like he'd been stabbed in the chest. "No. And I'm not thinking about the political ramifications. All I can think of is her. She is… She is impractical for me in every way. She's young. She was innocent." His body warmed just thinking of how far she had come in the past weeks. "She is soft and giving. She is everything I'm not. I shouldn't miss her. I shouldn't want her. And yet…"

"I could have told you that it is a grave mistake to take beautiful young women captive," Adam said, his tone dry. "I have a bit of experience with that."

"You were also the most humorless, angry man I had ever met before Belle came into your life. How did you change? I need to know. I need to know if it's possible."

Adam hesitated for a moment. "I was content to go through my life feeling nothing," he said finally. "The loss of my first wife was more than I could bear. At least, I thought so. I thought I had been damaged beyond the capacity for feeling. I wanted to be. But Belle came softly, and because of that I did not know I needed to arm myself against her. I was so certain that as her captor I held the upper hand. Ultimately, she was the one who captured

me. Her love changed me. And the fact that I had to become something different to be worthy of it. It does not
just happen as you sit idly by, Felipe. You must choose
it. You must choose love instead of darkness. Because
that's the only way that it can win in the end. But once
you do... Light wins every time. It swallows the darkness whole."

"Perhaps your brand of darkness, Adam. I fear mine
might have the power to absorb the sun."

"If that is how you choose to see it, if that is the power
you choose to give it, then I believe it. Light and dark
exist in the world, Felipe. Good and evil. Love and hate.
We must all choose, I suppose, which of those things we
give the most power. Which of those things get to carry
the most weight. In the end, I chose love. Because anything else was to submit to the unthinkable. A life without Belle. If you can imagine life without Briar, then I
suppose you don't need to change at all. But if this present darkness that you're in feels too suffocating, too consuming... Turn on the light, my friend."

"Talia." Queen Amaani walked into the room. It could
be no one else. After a week in Verloren she could recognize the other woman by the sound of her footsteps.
There was something about the way she glided over the
tile, even in heels. She was like an ethereal being.

And Briar looked like her. She was her daughter; there
was no denying it.

She was also the daughter of Dr. Robert and Nell Harcourt from New York, who had raised her and loved her
and done their best to protect her from a threat they'd
had no power against.

Living at the palace in Santa Milagro, then coming

here, truly underscored that fact. How much power the players in this game possessed, that Dr. Harcourt and his wife did not. It was strange, though. That realization didn't make her feel more indebted.

It made her feel…

Well, she felt as if it was the proof of love she'd always been looking for.

It had always been there. She'd just put so many of her own fears up in front of it.

She turned to face the queen, her heart pounding hard. "Briar," she said. "Call me Briar, please?"

The other woman's beautiful face looked shocked, but only for a moment. Then she smoothed it into rather serene calm. "If that's what you prefer, of course."

Briar smiled, knowing the smile looked as sad as she felt inside. "It's more…I've been thinking a lot. About who I am. And what I want. I'm so happy that I've been able get to know you and…and I'm sorry—" her throat tightened up "—I'm sorry that we couldn't have known each other better. I'm sorry that it…is this way. But I was blessed to have a wonderful upbringing with the people you chose to care for me. And…I became the woman they raised me to be. I wanted to be Talia for you. I wanted to please you. But I need to be Briar."

Felipe had always seen her as Briar. Always. Even when she'd told her mother and father to call her Talia, he had known.

He had known long before she had.

Funny how that wretched man could be so insightful about her behavior, and have such a huge blank when it came to his own.

Then the queen did something unexpected. She knelt down in front of Briar, her hands on Briar's lap, her face full of sadness. "I know. And it is… The reason we chose the Harcourts was because we had known them for years. Because we trusted them. Because we knew that they would help you grow into the woman you were meant to be. I'm sorry we failed you. I'm sorry you suffered at the hands of that madman…"

"He's not a madman," she said, surprised by her own vehemence. "He's…lost. And he's hurt. But he's…" Tears filled her eyes. "I love him. And I would be with him still except…it couldn't be like it was. With him convinced he had forced my hand. With me trying to earn his love. It has to be different. If he comes for me again, it has to be because he wants me. Not because he wants a wife he thinks will make him look good. And I need to go with him because I love him. Not because he kidnapped me from a hospital."

The queen's eyebrows shot up. "From a hospital?"

Briar sighed. "It's a long story."

The queen rose to her feet and sat in the chair next to Briar. Then she snapped her elegant fingers. A servant appeared. "Tea," she said. Then she turned her focus back to Briar. "I have time for long stories. The two of us have much catching up to do, Briar."

CHAPTER THIRTEEN

FELIPE HAD NEVER imagined coming to Verloren. Especially not without armed guards. Or an entire battalion. Not considering the relations between the two countries. It was one of the many reasons he had wanted Briar in the first place. She was a convenient human shield. One that forced the nations to be friendly.

But he was coming now as an enemy, with no defenses. With nothing. Nothing except a whole lot of darkness inside him that he wanted so desperately to shine a light on.

Briar's light.

Whether he deserved it or not, that was what he was here for.

He didn't expect a hero's welcome, but he didn't expect to be put in chains the moment he showed up at the palace, either. And yet he was. He also allowed it, because the last thing he could afford was the kind of scandal that would erupt if he committed an act of violence in a foreign palace.

And he also couldn't afford to do anything that Briar might disapprove of.

Especially not with her father, the king, looking on as he was led into the palace throne room.

"King Felipe," he said. "It is a surprise to see you. You will forgive the precautions. But last time you were around a member of my family without chains, you took her against her will."

He did not bother to correct the king by saying that last time he had been around the man's daughter he'd been the one to tell her not to return. And that before that she'd been in his arms—in his bed—willingly.

Felipe didn't want to die. Not today.

Perhaps after he met with Briar, perhaps if she rejected him. But not before he had the chance to try.

"I welcomed you to my palace without chains," Felipe pointed out.

"I was also invited. What is your business here?"

"I'm here to see the princess."

"You're here to claim a debt that isn't yours to claim, and was never meant to extend to my daughter," the older man said, standing. "I refuse. Even if it means war. I should have done that years ago."

"I am not here to claim her, as a payment or otherwise. I am here to speak to her. I'm here to tell her…"

"Here to tell me what?"

He looked toward the doors that led in deeper to the palace and saw Briar standing there. It was strange to see her dressed so casually. Wearing just dark jeans and a gray T-shirt, her hair loose and curly, her face void of makeup.

Strange, and yet she was even more beautiful to him now than she had been in the most beautiful of ball gowns. Because this wasn't a memory. This was now. She was here standing before him, and he had made a decision.

That made her the most beautiful she'd ever been to

him. It made this the most beautiful moment, in a world that had—to this point—been mostly darkness and pain for him.

"I am in chains," he said, lifting his wrists to show her.

"Oh, well…good. Now you'll have an idea of what it's like to be held against your will." She crossed her arms, cocking her hip to the side, her expression serene.

"Is there a chance, as I am in chains, I might speak to you alone? I can't do anything in this state, after all."

Her father's expression turned sharp. "Absolutely not."

Briar held up her hand. "Yes. I need to speak with him. I need to hear what he has to say."

The old king paused then looked at his guards. "Let us go. Briar, if you have need of us, you know what to do."

She nodded. "Thank you."

Once the king and his henchmen had exited the room, Felipe turned his focus back to Briar. "He called you Briar."

"Yes. I'm not Talia. I…explained that to them yesterday. I need to be…me. And that's Briar. Briar Harcourt. It doesn't mean I can't visit here. And I would like to get to know them. But…I'm me."

He knew what it meant. She didn't have to explain. Because he knew her. He could honestly say he had never known anyone else quite as well. And certainly no one had known him.

"Briar." He just wanted to say her name. Wanted to watch her respond to him. To his words. To his voice. Wanted to confirm that she wasn't neutral to him. No. No, she was not. It took three steps for him to close the space between them and when he did, he looped his arms around her, trapping her in the chain, pulling her up against him.

"I'm not here to steal you," he said, leaning in, pressing his lips to hers. "But I am here for you."

"You said…" Her voice wobbled.

"That I would not claim you. Not for revenge. Not for payment. But I want you." He drew her even closer, wrapping the chain around his wrists to make it so she couldn't pull away. "I *need* you."

"Why do I feel like you're trying to take me captive again?" she whispered, her dark eyes glittering.

"Impossible," he said. "I'm the one in chains. I suspect I have been for a very long time. But it took the desire to be free for me to truly recognize my limitations. When I wished so much I could hold you, but knew I could not because it would only harm us both. Because…because if I am in chains then holding you means having you in them, as well, and you were right. It would have only destroyed us both. That has long been my fear. That I destroy, rather than build. That I am my father's son, and I can only break things, even the things I love."

"And you're holding me in chains now," she pointed out.

"Yes, but this is literal, because I want you against me. Touching me. The other was metaphorical."

"I see," she said, the side of her mouth quirking upward. "But none of it matters if you haven't found the key."

"To my chains? Oh, I have. The metaphorical chains. Not these. Your father will have to release me from these."

She lifted her hands, taking hold of his face. "Unless you're going to tell me how you found the key, you can shut up."

He took that opportunity to wrap the chains yet another time around his wrist, hauling her closer as he dipped his head and claimed her mouth with his. When they parted, they were both breathing hard.

"You," he ground out. "You're the key, Briar. To all of this. To me."

"I am?"

"Yes," he said. "You. Not as a princess, but as a woman. You made me see…you made me see for the first time in years. You shone a light on my darkness. And even more than allowing me to see, you saw me. You saw me and you wouldn't allow me to hide."

"You saw me," she said, the words husky. "You made me stronger. You made me fight."

"It was in you all along," he said. "That fight. You just had to come up against a dragon to find it."

She smiled. "I like that."

"And I love you." The words scraped his throat raw. He couldn't remember if he'd ever spoken them before. He didn't think he had. "All my childhood I'd been too bound up in fear and abuse to…to feel much of anything. I dismissed it. I dismissed it as something that didn't matter because I didn't truly understand. I didn't know what it meant to love someone, or to have them love you. I didn't understand the power of it. I thought…I thought that perhaps my mother's death was something I could have fixed. If I had done more. If I had been better."

"No," she said, pressing her fingertips to his lips. "No. You were a little boy, Felipe. Of course you couldn't have stopped it."

"It felt like it was me," he said, his voice strained. "That I was the one who broke her."

"No, Felipe. It was him."

"I know. I know now. There was only ever one person who could have stopped the hell we lived in, and that was my father. And that small thing. That thing he taught me meant nothing…love. It would have healed so much, Briar. If he would have had it for me, for my mother. For anyone but himself. Love is not a negligible thing. I have come to believe that it is the only thing."

"I love you, Felipe." She smiled at him. And it was like the sun had risen after the darkest night, shining a light in the hidden corners of his soul.

He kissed her again, and he felt something lift away from him. A weight, a darkness that had rested upon him for longer than he could remember. He had tried to banish it with anger, with hate. With vengeance. But nothing had taken it from him. Until this. Until her love.

Love was stronger.

That was how the princess slew the dragon. Not with a sword. Not with a magic spell.

But with love.

And they lived happily ever after…

* * * * *

ONE NIGHT WITH HIS RIVAL

ROBYN GRADY

With thanks to my wonderful editor, Charles Griemsman, and literary agent extraordinaire, Jessica Alvarez. Professional, supportive and talented. I just love working with you both.

One

Last night was the best and worst decision of her life. On the one hand, it was ecstasy. On the other hand, disaster.

Veda Darnel couldn't get her head around it. She had practically sold her soul to spend one sizzling night with a man who had reinvented the word *satisfaction*. A consummate charmer who'd caused her to swap out her common sense for the thrill of unparalleled pleasure.

Lying together now, front to naked front, Veda studied the cocky cowboy in question as he continued to grab some much-needed sleep. Primal instinct was keeping his hand glued to her behind, pressing her hips against his. Each time he breathed in, that mouthwatering chest expanded and wiry hairs teased her nipples. Whenever his lips twitched with a dream-induced grin, she longed for just one more kiss.

Just one more time.

Well, sorry, universe. Not happening. Not now. Not ever

again. Damn it, she knew better. In the future, would *do* better.

Still asleep, Ajax Rawson drew in a sharp breath at the same time the fingers on her butt flexed, then dug in more. Veda had to bite her lip to stem the groan; her Benedict Arnold body wanted those expert hands everywhere and all at once. And if he woke up now, that could very well be where they'd end up. Making love like nothing else mattered.

As if there weren't already enough prices to pay.

Tippy-toe quiet, she reached behind her and found the big, hot hand cupping her rear end. She carefully coiled her fingers around his wrist, then tried to lift and shift it.

Seriously? His arm must be made of lead.

Knuckling down, Veda tried again. When she'd finally managed to ease herself away, she held her breath. But he didn't stir. Not an inch.

So, slide off the bed, dive into your clothes, bolt out the hotel suite's front door and never look back. Never go *back.* Still, a knot of bittersweet longing kept her hanging. Ajax was the best she'd ever had—the best there ever was.

And how many other women had thought the exact same thing?

He sucked in another sharp breath, rolled onto his back and scooped his arm under his pillow while his other hand gave those ripped abs a languid rub or two. Then his brow pinched, eyelids flickered open, and Veda's stomach dropped.

Too late to run now.

Ajax frowned sleepily at the ceiling, getting his bearings, before turning his gaze onto her. When one corner of his wholly kissable mouth eased up—when his lungs expanded on a breath that said, "Oh, yeah… I remember you"—Veda's resolve to do better wobbled like a thimble full of Jell-O.

Ajax's dreamy ocean-deep blue eyes smiled into hers

as he spoke with a sexy growl that was equal parts playful and deadly serious.

"You need to come over here." He cocked an eyebrow, smiling wider as the sheet tented over his waist. "On second thought, I can't wait that long."

When he rolled back toward her, heat rushed through her blood, pooling deliciously low in her belly. But tempted as she was, Veda didn't lean in. Didn't surrender. Instead, she brought her portion of the sheet higher and sat up.

"Actually," she said, "I have to go."

Ajax paused, then leaned up on an elbow, head in hand, biceps bulging. "You mean to the bathroom or something?"

"No. Not that."

"Ah, you need food," he said. "Me, too. I'll order up. Maybe some green pepper omelets, hot-off-the-grill bacon and chocolate-chip-banana pancakes drowned in syrup. We can eat breakfast in bed." He came near enough to brush his gorgeous stubble against her cheek. "Lunch and dinner, too, if you want."

Ajax was never lost for words—more specifically, the right words. He gave off a vibe that confirmed that everything good fortune had to offer came to him naturally. Like he never had to even think about trying.

If only she could say the same for herself.

Years ago, and more than once, a much younger Veda had watched Ajax from afar while daydreaming about being in this exact situation. Back then, as well as now, she hated to think what her father might say. Drake Darnel had an ax or two to grind with the Rawsons, the first dating back decades to a time when Ajax's dad, Huxley Rawson, was known as a stud.

What was the saying?

Oh, yeah.

The apple never falls far from the tree.

Now, as Ajax maneuvered to claim that kiss—as his

musky scent flooded her senses and all her pulse points started to throb—Veda felt her resistance begin to ebb. Thankfully, somehow, she managed to shore herself up and pull back in time.

Ajax pulled back, too, studying her like he couldn't work out what the problem was for the life of him. After the way she'd allowed herself to be so completely adored these past hours…really, who could blame him?

"Have I done something wrong, Veda? Have I hurt you somehow?"

She shook her head. "No. Nothing like that." He'd been a total gentleman. An incredible lover.

"Do you have somewhere else to be?"

"Not particularly, no."

His pained expression only made him look hotter, if that was even possible.

"Is this about family? About our fathers not getting along?"

She winced. "It's kind of hard to ignore."

"We did just fine ignoring it last night."

They'd met at a glitzy Saratoga Springs charity event held at a well-known venue. An hour in, needing a break from the hype, Veda had wandered out onto a balcony. Wearing a tux that fit his dynamite build to perfection, Ajax had been standing by the railing, finishing a call. Veda had swallowed her breath and promptly turned on her silver high heel. But he was already putting the phone away and asking in a rumbling voice that reduced her to mush, "Haven't we met somewhere before?"

Lamest pickup line in the playbook. Except he wasn't playing. While they had never spoken, of course she might look familiar. For years, at various horse races she'd gone to with her dad, she had been a shadow hovering in the background, fawning over Ajax.

So, had they met before?

Feeling like a tongue-tied teen again, Veda had murmured, "Not, uh, physically." Those beautiful blue eyes crinkled at the corners as he chuckled and replied, "Well then, pleased to make your acquaintance—*physically*."

After an exchange of names, of course the penny had dropped. She was a Darnel, he was a Rawson. Veda also mentioned that she had recently become friends with Lanie Rawson, his sister. Small world…and getting smaller.

With Ajax doing most of the talking, they had gotten to know each other more. Then had come the dancing and the kissing and, after midnight, *this*. The entire time, neither one had touched on the Darnel-Rawson feud. Frankly, Veda didn't want to spoil the mesmerizing mood. Apparently Ajax hadn't given the matter a whole lot of thought.

"Drake and Hux have butted heads over the years," Ajax reflected now, "but I can't remember the last time Dad even mentioned his name."

Was he joking? "I hear my father going on about Hux Rawson all the time."

"Wait. Didn't you say you're in New Jersey now?"

He was right. She hadn't lived here in New York with her father for years. "We keep in touch…phone calls, emails. I visit when I can."

Like this weekend. In fact, she was meant to have been her father's plus-one last night. Feeling under the weather, he'd backed out at the last minute.

Way to go, fate.

"Oh. Well…" Running a hand through his delectably mussed dark blond hair, Ajax blew out a breath. "I'm sorry to hear that."

"Sorry to hear that we keep in touch?"

"Sorry that your dad hasn't moved on. Must be tough holding on to a grudge like that."

Veda's cheeks heated up more. Drake Darnel was a whole bunch of things. *But c'mon now. Let's be fair.*

"I guess it would be difficult to move on when someone swoops in to steal the love of your life. The woman you'd planned to marry."

Ajax's tilted his cleft chin. "Did you say *steal*?"

"My father gave her a ring. Then Hux made his move and voilà." Game over.

"Uh, Drake *offered* a ring, which my mom declined. I heard that directly from her, by the way. And with regard to Dad casting some kind of a spell… Veda, it takes two to tango."

He gave the room a sweeping gaze, as if to say "case in point."

Veda wasn't finished. If they were doing this, she wanted to make the connection between then and now. Between player father and chip off the old block. Just one more reason last night had been a bad idea.

"I believe Hux had quite a reputation in those days."

Ajax frowned slightly. "He was a dude who dated before finding the right one and settling down."

Drake preferred to explain Hux's bachelor past in terms like *skirt-chaser, Casanova, cheat*, although that last dig was aimed more at the Rawsons' questionable business ethics. On top of the issue of how Hux had stolen Drake's would-be bride, the Rawsons and Darnels owned competing Thoroughbred stables. More often than not, Drake's horses were beaten by a nose by a Rawson ride.

Better training? Sporting luck? Or was something more going on behind the scenes with regard to performance?

As far as Veda was concerned, the entire horse racing industry was unethical. Cruel. That didn't even touch on the social pitfalls of gambling, where in some cases, entire paychecks were burned practically every week, leaving families in crisis. Long ago she had made a promise to herself. The day her father passed on, a for-sale sign would go up outside the front gates of the Darnel Stables and every horse would find a home without the threat of whips, injury or being shipped off to the glue factory when it was past its use-by date.

Shuddering, Veda refocused. Ajax was still talking about his folks.

"My mother and father were deeply in love. They were committed to each other and their family. Mom made a choice all those years ago. One she wouldn't hesitate to stand by if she was alive today."

Veda was sorry that Mrs. Rawson had died when Ajax was still a boy. Losing a parent at a young age changed who you were, how you coped. Every day Veda wished that her own mom was still around. She wished her childhood had been different—normal—rather than the screwup she had muddled and struggled through.

But now was not the time to go down that particular rabbit hole. She was vulnerable enough as it was.

Veda wound her hands tighter into the bedsheet she was holding close to her breasts. "I guess we'll just have to agree to disagree," she said.

"I guess we will." Ajax's gaze dropped to her lips as he added, "And if you want to leave… I get it. I do. Just please know that I don't have anything personal against your dad."

She wasn't done with being ticked off. The Rawsons had a lot to answer for. Still, Ajax's olive branch seemed so genuine, and the apologetic expression in his eyes looked so real… It wouldn't hurt to concede at least a small point.

"I don't hate your dad, either. I haven't even met the man."

"But you will. I presume Lanie invited you to her big birthday bash at home next month."

She nodded. "Should be good."

Though she wasn't looking forward to her father's reaction when he heard the news. While Drake knew that she and Lanie Rawson were more than acquaintances now, he was far from happy about it. He wouldn't care to hear that his daughter was looking forward to celebrating with her friend at her party.

And, of course, Ajax would be there, too, looking as magma-hot as he did right now.

His smile was just so easy and inviting.

"Wow. The Darnels and Rawsons finally coming together," he said. "Just goes to show, things change, huh?"

Veda gave in to a smile, too.

Just goes to show...

And because Ajax always seemed to know precisely when and exactly how to act, he chose that moment to lean in again. And when he slid that big warm hand around the back of her neck, this time Veda didn't resist. She simply closed her eyes and inwardly sighed as he pushed his fingers up through her hair and his mouth finally claimed hers the way it was always meant to. For better or worse, the way she must have wanted all along.

Two

"Eyes off. That means hands, too, partner."

Recognizing the voice at his back, Ajax edged around. Birthday girl Lanie Rawson stood there in a bright haute couture gown, hands on hips, a vigilant eyebrow raised.

Ajax played dumb. "Eyes and hands off *who* exactly?"

"If you don't already know, the bombshell you're ogling over there is Veda Darnel," his sister replied. "Drake Darnel's daughter *and* a good friend of mine."

When Ajax had gotten together with Veda four weeks ago in Saratoga, she had mentioned something about her and Lanie being tight. Frankly, in those initial few moments, he hadn't focused on anything much other than her amazing red hair and stunning lavender evening dress. Tonight, with that hair swept over one creamy shoulder and rocking a shimmering lipstick-red number, Veda looked even more heart-stopping.

Eyes off?

Never gonna happen.

Hands off?

We'll see.

Crossing his arms, Ajax rocked back on his boot heels. He'd had a full day at the stables before racing out to the track in time for the "riders up" call. After a thundering win, he'd made his way to the winner's circle to congratulate the jockey, the assistant trainer and their most recent champion, Someone's Prince Charming. Man, he loved that horse. Then he'd shot back to the on-site office to check messages and shower before driving the extra half mile here to don a tux. But first, he'd decided to take a peek at the party that was already getting under way in a glittering tented pavilion in the backyard of the estate.

Now, before he went inside to change, he had a question or two for Miss Lanie Bossy-Pants.

"How did you and Veda Darnel become pals?"

"We met at a women's business luncheon last year," Lanie explained, slipping her hands into the hidden pockets of her Cinderella gown. "Veda's a life coach. She talked about personal change through action rather than words. It was brief but powerful. Actually, I was blown away. Later, she said she recalled seeing us as kids at race meets when she tagged along with her dad. And then I remembered her, too. Or, at least, I remembered her hair."

Like the color of leaves in late fall, Ajax thought, doing some remembering of his own, particularly images of her moving beneath him in bed that night a month ago.

"Back then," Lanie went on, "Veda was like a mouse in a corner. Now she knows exactly what she wants. And I'm pretty darn sure that doesn't include being any man's flavor of the month."

Ajax chuckled to cover up the wince. "I'm not that bad."

Lanie had a skeptical if-you-say-so expression on her face.

"Anyway, I'm glad Veda didn't buy into her father's BS about all Rawsons being scum," she said. "You know she told me once that Drake is still steaming over Mom dumping him for Dad all those years ago. Just so sad."

Sad was one word. But Ajax didn't agree with Lanie. Veda had absolutely drunk the Kool-Aid when it came to believing her father's version of events.

During their one night together, she had gone to the mat for her father. According to Daddy Dearest, Hux was a slimy villain who had stolen Drake's girl. Ajax had set the record straight. His mom had made her own decision— because, duh, it was hers to make—after which she had married the far better man.

Veda had softened toward him again after that, and before vacating their suite around noon, they'd exchanged numbers. The next day, he'd sent flowers to her Best Life Now office address in Jersey. After a week not hearing from her, he'd called and left a message. A few days later, he'd sent a bigger bunch. Dialed again.

No response.

"She's smart, tough and to the point," Lanie said, looking Veda's way through the glittering party crowd. "Not someone who's desperate for a roll in the hay."

When Lanie pinned him with another look that said, *Don't go there*, Ajax coughed out a laugh. "You're seriously the sex police now?"

His sister tossed back her long dark hair the way she did whenever she was excited, angry or digging her spurs in. "I want to make sure that we're clear before I let you out to graze."

He threw her a salute. "Anything you say, Officer."

Lanie groaned. "Just go get changed. Not that the ladies won't drool over you in your boots." Walking off, his sister offered a fond grin when she added, "You're such a tart."

After parking in the designated area out in front of the Rawson property, Veda had followed a torchlit path that wove around the majestic Victorian mansion to a tent filled with conversation and music. She'd been taking in the swagged ceilings, which were awash with a million fairy lights, and looking out for anyone she might know when, larger than life, Ajax appeared at the entrance.

With hands bracing either side of his belt, Ajax was wearing a white business shirt rolled up enough at the sleeves to reveal his strong, tanned forearms. A sexy five-o'clock shadow highlighted the natural thrust of his jaw and cleft chin. Even from this distance, even in this light, his eyes radiated a hue that brought to mind ocean-deep waters sparkling with midsummer sunshine.

Following that whirlwind night in Saratoga, he'd sent two enormous bouquets of flowers. Both times when he called, Veda had ached to pick up. At some stage tonight, they were destined to run into each other. When they did, would Ajax try to reconnect? Were any sparks left on his side of the equation, or after her snub, was she already a speck in Ajax Rawson's rearview mirror?

Before he'd been able to spot her, Veda had inserted herself into a nearby circle of guests. Now she sneaked another look his way.

Lanie had joined him; given his sister's expression, their discussion wasn't particularly lighthearted. When Lanie walked off, Ajax left and Veda released a pent-up breath. She was safe—at least for now. Then Lanie headed Veda's way, which raised another question.

She and Lanie hadn't been in touch for weeks. Had Ajax mentioned anything to his sister about Saratoga? Lanie knew Veda wasn't the type to fall into bed with a guy for the heck of it. But after years of wondering, she had taken the opportunity to at last scratch her Ajax Rawson itch. And as much as she tried—as much as she knew she probably should—Veda couldn't regret a moment of the amazing time they had spent together.

When Lanie was a few feet away, she was joined by a man Veda recognized. Hux Rawson was tall and broad through the shoulders like his son, with neat steel-gray hair, complete with a widow's peak. He dropped a kiss on his daughter's cheek before he hooked an arm through hers and escorted Lanie on her way.

Right toward Veda.

Her head began to spin. From the way Lanie had described her dad, Hux would be gracious, even in welcoming Drake Darnel's daughter. In similar circumstances, she doubted her father would be as polite. Although he was aware that she and Lanie were friends now, Drake still disapproved of all the Rawsons. Always had.

Always would.

Red carpet ready in a tiered canary-yellow tulle gown and smelling like rose petals, Lanie gave Veda a hug and exclaimed, "You look positively gorgeous."

Veda was never good with compliments, so she simply passed on her best wishes, adding, "I left something on the gift table."

A glossy hard copy of the history of women in equestrian sports. Nothing Veda would ever want herself, but coming across it in a Princeton bookstore, she had known dressage champion Lanie would love it.

Lanie saw to introductions. "Veda Darnel, meet the most important man in my life."

An easy smile lit her father's bright blue eyes. "Glad you could make it, Veda. I'm Hux."

For a man in his midsixties, Hux Rawson cut a fine figure in his pristine tuxedo. The tanned face and smile lines bracketing his mouth suggested a long run of good health and personal happiness. Veda's father only ever looked annoyed—unless he was in his stables. Nothing against the horses, but there was more to life than work and stewing over the past.

Tacking up a smile, Veda replied, "It's great to be here."

"Hard to believe my little girl is twenty-seven today." Hux gave his daughter a wink. "So beautiful *and* conquering the world."

Lanie pretended to wither. "Pressure much?"

"You know I'm proud of you," Hux said, obviously referring to more than her riding achievements. "I know your mother would be proud of you, too."

Lanie's expression softened before something over her dad's shoulder caught her eye. Bouncing up on her toes, she signaled to a couple entering the tent.

"Will you two excuse me?" She snatched a champagne flute from a passing waiter's tray. "A hostess's job is never done."

Hux smiled as he watched his daughter hurry off, then returned his attention to Veda. There was a moment of uncertainty about kicking off the conversation again, which wasn't uncommon between newly introduced people. Except this man wasn't exactly a stranger. His decisions before Veda was even born had affected her life on so many levels, in ways he couldn't possibly know—in ways that could still leave her feeling a little lost.

Like now.

Looking directly into her eyes, feeling the weight of the past pressing in…

She wasn't surprised when a chill scuttled up her spine, then slithered around her throat—and squeezed.

The sensation wasn't new. It went back as far as elementary school when she had tried to learn her letters; they looked more like squiggling tadpoles in a white sea, no matter what her teacher had said. In later grades, whenever she was pushed to read in class or was feeling stressed, her ears would begin to ring and her throat would close. Feeling everyone's eyes on her, she would literally freeze, unable to speak. Whispers and open snipes followed her everywhere, even in her dreams.

Lazy.

Dumb.

Weirdo.

After a diagnosis of dyslexia in her teens, Veda had worked hard on herself. Not only was she determined to walk back all the damage that came from hellish anxiety, lack of confidence, few friends and less hope, she had vowed to be stronger for it. And looking on the brighter side, finding ways to reclaim her self-esteem had laid the foundations for her career as a life coach, the most rewarding job on the planet. While she still battled nerves and always would, Veda could speak in front of an auditorium full of people now. She hadn't suffered one of her attacks where she strangled on her words in years.

Until now.

Ringing ears…closing throat…freezing brain.

"This has been weeks in the making," Hux said, looking around at the tented pavilion and its high-end fairy-tale trimmings. "Lanie and Susan's efforts, of course, not mine. Have you met Susan yet? She came down early to make sure everything was set."

As Hux waited for a reply, Veda's throat remained squeezed shut. Cheeks flushed, she forced a smile and shook her head.

"Susan's a godsend," Hux went on. "Been with us for such a long time. She's phenomenal with the house and meals and, well, everything family."

Focused, trying to relax, Veda managed to squeak out, "I see."

Hux's smile dipped before he tried again. "When she arrived here, Susan knew nothing about horses or this kind of life. She loves the place now, of course, but she doesn't get much involved with that side of things."

Veda's mind was stuck. Words refused to come. And deep in her gut, tendrils of panic were spreading.

Lazy.

Dumb.

Weirdo.

Hux's eyes narrowed the barest amount before he tried a different approach. "I suppose you like horses, Veda? You've been around them most of your life."

"I... Horses are...beautiful."

He nodded like he hadn't worked her out yet and maybe didn't want to. "How's your dad doing?"

"Good. Busy." *Breathe, Veda. Just breathe.* "I'm staying there...this weekend."

"Right. The Darnel Stables aren't so far from here."

When she nodded again and took a sip from her champagne flute, Hux searched her eyes and then threw a look around. "Well, I'll let you get back to the party. Nice meeting you, Veda. Enjoy the night."

As he walked away, Veda let her smile and shoulders sag. Knowing next to no one here hadn't fazed her. She could even deal with seeing Ajax again, however that turned out. But being left alone to talk with the man who years ago had let loose a storm of demons that had ultimately torn her family apart...

Veda didn't like to dwell on how much she'd cried when her parents had split, let alone the bombshell that had landed after that. But now, snapshots of events leading up to her mother's death broke through. And with the music getting louder and the crowd starting to press in—

She needed some space, some air, and she needed it now.

Setting her glass on a nearby table, Veda escaped through one of the pavilion's back exits, and she didn't stop going until she was cloaked in shadows and certain she was alone. Out here, the night air was so fresh and freeing.

The beat of the music and drag of dark memories seemed just far enough away.

She was herding together more positive thoughts when, out of the shadows, a figure appeared. Dressed in a tuxedo now, Ajax was cutting the distance between them with a commanding gait. And the closer he got, the clearer the message grew in his gorgeous blue eyes.

You can run, sweetheart, it said, *but don't ever think you can hide.*

"If you want to leave, you're going the wrong way," Ajax said, tipping his head toward the house. "Cars are parked over there."

Taken aback, Veda blinked a few times before responding. "I wasn't leaving. I needed some air."

He forced a grin. "Like you needed air the night we met on that balcony a month ago."

Her knockout dress shimmered in the moonlight as she straightened. "Has it been that long?"

"Yup. That long."

After changing, Ajax had returned to the party pavilion in time to catch a flash of lipstick red as Veda dashed out the back. Of course, he had followed. He wanted to make sure she was all right. And, yes, he had also seen an opportunity to broach another sensitive matter. Namely, what the hell had happened after Saratoga? Why hadn't she accepted his calls?

Clearly, Veda wanted to avoid the subject.

"So, what are you doing out here in the dark?" she asked.

Ajax slid both hands into his pants pockets. "Psyching up for party mode?"

"Well, at least you're dressed for it now."

His smile was slow. "You saw me earlier?"

Her gorgeous green eyes widened before she visibly

gathered herself again and offered a cool reply. "You got changed in record time."

"I'd already showered at the office." Grinning, he propped a shoulder against a nearby oak and crossed one ankle over the other. "I don't mind the smell of hay and horse, but I'm not sure the guests would appreciate it much."

When her gaze dipped to his mouth, he remembered back to that night and words she had murmured while nuzzling him from his chest all the way down.

You smell so good. And taste even better.

As if she was remembering, too, Veda threw a glance toward the lights and music. "I should get back."

"I'll walk with you." He pushed off the oak before adding, "If that's okay."

After a second's hesitation, she made a face like it was no big deal. "Sure," she said. "Why not."

As they headed back down a lit path, he set a leisurely pace. After the flowers and phone messages—after the multiple times she had come apart in his arms that wild night—had she even considered dropping him a line?

He studied her profile—straight nose, lush lips, laser-beam focus. And then there was that jaw-dropping dress. He couldn't help but imagine sliding the fabric from her shoulders, tracing the contours of her breasts with his lips... with his tongue...

Focus, damn it.

"Did you get my messages?" he asked after clearing his throat. "I left a couple."

"I did. The flowers, too. They were lovely."

Uh-huh.

"I wanted to let you know how much I enjoyed our time together."

Gaze still ahead, she nodded. "Thank you."

He nodded, too, scratched his ear. "We left Saratoga on pretty good terms, wouldn't you say?"

Her heels clicked a little faster on the path. "We should get back to the party."

"I thought we could talk."

"Maybe later."

He pulled up. *Maybe now.*

"Is this still about your dad, Veda? Because I thought we'd worked through that."

The train of her red gown swirled as she spun back around. "We agreed to disagree. Not the same thing."

Really? "That conversation happened right before we made love again. Before you said, 'I wish we never had to leave.'"

Her nostrils flared as she crossed her arms. "If you're trying to embarrass me, it won't work."

For the love of God. "I'm trying to understand why you didn't pick up the phone."

He didn't get how she could be all prickly one second and turned on to the hilt the next. Was she an ice queen or too hot to be believed?

She hesitated before taking two steps closer. "I'm guessing you didn't tell Lanie about that night."

What the—?

"Of course not. That's between you and me."

Cringing, she darted a look toward the party pavilion. "So put away the megaphone already."

He rubbed the back of his neck, lowered his voice. "I'm confused, okay? We don't need our parents' consent. We're not kids."

"Right. We're adults making up our own minds."

He groaned. "Still confused."

"I don't regret what happened between us that night. In fact, I'll remember it as long as I live."

So he hadn't imagined it. He wasn't going insane. But when he stepped closer, happy to get back on track, her hands shot up, stopping him dead.

"Ajax, you are wonderful in every conceivable way," she said. "I love spending time with you. The problem is… I'm not the only one. You're always in news feeds with models, actresses, designers, female ranch hands, trainers… There's been an endless string of women over the years. For God's sake, you're known as the Stud."

Ajax exhaled. First he'd had Lanie bleating in his ear. Now this?

Sure, his brothers had ribbed him about that *stud* label, a name some features reporter had come up with for a story a while back. But Griff and Jacob knew who he was.

"I'm a normal and, let me emphasize, *single* guy. Like you're a normal single woman. Dating is not a crime." His shoulders went back. "And there's nothing wrong with us wanting to see each other again."

"Wanting something doesn't necessarily make it good for you."

"Unless it is."

She tried another tack. "I don't approve of the business that you're in."

Say what now?

"You mean the stud farm? Which has stables for race-horses, which is the exact same business that your father is in."

"That doesn't mean *I* like it." She asked him, "Do you have any idea how many people lose their shirts at the track?"

"Veda, I can't help that."

"Like a dealer can't help an addict who continues to use?"

"Not the same thing."

"I'll fill you in on the definition of addiction someday." She went on. "The worst part is the number of horses that are manipulated and hurt, too. Just last week, one of your own was put down after a fall."

He stiffened. "And let me tell you, I was upset about it."

"Not as upset as the horse."

He opened his mouth, stopped, and then sought clarification. "So you don't want to see me again because I own horses?"

"You *use* horses."

Whatever you want to call it. "That's not gonna change."

"No shit."

He had to grin. Veda could be direct when she wanted to be.

"Just please set me straight on one thing," he said. "You don't approve of keeping horses, but I don't hear you bawling out your bestie, the dressage champion."

"Lanie? That's...well, it's—"

"Please don't say *different.*"

"Ajax, I'm not sleeping with your sister."

"Right." Stepping closer, he lowered his head over hers and ground out, "You're sleeping with me."

His whole body was a heartbeat as she gazed up with eyes flooding with questions. Veda might have her reasons for staying away, but he could tell a big part of her wanted Saratoga again at least as much as he did.

Finally she stepped back, took a breath.

"We're here for Lanie. This is her night."

He cast a look toward the twinkling pavilion and nodded. "Agreed."

"So we need to put this aside."

"That won't work."

"At least for now. For your sister's sake."

He slowly smiled. "You're a shrewd negotiator, Darnel."

"And you're a persistent SOB."

"One way to fix persistentness...because that's absolutely a word."

She didn't hide her grin. "Okay."

"The point is, yes, we should rejoin the party, *and* have one drink together."

She cocked her head. "One drink?"

"Don't know about you, but I'm drier than a dust storm."

They continued down the path until Ajax had another thought and stopped again. "One more thing before we go in."

Veda sighed. "I'm going to regret this, aren't I?"

"I need to say how amazing you look tonight. That dress. Your hair." He slapped a hand over his heart. "And that's all I'll say on the subject. No more compliments."

And he meant it. Foot on the brake.

But one drink could always lead to two. Could maybe lead to…more.

Three

The woman who stopped beside Veda at the tent's buffet table came right out and said it.

"He's something else, isn't he?"

When the woman sent Ajax an approving look—he was talking with guests by the birthday cake—Veda's cheeks went warm. While looking over the desserts, every so often she had flickered a glance his way, obviously not as discreetly as she had thought.

And who was asking, anyway?

The woman was somewhere in her fifties and dressed in an elegant peach-colored sequined sheath. Her shoulder-length auburn hair was tucked behind an ear, revealing a dazzling teardrop diamond stud. Based on the woman's maternal smile as she continued to watch Ajax, Veda took a guess.

"You're Susan, aren't you? Hux Rawson's...housekeeper."

After many years, it was known among relevant circles

that the pair was less employee and boss these days and more a couple without the legal formalities.

Susan's dimpled smile grew. "I met Ajax when he was a teen. Now he's like my own. The other kids, too."

After Veda introduced herself—leaving out her last name, which might complicate things at this time of night—Susan looked Ajax's way again. As she leaned back against a column, her expression deepened. "Did you know that boy is the reason I'm here?"

"Really? How's that?"

The lights dimmed at the same time Veda settled in for what promised to be an interesting conversation.

"After their mom passed away," Susan explained, "the family was devastated, as you can imagine. With his father so lost in his grief, Ajax decided to step up to the plate. He placed an advertisement in the local paper. *We need a housekeeper*, the ad read. *Someone who would like a family to look after. On my word, we will look after you right back.*"

Veda's heart squeezed. "That is so sweet."

"I'd been going through some difficulties myself. Not a death, thank heaven. But enough to spin my world around 'til I didn't know which way was up. Life can be like that sometimes. Downright dizzying." Straightening, she resurrected her gentle smile. "I got the job and haven't looked back since. I've never felt more fulfilled. I'd always wanted children of my own, so those kids were the icing on my cake. Griff, Ajax, Lanie and, of course, Jacob."

Lanie had mentioned Griff, the Wall Street kingpin, as well as her adopted brother, whom she idolized as much as the other two. "Jacob's a lawyer, right?"

"With an outstanding reputation. He came to us through a juvie program." She toyed with the diamond stud as she clarified, "For years, Huxley ran a scheme here for boys in trouble who might benefit from fresh scenery and a little guidance. While they helped with chores, they learned about responsibility as well as what they were capable of and, more importantly, what they deserved out of life. Jacob had a terrible childhood, but Huxley saw something very special in that boy. He decided to fill the void and give him a real home."

Veda's chest tightened and expanded all at once. It was easy to tell that Susan had a generous heart, like Veda's mom, who had always been willing to see the best in people. Sometimes that kind of faith was uplifting. At other times, it was naive. Even foolish.

As the music segued into a slower, older tune, Susan glanced up at speakers hidden among the fairy lights. "Oh, I love this song."

The lyrics spoke of stars falling from the sky and longing to be close to someone.

Veda smiled. "I know it."

"I was so young when it came out. Back then I couldn't imagine having a gray hair or wrinkle. Time's so precious. The most precious thing we have." She held Veda's gaze when she emphasized, "Once it's gone, there's no getting it back."

Just then, Veda felt Ajax glance her way. While his gaze, curious and hot, locked with hers through the crowd, Susan straightened.

"Well, I'm going to find someone to share this dance with." As she headed off, Susan gave Veda a wink. "Maybe you should, too."

Perhaps it was the commanding picture Ajax painted in that crisp tuxedo, the knowing smile hovering at the corners of his mouth, or simply the song that amplified the moment. For whatever reason, when Ajax looked between her and the dance floor and then raised his brows in suggestion, Veda felt slightly light-headed. A little too eager to agree.

Since sharing that drink earlier, the anticipation had

only built…delicious, taut and unrelenting. Now, as Ajax extended his arms in the air in front of him like he was already slow-dancing with her, Veda felt an unraveling. Like a corset being unlaced. Like she could finally breathe out and relax.

Time *was* precious, and this night and its challenges were almost over. Wasn't this an appropriate and mature way to say goodbye?

She walked toward him. He met her halfway. After taking her hand in his much larger, far warmer one, he turned to escort her to the dance floor. Once they were surrounded by other couples, Ajax positioned their joined hands higher near his lapel while his free palm slid around to rest against the sensitive small of her back. As he smiled into her eyes, she quivered with the same kind of longing the song spoke about. Which was only to be expected, and nothing she couldn't handle. And when they began to move, his expert steps guiding hers, she was okay with his strength and his touch. She had no trouble owning her body's response to his scent and his heat.

"You met Susan," he said.

"She's a big fan of yours."

"Ah, she likes everyone. Heart of gold."

"She said you're the reason she's here."

His smile kicked up one corner of his mouth again. "The first time we met, I knew she'd fit in. Turns out, even better than I hoped. She and Dad have more than a professional relationship now. They're more than friends."

"But they never married."

While he thought that through, his hot palm shifted on her back—moving slightly lower, pressing harder. "I've never asked why. Not my business. They're happy. That's what it's all about."

As his gaze brushed her cheek, then her lips, the sexual pull tugged even more strongly. Everything about him was soothing, beguiling, on top of being sexy to a giddy fault. If he ever took a page from his father's book and settled down, all Veda could say was that his wife would be a very lucky girl.

Lanie was dancing nearby, but she didn't seem to notice them, or anyone else for that matter. Rather she looked besotted with her partner, a classic tall, dark and incredibly handsome type. Interesting. Lanie was supposed to be into her career way more than the opposite sex. It was one of the things the two women had bonded over.

Veda asked Ajax, "Who's Lanie dancing with?"

Ajax didn't turn around to check. Instead the two couples drifted farther apart.

"Lanie has a lot of friends."

Veda nodded at the crowd. "At least a couple hundred."

"You wouldn't know it now, but once upon a time she was shy. Guess we all outgrow that childhood stuff."

Veda recalled Susan's story about the kid who had taken over the reins in an effort to help his grieving family. She couldn't imagine Ajax ever being awkward, lacking confidence, doubting himself or not having just the right words. Having just the right *everything*.

The song finished up. As the DJ cued his upcoming selection, the moment stretched out. Veda and Ajax looked into each other's eyes and invisible strings worked to tug them even closer together. When the DJ played a faster, louder song, Ajax led her through the crowd to a quieter semi-hidden corner where blinking lights didn't quite penetrate and only the most curious eyes might see. As they faced each other again, with his hand still holding hers, the physical awareness zapping between them became fully charged. She imagined what might come next...

Would Ajax lift her chin and claim his first kiss of the evening?

If she let that happen, she'd be lost.

Sucking down a breath, Veda shored herself up and announced, "I'm going to call it a night."

His head went back. "You mean *now*?"

"It's getting late." They had less than an hour until midnight. "No one's left that I know."

"You know *me*."

Intimately. But better to avoid that fact.

"Lanie's obviously occupied for a while." Veda remembered how entranced her friend had looked with her dance partner. She wouldn't interrupt that chemistry to say goodnight. "I'll call and check in with her tomorrow."

"You're not staying over? I thought Lanie might have offered you a—"

"I'm staying at Dad's tonight."

A couple of days ago, she had called to give her father a heads-up. When she'd dropped in there earlier today to stash her overnight bag and change, he had been reading a book in his favorite chair. He had complimented her gown, adding, "It must be a swanky event." When Veda admitted that she was going to help celebrate Lanie's birthday at the Rawson property, her father's fingers had tightened around the book. He had restrained himself from trying to talk her out of entering enemy territory, although he had made it clear that he would be waiting up.

Now, from their tucked-away vantage point, Ajax studied the scene again. The party had changed gears, entering the phase when formalities were over. Plenty of guests were still here, happy to let loose. Plenty of women with whom Ajax could become well acquainted.

But he only tugged at his bow tie and released a couple of shirt buttons as he said, "I should call it a night, too. Big day tomorrow. I'll walk you to your car."

It had rained earlier. Crossing from the shelter of the tent onto a wet path, Veda scooped up as much of her mermaid dress train as she could. After a few steps, however, some of it slipped, dropping right into a puddle. She was about to dive and rescue what she could, but Ajax had already gone into action.

As if she weighed no more than a bagful of petals, he scooped her up into his arms. When Veda flipped the fabric up and over her lap, Ajax's gaze caught hers.

"All good?" he asked.

She almost sighed. "All good."

As they left the party noise behind, rather than focus on her body's reaction to being pressed up against so much Rawson muscle and heat, she did her best to concentrate on something else.

"When was the family house built?" she asked, studying the majestic shingle-style Victorian.

"The original place was built a hundred and forty years ago," he said, his big shoulders rolling as she gently rocked to the swing of his step. "It's still standing just a little north of here."

Veda wondered if it was anything like the original Darnel house, a gorgeous but pint-size stone structure that she used whenever she stayed over now.

"This house," Ajax went on, "was built around ten years later. It's been extended and modernized, but its heart is the same. Earthy. Solid."

Through some living room windows, she saw a wall filled with family portraits—some recent, others obviously going back years. There wasn't a single photo displayed in her father's house anywhere—not of family or graduation. Certainly not of a wedding.

As those portraits slid out of view, Veda sighed. "Lots of happy memories."

"Oh, man, I had the *best* childhood. This was a great place to grow up, and with fantastic parents." As they passed beneath an overhead light, Veda watched a pulse begin to beat in his jaw as his grin faded. "Things changed after Mom died, of course. But we got through it. In some ways, we're even stronger."

Veda was happy for them. Was even envious, as a matter of fact. What she wouldn't give to have been part of a big, happy family. How different her life would have been.

"I didn't get to meet Griff or Jacob tonight," she said, "but they looked proud standing behind Lanie with you all before the cake was cut." After a brief speech, she had thanked everyone for coming; some guests were from as far away as Argentina, Australia and the Netherlands. Lanie's dressage events took her all over the world.

"Yeah. Great night. And tomorrow morning, over a huge breakfast, all the highlights will be rehashed and new stories shared…until we're all asking about lunch."

When he chuckled, Veda noticed that her hand had come to rest upon his chest. Along with the gravelly vibration, she could actually feel his heartbeat against her palm. Then he looked down into her eyes and everything else receded into the background at the same time his gorgeous grin seemed to gravitate a smidgeon closer.

If I wound my fingers into his lapel… she thought, *…if I edged up a little and he edged down…*

Then—thank God—they arrived at her SUV. Ajax lowered her onto her feet and, as Veda admired his profile—the high brow, hawkish nose and shadowed granite jaw—he gave a thumbs-up to the ad panel for her business painted on the door.

"Best Life Now," he said. "I like it. Real catchy." He nodded like he was invested. Like he sincerely wanted to know more. "So how does a person do that—have their best life now? Do you give talks? Teach classes?"

"I do both." She delivered her automatic line for anyone who showed interest. "You ought to come along to a self-improvement seminar sometime."

Not that she could possibly tutor him on anything in

that regard. Ajax had his life all sorted out. He was exactly where, and how, he wanted to be.

He crossed his arms and assumed a stance that said she had his full attention. "Give me the elevator pitch."

"You can achieve your best life now by behaving your way to happiness and success," she replied. "Start with healthy habits and surround yourself with the best. The best friends, the best information, the best advice, *and* be smart enough to take it. You should also go after the things that matter to you the most. Everyone needs to get behind themselves and push."

"Sure." He shrugged. "Get up in the morning and get things done."

Spoken like someone who'd always had his shit together.

"Did you know that some people struggle to even roll out of bed in the morning? And you need to look beyond the rationale of just being lazy."

"Look beyond it to what?"

"Maybe past trauma, dysfunctional family, learned help-lessness."

His eyebrows drew together. "You can learn to be help-less?"

"Sure. It can happen if a person feels like they can't stop the bad stuff from happening, so they just give up."

The same way Veda had wanted to give up after her mom had died. She wasn't able to save the person she had loved most in the world. Worse, she had felt responsible for the accident. Constant feelings of worthlessness coupled with guilt had added up to a *why the hell bother?* mind-set.

Ajax's expression changed as his eyes searched hers. "There's a whole lot more to you, isn't there, Darnel?"

"A few layers. Like most people."

The perfect Ajax comeback line might be, *And I want to peel back every one, starting here, tonight.* But there were parts of Veda no one would ever know. Not her father or

Lanie. Not Veda's Best Life Now clients or blog followers. And certainly not Ajax Rawson...family rival, player extraordinaire and proponent of an industry that she wished would disappear.

As if he'd read her mind, Ajax's jaw tightened and his chin kicked up. Then, rather than delivering a line, he did something that pulled the rug right out from under her feet. He took a measured step back, slipped both hands under his jacket and into his pants pockets. The body language was clear.

Nothing more to say. Won't hold you up.

After a recalibrating moment, Veda got her rubbery mouth to work. "Well, Ajax...it was good to see you again."

"You, too, Veda. Take care. Stay well."

When he didn't offer a platonic kiss on her cheek—when he only pushed his hands deeper into his pockets—she gave a definitive nod before climbing into her car. But she hadn't started the engine before his face appeared inches away from her window.

The nerves in Veda's stomach knotted even tighter. Damn, she had to give it to this man. He'd waited until the very last minute, wanting to catch her completely off guard to ask if he could see her again.

Channeling *aloof*, Veda pressed a button. As the window whirred down, she got ready for an extra-smooth delivery. But Ajax only pointed down the driveway.

"Take it slow down the hill," he said. "There's a sharp bend near the office."

She blinked. "A bend?"

"It'll be wet after the rain."

When he stepped back again, Veda took a moment before winding the window back up, starting the car and driving away.

So...

Score, right?

Rather than trying to charm or argue with her, Ajax had given her what she wanted. A cut-and-dried goodbye. And the bonus: she wasn't the one receding in Ajax's rearview mirror. *He* was receding in *hers*. In fact, watching his reflection now, she saw how he was literally walking away.

Sighing, Veda settled in for the drive home—or tried to. After being so close to Ajax and his drugging scent, the car smelled stale, and following hours of music and conversation, the cabin was too quiet. Veda flicked on the radio, but she only heard that song playing in her head…the one she and Ajax had danced to all of ten minutes ago.

She shook herself. Thought ahead.

In thirty minutes, she would be turning into the Darnel driveway. She would find her father reclined in his tufted high-backed chair by an unlit fire. After inquiring about her evening, he would calmly regurgitate how he felt about his daughter consorting with the enemy. The Rawsons were cheats who would have their comeuppance. Drake never tired of admitting that he couldn't wait for the day.

Veda sat forward and looked up. Raindrops were falling again, big and hard on the windshield. She switched on the wipers, imagining her father's reaction should he ever discover the truth. Not only was his daughter friends with a Rawson, she had also—shock, horror!—slept with one. In his chilling way, Drake would let her know his verdict. She was no better than the woman he had loved *or* the woman he had married. To his mind, both had betrayed him with a cowboy. Then her father would disown his daughter, the same way he had disowned his wife. And there wouldn't be a thing she could do about it.

You are dead to me.

Dead. Dead. Dead.

Suddenly that tricky bend was right there in front of her. About to overshoot, Veda wrenched the wheel, slammed on the brake. As her tires slid out, she pulled the wheel the other way and the SUV overcorrected. A surreal moment later, it came to a jolting stop on the grass shoulder, at right angles to a heavy railed fence and the sweeping river of asphalt.

With those wipers beating endlessly back and forth, Veda white-knuckled the wheel, cursing her inattention. Her stupidity. But thankfully, she hadn't crashed. There was nothing that couldn't be undone. *So pull up your big-girl panties and get back on the road!* And she would…as soon as she'd dealt with the tsunami of déjà vu rolling in.

Mom sitting in the front seat of a growling pickup truck. Her cowboy boyfriend looking over his shoulder at Veda in back. A terrifying screech. A crashing, blinding jolt—

When her ears started to ring, Veda pushed open her door and scrambled out.

There were plenty of motels around. Or maybe she should simply drive on through to Jersey. She was under no obligation to see her father tonight. Damn it, her only obligation was to herself.

Not my fault, not my fault, not my fault.

At that moment, just as the skies opened up in earnest, a pair of big hands clamped down on her shoulders and spun her around. With hair whipping over her eyes, it took a moment to recognize the masculine figure, and then the concerned face streaming with rain.

Ajax raised his voice over the downpour. "What the hell are you doing?"

Veda thought about it and shrugged. "I don't know."

His brows snapped together before he threw open the back car door and waved an arm.

Get in.

The next second, he was behind the wheel, getting the vehicle back onto the driveway before turning, not toward the house or the main road, but into an offshoot lane. A moment later, they'd pulled up outside a building. After helping Veda out, he handed over her evening clutch from the front passenger seat and led the way to the building's main entrance.

Soaked through, her soles sliding in their heels, she asked over the noise of the rain, "Where are we?"

"Somewhere safe."

And yet, as Ajax punched numbers into a control pad by the door, the sign mounted next to it seemed to both mock and warn her.

Rawson Studs.
Satisfaction guaranteed.

Four

Entering the office reception area and flicking on the lights, Ajax was torn between a slump of relief and thinking, what the hell?

So much for carrying Veda over those puddles earlier. Now her hair and dress were drenched. Worse—and no surprise—she was visibly shaken. He could practically hear her teeth chattering. Had she been playing with her phone or simply off with the fairies when she'd overrun that bend? The bend he'd specifically told her to watch out for.

With Veda close behind, he strode down the corridor, past some other offices and into his private office suite—his home away from home. Running a hand through his dripping hair, he took it down a notch. And then two. The last thing she needed was a grilling. Far better that he shake it off.

"I vote scotch," he said, making a beeline for the wet bar and pouring two stiff ones. But when he brought hers over, Veda's nostrils flared like he was offering week-old hog feed.

"I don't drink hard liquor," she said.

"Fine." He lifted the glass and tossed it back. "Bottoms up."

After the heat hit his gut, Ajax found the bar again. "I'll get you a wine."

"Just water," she said. "Although… I've probably had enough of that for one night."

Enough water? Because of the rain and almost killing herself? But he didn't laugh.

Despite dancing together and their too-hot-to-ignore connection, by the time he'd escorted—no, literally carried—her to her vehicle, he'd made a decision. If Veda really wanted him to take a hike, he would comply, at least for now. So he had played nice and said good-night. Thank God he turned back around when he did. Seeing her almost take out that fence had scared the living daylights out of him. Veda must have gotten the fright of her life.

But now as she accepted the tumbler of water, he noticed her hands had stopped shaking. After taking a long sip, she let her head rock back and eased out a breath.

"I'm sorry, Ajax," she said, looking so vulnerable and bedraggled and all the more beautiful because of it.

With the tightness easing in his chest, he hitched up a shoulder and swirled his drink. "Ah, you're not hurt. That's what matters."

"I'll get out of your hair as soon as the rain stops. Promise. I don't want to hold you up."

Veda wasn't an inconvenience. He wished she'd just relax. That was sure as hell what he intended to do.

She pushed aside the wet hair clinging to her cheek and neck. "Do you mind if I take my shoes off?"

"Be my guest."

While she sat down on the couch to slip off her heels, Ajax shed his jacket and plucked at his soaked shirt.

"I need to change." He considered her soggy dress. "I can offer you a towel and a clean shirt."

Getting to her bare feet, she held up the waterlogged hem of her dress. "I'll take it."

Ajax slipped into the attached private suite where he spent most nights, and grabbed a freshly pressed shirt from the walk-in closet next to the bed. Back in the main area, he held the button-down out to Veda.

"How's this?"

"It's dry—so, perfect."

He pointed her to a guest bathroom with plenty of towels. As soon as she disappeared behind the door, he headed for his room again, ripping his shirt off as he went. After ditching everything else in a corner—shoes, socks, pants— he towel-dried his hair in the attached bathroom, then found a pair of drawstring pants. That's when his phone sounded in the next room. He recognized the ringtone.

Griff.

Hopping as he slotted each leg into the pants, he recovered the phone from his jacket's inside pocket.

"Your lights are on," Griff said when Ajax connected. "Want company? I have some stuff to unpack."

Glancing toward the guest bathroom, Ajax lowered his voice. "What's wrong?"

"Not so much outright wrong as possibly troubling."

"To do with family or business?"

"Both. I'll come down and we'll hash it out."

Ajax grasped for an excuse. "It's raining."

Silence on the other end of the line ended with a grunt.

"Okay. Got it. You have someone squirreled away with you down there."

Ajax was shaking his head. "Not what you think."

"Bro, you don't need to play Boy Scout with me."

"She had a little accident going down."

Griff cleared his throat. "Okay. Not touching that one."

"Going down the entrance road. Her car skidded out."

Griff's tone changed. "Is she all right?"

"Shaken, but otherwise fine."

"I'd ask if there was anything I can do but I'm sure you've got it in hand. Or she has."

He and Griff were of a similar mind where the opposite sex was concerned. Unlike their brother Jacob, who had recently found the girl of his dreams, neither Ajax nor Griff was ready to settle down. They dated freely and widely and, more often than not, were with women who shared the same philosophy.

Given what Lanie had said earlier, and Veda's comments about men with reputations, his current guest did not subscribe to that particular point of view, which didn't gel with her enthusiasm in Saratoga, but whatever.

Absently pulling the string on his pants tighter, Ajax said again, "Griff, this is not a hookup."

"So you two definitely won't end up naked together tonight."

Ajax looked down at his bare chest at the same time he imagined Veda's dress puddled on that bathroom floor as Griff went on. "Look, we'll catch up over breakfast. You ought to bring her along."

"Why would I do that?"

"Gee, I don't know. Manners? Food?"

"Veda won't be here in the morning."

Even if he and Veda *did* spend the night together—say, she curled up on a couch, shut her eyes and fell dead asleep—neither would want that kind of morning-after scrutiny. Yes, they were adults who were more than capable of making adult decisions. But after that "eyes and hands off" talk, Princess Lanie would blow a gasket if he walked into the house with her bestie hanging off his arm.

And Veda had that thing going on in her head about Hux—the story where he was supposed to have stolen Drake's future bride. *As if.*

"Wait a minute," Griff said. "Did you say Veda? As in Darnel's daughter?"

Ajax groaned. "Don't tell me you've got problems with that, too?"

"I, uh…" Griff exhaled. "Jax, we'll talk in the morning, okay?"

Ajax was signing off when the guest bathroom door fanned open. As Veda stepped out, every cell in his body stood to attention. The button-down shirt she wore was ten sizes too big, her towel-dried hair was a flaming mess, and what he could see of her legs made his mouth water. The unconscious way she used both hands to push back all that hair told him she felt more relaxed. Then she stopped, her eyes grew to saucers, and Ajax remembered.

She was the only one wearing a shirt.

He'd swear on the Bible that was not intentional.

"I, uh, got caught up on a call," he said, waving the phone.

Veda's gaze slid up from his chest.

"It was Griff," he said. "My brother. He saw the lights on here, so I filled him in."

"As in, I'm an idiot?"

"As in we need reflector lights on that curve."

When her eyes dipped to his chest again, Ajax reevaluated his position. He definitely had *not* brought Veda here to seduce her. Before his phone had rung, he'd had every intention of slipping on a T-shirt. But now he got the distinct impression that Veda wasn't about to freak at his lack of clothing. Hell, she'd seen him in way less than this.

Veda was crossing over to his desk. He'd left his hat by a stack of papers. Now she ran a finger around the black brim, then sent a bland glance his way.

"Every cowboy needs one."

"At *least* one. That particular hat's for dressing up." Like for meetings, events. He nodded at another Stetson on a vintage hat stand. "That one's for work." For when he was hands-on in the stables with the horses and his team.

She picked up the formal hat and sussed out its lines as he wandered over.

"I reckon it'd suit you," he said.

"Pretty sure you're wrong."

He took the hat, but when he placed it on her head, the brim fell low enough to cover her nose. He saw her grin before repositioning the inner band so that it was propped against the front of her crown.

"There now," he said. "Not too big at all."

"All I need is a set of spurs and a big ol' buckle on my belt—"

The hat slipped again. As she caught it and pushed it back up, he angled her around toward some mirrored wall tiles. Setting her hands on her hips, she struck an Annie Oakley pose, then pulled a face.

"Yeah, nah." She lifted the hat off her head as she turned back around. "Bend down."

She set the Stetson square on his head, then stepped back to inspect her work. As she took him in from top to tail, her grin changed from light and playful to *we're having too much fun here*.

Putting her weight on one leg, she crossed her arms. "Your other hat's black, too."

"Yep. All of them from day one."

"Which was…?"

"When did I get my first real cowboy hat?" He scratched his temple under the brim. "I can't remember ever being without one." When her lips twitched, like he'd said something funny, he frowned. "What's the joke?"

"It's just…at the risk of inflating your ego, you look like you ought to be on a billboard right now."

He flicked a glance up at the brim. "You like the hat that much?"

"I like the overall picture. Who wouldn't?" She seemed to gather herself, adjusting the oversize shirt's collar, before assuming an indifferent expression. "Just an observation."

Ajax's smile grew. "An observation, huh?"

"The hat, the smile. You know…" She fluttered her hands at his chest.

Chewing his inner lip, Ajax grinned more.

"I think you're flirting with me," he said.

She rolled her eyes. "I am not."

"You definitely are, and you know it."

"Ajax, I've never said you weren't sexy."

"Double negative, but go on."

"That's it." She glanced at his chest *again*, then, just as fast, looked away. "You can stop fishing for compliments."

"Well, I have something to say."

"Of course you do."

"You seem okay now. After that incident in your car."

"I am. Thanks again."

"And one other thing."

"Let me guess. You think I'm sexy, too."

Well, yeah. But that aside…

"Just thought you'd like to know—" he nodded toward the window "—the rain stopped five minutes ago."

Ohmigod!

He was doing it again. Being all mind-bendingly gorgeous, having her believe he was about to make a big move, and then—

And then—

Veda spun toward the window.

The rain had stopped?

"I thought it was still pouring."

"Nope." He rubbed his knuckles over his shadowed jaw as he peered out the window, too. "Guess it could start again, though."

Before she thought to stop herself, Veda smiled. "Yes, it could."

"But you said you wanted to leave as soon as it eased off. So, to be safe, you should probably make a break for it now."

That teasing grin, the mischievous glint in his dreamy blue eyes... He was just so full of it.

"You love playing with me, don't you?"

His smoldering grin spread wider. "I'll go with yes."

She'd put it another way. "You don't really want me to go."

"Wait. *You* were the one who said you wanted to leave. I'm merely respecting your wishes. Keeping you up to date. Making sure any possibility of you and me getting together again tonight is categorically off the table." He shrugged his broncobusting shoulders. "That *is* what you want, right?"

While his chin tilted downward so that the brim of his hat almost covered the gleam in his eyes, Veda froze. What was the right response? She wasn't completely sure anymore. The spinout in her car had brought back some ugly memories. Now she was with the man who had stormed down that hill in the rain to rescue her, which had made her feel not just good but safe.

And yet Ajax was the furthest thing from that. He was a prince in the art of seduction. He was in love with an industry she loathed.

For God's sake, he was a Rawson.

"I can see you're frustrated," he went on.

She grunted and shifted on her feet. "A little."

"Would you like me to fix that for you?"

Like how? By kissing her senseless?

He was blindly laying the hat on the desk while he studied her face and hair like she was a fine piece of art. Like he could devour her whole in one big-bad-wolf bite.

"Veda? You okay?"

She held her nervy stomach. "I'm not sure."

His gaze raked over her again, drawing out the moment, leaving her to wince and wonder and wait.

"You know," he finally said, "I wasn't going to push it, but we need to do this. We need to quit playing games."

"Playing games?"

"Come on, Veda. You know what I'm talking about. Just be honest and say it—"

"Okay, okay! We do. We need to talk."

A muscle in his jaw jumped before he gave a slow, approving nod. "So you agree. We need to be open about how we feel."

"And then what?"

"Then we need to do something about it."

"You mean the same something we did in Saratoga."

He moved closer, until his breath warmed her brow and the energy arcing from his body to hers could be measured in megawatts.

In his lowest, sexiest voice, he said, "I'm going to kiss you now."

Her insides began to throb. To beg. "Why…why are you telling me that?"

"I want to know you're okay with it."

"You didn't ask the first time you kissed me."

"Did you want me to?"

"No."

"And now?"

She blinked, then gave it up. "I suppose you can tell me what to expect."

His lidded gaze dropped and locked on her mouth. "This kiss will be soft and light. Just a taste. Just in case. Then, if you're absolutely sure, I'll kiss you again. Deeper and longer next time."

She croaked, "And then…?"

"Then…" He studied her shirt. "That'll need to go."

She swallowed and pushed out a quivery breath.

"Ajax…?"

"Yes, Veda?"

"I'm not wearing anything underneath."

His grin grew. "I was hoping you'd say that."

Five

This time four weeks ago, she and Ajax had been in Saratoga Springs. As they strolled around a garden after the charity event, there hadn't been a cloud in the jasmine-scented moonlit sky. She remembered how he had stopped to cup her face and then kiss her like no woman had ever been kissed before. In that instant, it was all over.

She was his.

For years, she had dreamed of Ajax Rawson telling her she was beautiful, making her blush. But that night he'd done so much more than that. He had lifted her up. Helped her to fly.

After parting ways, she'd decided that had to be a one-time-only experience. And yet, as his lips met hers now and sparks began to ignite, Veda only wanted to know that kind of ecstasy again. Suddenly all she cared about was Ajax, all night long.

That didn't change when his mouth claimed hers and she found out he had lied. This wasn't soft and light, or just a taste just in case. This was as deliberate as any kiss got. And then his arms wound around her, urging her in, and her hands found his chest, hard and hot just as she re-membered. When her fingertips grazed his nipples, she felt his grin before he deepened the kiss…so penetrating and skilled, her blood felt on fire.

While she reacquainted herself with his shoulders and pecs, his hands trailed down her back until they were under her shirttails, kneading her buns. After each lov-ing squeeze, his fingers slid together, scooping between the backs of her thighs. When Veda lifted a knee against the outside of his leg, his tongue stopped stroking hers for a beat before his touch went deeper, sliding along her sex. Each time he dipped a finger inside, pressing on just the right spot, she inched that knee a little higher and held on that bit tighter.

"I've thought about you every day," he murmured against her lips.

"Me, too," she sighed. "I've thought of you."

His jaw grazed her cheek. "Next time, you'll answer my calls."

She couldn't stop grinning. "Just try to get me off the phone."

He hooked both hands between the backs of her thighs, coaxing her legs apart as he effortlessly raised her up. As her feet left the floor and her legs looped around him, she clung to his neck before his mouth took hers again. Cra-dling her seat, he rotated her hips, pressing her closer, stok-ing that heat.

And as his hold grew firmer and the grinding got more intense, the friction began to climb…dear Lord, it began to blaze.

That night in Saratoga, Veda had given herself to him completely despite being nervous as hell. Ajax remembered how she had blushed while he'd gotten her out of that dress…how she had hesitated that first time climbing on top. Being with Veda had felt different.

Had felt…new.

Tonight, however, the training wheels were off. In no time, they had gone from kissing to full steam ahead. Now her legs were lashed around his hips, and every time he pushed in against her, the bulge in his pants just grew and grew.

Breaking the kiss, he set his chin on her forehead, found his breath and drilled down on necessities.

"Protection," he said.

Her teeth grazed his Adam's apple. "We need that."

As he resumed their kiss, her hand dipped under his waistband and coiled around his erection. It felt good. *Very* good. Dropping his weight a little, he balanced her on his thighs to give her a little more room.

A moment later, he fought through the pheromone fog to ask and be sure. "You're on the pill, though, right?"

Her grip on his neck slipped. At the same time he caught her, he moved to brace a palm against the nearest wall. A heartbeat later, she eased up and positioned the tip of his shaft precisely where it needed to be.

After that initial bolt of pleasure, he began to move. Not in careful, gentle *we'll get there* pumps. Tonight she obviously didn't need slow and steady, and you'd better believe, neither did he.

Her fingers were in his hair, knotting through the back, plowing up the sides, and he was wishing it hadn't been so long between encounters because nothing felt like this… Veda here with him now and all brakes off, letting him know that her reasons for staying away didn't matter anymore.

Or at least didn't matter tonight.

As her legs vised tighter and his hold on her butt grew

firmer, perspiration broke out on his brow, down his back. And then the responsible side of his brain kicked in again. *No glove, bro, no love.* Being inside her again was better than anything. But he needed to rein it in. For a start, he wanted to satisfy her first.

But it seemed, on that score, she was way ahead of him.

He was about to pull out when she ground in that much harder, deeper, at the same time her legs locked around him extra tight. When her head arced back, she shuddered and convulsed as her mouth dropped open and her nails bit into his neck.

God! There was so much steam and energy. Such intensity and blinding, shooting heat.

That was the second Ajax realized he'd just crossed the finish line, too.

Six

Amazing wasn't the right word. It wasn't nearly big or, well, *real* enough. With early-morning light filtering in through the windows, and Veda still asleep, the best Ajax could come up with to describe last night's reunion was explosive.

Lying beside her, facing her, he played with a wave of her hair as he recalled the conflagration when they'd come together. He'd been acutely aware of the heat as it built, the speed with which it had grown. But that tandem climax had caught him completely off guard.

Afterward, Ajax had carried her in here to the bedroom where they'd scrapped her shirt and his pants and played around in a warm sudsy shower. There'd been plenty of exaggerated lathering and just as much kissing. But after toweling off, they'd slipped under these sheets, snuggled up and fallen asleep.

As he'd drifted off, Ajax had embraced the feeling. Absolutely, without question, he'd been satisfied like never before. Now he wanted to coax her awake and not only re-capture it all, but go harder and deeper.

He wanted to know so much more.

Veda stirred. Tangles of red hair glistened in the muted light as she stretched and sighed and eventually blinked open her eyes. She smelled of soap, remnants of her cit-rusy perfume and a natural scent that aroused him possi-bly even more than the sight of her breasts peeking above the rumpled sheet. He wanted to trace the tip of his tongue around each nipple, nip and gently suck the tips.

Instead he brushed his lips over hers. When she sighed again, sleepily smiling into his eyes, he ran a palm up her side. As he found her breast, she slid her fingers back through his hair.

Angling his head, he kissed her slowly and emphatically while he rolled her nipple between a finger and thumb. Then, moving closer, he pressed in against her belly, letting her know how darn turned on he was. He loved making her come, making her happy. He couldn't think of a better way to kick off a lazy Sunday morning. Hell, if it was up to him, he'd spend the whole day here. The whole week.

Then Veda paused and shifted onto her back. Maybe she wanted him to use his mouth instead. He was only too happy to oblige.

But as he moved to go down, she caught his shoulder. Her voice was croaky but firm.

"What time is it?"

Ajax leaned in to circle the tip of his nose around hers. "Doesn't matter."

"It *so* matters."

A few moments earlier, he'd caught the time on his wristwatch on the bedside table. "A little after seven."

She shut her eyes and groaned. "I need to go."

"You do not need to go." He knew where she was headed with this, but right now they needed the outside world to butt out. "If you're worried about what anyone might think—" like Lanie or Hux, or Griff, who'd called it last night on the phone "—this is none of their business."

"It would just be so much easier—"

"You know what would be easier?" he cut in, edging closer. "If we finished what we're doing now. And later, you come up to the house and have breakfast."

She blinked like he was talking Mandarin. And, yes, he'd baulked at that breakfast idea, too, when Griff had suggested it. But now, after being with Veda again, extending that invitation seemed like the obvious thing to do. He didn't want to shoo Veda off like he was ashamed or some kind of prick.

"Sorry," she said, pushing up onto an elbow. "I don't work that way. I'm not going to flaunt it."

Ah, hell. He'd come right out and say it then. "You mean because your father wouldn't approve?"

Her eyes widened. "My father wouldn't be the only one knocked off his chair." She stopped, seemed to remember something and then cursed under her breath. "I forgot to call to say not to wait up."

"Your father was waiting up for you?" Really? How old was she again?

"It's his house. I am his daughter."

"And you're over twenty-one."

She switched tacks. "What about Lanie? What's she going to think?"

When she found out that her friend and brother had spent the night together? "Lanie wouldn't expect this. But she'll support you because that's what friends do. Siblings, too, for that matter."

He pushed up to sit against the headboard. Veda took her time but finally joined him. Wrapping his arm around her, he nuzzled her sweet-smelling hair and waited. He'd said enough. Time for her speak.

Bit by bit, he felt her relax. Eventually, she laid a palm on his chest.

"When I drove away last night," she said, "I was…distracted. Thinking about Dad and how he would react if he knew…"

Drake might get his nose out of joint, but dude. Suck it up. Except Veda didn't need to hear that.

Ajax stroked her arm, nuzzled her again.

"I'm sorry," he said.

"Sorry we got together, or sorry that my father's against anything Rawson?"

"Veda, I don't care what Drake thinks about me or my family. I care about how you feel."

She paused before she rubbed her cheek against his shoulder, nodding.

"I want to tell you something else," she said.

He held her a little tighter. "Shoot."

"When we were younger, I had a massive crush on you. I'd go to a race with my father and see you there with your dad. You were this tall, blond, muscle-ripped dream. Always smiling and talking. But I think an even bigger part of the attraction was knowing you were taboo. Forbidden. And even though I've moved away and have my own place and my own views, I always felt that was a place I could never go."

Ajax's gut was in knots. Imagine growing up in the cold shadow of a father like Drake Darnel. Sure, Ajax liked having his own father's approval, particularly when it came to looking after the farm and the business. Hux's middle name was High Standards. But they were still their own people who enjoyed a mutual respect. There was trust. A certain understanding.

Which was obviously not the case where Veda and Drake were concerned.

"So don't tell your father," he said. The silly old coot didn't need to know.

"It's too late for that. My car is parked right out front. Whether or not I sit down for breakfast with your family, rumors will spread. They always do."

"My family isn't into gossip, Veda."

"Maybe not. But you have how many employees? Riders, assistant trainers, grooms, barn and breeding managers? I just want to get in my car and drive away." She winced before giving a small, surrendering smile. "But I guess I'll stand tall and stay."

He got that this was hard for her, and maybe she was right. Maybe she should just jump in her car and forget the whole breakfast-with-the-Rawsons thing.

"Are you sure?" he asked.

A wave of red fell over her cheek as she nodded. "Except... I can't wear an evening dress or a man's shirt to your family's table."

"Well, I know how to fix that."

She was already onto it. "You mean contact Lanie and ask if she's got anything I can borrow."

Veda looked like she'd rather pull out her toenails.

"I can do it," he said.

"Thanks, but it'd seem less weird coming from me."

Just then his phone sounded. A text.

"Princess Lanie's morning ride must have taken her by here," he said, putting aside the phone after reading his sister's message.

Veda slumped. "She saw my car."

"She says that she just dropped off a selection of clothes at my front door, and she expects to see us both at breakfast." He cocked a brow. "Or else."

People openly talked about anxiety these days. No matter how infrequently, everyone experienced the sensations.

Racing heartbeat. Increased blood flow. Feeling uneasy, flustered. Even panicked.

On her blog, Veda often addressed the issue. Her philosophy? Accept that you're only human and embrace the idea that you can work through it. Having grown up with a learning disability, a self-absorbed father and a mother who "loved too much," Veda felt as if she had earned the right to give advice on the subject.

As an adult, she continued to feel the fear and come out the other side, like last night when she'd been left alone to speak with Hux Rawson. Or now, walking into the Rawsons' dining room with Ajax as everyone's attention turned their way. Even the golden retriever lying by the closed porch door lifted its head to check her out. Just like last night with Hux, Veda's throat closed while her heart punched her ribs like a heavyweight champ. But she would get through it.

She always did.

The stunned silence ended when Lanie called out from a separate buffet table adorned with silver-domed platters.

"You guys want a coffee?" she asked. Her attitude was, *Nothing to see here, folks. Just my lady-killer brother with his latest conquest, who just happens to be my friend and a Darnel.*

As promised in the text, Lanie had left an assortment of clothes on Ajax's office doorstep; Veda had chosen a mustard-colored sundress and matching sandals. And yet as Lanie laid two brimming coffee cups in front of a pair of vacant chairs, she avoided Veda's gaze. Didn't so much as try to return the smile.

As if Veda hadn't felt awkward enough.

From his vantage point at the head of the massive table, Hux Rawson nodded a greeting as Veda and Ajax took their seats to his left. Brother Griff raised his cup and muttered, "Morning," while Jacob offered an easy smile, as

did the beautiful woman beside him. A high chair sat between the pair, occupied by a little boy playing "squish"
with a banana.

Veda expected Hux to rise above any perceived awk-
wardness and say something inclusive...welcoming. But
he was looking off toward an adjoining doorway—perhaps the kitchen—as if someone had just called his name.

As relaxed and charming as ever, Ajax did the honors.

"Everyone, for those who don't know, this is Veda."

No surname supplied, which set off a tug-of-war in the
pit of Veda's gut. She would rather Darnel wasn't mentioned, but like it or not, it was a big part of who she was.

Jacob was the first to speak up.

"I didn't get over to say hi last night. I'm Jacob." He ruf-
fled the boy's mop of dark hair, an identical shade to his
own. "This is my son, Buddy. And next to him, the other
love of my life."

The woman's eyes sparkled with obvious affection for
them both before she met Veda's gaze. "I'm Teagan. Great
to meet you, Veda. Can I just say—I love your hair."

Veda had brought a small comb in her evening purse.
Not nearly enough to get through this morning's whole
new level of tangle. Then she had used Ajax's brush to
sort through as many knots as she could, which still hadn't
taken care of things.

Smiling, Veda ran two fingers around a thick wave.
"There's lots of it, and it's all red."

The oldest Rawson brother introduced himself. "I'm
Griff."

Veda returned his smile, which looked a little wooden.

"Nice to meet you, Griff," she said.

"Did you have a nice time last night, Veda?" Hux asked
as Susan entered the room. Upon seeing the additional
guest, she hesitated before recovering to take a seat alongside Hux.

"It was a lovely evening," Veda replied without a stumble, although her hands in her lap were clutched tight enough to strangle someone. "Just beautiful."

"I got to bed around three." Having set down her plate of hash browns and avocado toast, Lanie took her seat between Susan and Ajax at the same time she blew a kiss to her dad. "Positively the best night ever."

Susan was looking past Lanie and Ajax to Veda. "We discussed a song, you and I."

Veda nodded and smiled. Susan was such a sweet lady. "It's still doing rounds in my head."

Ajax finished swallowing a mouthful of coffee. "What song?"

Susan sang a couple of lines about creating a dream come true, and then winked at Hux while everyone else either chuckled or grinned. Veda felt her own smile warm her right through. Yes, this was awkward. She and Lanie would need to talk later. But the overall energy said *togetherness*...said family ties and lots of love.

When Ajax pushed back his chair and nodded toward the buffet table, Veda followed his lead and stood up. While she put some strawberries and a lemon muffin on her plate, Ajax gathered enough food to stock her refrigerator for a week. Meanwhile, at the table, the Rawsons were back to discussing the party. The focus was off her, thank God.

While taking their seats again, Hux kicked off a different conversation, speaking directly to Ajax.

"I've had an interesting chat with Yvette Maloney. She wants to buy a few acres that butt up against her property, and for an eye-popping price, I gotta say."

"You mean the parcel with the original house," Ajax said, squeezing a pool of ketchup onto his plate. "Not for sale."

"That old place needed a bulldozer when Dad was a kid," Griff said.

"Not anymore." Ajax collected his silverware. "I've done some work on it over the years."

Hux's eyebrows shot up. "Where'd you find the time?"

"A day here and there." Ajax cut into a fat sausage. "In my opinion, those acres are the best we have. Yvette Maloney knows that."

The men back-and-forthed for a while. When the subject ran out of steam, Jacob took a fork and pinged it against his glass.

"Everyone, I have an announcement to make."

Hux swallowed a mouthful of waffle. "We're all ears, son."

Jacob reached past the high chair to squeeze his partner's shoulder. "I gave Teagan a ring this morning." He caught her gaze and smiled like only a man in love could. "We've set a date."

The room erupted as everyone got to their feet to give Teagan hugs while Buddy's plump cheeks pinked up with excitement and he slapped banana all over his bib. Veda remembered Lanie mentioning their situation. Jacob had been given full custody by Buddy's mother while Teagan—a billionaire's daughter, no less—was relatively new to such a family dynamic.

Veda didn't insert herself among the well-wishers. She simply smiled, letting the newly engaged couple know how happy she was for them both. The way they gazed at each other—with respect and pure adoration—it was clear they had a wonderful future ahead of them.

Suddenly the backs of Veda's eyes began to prickle. It happened sometimes when she thought about marriage. Kids. Of course all that was way down on her to-do list. Right now her focus was on her work and helping her Best Life Now clients achieve their goals. But one day she *would* like a family of her own.

And, boy oh boy, would she do it right.

Jacob reached across and lifted Teagan's left hand; a multi-carat emerald-cut diamond sparkled on her third finger. Standing behind the couple, Ajax glanced across the table and caught Veda's gaze. His brows nudged together and his head slanted before he returned his attention to the happy couple and their child.

"We'll need to celebrate," Susan said, drifting back to her seat. "An engagement party."

"My father wants to give us a party in Australia," Teagan said, mopping up banana from around Buddy's mouth. "You're all welcome, of course."

"A trip Down Under." Griff scratched his head. "What's that? A twenty-two-hour flight?"

"From this side of the country," Teagan replied. "I live in Seattle. Or *did* live there."

Jacob explained for Veda's sake. "Teagan's moved to Connecticut to be with Buddy and me."

There was more talk about the wedding, which would take place on the Rawson property, the same kind of elaborate party pavilion-style event as last night's birthday do. Veda thought about the distant future and the possibility of having a wedding at the Darnel estate. Her father was often so cynical and miserable, she couldn't see him offering his home, let alone being truly happy for her no matter who she married. Drake didn't believe in that kind of love.

Everyone returned to their seats and their various conversations. But Lanie still avoided Veda. Was her friend that taken aback at this turn of events between Ajax and Veda or was she simply annoyed?

Ajax was finishing the last of his hash browns when Griff caught his attention from the other side of the table.

"Ajax, you got a minute?"

Dabbing his mouth, Ajax looked Veda's way. She nodded. Of course he should go talk with his brother. It opened the door for her and Lanie to have a chat, which would include an explanation of how Ajax and she had first met. Simply put, she had fallen for Ajax Rawson's charms not once now, but twice. He made her feel so good. Like when they were alone, and in the zone, she didn't have to try.

Didn't have to think.

And, yes, she knew he'd made a lot of women feel that way.

Someone's phone was ringing. Hux pulled a device out of his top pocket and studied the caller ID with a quizzical look on his face.

Getting to his feet, Griff asked, "Who is it, Dad?"

"Matt Quibell. From the State Gaming Commission."

Veda didn't miss the look Griff slid Ajax's way before he said, "Maybe you should call him back."

But Hux was connecting the call. "Matt's a friend. He might want to congratulate us on yesterday's win."

Griff lowered himself back into his seat and motioned for Ajax to do the same as Hux Rawson swiped his phone screen to pick up. Lanie and Teagan talked across the table while Buddy sucked a piece of toast and Jacob looked between Griff and Ajax. Veda got that receiving a call from anyone at the Commission, particularly on a Sunday morning, was a big deal. But Hux had said this guy was a friend.

However, by the time Hux finished the call, with only a few mumbled words from his end, his face was gray. He dropped the phone on the table and fell back in his chair like he'd caught a bullet in the chest. Susan reached to hold his hand.

"What happened?" she asked. "Huxley, what's wrong?"

"Yesterday after the race, an objection was lodged regarding our runner in the twelfth," he said.

Ajax gave a slanted grin. "It was a dry track. A clean race."

"Matt wanted me to know the objection relates to allegations of horse doping." Hux's brows knitted as he eye-balled his son. "Those allegations, Ajax, are against you."

Ajax was lost for words.

He felt everyone's questions drilling into him and, holy shit, he had them, too. Overmedicating, doping…no question, it happened in the industry. But everyone knew that Ajax Rawson's horses won fair and square or not at all.

Shaking his head again, he tried to resurrect his smile, shake everything off, because this was crazier than purple snowflakes in June. It was crazy to think he would throw away his sterling reputation, and for what? A Grade 1 purse? Yes, his was a nice cut. But Rawson horses had won plenty and would win plenty more.

"That's a crock." Ajax scanned the table of shocked faces and shrugged. "It's a mistake."

Jacob asked their father, "Who made the allegation?" like he was already taking notes in his head for a legal defense.

"An assistant trainer." Hux was focused on Ajax. "He claims he saw your float driver, Paul Booshang, using a syringe."

Ajax heard Veda's sharp intake of air as he held up a hand. "Stop right there. Paul is a good guy. I trust him like everyone I allow near my horses. That assistant trainer is full of it."

"You left right after the usual samples were taken from Someone's Prince Charming," Hux said.

"Sure." Ajax shrugged. "I needed to get back for the party."

"Later, Booshang was questioned by a steward. Apparently he wanted to come clean. He said you'd done this kind of thing before. That you must've gotten away with false negatives in the past. Or you'd paid someone off."

Ajax's heart was pounding in his chest and in his ears.

Gravity wanted to suck him back down into his seat. But he lifted his chin and stood firm, even as steam rose from around his collar. Even as his hands fisted into mallets by his sides.

"I need to talk to Paul." Now.

"Good luck finding him, because I'd bet my right leg he won't be anywhere around here." Hux threw his linen napkin on his plate. "Expect a call after the EDTP results are in."

Ajax heard Teagan ask Jacob in a near whisper, "What's EDTP?"

In a low voice, Jacob replied, "New York's Equine Drug Testing Program. Postrace testing is performed by Morrisville State College under contract with the Gaming Commission."

While Ajax digested the news, Hux looked somehow resigned. Or was that disappointed? Impossible. Ajax's ethics were as sound as his father's. Hux couldn't possibly believe...not for one second...

Ajax remembered Veda sitting beside him. She was gripping the edge of the table, looking up at him like he'd grown a pair of horns. Like he was already guilty as charged. And if for any reason those results came back positive for banned substances, as owner and trainer, he would be held legally responsible. Whether he was involved or not, the buck stopped with him.

Sitting forward, Griff clasped his hands on the table. "I don't think Booshang acted on his own."

"He's in this with someone else?" Jacob's amber-gold gaze burned into his brother's. "Why would you think that?"

Griff's jaw flexed. "I overhead something at the party last night."

Ajax's head snapped back. *My God.* "You knew this was coming, didn't you?"

That's why Griff had wanted to talk last night. Why he'd been so eager to get him away from the table a minute ago. He wanted a huddle before this all hit.

When he was thirteen, Griff had decided to befriend a stallion named Devil's Fire. Now he absently rubbed the scar above his left eye that had resulted from a secret bareback mount and subsequent fall.

"I caught a few words of a conversation between two guests you'd invited, Dad," Griff said. "One had a horse in the same race. I heard him say that a steward was speaking with one of our drivers who had links to...certain people."

Hux's voice rose. "Speak up, son. Links to who?"

Griff averted his gaze when he ground out, "Drake Darnel."

As blood drained from his head, Ajax shut his eyes. Booshang had worked for other stables in the past, including Darnel's. Obviously he hadn't held it against the guy. But now Ajax was boiling mad inside. Not only had Booshang abused his trust on so many levels, now Drake Darnel was involved? Was he that jealous of Rawson's impeccable reputation and list of wins that he would try to frame them? Or was this some warped form of revenge for Hux supposedly stealing Drake's girl all those years ago?

Like, seriously—get a life!

Ajax strode for the door. "I'm going to find Booshang, wherever the hell he is, and tell him he's got two choices. Talk, and fast, or—"

"Being a hothead won't solve anything," Jacob said, shooting to his feet. "We need some kind of strategy going forward."

Ajax took a breath. When Jacob had first arrived at the farm all those years ago, Ajax had been less than taken with the juvie kid from Brooklyn. Jacob had been defensive, on the edge. But Hux had seen something in the troubled teen.

Jacob had had to work to gain their father's trust but, hey, hadn't they all?

Hux pushed back his chair. "Let's get on it then. We'll need vet records for a start. And a detective to dig around and see if there's anything to a Darnel connection." He squeezed Susan's hand before he stood and nodded toward his den at the back of the house. "Giddyap, boys."

When Ajax saw Jacob ruffling his son's hair and kissing his fiancée, he remembered Veda again. He strode back over and took her hand. Hux's dog, Chester, scrambled out of the way as Ajax swung open the door and ushered Veda outside onto the porch.

"And you thought this wasn't going to be easy," he joked as he shut the connecting door for privacy's sake.

Releasing his hand, Veda continued to give him an unimpressed look.

"I need to go."

Ajax couldn't argue. He had business to take care of, no getting around that. And, irrespective of whether her nut-job father was actually involved in this mess, now Veda needed some time and space.

"I'll walk you down to your car."

"I can walk myself." Her stony mask eased a little. "I wanted to talk to Lanie, but that can wait."

What a mess. This morning couldn't have ended worse. "I'm sorry this happened."

"It's almost poetic justice, don't you think?"

"Meaning…?"

"You and I…not the best idea."

His chest tightened, but he managed a stoic smile. "Let me sort this out."

When he took her hands, she pulled away.

"Do what you need to do. I don't want to be involved."

He held her gaze. "Just so we're clear, I don't dope my horses."

"You mean with steroids? Or just with too much of the legal stuff? Everyone knows it happens, and way more than the establishment cares to admit. No one even talks about the jockeys' lives that are put at risk when a juiced-up horse breaks down."

Ajax shot back, "In case you missed it, your father could be implicated." Her comment stung, and he couldn't help himself.

"Go ahead and join the dots for me." She crossed her arms. "I know you want to."

"Booshang worked at Darnel Stables in the past. Given how much your father hates Hux, maybe it's a frame job."

"Why would Booshang risk his job and a fine to help set you up?"

"Geez, I don't know. Maybe *money*? Your father is loaded. And he still has it out for Hux. Poor jealous bastard."

When her eyes flashed and nostrils flared, Ajax knew he'd gone too far.

"I need the entry code to get into the office building," she said.

To get her belongings. He'd left his private suite unlocked, so fine.

But then Ajax paused. He couldn't be sure if Booshang was indeed still on Drake's payroll. Regardless, Veda wasn't involved. And the vast majority of his records were electronic. But if he allowed her unsupervised access to his office, to his hard files, would she be tempted to snoop? Not that she would find anything untoward. And he had cameras installed outside so he could check the footage later if need be.

He passed on the code and watched her stride off, red hair swishing, before he kicked a porch post as hard as he could. But he had to focus on his number one priority now.

He needed to clear his name, and if that meant taking down
Drake Darnel as an accomplice in this lie...

Ring the bell.

Bring it on.

Veda felt as if she had escaped a war zone. Breakfast
with the Rawsons was supposed to have been a little shaky
but ultimately fine. She should never have agreed to go.
She should never have gotten with Ajax again, full stop.
For whatever reason—and there were a few—it was always
going to end badly.

She took a shortcut to the Rawson office through a lush
connecting paddock. Inhaling fresh air mixed with the
smell of horse, she held each of her cheeks in turn, trying
to pat away the heat. She had no prior knowledge of this
doping incident. As for her father? Drake hated the Rawsons, but he wouldn't stoop to criminal behavior to discredit
them. Absolutely not.

The Rawsons were the ones incriminated here, not the
Darnels.

As for Booshang being the one at the heart of this matter...she wasn't about to blurt out her personal association
with Paul in front of Ajax or anyone else; how suspicious
would that look? She didn't know whether Ajax had worked
with Booshang to dope that horse, whether he'd done it before, and she didn't *want* to know. As far as she was concerned, this was the end. Ajax could send as many flowers
as he liked. He could call her until his redial finger dropped
off. She would never buckle and see him again.

She couldn't get out of here fast enough.

Using the code, Veda let herself into the building. She
grabbed her gown, shoes and purse and headed for the
door again. But then a series of glaring thoughts stopped
her dead.

Ajax's denial of involvement had seemed genuine, but

if he *was* involved, she doubted he would simply throw up his hands and confess, particularly in front of his family. His father. Could Paul Booshang prove Ajax's involvement? Might there be some kind of evidence hidden away within these walls? A signed contract between the two men, maybe? But where would a person begin to look? If she dared, how much might she find?

Veda's ears pricked up. Through the open door, she heard a dog bark and hooves galloping nearer. She hurried out.

On the back of a magnificent black Thoroughbred, Lanie was closing the distance between them, her long dark hair streaming behind her.

Lanie had been kind enough to lend her these clothes. Her friend had also offered a welcoming comment when she and Ajax had entered the Rawsons' dining room earlier, but she hadn't met Veda's gaze once. Obviously she wasn't happy about her friend's overnight arrangements. How much less impressed would Lanie be when she found out that this wasn't the first time?

With an armful of red evening gown, Veda was opening her car door when Lanie jumped out of her saddle.

"I thought you and I should talk," she said, tossing the reins over a rail as the Rawsons' golden retriever scooted to a stop on her heels.

"This isn't the best time," Veda said, dumping her belongings on the back seat.

"You stayed with Ajax last night." She was stroking her horse's neck. "I had assumed he wasn't your type."

"But then Ajax is every girl's type, right?"

Lanie's hand dropped. "Who exactly are you angry with?"

"I'm angry with myself."

"Because you made a mistake?"

"Because I made *two*." When Lanie's eyebrows shot

up, Veda slammed the door shut. "Don't look at me like that."

"Well, see, here's the funny part. Early last night, I caught him looking at you like a wolf might drool over a juicy lamb chop. I told him you were off-limits."

So Lanie had been looking out for her, defending her from her stud brother, while Veda had lied to her friend by omission.

Veda slumped back against the car. "I should have told you."

"You don't owe me an explanation. Women find my brother exceedingly attractive—irresistible, in fact—and he knows it."

"That makes me feel so much better."

"As long as the two parties involved are consenting adults who know the stakes, it's off to the races, as they say."

Veda opened the driver's-side door. "I don't intend to see him again."

"Because of this doping business?"

"Among other things."

"Playing hard to get will only make him chase you more."

Veda sank in behind the wheel. "I'm not playing."

The glint in Lanie's bright blue gaze softened. "You're my friend, no matter what happens between you and Ajax. And remember… I'm his sister, not his keeper. I don't control what he does, how he feels. No one does." Lanie shrugged. "And who knows? Maybe in you, the mighty Ajax will finally meet his match."

Veda was buckling her seat belt. "Don't be facetious."

"I'm serious. Although if it's proven that your dad is behind this doping plot…"

"My father is *not* involved."

Lanie's smile was wry. "For everyone's sake, I hope not."

As Lanie rode off over the hill, Veda counted to ten. She liked Lanie but she didn't like the conversation they'd just had. It brought back memories of her first-grade teacher, and others, telling her that she needed to be smarter. Try harder. It made her feel like she wasn't sure about their friendship anymore.

Like maybe all the Rawsons were more trouble than they were worth.

Seven

Ajax got to his feet as Veda made her way through the sea of round tables set up for the Best Life Now "Motivation Is Key" seminar.

"Surprise," he said as she jolted to a dead stop in front of him.

Veda's eyes were wide and her mouth was hanging open like she'd just seen the ghost of lovers past. Two weeks had gone by since Lanie's party, which had ended with him and Veda enjoying one hell of a reunion. While he hadn't phoned or sent flowers, he hadn't forgotten her. Along with the pain-in-the-butt doping scandal that hadn't found a resolution yet, Veda had been at the forefront of his mind, particularly when he lay in bed at night. It would have driven him nuts if he hadn't come up with this plan B.

Veda's presentation had ended ten minutes ago. While she had spoken with interested attendees who wanted to personally introduce themselves, the majority of the audience had left the room. Now Veda flickered a glance around, taking in the stragglers while running a palm down the side of her emerald-green pantsuit.

"What are you doing here?" she asked in a hushed, harried tone.

"You invited me," Ajax explained.

Her eyes widened again as she hissed, "I so did not invite you."

"You said I ought to come along to one of your seminars. I looked up your website, saw this gig, in beautiful Barbados no less, and ta-da!" He held out his hands. "Here I am."

Her chest rose and fell a few more times before she returned a smile laced with venom. "Well, I hope you found my talk enlightening. Now, if you'll excuse me…"

As she breezed past him and through one of the opened doors, Ajax drank in the vision of her swaying hips before he nodded goodbye to the kind and still curious ladies who had allowed him to join their table when he had arrived halfway through Veda's talk.

"If you're through for the day," he said, catching up, "I thought we could have a drink."

Veda smiled at attendees who nodded and waved at the same time she cut Ajax a response.

"I think not."

"Veda, we need to talk."

She hitched the strap of her carryall higher on her shoulder. "Nothing to discuss."

"You're not curious about the horse doping thing?"

Her step faltered before she strode on, chin even higher. "Not curious enough to get involved."

When they had spoken last, he'd said Booshang might be on the take with her father offering the bribe. He still had no proof of that, and there'd been some kind of delay with the test results. He only knew that given Drake's grudge, a conspiracy theory fit, and his family agreed.

Veda pushed open another door. Ajax was ready to follow her inside until the restroom sign stopped him dead.

Five or so minutes later, Veda emerged from the women's bathroom and strode past again, this time heading for the elevators. If she got inside, that was his cutoff point. He'd come here to talk, not to flat-out stalk. He was slowing his pace, backing off, when she ducked behind a huge framed poster set up in a largely unpopulated corner of the lobby. Then her arm slid out and a curling finger beckoned him over. Ajax darted a look around, wondering if this was some kind of trap, and joined her.

"I'll be clear," she said. "Ajax, I don't want to see you again."

Given the circumstances under which they had parted, he'd expected that. Now was the time to lay all his cards on the table. No holding back.

"I came here in person to let you know face-to-face how I feel about you. How I feel about *us*."

She looked unmoved. "I already know how you feel. You think we're good in bed."

"We aren't *good* in bed, Veda. We're *phenomenal*."

"Like you haven't said that to a woman before."

"I know you feel it, too," he said, ignoring that last dig. "Maybe it's because we both grew up in families who own stables. Or maybe because we're opposites in lots of ways, and opposites are meant to attract."

"Sometimes they repel. Like water and really oily slime."

He wouldn't take offense. "That's not how this is." He edged closer. "That's not you and me."

She hesitated like he might be getting through, but then she straightened and seemed to shake it off. "It doesn't matter that we share an attraction."

Damn it. "The point is I miss you. And I think you miss me."

When she didn't try to deny it, Ajax felt pressure as

well as relief. Taking in every beautiful inch of her face—apple cheeks, cute nose and lips that were parted the barest amount—he knew this was the moment to act. So he set a palm against the wall near her head and oh so carefully leaned in. When he thought she might surrender, before he could actually connect, she dodged under his arm and was gone.

But when he emerged from their hidey-hole behind the poster, he found that she hadn't run away. Her expression wasn't *I'm yours*, but she didn't look like she wanted his balls on a chopping block anymore, either.

She adjusted her bag strap again and conceded, "I guess...now that you're here..."

Ajax tried to hide his grin when he prodded.

"Yes, Veda?"

She blew out a resigned breath. "Well, I guess you can buy me one drink."

While they found a table in an open-air bar with a spectacular view of the ocean, Veda told herself to calm the heck down. Her hands wanted to shake. Her heart was pumping like a steam train piston. After two weeks with no word, she had assumed Ajax had lost interest. Which had hurt—a lot—but was better than the alternative, which entailed finding the wherewithal not to answer if he called.

She'd been beyond shocked—and pissed—that he had taken it upon himself to show up at this exclusive seminar out of the blue. How rude. How presumptuous. On the other hand, yes, she was also a teeny bit flattered. He had obviously been thinking about her, and God knows she'd been thinking about him, too...in more ways than one.

"So, you really don't want to know what's happening with that ridiculous doping allegation?" Ajax asked, like he'd read her mind.

"Let me guess." Sitting across from him, she inhaled the

fresh, beach-scented air and set her bag down. "Your lawyer brother hasn't found any link to my father."

The gleam in his eyes said *not yet.* "Although Drake was happy to make a comment to the press when asked."

"Unfavorable, I suppose."

"You could say that." He sat back, looking like a dream in a shirt the same color as the water, a light breeze combing through his hair. "Jacob has tried to speak with Booshang. He's not cooperating."

"Which doesn't let you off the hook."

Paul Booshang had implicated Ajax, but he had worked for the Darnel Stables in the past, when she was a girl. Back then, if her father had ever found out that Paul was up to no good, he'd have been out on his ear.

Then again, Drake didn't know everything, did he?

"So I presume the results were positive," she said.

"They haven't come back yet. Some kind of delay at the lab. In the meantime, Jacob has his people digging around, trying to get to the bottom of it all. Other than Booshang's claim that I organized the whole deal, there's not a shred of evidence."

"Or evidence to the contrary."

"And thanks for the continued vote of confidence."

Her smile was tight. "You're welcome."

An impeccably dressed waiter appeared, setting down the drinks as Ajax asked, "Have you spoken to your father?"

"I dropped in before driving home that morning. Word travels fast in the racing industry. He'd already heard."

"And he asked you to pass on his best wishes, right?"

"Actually, he said that he'd always known this kind of thing would come out."

"Particularly if he helped set us up."

She stirred her creamy mocktail with her straw. "When

you find out that my father had nothing to do with this, I'll accept your apology."

"I'll look forward to his apology as well."

That would never happen. Never in a hundred years. In a million.

"So have you and Lanie spoken?" he asked, changing the subject as he picked up his glass.

Veda remembered their talk outside the Rawsons' office building that morning.

"She said whatever happened between us was our business. But she wasn't exactly cheering from the sidelines. She said she is in no way responsible for your behavior."

He paused before setting his beer back down. "I don't need to defend myself."

"Then don't."

He got back on point. "I care about you, Veda. I wouldn't be here if I didn't."

Veda remembered Lanie's parting remark about her being the one who might bring the mighty Ajax Rawson down. Before that, Lanie had said that playing hard to get would only make Ajax more determined to see her again. She hadn't been playing, and yet here he was.

Which raised an obvious question.

"You must have pursued other women," she said, stirring her drink some more.

"The point is I'm pursuing *you*. Pursuing *us*."

With those seductive blue eyes smiling into hers, he looked so convincing. But if Lanie was right, Ajax's relationships were largely about the chase. Veda had been putty in his hands the first time; she'd been won over the second. If she gave in a third time *and* let him think that she was seriously falling for him, would the Stud pull back on his reins? If she upped the ante and said she wanted a future together, would he turn tail and run?

Pursuing him rather than the other way around was an

insane idea. Even dangerous as far as her heart was concerned. But now she couldn't help but wonder.

Ajax cared about her?

Exactly how much, and for how long?

"The seminar's organizers are putting on a dinner tonight," she said, really curious now. "I can take someone."

His eyebrows shot up. "You're asking me?"

"You want to spend time together, right?"

"Right. Except…"

Except, suddenly this was too easy?

"You don't want to come?" she asked, feeling bolder now.

He gave her a smoldering, lopsided grin. "Of course I want to come."

Veda's stomach jumped before she manufactured an encouraging smile.

"So, dinner tonight?"

His cocky grin widened. "It just so happens that I'm free."

Eight

Ajax finished fastening the Tiffany cuff links before swinging the formal jacket off its hanger and slotting his arms into the sleeves. Standing before his hotel suite's full-length mirror, he ran his fingers through his shower-damp hair, then blew out a long breath.

To the starting gates, boys.

Following Veda here to Barbados had seemed like a no-brainer. It was either make a big gesture or continue to have her sail right out of his life. He couldn't let that happen. Not without giving it his all. But he hadn't thought that getting her back would be this, well, easy.

As he sat on the edge of the bed, slipping his feet in his shoes, Ajax remembered how he'd imagined Veda's initial reaction: shock followed by a flip of the bird. He'd been stoked when she caved and agreed to a drink instead. Tying the first shoelace, he recalled how she'd warmed up more at the bar. Not only had she agreed to see him again, she'd invited him to this dinner. It had crossed his mind to suggest that she come up to his room beforehand, because by that time, he'd gotten the impression she wouldn't say no.

Pulling the second shoelace taut, it snapped right off in his hand. Ajax tossed the piece aside and got on the phone to the concierge.

"Strange request. I need a shoelace," he said as his gaze landed on the king-size bed. He imagined Veda lying there naked among the cushions, calling him over, and couldn't they please stay the whole week?

The concierge was saying it could take up to thirty minutes to have a shoelace delivered.

"I'll come down and grab one. Thanks."

This would be a good night, Ajax reaffirmed to himself as he left the room with one loose shoe. Better than their night in Saratoga. Even better than after Lanie's birthday party.

And tomorrow morning…?

The elevator doors slid open. After stepping inside, he dug his socked toes into that loose shoe while visualizing the most obvious outcome. Tomorrow morning they would make love for the third or fourth time since returning from dinner. Then they would talk, probably about setting a date to see each other again.

But he was snowed under at the moment. It didn't make things easier that Hux had been weird since that phone call from his pal at the Commission. And Drake's recent comments to the press questioning the legitimacy of Rawson's long list of wins certainly didn't help.

For years, his father had left the majority of business decisions to Ajax. These past couple of weeks, however, Hux was always in the office or hanging around the stables. Asking questions. Going over things. Once he'd even enquired about Veda, and not in a supportive way.

When Ajax left the elevator, he finally lost the unlaced shoe. Picking it up, he continued across the extensive lobby floor. He didn't want to think about that other situation back home now. He wanted to focus on Veda because he absolutely couldn't wait to see her again. The thought of her made him buzz all over, like his blood was vibrating, it was pumping that hard.

Sure, he liked playing the field, like Griff. And, yes, like their father when he was younger, although that had changed when Hux had met "the one." Apparently, back then, Ajax's mom had let her future husband know early on that she wasn't letting go. Hux said that after a couple of dates he had known it would be until death do us part.

Gripping that shoe, Ajax shivered to his bones. Committing to a woman for life was one thing. Having her taken away far too soon was something else again. Losing his sweetheart had broken Hux in two. Ajax had never contemplated testing fate the same way. He had never imagined himself, well…risking that much.

One lousy misstep and everything could be lost.

A man behind the reception desk ambled over. After Ajax had explained about the shoelace, the clerk went off to hunt one down and Ajax's thoughts returned to Veda. When he'd texted earlier, she'd said they should meet here in the lobby. He smiled to himself wondering what she would be wearing? The lipstick-red number was a hard one to beat, but then Veda looked amazing no matter what she had on. In fact, his favorite getup had to be that oversize men's shirt and black cowboy hat.

What man in his right mind would pass that up? Who wouldn't want to grab on and never let go?

Still holding the shoe, Ajax crossed his arms and exhaled. What a night that had been. It made him wonder how this evening would compare. Guess he'd find out soon enough.

And in the morning…

Tomorrow morning…

* * *

Leaving the elevators, Veda saw him standing by the front desk—holding a shoe?

Ajax looked particularly gorgeous in a dark blue suit that accentuated those beautiful broad shoulders all the way down his long, strong legs. But his usual cheeky grin was nowhere to be seen. In fact, his eyebrows were drawn together and his freshly shaved jaw was thrust forward.

She couldn't have anticipated Ajax showing up uninvited, for all intents and purposes, at the seminar. The bigger shock was her asking him—and in record time—to be her date for this evening's dinner. But she was determined to go through with her plan. Either way, this had to end. Better it be sooner rather than later and with her in the driver's seat.

Following Lanie Rawson's insider opinion, when a woman pursued Ajax rather than the other way around, he lost interest. This class of male was all about the chase. When she fully leaned in to grab Ajax's charms with both hands—when she let him think that she was ready to be his happily-ever-after—he would choke and retreat. Problem solved.

Of course, in order for this plan to play out, she would need to end up in his bed again. She wouldn't complain. Nor would she hold back. Tonight she had a valid reason to really let loose. In the afterglow, she would bring up the possibility of marriage.

Come tomorrow morning, Ajax Rawson would be running for the hills.

After a uniformed man behind the desk passed something over to Ajax, he took a seat in the lobby lounge. Now she could see that he was rethreading his shoe with a new lace. Drawing nearer, Veda watched the jacket stretch taut across his broad back as he worked. Even doing such a mundane chore, his moves were close to hypnotic.

She was closing the distance, almost upon him, when he looked up and sent over the slowest, sexiest smile. Veda flushed—cheeks, breasts. *Everything.*

As he got to his feet, she put her plan in motion, giving him an openly salacious once-over. When his smile faltered, she read his thoughts. *What exactly is going on here?* he was wondering. Then she stepped into the space separating them, set her hand on his lapel, pushed up on tiptoe and brushed her lips over the fine-sandpaper feel of his jaw.

"God, you look hot," she murmured near his ear.

When she pulled back, she could barely contain her grin. Ajax looked shell-shocked. It would sting like hell when this ended, but in the meantime she was good with having an obscene amount of fun. Call it payback for all the girls who had been left behind in the Stud's wake.

He cleared his throat, resumed that dynamite smile and acknowledged her dress—a sheath made from a shimmering Caribbean print fabric with a corset back. She had planned to wear a matching cap-sleeved bolero jacket, but in this case, less was definitely more.

"And you look absolutely beautiful," he said. "Breathtaking, in fact."

Playing it up, she glanced down at her bust. "You don't think it's too…snug?"

She had laced herself up extra tight to get the maximum advantage from her cleavage.

"Not too snug," he assured her. "Just right."

She glanced down at his feet. "You had some kind of problem?"

"Would you believe I threw a shoe. All fixed now, though." He stomped like a horse and then offered her his arm. "Shall we?" As they walked to the elevators, she was aware of heads turning, men's as well as women's. Aside from looking like Hollywood's top leading man,

Ajax oozed charisma and smelled divine. This might not end well, but right now it felt good to be the one on his arm.

A woman joined them in the elevator going up. Her bobbed honey-blond hair and black evening gown with its halter neckline made for a stunning combination. But all of Ajax's attention was focused on his date. On Veda. Given the famished look in his eyes, she wondered whether he might tell her there was a change of plans. That he was taking her straight up to his room and staying there.

When the doors slid open, Veda let out her breath. She'd been full of confidence earlier, but he was the one with all the experience. Had she bitten off more than she could chew?

They followed the woman out and headed toward the ballroom's open doors.

"I've already told you how beautiful you look, haven't I?" he asked in a voice that suddenly sounded deeper and slightly rougher.

She pressed a palm against her stomach to ease her nerves. "Breathtaking, you said, and not too snug."

"You smell beautiful, too," he said as they entered the room. "What is that? Something French?"

"It's domestic." And hardly expensive.

"Want to know something?"

He looked so intense and sincere, like he had a juicy big secret he needed to share. She smiled, nodded. "Sure."

"I want to thank you."

"Thank me for what?"

"For trusting me. For not walking away."

It was on the tip of her tongue…snide and a little bitter. *Has any woman ever walked away, Ajax?* But tonight was all about an experiment that had only one logical conclusion. She would continue to come on to him, strong and relentless, and be the victor when she scared him away.

* * *

Throughout the evening, Ajax tried to look interested. And he had to admit, there were some high points. Like the main course, which featured the freshest lobster on earth. Veda seemed happy with her vegetarian option. He guessed tofu actually worked for some palates.

The conversation around the table was…interesting. Their dinner companions were well-heeled folks involved in the self-help business. There was a psychologist guru and his wife, a personal budget planning person and her high-profile chiropractor partner. The rest were people who had enjoyed being part of the exclusive seminar audience today.

While awards for best this and most acclaimed that were presented, Ajax tried to remain present. Rather than let his mind wander to the challenges that awaited him back home, he focused on Veda. Along with that dress, which was stimulation enough, she was doing all kinds of suggestive things, like when she'd held his eyes while licking her dessert spoon real slow and all around. Or when she'd "accidentally" missed her mouth and spilled water between her spectacular cleavage. Either Veda was trying hard to let him know something or he was losing his grip.

A waiter was removing their dessert plates when Veda settled her hand high on his thigh. And squeezed. Ajax slid her a pointed look while what was behind his zipper paid attention, too.

"I guess you're ready to go then?" he asked as her nails circled, then slid higher.

Her smile said, *You'd better believe it.*

He was pushing back his chair when she said, "I need to have a word with someone first. I won't be long. Can you wait a couple of minutes?"

He scooted his chair back in. A couple of minutes? Sure. "I'll be here."

He watched her weave between the tables and people milling about, some leaving, others heading for the dance floor. He would have liked a cheek-to-cheek but she was obviously keen to slide into home base. Which, of course, ratcheted up his anticipation levels. Because this was a sure bet.

Like really, *really* sure.

"Excuse me. I saw you earlier in the elevator."

He focused on the woman standing by his chair. "Oh," he said. "Hi."

"But I feel as if I've seen you before that," she went on.

He smiled. Shrugged. "I'm not sure."

She took Veda's vacant chair. "Maybe in a movie or a magazine."

Ajax chuckled. "Afraid not."

"Perhaps I've seen you at a previous event."

"This is a first for me."

Ajax flicked a glance Veda's way. She was deep in conversation with a couple on the other side of the room.

"The woman you're with…"

He replied, "Veda Darnel from Best Life Now. She spoke today."

She glanced at his left hand. "You two aren't married."

He shook his head. Definitely not married. "Veda and I are…good friends."

Her eyes suddenly rounded. "Oh, now I know where I've seen you before. You're Ajax Rawson. The Stud."

Ajax gave a wry grin. Would he ever live that tag down? "I'm Ajax. Right."

"You own a big ranch. A stable." She sighed. "I love horses. I went to the Kentucky Derby last year. What an amazing day."

He paused, then turned a little toward her. "We lost by a nose last year." He mentioned the name of the horse.

"Oh, so close!" she agreed before arching a brow. "So which Rawson ride should I keep an eye out for next?"

"Actually, I have a good tip for the Breeders' Cup."

"So hopefully an Eclipse Award, too."

He looked Veda's way again. She was still talking. So he settled back and continued to share his tips.

When Veda turned back toward the table, her stomach dropped. Her falling-all-over-Ajax plan was working better, and faster, than she had even hoped. He was talking with a woman—the same woman who had shared the elevator ride from the lobby up to this floor—and looking more animated than he had all night. Like this woman was so entertaining, he couldn't get enough of her conversation. Like he was already over Veda after she'd lavished attention on him.

With measured steps, she approached their table and, gritting her teeth, joined them. It took a second for Ajax to realize she was there.

"Oh. Veda. This is Charlotte."

Charlotte continued to smile into Ajax's eyes and explain for Veda's benefit, "I'm a huge horse racing fan."

Perfect.

As Veda collected her purse off the table, Ajax got to his feet. "Did you catch up with your friends?"

"I did." Veda exhaled. "I think I'm done here."

When Charlotte got to her feet, too, Veda fought the urge to push her back down. "Please," she said. "Keep talking."

Charlotte tipped her head Ajax's way. "Your call."

Ajax actually took a moment before he replied. "It was great meeting you. Might see you at the Derby one year."

As Charlotte took her leave, Ajax reached to take Veda's hand. She stepped away. Frankly, she wanted to kick his shin. Lanie was right about her brother in spades. All about the chase.

"I really don't want to get in the way," she said, overly sweet.

He had the audacity to look confused. "What…you mean get in the way of me and that woman?" His grin was pure charm. "I met her two minutes ago."

"Well, you do work fast."

His look said *you've lost a screw*. Like she was cranking the crazy for believing her eyes, knowing his record the way she did. Her plan tonight had been to come on so strong that he lost interest. But now she wondered. Would he have flirted with that woman regardless?

"Veda," he said calmly, sincerely, "she came over and recognized me. I was filling in time, waiting for you."

As she studied those blue, blue eyes, her throat began to close. Irrespective of whether that was true, she felt like a loser. Like a lost, misunderstood teenager again.

She blew out a shaky breath. "Ajax… You do my head in."

He kept his gaze on hers, looking as if, for once, he didn't know what to say. It was her move to make, and she knew what to do. What she should have done when he'd shown up unannounced earlier.

She walked away.

"I'm going to bed," she said, and then added, "*alone*."

An hour later, she had changed into her pj's and was staring blindly out over the quiet moonlit waters, feeling lower than low, when she heard a knock. Knowing who it was, she walked to the door, opened up. Ajax stood there, his tie hanging loose, shirt half-undone, making *remorseful* look so sexy that she quivered.

"I'm sorry I hurt you," he said. "I honestly didn't mean to."

While her heart continued to break, she took a long, agonizing moment and finally stepped aside.

He crossed the threshold and, before the door had even

swung shut, somehow she was back in his arms, both hating and consoling herself for wanting this man more than ever.

After Veda had left him in that ballroom, Ajax went down to the bar and thought the whole thing through over a double scotch. She'd been open about her feelings and insecurities where his dating history was concerned. Talking to that woman... He hadn't done anything wrong. But, hey, he got where Veda was coming from.

He could see, he supposed, why she'd been upset.

Finally, he'd knocked back that scotch and then knocked on her door. After his apology, she had buckled and let him in. As soon as their lips touched, she melted in his arms. And as the kiss deepened and he brought her closer, he felt a tremor run through her as if she was feeling the same relief that he did.

"I didn't want you to come back," she said against his lips. "I prayed you wouldn't because I knew I'd give in."

His hold on her shoulders tightened as his gut clenched. "Veda...don't you know how much I care about you?"

She cupped his cheek and almost smiled. "You should show me."

Ajax slipped the tie from his collar and let it fall on the floor. Veda wasn't asking for sex. She wanted him to make love to her. She needed to know she wasn't just one in a line. Now he needed to know that, too.

As she led him into the bedroom, he took a quick inventory...muted light, turned down bed. Then he held her face with both hands before brushing his lips over hers, feathering kisses on each side of her mouth until her eyes drifted shut and her hands covered his. Then he kissed her more deeply, but not the way he had at the door.

He stroked and teased her tongue with his, every now and then adjusting the angle and taking as much time as he could. When his lips finally left hers, her breathing was heavy and he was aching to move things along. But this wouldn't be like the last time when he'd jumped off that cliff way too early. He wanted to arouse her to the point of begging, then leave her satisfied beyond ever needing to question again.

He coaxed her around until her shoulder blades rested against his chest. After sweeping her hair to one side, he nuzzled a trail up the slope of her neck while his palm skimmed up and down over her pajama top. Nibbling her lobe, he undid three buttons and then slipped his hand in under the silk.

When Veda sucked in a breath, he shifted to rest his cheek against hers and slid his other hand into the opening, too. Veda's head fell back against his shoulder as she trembled and sighed. And when she pressed her behind against his thighs and undid the rest of the buttons herself, he coaxed her around to face him and kissed her again.

He blindly stepped her back until her legs met the bed. Then, easing the silk off her shoulders, he kissed her a little harder. When the sleeves caught at her elbows, he guided her down until she sat on the bed's edge. Lowering onto his knees, he drew one nipple into his mouth while she held on to his head, grazing the back of his leg with her toes.

"Take your shirt off, Veda," he said sometime later. "Honey, lie back flat on the bed."

Getting to his feet, he ditched the shirt and belt while taking in the picture of her doing as he'd asked. Her hair was a burnished halo. Her expression said, *I want to please as much as be pleased.* Leaning over her, one arm bracing his weight, he hooked three fingers into the waistband of her shorts and, little by little, tugged them down. Dropping the shorts by his feet, he studied that part of her he ached to know again.

Taking his time, he trailed a fingertip over her smooth, warm mound before tracing a teasing line down the center and between her thighs. Then, kneeling on the floor again, he caught her ankles and set her feet on the mattress. Savoring her sweet, heady scent, he used his thumbs to part and expose her further.

When he finally went down, she held his head while he stroked her with his tongue and slipped two fingers inside. It wasn't nearly long enough before she was gripping his ears, beginning to tremble. And as he reluctantly drew away, she held out her hand.

"Where are you going?"

He showed her the foil wrap he'd retrieved from his wallet before tossing it on the bed and ditching his clothes. When he stood before her again, she sat up and immediately coiled her fingers around the base of his shaft. Ajax groaned at the rush of heat as she angled him toward her mouth and ran her tongue around the tip three times. When she gripped his thigh, Ajax closed his eyes as, shifting forward and back, he cupped and held her moving jaw.

Before he got too close to that edge, he eased away and saw to the condom. He thought about swinging her on top of him but instead went the more traditional route. As she reached to link her arms around his neck, he positioned himself on top and eased inside…a long, deliberate stroke that felt like it lasted forever. Then he covered her mouth with his, matching the rhythm of the kiss to his thrusts.

When he thought she might be close again, he murmured a warning against her lips. "I wouldn't count on much sleep tonight."

On the brink, she grinned as she asked, "So what about the morning?"

He wanted to answer that question but he only picked up the pace.

Now just wasn't the time.

Nine

For as long as Ajax could remember, he was always up with the birds. And yet catching the time on his watch now—

Really? Was it after eight?

On any other day, he would be wrapping up track work and thinking ahead to checking on his foaling mares and attending to the books. But this morning he was with Veda. Although she was obviously already awake.

Ajax rubbed each eye and looked around the palatial plantation-style bedroom until his focus landed on the open door of the vast marble bathroom. Veda stood with her back to him, brushing out those gorgeous red waves. She was dressed in a romper that showed off her legs and was perfect for this setting. While relaxed, the resort was known for its luxury and pampering. Its facilities included three golf courses, a dozen spa treatment rooms, each with its own garden and plunge pool, and a massive, multi-layered swimming pool surrounded by coral-rock walls. There was plenty to do.

Right now Ajax was only interested in private pursuits.

As he pushed up on an elbow, every cell in his body told him he needed to get Veda back here in this bed. And later, when she wanted to talk about walking out on him after dinner last night, he'd happily listen.

She stopped brushing her hair midstroke and turned around. Finding his gaze, her expression stilled before a soft smile touched her lips and she headed back into the bedroom.

"Morning," she said.

"Morning back."

Getting ready for her to join him, he readjusted his position, sitting forward, resting his forearms on raised knees and lacing his fingers between his legs. But she crossed to the wardrobe instead, finding sandals to slip on her feet. Then she went through her open suitcase. Was she searching for sunscreen? A hat?

Or was she just filling in time?

"You're ahead of me this morning," he said, combing a hand through his bed hair.

"You should see the sky. So blue, it's unreal. The water, too."

Her tone matched his—light and easy. Which was in stark contrast to the intensity of their bedroom marathon the night before. And when she continued to fluff around in her suitcase and the silence got awkward, Ajax's thoughts returned to the previous day when he had wondered how things would be between them *this* particular morning after the night before.

Yesterday she had gone from *please disappear* to *I'm totally yours* in ten minutes flat. And she had continued in that steamy vein until that woman, Charlotte whoever, had sat down with him to share an innocent chat.

Veda had a thing about his "reputation." She didn't trust him. Apparently not for a New York minute. He had hoped that the time they'd spent together here last night would help, but now he wasn't getting that vibe.

As he got out of bed to pull on his pants, she wandered out onto the furnished terrace. When he joined her, he was taken aback by the view of golden sand and, farther out, turquoise water scattered with diamond drops of sunshine.

"I love the hills back home," he said, breathing in the warm salty air. "But this is pretty darn special."

"It's supposed to be hot today," she said, gazing out, too. "But I don't feel it. I think it'll be pretty mild."

He studied her profile, the small straight nose, elevated chin, determined green eyes that were sparkling as much as the water. Her hands were clutching the rail like nothing and no one could pry them free.

She was right. He wasn't feeling the heat, either. Not like last night.

Making love, he had wanted to give her more, give her everything. Physically, they had never been closer. And yet now, he was up against that wall of hers again.

He rested his hand next to hers on the rail. "What have we got planned for today?"

"I'm going to relax," she said, closing her eyes and tipping her face more toward the warmth of the sun.

"Relaxing sounds good."

She took in a deep breath but kept her eyes shut. "What are you going to do? I guess you need to get back. Work to do."

He took in a group of guests relaxing on sun loungers on the beach. "I'll stay on. Hang out."

When she finally opened her eyes and slid him a look, he moved to cover her hand with his. But she was already turning away, heading back inside. He frowned at his bare feet for a moment, weighing things up. Did she want him to simply say, *Thanks for the sex, see ya later,* and walk away? That would make her evaluation of him right, but it was an empty victory if you asked him.

Inside, he found her flicking through some hotel literature. Hitching up his shoulders, he shoved both hands in his pockets and got the words out.

"I meant what I said last night, Veda. The last thing I want to do is hurt you."

The brochure crinkled as her grip tightened. Then she shook her head slightly. "Doesn't matter."

"It matters."

Her eyes met his. "Don't you want to know why I was suddenly falling all over you yesterday?"

Well, yeah. "I was curious."

"I was testing a theory. The one that goes, 'girl full-on chases Ajax. Ajax gets bored and gets another girl.' It didn't take long."

"Veda, that woman and I were just talking. I wasn't bored."

She crossed her arms. "Really?"

He hesitated.

"Look, I've had more exciting evenings," he admitted, "but that had absolutely nothing to do with you." And about that theory… "You decided to throw yourself at me so I'd get bored? Why?"

"To speed up the inevitable. To prove the theory right. Just look at your track record. You *must* be all about the challenge."

He crossed over to her, took her hands and held on. "I came here to be with you. No one else."

"For however long that lasts."

"Well… Yeah. That's right."

Her eyebrows shot up. "At least you're admitting it now."

"Yesterday, after our drink at the bar," he explained, "I felt on edge. If we ended up in bed again, I wasn't sure how it would be the next day between us. I wasn't sure how I would feel come morning. Not because I was bored, Veda." He put it out there. "Because I haven't felt like this about anyone before."

She blinked several times, then pressed her lips together.

"That's another line," she said.

He smiled into her eyes. "Let's just go with the flow. See where this takes us."

"You mean despite my father despising your family, and Hux probably thinking I'm some kind of spy?"

"Don't forget the fact that you hate the profession that I love."

"And neither of us wants anything serious."

That got him. *Serious* was an interesting word.

And best not think about that now because he could see that he might have turned this ship around.

Her lips almost twitched. "So, what's your idea of going with the flow while we're here?"

Squeezing her hands, he winked.

"Put on your swimsuit," he said, "and I'll show you."

"Here's something you don't know about me," Ajax said, while they settled into a pair of sun lounges set up in a quiet nook of the extensive pool area. "It's my biggest secret. You'll never guess."

As Veda heeled off her sandals, she slid him a look. Now this could be interesting. Ajax was pretty straightforward. Openly charming. Explicitly sexy. Here for a good time, not a long time. Whether he was actually flirting with that woman last night wasn't the point. His history of short-but-sweet was the problem.

And yet when he had knocked on her door, Veda had looked into those dreamy blue eyes and rolled over. Which could be viewed as weak or simply taking what she wanted. And, of course, she hadn't been disappointed. Ajax had a way of bringing out the very best in her, with his hands and his tongue and his…well, *everything*. This morning, however, she'd been torn between wanting to jump on him again and wondering whether he was thinking she was way too easy.

And that's how she had ended up here, making the decision to simply relax in the Barbados sunshine with Ajax and his drool-worthy body. This man was her Achilles' heel, and ultimately, there would be a price to pay. But not today.

Not today.

He was talking about his biggest secret…

"Let's see." Pretending to think long and hard, she tapped her chin. "You love soppy movies?"

"Other than *The Longest Ride*, not a chance."

"You're an alien conspiracy diehard."

"Really good guess, but no tamale."

"You think only one game of football should be televised per week."

He chuckled. "My secret is that I used to be afraid of water. Couldn't swim. Not a stroke."

Veda slid her gaze from him to the pool, then back again. "You did say used to be, right? How'd you get over it?"

"Hux had the same fear when he was a kid," he said, flipping the lid open on the sunscreen. "Want me to do your shoulders?"

After ditching her wrap, she swept her hair to one side. Her swimsuit wasn't anything outrageously sexy—just a semi-fitted white tankini top that fell to her navel and black bikini bottoms that pretty much covered both cheeks.

"Is Griff afraid of water, too?" she asked, turning around. "I haven't heard Lanie ever mention it."

"Just me and Dad," he said as a big, hot, borderline rough hand smeared cream between her shoulder blades. "We have a huge pool at home. One summer when I was eight, he had me in there every day. It took a while but he was patient."

Veda's eyes drifted shut. He was using both hands now, working over her shoulders and down her arms.

Feeling a little dreamy, she asked, "So you went on to win every race at the school meets?"

"I never won a ribbon in the pool." He was close behind her now, reaching around to rub her thighs. "But I no longer freak out at the thought of my head going under, so all good." He made a shivering sound. "I'll never forget the feeling, though. Total panic."

"I can identify."

"You needed heavy-duty swimming lessons, too?"

"Heavy-duty *reading* lessons." She took a breath and let it all out. "I'm dyslexic." When she felt his hands draw away, she turned back around. "I get letters confused," she said. "Jumbled. Back to front."

"Dyslexic. Right." He nodded, then nodded again. "I mean, I've heard of it."

"It set me back when I was younger, in a whole lot of ways."

"You mean at school?"

"I didn't understand why other kids weren't turned off by books or writing the way I was. I didn't get how they put letters together to make words, let alone sentences. I actually thought it was some kind of joke and I was the punch line."

"So when did the teacher tell your parents?"

"I wasn't diagnosed until years later."

He rocked back. "You mean you went all the way through struggling like that?"

The sunscreen bottle lay on the lounger next to his leg. She grabbed it up and explained, "I did really well in math. Maybe it's a compensatory thing, but my brain does way better with numbers."

"Getting through something like that… It must be a huge inspiration for the people you coach."

She held off squirting sunscreen into her palm. "We were talking about secrets, remember?"

"Oh. So who else knows?"

"My dad. Now you. Turn around."

He swung his legs over to the lounger's other side and then there was his back...bare, broad and perfectly bronzed. As she rubbed the hot, smooth slopes on either side of his neck, she imagined him working in the sun with his horses, sans shirt, jeans riding low.

"So you're obviously over it," he said as she continued to stroke and rub.

"You don't get over dyslexia. But you can learn to work with it. In a lot of ways, I don't think of it as a disability. I had to try harder at a lot of things. Some of my grades sucked. But along the way I've learned other stuff like keeping things clear-cut and how to delegate. I've honed my concentration skills and try to listen to intuition."

His beautiful shoulders rolled back. "How did your parents react when they found out?"

Her stomach balled up before she squeezed more sunscreen into her palm. "It was after my mom died."

He paused before asking, "Did your dad help?"

"Not like yours with the swimming." Her father hadn't been hands-on. "He took me to professionals." For her dyslexia and also to help manage her grief. "He's never been big on communication." She rubbed Ajax's back again, painting a big circle, then sweeping her hand up and down. "Maybe that's where I get it from." Maybe Drake was dyslexic, too. Sure, she saw him with books, reading. That didn't mean it was easy.

"Veda, you're a great communicator. I was glued to my seat listening to you on that stage yesterday."

"Ha! You were not."

He turned back around. "No lie."

"Well, I'm not a natural at it. The big D held me back in

a lot of ways other than schoolwork. I was socially awkward through the roof. I never felt like I fit. Some kids at
school made it way worse."

"You were bullied."

She nodded. "Whenever I got stressed, like if I had
to read in front of class, my brain would freeze. It literally wouldn't work. I'd get this feeling like fingers closing
around my throat. No words would come out. I was completely mute."

He leaned closer. "When was the last time it happened?"

"Not for ages. Until a little attack at Lanie's party when
she introduced me to your dad and then left us alone."

"But Dad's easy to talk to."

"He is. But remember our family feud? Huge trigger. I
got a few words out but by the time he left, Hux thought
I was a kook. That's the other thing. When you have this
problem, which is *not* the same as being shy, people don't
know what to make of it. Make of you. Some wonder if
you're just too stuck-up to talk to them, or maybe your IQ
must be low." She winced. "Really not a nice place to be."

When he took her hand and smiled, her everything, inside and out, smiled, too.

"This is what we're going to do," he said. "We're going
to swim out into the middle of that pool. I'm going to keep
us afloat and listen while you tell me all about what's next
on the Veda Darnel Kick Ass agenda."

Still smiling, she nodded. "I like that idea."

Hand in hand, they waded in and then freestyled out
until the water was up to his chest and she couldn't touch
the bottom. Then he wrapped his arms around her waist
and twirled.

"Not feeling anxious?" she asked, holding on to his
shoulders and winding her legs around his hips.

"Not in the least. Feeling good. Feeling *great*. And I'm
listening."

"Well, if you really want to know, large scale, I do have a dream. I don't know when but I feel it'll happen some-time, even if it's when I need dentures and three naps a day. I would love to have a quiet acre or two for a rescue farm," she said.

"What kind of animals? Because I can't possibly guess."

"Right. Horses. But also sheep, chickens, ducks, pigs. Actually, did you know pigs are supposed to be more in-telligent than dogs?"

A sexy grin hooked his mouth. "I did not know that."

"Some say pigs are the fifth most intelligent animal in the world. They're capable of learning how to do simple jigsaw puzzles and work basic remote controls."

"*Sold.* We definitely need lots of pigs."

She laughed at his gorgeous smiling eyes. "Lots of ev-erything."

"You might need more than a couple acres then."

"Sure. Like I said. It's a ways off yet."

His hands were sliding up and down her back, making her tingle…making her hot.

"So, what are you going to call your first pet pig?"

"Well, Wilbur and Babe are already taken."

"Porky, too." Sliding and swirling, he touched his nose to hers. "I've got one for a sheep. Baa-bardos."

She smothered a bigger smile. "And people say you aren't funny."

"Oh, yeah? Want to hear a dirty joke?"

"Do I have a choice?"

"A white horse fell in a puddle of mud."

Before she could roll her eyes, he started tickling her ribs until she was splashing around, laughing so hard.

"I can do this all day," he said. "Take it back. Take it back."

"Okay, okay! You're funny. *So* funny."

"And you're beautiful. And really easy to tickle." He

came in to graze his lips over hers. His deep voice rumbled through her when he said, "I'm glad we're here together."

Catching her breath, easing out a sigh, she ran her palms over his warm, wet shoulders. "I'm glad we are, too."

As he held her by the hips, his eyes drifted shut. Then he nipped her lower lip and ran the tip of his tongue over the seam.

"What's your intuition saying now?" he murmured, staying close.

"That you need to prove just how good you are in the water."

When she found his arousal well below the surface, his mouth automatically claimed hers. By the time he broke the kiss, in Veda's mind, they were completely alone. In their own world.

She shivered as he nibbled that sensitive sweep of her neck.

"Veda?" he asked.

Eyes closed, she cupped his scratchy jaw. "Hmm?"

"I think we need to go back to the room."

And then he was kissing her again, and in that wet, steamy, crazy-for-you moment, she was already thinking about next time...dreaming about seeing her Ajax again.

Ten

Early the next morning, Veda and Ajax said a reluctant goodbye at the airport before boarding separate flights. Back in New Jersey hours later, still unpacking while smiling over the memories, Veda answered a knock on her condo door and almost fell over. This was the last person she expected to show up unannounced today. And, given her ongoing fling with Ajax, pretty much the last person she wanted to see.

"I was down this way," her father said, placing his tweed duckbill cap on the hatstand as he made a point of stepping around her to walk inside.

She took a moment to remember to breathe while Drake assessed the surroundings, taking a token interest in the bookshelf while running a fingertip over the self-help titles. He had asked for her address ages ago but had never arranged to visit, let alone simply dropped in.

"Well…can I get you something to drink?" she asked.

"Green tea?" He retrieved a handkerchief from his dress pants pocket and wiped his fingertip clean. "Very hot."

"I have coffee. Freshly brewed."

He took a moment to accept that option and then added, "No sugar, of course."

Walking to the kitchen, she felt rather than heard him behind her. For as long as she could remember, Drake had worn the same aftershave. More often than not, the scent stirred feelings of unease. As she had told Ajax yesterday, Drake wasn't a total monster; after her mother's accident, he had gotten her help. But he wasn't demonstrative as far as fatherly affection was concerned. He certainly hadn't shown love toward his wife.

Now the nostrils of his long thin nose flared like he was either opposed to the aroma of her coffee or, more likely, the space in general. Her condo was the polar opposite of Darnel Manor, as in modern and personal rather than ridiculously grand and, in so many ways, stuck in the past.

"There's a courtyard," she said, retrieving cups from the cabinet. "It's such a nice day out."

He nodded, then asked, "How long have you been here now?"

"Three years. It's home."

He grunted—the sound someone might make when they were on the verge of being bored stiff.

She led him through to the courtyard, which was littered with fallen leaves and petals from a vine. As she set down their cups on the tabletop, Drake snapped out his handkerchief again to dust down his seat.

"Are you staying in the city?" she asked, taking a chair. Drake had friends in Manhattan.

"I'm here to speak with you."

Veda caught something knowing lurking in the shadows of his eyes and then, of course, this shock visit made sense. Drake must have heard through the grapevine that she was romantically involved with a Rawson and couldn't wait to express his opinion. On the outside, he was his usual up-tight self. On the inside—oh, how it must bite.

His question, "Is it true?" confirmed her guess.

She wasn't after a fight. Nor would she lie or shrivel up in a corner.

"Yes." She lifted her cup. "It's true."

He carefully lowered himself into his chair. "You're asking for trouble. You know that, don't you? It was bad enough when you became friends with the girl."

"You mean Lanie Rawson."

"Yes. *Rawson*." His lips pursed and twitched. "I can't believe it. Can't believe it of my own daughter. You know the kind of people they are. The kind of *men*. The father has no scruples. And the sons…" He made a face like bile had risen in his throat. "I wouldn't be the least surprised if they all had diseases."

"Like Ebola?"

"Sexually transmitted."

After tsking, he took a mouthful of coffee, rather inelegantly, Veda thought.

"That boy is even worse than his father," he said.

"Worse?" She arched a brow. "Or better?"

Drake's chin began to quiver. Not because he was going to cry. Because he was livid and showing it.

"I didn't think you could ever betray me like this. Not like this."

Using that grudge from his past as an excuse to act out had been warped enough when he'd used it against her mother.

"You do realize that I'm your daughter, right? Not the woman who left you for Hux Rawson."

Getting to his feet, he retrieved something from his shirt pocket—a page torn from a magazine—and read it out loud.

"'Ajax Rawson, also known as the Stud, was spotted

with another beautiful female companion. Life coach Veda Darnel, daughter of longtime Rawsons critic Drake Darnel, looks smitten. We wish her luck.'"

Her father was coming around the table, standing beside her, almost begging.

"Veda...darling...he'll hurt you. Then he'll leave you."

She glared at him. "Because everyone leaves you, Dad?"

She and Drake had words after that. She said some things that she'd kept buried for way too long. And she was still pacing, fuming, long after he'd left.

She didn't owe that man an explanation. This was her life now, not her mother's and certainly not his. And yet in some ways she felt fourteen again, when her father could barely look at her because she had sided with her mom. Now she wondered more than ever: Would Drake have loved her less or more if he ever found out she was responsible for the death of his wife?

When her cell phone rang later that day, Veda had almost succeeded in pushing her father out of her mind. She needed positivity in her life, not smothering and controlling.

When she answered the call, an official-sounding woman asked to confirm with whom she was speaking. Then this woman passed on all the information that she had...said she was sorry...and, yes, most definitely...it would be wise to come to the hospital right away.

When Ajax arrived back at the farm, all kinds of shit was hitting the fan.

Even before entering the office building, he heard the raised voice. Striding through, he found his private door open. When he saw papers and files strewn all over the damn place, he was so taken aback, he couldn't contain the growl.

"What the hell is going on?"

Hux sat behind Ajax's desk, poring over an assortment

of splayed documents. When he looked up from the mess, his eyes were more unhinged than blue.

"What do you *think* is going on?" Hux fell back in the high-backed chair. "Did you even bother to open Jacob's messages?"

Charging forward, Ajax started stacking papers. "I spoke to Jacob an hour ago."

"So you know they want to look through your veterinary records."

"We went over them two weeks ago. There's nothing to see."

"The stewards have scheduled a meeting with you and Booshang this Friday. After the delay, the test results are expected to land that morning."

"We'll be ready. If there's a fine or suspension, we'll deal with it."

Hux shot to his feet. "Damn it, Ajax! This is serious."

For God's sake. "My books and stables are *clean.*"

"A Triple Crown trainer…and now your reputation will be—"

"Hux, get off my back!"

His father's eyes blazed before he moved to the window to gaze out over the stables. "Yesterday, two clients loaded their horses and took them away."

Which clients? What horses?

Exhaling, Ajax shoved the documents aside. "They'll come back when this is sorted out."

"And if there's a next time?"

Ajax studied his father and said it out loud.

"You can't seriously think I'm actually involved in this."

Hux slumped and shook his head. "No, no. Of course not."

"Then what were you thinking going through all this? There's nothing to find here. I told you. I'm clean…even if a lot of other trainers can't say the same."

Hux waved that away, but it was a valid point. As much as he loved horse racing, Veda was right. Everyone in the industry knew that doping, or at the very least overmedicating, was a problem.

Hux visibly gathered himself before asking, "Where were you this weekend?"

"I haven't had a day off in months. I needed a break."

"With the Darnel girl?"

"Her name is Veda." He grabbed his work hat, stuck it on his head. "And she's not a girl."

"Don't you think it's strange that she suddenly befriended Lanie and now you? When we spoke alone at the party, frankly I thought she was hiding something."

"Like she'd joined her father and Booshang in a vendetta against us?" *Oh, please.* Ajax headed for the door. "We don't know that Drake is involved in any way."

"Griff heard his name mentioned that night. Darnel is spouting off to the press."

Ajax had his doubts, too, but, "That's not proof. And it's certainly not any reason to ransack my office and send the hounds after Veda."

While Ajax stood at the door, his demeanor more than implying that Hux needed to leave, Hux's expression changed from frustration to something akin to enlightenment. His voice was a disbelieving rasp.

"My God. Ajax…you're serious about her, aren't you?"

"Dad, that's none of your business."

"You've always wanted to do things your own way," Hux said, moving closer. "Always wanted to lead the pack. Make an impression."

"If you mean like working my ass off to keep this place afloat when you could barely drag yourself out of bed—" Ajax thumped the door "—yeah, I lead the pack."

"Your mother had died—" Hux snapped his fingers "—just like that."

"She'd been sick for months." Ajax swallowed hard. "And she was my mother as much as your wife. Damn it, I was hurting, too. But I kept pushing forward." He gritted his teeth, shook his head and ground the words out. "I never understood why you resented that."

"I'm sure I've thanked you, and way more than once."

"With a clap on the back and a wage that hardly reflects what I bring in for this place. Griff just has to smile and you gush over how brilliant he is. I'll puke if I have to hear again how proud you are of Jacob."

Hux pulled a pained face. "You're jealous of your brothers?"

"I'm tired of bending over backward trying to please you." Ajax squared his shoulders. "This place would fall apart without me."

Hux's chin lifted. "Please don't think you're indispensable, because, I can assure you, none of us are."

When his father stormed out, Ajax fought the urge to follow and bawl him out some more. It hurt like hell to have that conversation. Hux was a good father, but this had been brewing for too long. Since his mother had passed away, rather than a son, Ajax had felt like an employee needing to jump through higher and higher hoops. Well, he was sick and tired of proving himself.

He slammed the door and wandered over to the window. An assistant trainer was working with a new boarder in the arena. In the lower paddock, a stallion was shaking his mane, enjoying the sunshine. Ajax loved this life, from keeping a close eye on foaling rates to writing up owner updates and finalizing racing nominations.

But what was his future here? He wanted his father to live to a hundred, but was he prepared to do pretty much all of the work only to be reminded in times like these that he wasn't really in charge? Had Hux ever truly considered handing over the reins one day?

And Veda…

No one would tell him whom he could or could not see. And if his father didn't like it—if Hux had suspicions with regard to Veda's motives—he could blow it out his pipe. Because Veda was not working with her father to bring them all down. She had way more integrity than that. He'd bet his life on it.

Ajax drew out his phone.

He might come across sounding needy, but he had to hear her voice about now. Although it had started off shaky, their time in Barbados has been the best. They had parted with an understanding that they would see each other again soon, and he appreciated that was a huge deal for her.

It was for him, too.

"Ajax?"

The boost he felt from hearing her say his name didn't last long. Rather than sounding pleased that he'd called, in that single word she sounded upset. Panicked even. He pressed the phone closer to his ear.

"Veda, are you okay?"

Obviously on speaker, she talked in a series of halting phrases. There'd been another phone call. She had left immediately. Would be there inside half an hour.

"Whoa. Hold on. You're driving up here? I'm guessing this has something to do with your dad."

"There's been an accident," she said, followed by a sharp intake of breath. "He's in the hospital."

Ajax's priorities did a one-eighty.

"Which hospital?" He was already rushing for the door, car remote in hand. "Don't worry, honey. I'll meet you there."

Eleven

Veda had kept it together the entire drive from Jersey, but when she saw Ajax waiting for her as she ran from her parked car to the hospital's entrance, all that built-up emotion threatened to break through. Being told that her father had been in a serious car accident had thrown her like nothing else could. Now she flung herself into Ajax's open arms and dissolved as he stroked her hair and murmured her name.

"It's okay, Veda. We'll go in together. I'm sure he'll be fine."

She dashed away tears she'd held back until now. "Apparently he was only a few minutes from home when he ran off the road. He said he thought he saw something…"

"So he's conscious?"

She nodded as they headed inside. "He hit a tree."

Walking to the elevator, Ajax held her hand so tight, it almost hurt. But she only gripped his hand back in return. God, how she needed an anchor…this depth of support.

Earlier on the phone, the administrator had passed on ward details. At the nurses' station, Veda provided her father's name, approximate time of arrival and reason for admittance. When the nurse looked up from the computer screen after checking, Veda knew something more was wrong.

The nurse adjusted her eyeglasses and tried on a smile as she got to her feet. "I'll see if I can find a doctor. Please, take a seat."

Veda's face began to tingle and go warm. As she turned to Ajax, the room seemed to slope and wobble on its axis. This wasn't the hospital her mom had been rushed to after that other accident, but it looked the same, smelled the same, and the look on that nurse's face…

Veda was aware of Ajax's hands bracing her upper arms as he rushed to reassure her. The nurse wouldn't be long. He was sure that Drake was all right. The entire drive here, Veda had told herself that same thing: as big a shock as this was, her father would be fine. But her thoughts were bombarded with phrases like *Fate can be cruel* and *History might not repeat itself but it often rhymes*. She seemed to have always been at war with Drake, but that didn't mean she wanted him taken from her, particularly the same way she had lost her mom.

A tall man with a lilting voice was introducing himself… the name badge said Dr. Wasley…or was that Sawley?

Veda couldn't wait a second longer. She had to know. "Is he dead?"

The doctor's onyx eyes smiled as he reassured her. "Your father is very much alive. Apparently a deer leaped out and collided with his vehicle. No fractures, although we want to keep an eye on a minor head injury. A graze and bump on his head. He's a lucky man to have gotten off so lightly."

Ajax asked, "When can Veda see him?"

The doctor's mouth pressed into a harder line before he replied. "Ms. Darnel, your father has asked that he not be disturbed at this time."

Veda blinked, shook her head. "But does he know that I'm here?"

"He gave your name as next of kin." The doctor paused. "But I'm afraid he doesn't want visitors."

Veda was ready to ask that someone look into that again. But then the nurse's expression a moment ago began to make sense. She'd been reacting to the situation of a daughter rushing to an injured father who didn't want to see her. It was sad. Awkward.

The doctor tried to rationalize. "Oftentimes, people are embarrassed at having lost control of a vehicle. They might need time to overcome feelings of having let others down, as they perceive it." He offered a reassuring smile. "I'm certain he'll come around."

As the doctor left, Ajax looped his arms around her and Veda leaned in. He felt real when, at this moment, nothing else did.

"We'll hang around," Ajax said, stroking her arm as she nestled against him. "You can be here when he comes to his senses."

"And if that doesn't happen?"

"Like the doctor said...he's got issues with having screwed up."

"So he shuts me out. Typical." She stepped back. "Well, I'm not going to give him the satisfaction of being pathetic enough to wait."

Ajax's gaze softened further. "Maybe just a few minutes. He knows you're here. Let that sink in. He's obviously not thinking straight."

"He's thinking like he always does. About himself."

After their argument this morning, had Drake purposely wrecked his car for a sympathy vote? To snap his recalcitrant daughter back into line? Hell, she'd dropped everything to race here, hadn't she?

"Sorry," she told Ajax, heading off. "I've got to go."

"You can't drive back to Jersey," he said, catching up. "You shouldn't be driving anywhere right now. Your father might be acting like a dick, but you're smarter than that."

Stabbing the elevator call button, she tried to settle her emotions.

"You're right. I'll take a cab. Go back to Dad's place… catch my breath."

"I'll drive. And sit with you for a while."

She darted him a look. "You mean actually come into enemy territory?"

The corners of his mouth twitched. "Boy, wouldn't that piss him off."

Veda hesitated. Then she smiled. Finally she laughed because, hell, what else could she do.

As the elevator doors slid open, she linked her arm through Ajax's and, after this crazy, stress-filled morning, announced to the world, "Let's really tick Drake off. My God, let's make him howl!"

Veda had gotten her spark back before they'd left the hospital, but she'd gone quiet while he'd driven her car back to Darnel Manor. Obviously she was still dwelling on the accident, as well as Drake's latest dick move. He had manipulated a highly emotionally charged situation by refusing to see, and comfort, his own daughter.

Ajax didn't buy into the doctor's explanation about her father feeling embarrassed over totaling his car. Something major was up between father and daughter, and Ajax had the feeling it centered on him.

Passing through the open Darnel gates, he took note of the endless stream of soaring pines lining the drive. At the top of the first hill stood a massive stone-and-shingle structure that captured the essence of an over-the-top bygone era. After parking the SUV out front, he escorted Veda to the colossal cherrywood double entry doors. Looking around, Ajax couldn't make out any sign of the stables, arenas, paddocks—no horses or people were anywhere to be seen.

Then they stepped inside and Ajax almost lost his breakfast.

This place was the Gilded Age on steroids. The foyer was three stories of imported marble, gold trimmings and hardwood parquet flooring and had enough classical sculptures to man a football team.

He realized Veda was studying him and snapped his hanging jaw shut. "A wood shack this is not."

She hugged herself as if battling a chill. "It feels like a huge, creepy mausoleum, right?"

"I wasn't going to say that." *Out loud.*

"Mom never felt comfortable here. But that wasn't totally the house's fault."

"Must take an army of people to keep up appearances," he said, blowing imaginary dust off a Greek goddess's head.

"My father gets someone in three times a year to give everything a resounding polish. Other than that, I can't tell you whether anyone walks through those front doors anymore. Aside from me on occasion. And, I guess, someone to drop off groceries."

So Drake didn't allow his trainers, grooms, riders, farriers and other employees to enter his sanctuary. He preferred to conduct business at the stable office. A little Howard Hughes, but sure. Okay.

"Doesn't he at least have a cook?"

"Far too intrusive," she said with a manufactured air. "And he is the world's best chef. Just ask him." She cocked her head. "Ajax, are you hungry?"

Come to think of it. "I could squeeze in a little something."

She led him into a kitchen that continued the lavish theme, with an exclamation point. Compared to Susan's kitchen, this room looked so *big*. And lonely. The word *haunted* also came to mind.

Veda opened the refrigerator door and cobbled together ingredients for sandwiches. While he slapped mayo on the bread and she cut lettuce, tomato and cheese, he tried to picture her growing up in this place. He felt ill just thinking about it. But the stark formality fit with everything he knew about Drake Darnel, including his rebuff of Veda today.

He thought he was pretty darn special.

"I never felt like this was a home," she said, laying fillings on the bread. "I don't know how my mother suffered it for so long."

"What was the tipping point?"

"In the marriage? Drake accused her of having an affair with one of the stable hands. My father isn't much of a conversationalist at the best of times. After that, it was the silent treatment every night." Veda sliced the sandwiches, and while Ajax put them onto a plate, she found a chilled bottle of juice. "I challenge anyone to live in this kind of environment for any length of time," she said, leading the way through a door that connected with a colossal-sized sun room. "Slowly but surely, let me tell you, it drains the soul."

The hexagonal room was surrounded by soaring floor-to-ceiling French windows. Ajax could admit that the view of the hills was pretty—similar, of course, to a view from his home.

They sat together on an ornate red velvet couch and dug in while looking out over the vista. On his second bite, Ajax's phone rang. After checking the ID, he put the phone away.

"You can take it," Veda said. "Don't mind me.".

"It was Hux."

"You didn't want to lie about where you were?"

"I don't give a crap whether he knows or not."

She lowered her sandwich. "That doesn't sound good."

Recalling their argument earlier that day was almost enough to put him off his food. "I love that man. He's a great father and mentor. But sometimes…he just doesn't get it."

"This is about that doping allegation."

"Yes. And no."

Ajax explained how he'd gotten home that morning to find Hux riffling through his office files, and then shared the news that a meeting regarding those allegations was scheduled for the end of the week, *and* some clients had decided to take their horses elsewhere.

"Hux and I have never had an argument like that before, and I'm over it. I love what I do, but sometimes, like today… He doesn't know how much I give."

Veda looked taken aback. "Sorry. I thought everything was hunky-dory in the Rawson camp."

"Ask the others and they'd agree. Griff, Lanie, Jacob… he supports and encourages them without a second thought. But me? I feel like I have to earn his approval every day."

"Have you always felt that way?"

"Since Mom passed. You know about me putting that ad up and finding Susan."

"That was so brave."

Ajax didn't see it as courageous but simply as necessity. "Everyone was so down. Someone had to get things moving again. I had to at least try to make people smile and forget." He flinched. "I sound like I'm whining, don't I?"

"No. Not at all." She smiled softly. "Ajax, you found a way to save your family. I think that is the noblest thing anyone can do."

His throat was suddenly thick. No one would ever know, and he would never forget, how desperate he'd felt at the time. He had wanted to save his family. What was left of it, at least.

"I felt so stifled living under my dad's say-so," Veda said, and then clarified, "I know Hux isn't anything like my father… Just saying."

"When did you leave?"

"Freshman year of college. Never looked back."

"I didn't do college. Too much to do at home."

"Did you want to go?"

"When I was young, I wanted to be a vet."

"Well, there you go!"

"That was a long time ago."

"Hey, there's nothing wrong with starting a little late." She thought a moment before squeezing his arm then getting to her feet. "I'd like to show you something. I mean if you're not in a hurry to get back or anything."

Ready to shake all the bad feelings out, he jumped up. "Veda, I'm all yours."

Seeing the tree house again brought back a flood of memories and emotions. Perched in a rambling old oak ten feet above the ground, the timber hideaway was the size of a modest bedroom and had once been home to Veda's favorite dolls and games. Here she had felt totally happy. Truly safe.

"I had a little dog growing up," Veda said as she and Ajax drew closer to the tree house. "Gus was my best friend. I used to climb up this ladder and he'd jump in that." She crossed over to a faded blue plastic bucket with a hairy old rope tied to its handle. "Then I'd pull him up."

"Gus… I'm thinking a beagle."

"A cream teacup poodle. He had apricot smudges on his cheeks like an old lady had done his makeup. Dad brought him home for me on my fifth birthday. I even caught Gus snuggled up on Drake's lap a few times."

Looking up at the tree house, Ajax grabbed a ladder rung. It snapped, rotten all the way through.

He winced. "I'll fix it for you."

"Don't worry. This must be fifty or sixty years old. An employee from the stables used to patch it up for me."

"Sounds like you had a friend."

She arched a brow. "It was Paul Booshang."

His head kicked back. "Get outta here."

"And he *was* a friend. Mom's, too. I don't think he liked the way Drake ignored my mother and me."

"I don't suppose you knew anything about him doping horses back then."

She shook her head. "And neither did my father, or Paul would've found a boot up his backside. In case you haven't noticed, my father is not a tolerant man, even where family is concerned. I'm sure Paul wasn't the only staff member to feel sorry for me and Mom. It got worse after she said we would leave if things didn't change. Once it got so heated, he slapped her."

She kicked the bucket and the old plastic split into brittle pieces at the same time Ajax drew up to his full intimidating height.

"Did he ever touch you?"

"Never. In fact, the night we packed up to leave, he asked me to stay." Remembering how torn she had felt... how lost... Veda shuddered. "Believe it or not, I cried walking out the door."

Ajax stepped closer. "I'm sorry you had such a hard time growing up. It must seem like a long time ago now."

Actually, it didn't feel that long ago at all.

"Dad came by to see me earlier," she said.

"You mean in New Jersey? Today?"

"We argued. And yes, it was about us."

He blinked as he put it together. "Veda, if you feel

guilty over your father's accident because he might've been upset—"

"I don't feel guilty." She fought down a shiver. "I absolutely don't."

Anyway, that was enough about Drake. Enough about the past.

"When I stay over now, I use the guesthouse." She nodded toward the beautiful old stone building. "It was here before the main house was built."

Following her gaze, Ajax's eyebrows shot up. "The Rawson original has a long way to go before it looks anywhere near as good as that." He brought out his phone and pulled up a few photos.

"Oh, it's sweet," she said, taking in the Cape Cod with its steep pitched roof and big front door centered below a massive chimney.

"I should show you around sometime," he said, slotting the phone away.

"My turn first," she said, grabbing his hand and heading toward the guesthouse.

"We'll need keys."

"Got them in my pocket."

He grinned. "I like how you think."

"I like how you feel…" Turning back and into his arms, she nuzzled his warm, salty neck. "How you taste."

When he kissed her, Veda felt her world shift that much more toward a new way of thinking and feeling. Once she had been happiest here alone, just her and little Gus. Now she was happiest when she was with Ajax. Right now, she felt safe.

Maybe even loved.

Twelve

When Ajax drove his truck up to the house early the next morning, an unfamiliar vehicle was parked in the guest area.

If Hux had company, Ajax was happy to take a coffee on the back porch and wait until his father was free. He'd been mad as hell after their argument. Since talking it through and spending the night with Veda, however, he had calmed down.

Not that his opinion had changed on anything, Ajax thought, taking the front steps two at a time. He hated the doping allegation hanging over his head. He was sorry that some clients had opted out. But he wasn't unhappy that this episode had brought to the fore his growing concerns regarding his standing here at Rawson's. He had felt like the hired help for too long.

So now it was crunch time, Ajax reaffirmed as he headed for the kitchen and the coffeepot. He and Hux would have a conversation today highlighting the fact that fair was fair.

He wanted a partnership agreement drawn up by the end of the week or he would need to consider his other options.

When he pushed through the swing doors, he found Susan standing by the center counter. Her eyes widened before her usual welcoming smile took over.

"Ajax. What good timing."

That's when he noticed their company. Five foot one. A hundred and ten pounds. Thick shoulder-length blond hair that she usually wore in a ponytail but was loose today. He was used to seeing her in training gear or jockey silks, not a dress. But her smile was the same. Big. Contagious.

He headed over and gave their guest a big, warm hug. She didn't smell a bit like leather and horse sweat. In fact, her scent brought to mind a summer garden.

"Fallon Kelly." Pulling back, he took his friend in again. "This is a surprise."

Fallon's chocolate-brown eyes were dancing. "I was driving through on my way to Vermont. I hoped y'all wouldn't mind if I dropped in."

Susan set a cup of coffee on the counter beside Ajax. "She looks well, doesn't she?"

"She looks *amazing*," Ajax replied.

Susan was headed for the swing doors. "You two get caught up while I tell Huxley you're here, Fallon. And I'll let him know you're home, Jax."

Susan and Hux didn't have secrets; she would know all about yesterday's blowup. Not that she ever inserted herself into family matters, which was nuts given she *was* family.

Ajax led Fallon out back and they took seats that offered a magic view of the hills. Dew was still glistening on everything green. The sky was a dome of early heaven-sent blue. If he squinted, he could even see the roof of the original house from here.

"It must be a year since we saw you last," he said. "Just after you gave up riding."

"Doesn't seem that long ago."

He thought about his own situation—about weighing up his choices—and asked, "Do you miss the racing scene?"

"I miss the special bond I have with a horse. I don't miss those early mornings and worrying about every little thing I put in my mouth."

Ajax hooked an arm over the back of the bench as he turned more toward her. "I'll never forget our big win at Belmont Park."

"I had a great ride. Kudos to the wonderful trainer." She tipped toward him, grinning.

And then, for just a second, her gaze dropped from his eyes to his lips, which prompted a whole other line of recollection. After that win and celebratory drinks, he and Fallon had gotten together—a single night that hadn't developed into anything more. Her career was her main focus. Or so he had thought. He'd been blindsided when she'd said that she wanted to pursue other goals.

"So what are you up to now?" he asked.

"I've been in Kentucky with family, thinking about starting a riding school. Nothing snooty. I'm more interested in being laid-back. In having fun."

Sounded good compared to the ruckus going on around here of late.

"What's been happening in your life, Jax?" she asked, before taking a long sip from her steaming cup.

"I'm surprised you haven't heard the rumblings, even all the way down in Louisville."

"You mean the rumor that you're into doping now?"

His grin was entirely humorless. "So, you *have* heard."

"I want you to know that I support you one hundred percent. And what the hell is with Paul Booshang anyway? I'd always thought he was a good guy. Trying to fix a race is bad enough. Dragging you into it is unbelievable." She took another sip and then asked, "Do you think Booshang is a lone wolf, hoping he could make a sure bet on the side, or is he in cahoots with someone else?"

"I'm not sure I should go into that."

Fallon's eyes rounded. "So there *is* someone else."

"Nothing's been proven. Not by a long shot." When she arched a brow, he grunted and gave it up. "We've heard Drake Darnel's name mentioned."

But after hearing Veda's tree house story, it didn't sound as if Booshang had ever been a fan of Drake's. So why would Paul work covertly with him now?

"Darnel Stables has an impeccable reputation. But as far as the man himself is concerned..." She visibly shuddered. "Do you know, after our win in Elmont, he flat-out scowled at me."

"His filly finished second."

"Drake Darnel is a stinking bad loser." She shrugged. "Still, I can't see him shooting his horses up. He's too darn self-righteous. But he does hate your dad. He'd tell anyone who listened that good training was not the reason your horses won."

"Meaning we had to be using performance enhancing drugs."

"I guess no one's surprised that his daughter thinks the same."

Ajax sat up. "Veda?"

"Uh-huh." Fallon sipped her coffee. "That's her name."

"So, you've heard that with your own ears? Veda saying that we break the law? Cheat?"

Fallon looked taken aback. "I've never spoken to her personally. But I think it's common knowledge what she thought of the industry."

Susan appeared at the door.

"Huxley is on a conference call," she told them. "He'll be a while. But I've pulled a batch of blueberry muffins out of the oven if anyone's interested."

Fallon smacked her lips. "I can smell them from here. Can you put one away for me?" she asked, getting to her feet. "I was hoping Ajax might take me on a tour of the stables while the sun's not too high in the sky."

"I'll let Huxley know where you're at," Susan said, heading back inside.

"I'll come and see him when we're through," Ajax said. His business with Hux could wait for now.

Walking along the path that led to the foaling barn, he and Fallon were stopped a couple of times, first by a rider and then a groom who wanted to say hi. She'd been popular with the team, and it had been a loss to his stables when she left.

"I miss this place," she said, gazing out over the hills and paddocks.

"Kentucky's pretty, too."

She nodded. "Dad still has half a dozen horses. Still rides every day."

Fallon's trainer father had enjoyed some success a couple of decades ago, which was how Fallon had found her way into the game.

"He always wanted you to ride in the Derby," Ajax recalled.

Fallon laughed. "I was never that good."

"You could have been if you'd kept going. Absolutely."

When she elbowed his ribs and laughed some more, Ajax got a funny feeling in his stomach. They'd always gotten on well. Common interests and parallel dreams. Which was hardly the case with Veda. But after yesterday, and particularly last night, they seemed to be overcoming their obstacles. Whenever they were together, he felt as if nothing else in the world existed. Like the only thing that mattered was making her happy.

But given the way she had cut him off at the knees in Barbados because of his innocent chat with that woman, how would Veda react if she saw him with Fallon when their relationship hadn't always been platonic?

Of course that was ancient history. Other than Griff, no one knew about their fling, and Ajax wouldn't go out of his way to mention it. Why upset Veda when there was absolutely nothing to worry about?

When they passed a stable hand leading a cream four-year-old, Ajax pulled him up.

"We need to check that left hind leg," he said, running a hand down the limb. "The hip's hiking when the leg hits the ground."

"The owner's already made up his mind about this one," the stable hand said.

Ajax frowned. "Made up his mind about what?"

"I thought he must've talked to you." The stable hand rubbed the horse's neck. "This guy's retiring. I'm about to load him up for the last time."

If a horse wasn't earning enough, an owner decided whether he would literally be put out to pasture, retrained for a new career or…that other lesser-talked-about alternative that meant a one-way trip to Canada or Mexico. When he spoke to the owner to square the accounts, he would make an offer for the cream.

If it wasn't too late.

"Come on," he said to Fallon, focusing on the now. "I'll introduce you to Someone's Prince Charming. I'm backing him for a Triple Crown next year. He's a star, and just so smart and wanting to give his all."

He'd certainly known a few in his time, but Ajax loved that horse like he had loved no other.

Ajax stopped and turned around. Hux was trotting down the path, calling out his name. When he arrived, Hux gave Fallon a hug.

"Is this a professional visit?" he asked. "Looking to get back into your silks?"

Fallon gave him a good-humored grin. "My racing days are over."

"Well, we all want to hear what you're up to, so you're staying for dinner," Hux said. "No arguments."

Fallon caught Ajax's gaze and nodded. "I'd love to."

"Do you mind if I steal Ajax for a second? There's some business we need to discuss."

"Sure. I'll catch you up at the stables," she told Ajax, heading off.

When she was out of earshot, Hux pinned his son with a look. "Nice of you to show up today."

Wow. "I'm actually taking some time off. So sue me."

"Don't speak too soon."

Was he referring to the doping business and possible sanctions?

Man, he was so over this.

Ajax was walking away when Hux added, "She must be good."

Bristling, Ajax slowly turned back. "If you're talking about Veda—"

"It could be part of Darnel's plan, you know," Hux said, cutting in. "Make sure you're sidetracked while it all crumples down around me."

"Around *you*? Like I don't put my heart and soul into this place?"

"Not lately. This time of year, you need to be here, doing your job. Once I didn't have to tell you that."

"Right. Once all I did was beg for every crumb of approval you'd toss my way."

As a groom hurried past, eyes cast down, Hux lowered his voice. "You need to get your head on straight."

"Which means?"

"Priorities. Open your eyes to what could be happening here."

As Hux strode off, Ajax remembered how good Veda

had felt in his arms last night, and then Fallon's recollection that Veda believed the Rawsons were unscrupulous, too. Perhaps that had come from her dislike of all things horse racing–related. It didn't mean that she would conspire to sell him out. Veda wouldn't do that.

No way, no how.

That evening, Veda was thinking she might have to leave a message when Ajax finally picked up.

"Hey there," he said, sounding beyond sexy.

"Hey, back." She set aside her laptop with images on the screen of teacup poodles available from rescue groups. "Just thought I'd check in and see how it went with your dad today."

"Hux is being a giant paranoid pain. I know we lost some business because of Booshang but…" He cursed under his breath. "I don't want to talk about any of that."

He sounded short, but she knew that wasn't about her. If she was in his position, she'd be stressed, too.

After an amazing night spent together here in the guest-house, after the way he had supported her yesterday when Drake was being so, well, *Drake*, she was feeling even better about her relationship with Ajax. There might be a mountain of things standing in their way, but at least now she felt more secure about his feelings for her. Yes, he'd been a stud in the past, but that didn't mean he would always play the field. Hux had settled down eventually, hadn't he? So maybe this liaison wasn't as doomed as she had once thought.

"Did you speak with your dad today?" he asked.

"After we drove down to the hospital to get your car, I hung around for a while but he was still sulking, so I just dropped off those personal items I knew he'd need. He should be out in the next few days. I'll stay here until then."

She clicked on an image and sighed as a pair of adorable baby-blue puppy eyes melted her heart.

"You know, talking about Gus the other day got me thinking," she said.

"Gus who?"

"My little poodle, remember?" she reminded him. "He was just so loving and cuddly and cute. I've always wanted another one."

"Do it," Ajax said. "Animals are great company."

"As a matter of fact, I could use a little human company right now." She shut her laptop lid. "Wanna hang out?"

There was a beat of silence.

"Actually, we had a visitor from Kentucky drop in out of the blue. Someone I haven't seen in a while."

Veda let out a breath as all her built-up anticipation deflated. The way he had kissed her goodbye this morning, the promise he'd made about seeing her again... Well, naturally she had hoped...she'd assumed...

But she didn't want to act like a clinging vine.

"Oh, sure," she said, opening her laptop again. "I understand. Did you work together?"

"Uh-huh. A jockey."

"Would I know his name?"

"Fallon Kelly. She retired last year. Hux invited her to stay for dinner."

Last year, after a Drake rant about being swindled out of a Belmont Stakes blue ribbon by a Rawson horse, Veda had googled the story. Fallon Kelly was not only a talented jockey, she was a beautiful and obviously self-possessed woman. In the story's accompanying picture of Fallon with Ajax, she had radiated confidence. They obviously made a great team.

Putting aside a twinge of unease, Veda said, "Well, I'll let you get back to your guest then."

"I'll call tomorrow."

There was a long silence when something else needed to be said. *Have fun* didn't fit. *Be good* was even worse. *Love you* was way too much, too soon. Although she was heading in that direction, which could hardly be a surprise. It was what she had feared from the start. Now…it was too late to try to push those growing feelings aside.

Finally he said, "Sleep tight. And good luck with the puppy search. Can't wait to meet him."

Veda put down the phone on a sigh. If the Rawsons and Darnels weren't enemies, he might have invited her over to meet his guest. She would feel included rather than shunted aside. But it was only one night. This time tomorrow Fallon Kelly would be gone and Veda would be in Ajax's arms once again.

Thirteen

Finally Drake deigned to see his daughter.

Sitting up in his hospital bed, Veda's father was freshly shaved, wearing the pajamas she had dropped off for him two days earlier. Other than a bruised color around his eyes, he looked remarkably well and more than prepared to hold court.

As Veda entered the private room, he kept his stony gaze glued to hers, but he didn't speak, which was clearly a tactic to make her sweat. Although Veda's stomach was churning, she didn't shrink away.

Taking a seat by the window, she let the seconds tick by as he continued the stare-off. Finally, his lips sucked in and he cleared his throat.

"I'm dry. Pour me a water, please."

Veda got to her feet, poured a glass from a jug and handed it over.

"The doctor said you can leave in a couple of days," she said while he sipped.

"I can find my own way," he said, and then covered his mouth to cough.

"If you're not feeling up to it, don't rush yourself." Making sure she looked unconcerned, she crossed her arms. "I imagine you've spoken to the stable manager and trainers so things would be sorted out there."

"Did your boyfriend want you to ask me that?"

Veda was so taken aback, she almost fell sideways.

"I beg your pardon?"

"You invited him onto my property, didn't you?" he bit out. "My God, a Rawson in my house. Did you think I wouldn't find out? That my people wouldn't pass on what they saw?"

She hadn't noticed anyone around. Had Drake sent someone over from the stables to literally spy?

"It was bad enough," he went on, "that you spend time with a Rawson boy. But it had to be Ajax, didn't it? The biggest bastard of the pack."

An impulse shot through her: she wanted to leap over and slap his face. But she wouldn't stoop to his level. Instead, she bit her lip and, outwardly cool, simply tipped her head.

"He makes me happy," she told him, recalling her mother saying the same thing about her cowboy once upon a time.

Drake sneered. "He's even worse than his father. Always charming the women. Seeing who he can fool. Rawson men don't care."

"Hux Rawson cared about the woman he married. I've been told that they loved each other deeply."

But this conversation was absurd.

"You've just survived a car accident, for God's sake. Can't you ever move on?"

Given his next question, clearly not.

"Married, you say?" Her father snickered. "Has Ajax asked you to marry him then?"

"Of course not!"

"Didn't think so."

Veda's hands fisted at her sides. "Bitterness destroys a person, Drake," she said. "It turns them rotten from the inside. It turns them bad."

Her father's eyes flashed at the same time he hurled his glass into a corner. As shards and water flew everywhere, Veda barely flinched. In fact, she stepped closer to the bed.

"Ajax is funny and laid-back. He's charming and brave. People are naturally attracted to men like that."

The corners of Drake's mouth pulled down more. His words were a harsh, hateful whisper. "You like to hurt me."

Veda withered. "You really are deluded."

When she was halfway out the door, he called out. "I'm going home tomorrow. Friday."

"Don't worry. I'll be gone."

"Veda."

She counted to ten before she turned back around. "What now?"

"I've changed my mind."

She looked at him hard. "Changed your mind about what exactly?"

"You can drive me home." He fluffed the sheet. "Be here by nine. Don't be late."

Lanie was lost in her thoughts when the cab driver kicked off a conversation.

"Said on the radio there's supposed to be a thunderstorm rolling in later today."

Glancing out the window, Lanie spotted a distant bank of clouds. "Rain is always nice."

"Oh, sure. As long as it's not too fierce." The driver added, "I have a vegetable patch at home so I take notice. Beets and peas and onions this year."

Lanie had gone back to her thoughts, trying to find a

solution to her nagging problem, when the driver spoke again.

"Was it fine weather where you flew in from today? The rest of the state's supposed to be clear."

"I'm just back from visiting a friend in Germany."

"That's a long way to visit a pal," he said with a gravelly chuckle.

"We have a lot in common. And it was a special occasion."

Lanie had met her German friend at the Dressage World Championship in Tryon, North Carolina. She wasn't able to attend Lanie's birthday party, but with good reason. She'd been preparing for her wedding, at which Lanie had just been a bridesmaid.

Although not too many people knew, Lanie really wanted a family someday, and the ceremony, which was held in the private courtyard of a centuries-old winery estate, had pulled all her romantic strings. Aside from the scenery and the couple's heartfelt vows, she couldn't help but remember the other special person she met during that trip to North Carolina. Kade Wilder had been a guest at one of the events held at the championships. He was handsome, articulate and passionate about running for Congress.

They had spent the night talking and later followed each other on social media. When Lanie had posted about her party, Kade had messaged he would be in town and would love to personally pass on his wishes. He had arrived late but the dance they had shared was worth every second of the wait. As he'd held her in his arms, she had practically drowned in the dark blue pools of his eyes.

She wasn't the type to get goofy over a man, but her stomach had been filled with so many butterflies that night on the dance floor, and later when they had spoken alone. Perhaps the attraction was one-sided, though. Kade hadn't tried to kiss her that night, and he hadn't tried to contact her since.

"We'll be there in thirty," the driver said. "I've heard of Rawson's farm. They've had plenty of winners over the years."

"It was a great place to grow up, especially if you love horses."

Finding her phone, Lanie logged in to see whether Kade had posted anything since the last time she'd looked.

"So you're a Rawson kid?" the driver asked.

"I am."

"Must be hard right now with all those rumors about drugging and race-fixing floating around. Even money laundering. That's what some Darnel guy was hinting at on the radio this morning."

Lanie almost dropped her phone.

What the hell?

"Rawson's is one of the most reputable stables in the state. In the country."

The driver shrugged. "I'm sure it is, lady. Just sayin'."

Growling under her breath—at the situation, not the driver—Lanie swapped to another social media platform and swiped through the feed. She shouldn't be surprised that word of those doping allegations had leaked. People loved a scandal. But Hux and Ajax would have it sorted out soon enough. The Rawsons had overcome battles far tougher than this.

She stopped at a post from Veda. The caption indicated it was a view from Darnel Manor. The last time she and Veda had spoken was the morning after the party. Lanie had been stunned to learn that Ajax had scored that particular notch on his bedpost. Later, Veda had admitted that it hadn't been the first time.

Lanie had given her opinion on the subject, after which Veda had claimed that she wouldn't see Ajax again. Veda was a strong woman, but Ajax was a pro. If her brother set his mind to it, Lanie would bet her lucky saddle that Veda would fold.

Lanie focused on the photo again. If Veda was in town, they should catch up. Veda might want to talk about Ajax. Lanie could use a sounding board, too. Was it better to file her feelings for Kade away under Obviously Not Happening, or should she be the one to reach out this time?

Lanie speed-dialed her friend. Veda answered with her usual direct style.

"Lanie. I'm glad you called."

"I've just flown in and caught your feed. Are you visiting with your dad?"

"Kind of. He's been in a car accident."

Lanie gasped. "God. Is he okay?" She didn't personally know the man, and if she did, she probably wouldn't like him, but she still felt for her friend.

"He was lucky," Veda explained. "He's in the hospital, though, so I'm house-sitting between visits."

Lanie sat forward, peering out the windshield down the road ahead. "I'm not far away. I should drop by."

There was a grin in Veda's voice when she replied, "You definitely should."

Ten minutes later, Lanie was out of the cab and enjoying Veda's welcoming hug. Lanie came right out and said it.

"I need to unpack about a man."

Veda groaned. "Same."

While they sat out back with a glass of wine and the sun arcing more toward the dark clouds traveling in from the north, Veda and Lanie played rock-paper-scissors to decide who went first.

Lanie won.

After listening to the whole gorgeous-but-MIA-man story, Veda wanted to highlight a point.

"I saw you two on the dance floor the night of your party. You were literally floating on air."

Looking off, Lanie swirled her wine in her glass. "I don't carry on with something if the feelings aren't right. I was beginning to think I was incapable of going all weak at the knees."

Veda raised her glass. "Guess no one is immune."

"Which brings us to my brother. He's the man you want to talk about, right?"

Veda filled her friend in. She didn't leave anything out, including playing *not* hard to get in Barbados, followed by the *getting jealous over probably nothing* episode at that dinner. She wrapped up with how Ajax had met her at the hospital after her father's accident and, later, had come back here to keep her company.

"He stayed over that night, and we've spoken on the phone since."

Lanie prodded. "But?"

"We haven't seen each other since Tuesday morning." This was Thursday afternoon. "After having a long weekend, I know he'd be busy with work, catching up. And there's that Booshang thing to deal with. A stewards' meeting is set for tomorrow. On top of that, some Rawson clients have removed their horses from the stables."

Lanie grunted, surprised, and then tossed back her hair. "They'll be back."

When Veda only bit her lip, Lanie frowned and tipped closer.

"Wait. You don't think Ajax actually doped that horse, do you?"

Veda admitted, "I wasn't sure at the start. I mean that kind of stuff happens all the time."

"Not at Rawson's."

"But that's not technically true. Paul Booshang was working for Ajax when he was caught."

Lanie paused before she got to her feet and looked out over the hills like she was daring them to point out the facts, too.

"Ajax and Jacob will clear our name," she said. "Dad'll make sure of it."

"Ajax says that Hux is giving him a hard time, too."

Lanie swung around. "Well, it seems as if I came home just in time then. Far too much testosterone flying around."

When Lanie grinned, Veda smiled, too. "*Way* too much testosterone," she agreed before she sobered again. "Maybe I'm being selfish or needy, but I wish Ajax could find a minute to come over and see me."

Lowering back down into her seat, Lanie made a suggestion. The most outlandish notion in the history of anything.

"Why don't you come over and see him instead?"

Veda almost spluttered her wine. "That's such a bad idea."

"Veda, it's my home, too. You're my friend, and I'm inviting you."

"Forget about Ajax maybe feeling like we're treading on his toes. My father was mentioned in connection to those allegations. I'm sure Hux doesn't want a Darnel shoved in his face any time soon."

Or ever.

"My father is an alpha male who's not afraid to stand up for what's right. But Veda, he's not a tyrant. In fact, he can be a big ol' pussycat where I'm concerned." She took Veda's hand. "I know there's talk about your father being involved in this somehow. But even if that's true, it's no reason to hold it against you."

"I'm not so sure."

"Spurned by association? My mother dated Drake but Hux didn't hold it against her, did he?"

Veda had to think that through. "I guess not…"

"So it's settled." She took Veda's glass and set it down. "You're driving me home."

Veda's throat convulsed. "I'm still not sure that's a good idea. He has that meeting tomorrow, don't forget."

Lanie's determined expression softened. "From what you told me, you and Ajax are getting over your hurdles. I'm sure he would appreciate the visit. In fact, he'll probably be blown away."

Veda had something else she needed to say. "I'm sorry I didn't tell you about me and Ajax after that first time."

Lanie waved it off. "We're friends. Not Siamese twins."

"But we've always been open with each other."

"That hasn't changed."

"I'm just saying…if you ever found anything out about Ajax…something that you might think I ought to know…"

When Lanie read between the obvious lines, her expression filled with understanding as well as conviction. "No secrets between friends. Promise."

Smiling, Veda nodded. "I promise, too."

After another long day taking care of business, including rolling calls from clients who were growing ever more curious about those pending test results, Ajax was happy to kick back. When Fallon arrived at his office, saying that she had brought along two saddled horses that were raring to go, Ajax didn't waste a moment pulling the whistle on quitting time.

He needed to stop thinking about the stewards' meeting set for tomorrow. Jacob would be sitting beside him, and Griff was taking a day off work to show his support for the team. Of course, Hux would be there, too. Frankly, Ajax wished he would simply stay the hell away.

Since their confrontation earlier in the week, Hux's mood had tanked even more. No one knew what the test results would reveal, or what penalties would be handed down. But, yes, mud tended to stick, particularly when Drake Darnel was slinging it around every opportunity he got, like in that absurd radio interview this morning.

Money laundering.

What a crock.

None of that impacted his feelings for Veda, but it had held him back from seeing more of her these past days. At this point in time, Hux didn't need the added aggravation of having his son flaunt the fact that he was sleeping with the enemy's daughter. Hux had never let Drake get under his skin before, either professionally or personally, but this was a whole other ball game.

The big question was whether Darnel was shoveling his crap onto the Rawsons to divert attention from his own part in this doping episode. If that was the case, when would the truth be revealed?

Ajax was glad that Fallon had accepted Hux's invitation to stay on a few days. She understood the industry; whenever he vented about this, she was only ever supportive. And she helped in other ways, Ajax thought as he stepped outside and glanced at the clouds rolling in.

She came along on his rounds and helped out with track work. Best of all, she managed to bring the occasional smile to Hux's dour face.

Once those results were in, Ajax thought as Fallon spurred on her horse through the open paddock gate, everyone would be free to get on with their lives. He could properly pick up with Veda where they had left off. And if Hux wasn't happy about that state of affairs, too damn bad.

Ajax would always love and respect his father, but these past weeks had put a different spin on how he viewed their relationship. He'd given his heart, blood and soul to this place. Irrespective of those test results, he needed a partnership contract now. Tomorrow after the meeting, he would give Hux the news.

"Hey, Jax, I'll race ya!"

Fallon, who was handling that chestnut two-year-old like the pro she was, was already springing into a gallop. As she bolted off, throwing a goading look over her shoulder, Ajax swung into his saddle, and Someone's Prince Charming took off after them. Fallon was such a natural; hanging up her silks seemed a waste. Which brought to mind the other reason he was glad she had stayed. Having her own riding school was cool, but having their horse wear the Kentucky Derby's rose blanket next year would be monumental. And she, along with the Prince, had the goods to deliver.

Fallon just beat him to the oak at the top of the next slope. As her horse snorted and lowered his head to tear off some grass, Ajax pulled up, too. Breathing in air scented with approaching rain, he gazed out over the hills he called home.

"I'm going to miss this place," Fallon said as the sun disappeared behind the bank of rolling clouds.

"You don't have to go," Ajax said, leaning on his saddle's horn while she dismounted.

"I have a life to get back to."

"Don't you miss the one you left behind?"

Fallon swept up a wildflower and twirled the stem. "We've talked about that. I made a decision to move on. I don't regret it."

Climbing down to join her, Ajax asked, "Not even a teensy bit?"

"I need to do something different. Something for me."

"But you loved being a jockey," he said, stealing the flower and slotting the stem behind her ear.

"The truth is I did it for my father. It was always his dream."

Ajax blinked. "I didn't know that."

"As a boy, Dad dreamed of bringing home a Derby win, but he was never the right build to ride. I was."

"Winning the Kentucky Derby..." Ajax playfully punched her arm. "You could still do that. I have the ride right here."

While Ajax stroked his horse's warm, strong neck, Fallon searched his eyes for a long moment.

"Ajax, are you trying to talk *me* into staying or you?"

Muscles in his chest locked before he reevaluated those hills, which were fast becoming covered in shadow rather than sunlight.

Shaking his head, remembering how it used to be, Ajax growled. "I wish this had never happened." Booshang's behavior that day and his ridiculous allegations had turned the world upside down.

"This all could be a blessing in disguise," Fallon said. "A new opportunity for you. A new start."

If, or rather when, Hux signed that partnership agreement... "Yeah. I suppose it could."

"So you'll consider my suggestion."

"What suggestion?"

"That you help me with my riding school. We spoke about it the other night."

Over dinner. But they'd been joking around.

"I'm not saying give up what you do here, just lend a hand when you can. I think we could have fun." Fallon's smile changed as she adjusted the flower in her hair. "I think we could be happy."

A lightning bolt ignited the sky, cutting a jagged line through the churning clouds. Seconds later, an almighty clap of thunder split the air. Whinnying, Fallon's horse reared up, then charged back down the hill toward the safety of its stall. Ajax caught the Prince's reins as another bolt struck and an even worse clap shook the ground. The next second, hard rain began to fall.

Ajax jumped up into his saddle then threw out his hand to Fallon. "Want a lift?"

She caught his hand. "Bless your heart!"

She swung up behind him and they lit a trail back down the hill.

With rain hitting his face, Ajax let out a whoop. This was what life was about. Feeling free...even reckless. Like you could do anything when you decided nothing would hold you back.

Fallon was an amazing woman—beautiful, talented. He'd known that when she'd won the Stakes as well as later, when they had slipped away to be alone. He had loved catching up with her these past days.

But he had seen the look in her eyes a moment ago. When she'd said they could be happy, she was talking about more than working together on a riding school. If he had stepped into her space...if he'd kissed her...she wouldn't have pulled away.

But Fallon wasn't the one he wanted right now, and when they were under cover, he would be clear in letting her know exactly that.

Veda was driving up the Rawsons' private road, heading toward that fateful bend, when the heavens opened up and dumped big-time. As the sudden rain smashed against the windshield, Lanie readjusted her seat belt.

"This is one serious summer shower."

Veda switched on the wipers and shifted closer to the wheel. "Reminds me of the rain the night of your party."

"When your car spun out."

"Right here, actually," Veda said as the SUV rounded the corner and her stomach lurched.

"You must've been happy to see Ajax charging down to rescue you."

Remembering it all very well, Veda wanted to smile. But other older memories made her shudder instead.

"I wonder what would have happened," Veda said as

the vehicle climbed toward the house, "if it hadn't rained that night."

Lanie shrugged. "What's meant to be is meant to be."

Then the belting rain stopped as quickly as it had started, and the guest parking area appeared before them. As Veda pulled into a spot, she noticed some movement on an adjacent hill. Soaked through, Ajax was riding toward the house on the back of a magnificent-looking steed.

With his hair flying back and his shirt wet through, tugging against all those gorgeous muscles, he had never looked so handsome. So capable and in charge. She couldn't wait to feel those arms around her again.

Veda was hurrying to shut down the engine and jump out when, beside her, Lanie groaned out an expletive. Her eyes were bulging like she'd swallowed a toad. A chill rippled over Veda's skin as she reached across to hold her friend's shoulder.

"Lanie? God, what's wrong?"

"Nothing. Not a thing."

Lanie pasted on a limp smile that only made Veda worry more. She looked out through the windshield again as another chill swept over her. Ajax was bringing his horse to a showy stop. Someone was hooked up behind him. As he helped the other rider down, the woman looked up at him as if no one else compared.

As if he was the best.

Veda's scalp started crawling. She didn't want to jump to conclusions, be overdramatic. But come on. She wasn't a fool.

Without taking her eyes off the woman, she asked Lanie, "Is it someone from his past or someone new?"

Lanie exhaled. "You and Ajax should probably talk."

Veda clenched her jaw and drew down a big breath. *No secrets between friends.*

"If you know anything…"

Lanie shut her eyes and dropped her chin. "Griff mentioned something last year…"

Ajax was dismounting. He'd seen her car and was heading over with an uncharacteristically measured stride. She felt strangely hypnotized by the way those wet jeans clung to his thighs and his narrowed gaze held hers.

"What's her name?"

"Fallon Kelly," Lanie replied. "She's a jockey. Or was. She'd hung up her whip last I heard."

Veda felt as if she was folding in on herself and melting away. The surprise guest had stayed on longer than a night. Longer than Ajax had said she would or had mentioned in his calls.

By the time Ajax reached the car, the shock was ebbing. In its place, Veda felt those familiar fingers curl around her throat at the same time her brain began to shut down. But she needed to speak with Ajax. No games. No blinders. She simply wanted the truth.

Getting out of the car, she took in Ajax's plastic grin and the way his big shoulders in that chambray shirt slouched just a bit as he shook out his wet hands. He went to take a step closer, but then blinked and rocked back on his boot heels instead.

"Well, this is a double surprise," he said, acknowledging Lanie, who was out of the car now, too. "Veda." He jerked a thumb over his shoulder. "I mentioned Fallon Kelly was staying over. She used to ride for us."

Still standing by that magnificent horse, obviously realizing that Veda was Ajax's latest squeeze, Fallon sent over a half-hearted wave. Veda recognized her face from that story she'd read about her online. While Lanie joined Fallon, Veda and Ajax simply stood there, drilling into each other's eyes.

"You want to come down to the office?" he asked her.

"I'm not holding you up?" Veda replied.

His eyebrows drew together before he nodded toward the path. They walked side by side, neither saying a word the entire way. When they got inside, they moved through to his private office, and he shut the door.

She wanted him to talk first. Would he try to say this was completely innocent, or that it was all in her head? Maybe the time had come where he would simply say that he felt bad about them not working out. That would definitely fit.

"I know what you're thinking," he said.

"What's that?" she asked.

"That Fallon and I… That something's going on." He gave an exaggerated shrug. "We're just friends."

"If I could make an observation…"

He exhaled. "Go ahead."

"I would put my money on her wanting way more than friendship."

Veda almost expected him to deny knowing it, too. But he only searched her eyes as his bristled jaw worked from side to side. Veda's stomach went into free fall.

"We went for a ride," he said. "There was a clap of thunder. Fallon's horse freaked and galloped home. That's all there is to it."

Veda's throat was blocked with emotion. At the same time, she felt something akin to relief. This was really over. He didn't want to admit that he and Fallon Kelly had slept together in the past. And it sure as hell seemed like they were sleeping together now.

"Okay," she said.

His eyes narrowed. "Okay?"

"It doesn't matter."

"I'm getting the impression that it matters a lot."

She tried to ignore the tears pounding away at the backs of her eyes, threatening to break through.

"The bottom line is that I don't trust you."

His eyes grew darker as the line of his mouth hardened.

But his voice remained level. She guessed he might actually be hurt. The Stud always did the dumping, not the other way around.

"So I'm the only one who's supposed to embrace blind faith?"

She frowned. "What the hell are you talking about?"

"The Booshang fiasco. I keep defending you when other people think you might be involved."

Talk about deflection. How dare he throw that other stuff in her face now.

He cut her off before she got to the door.

"We need to talk, Veda."

Her unshed tears kept building up, but she held them back.

"I have nothing more to say."

"I don't know what you want from me." He drove both hands through his damp hair. "Galloping down that hill, I swear I was only thinking of you."

"Don't worry." She shoved past him. "You'll get over it."

Veda hated to think just how quick.

Fourteen

The next day, the stewards' meeting was over in record time.

As Ajax left the building, he didn't have a chance to re-hash the findings with his family before a tidal wave of reporters descended. There were TV cameras crowding him in while microphones got shoved in his face.

"How do you feel about the decision?" one reporter asked.

"What's your next move?" asked another.

"Clients have left Rawsons," someone cried out from the back of the mob. "How badly has this discredited your name?"

In his faultless attorney style, Jacob stepped forward and spoke for the family.

"This meeting was a courtesy to let Ajax Rawson know that samples taken from Someone's Prince Charming confirmed that no State Gaming Commission regulations were violated with regard to illegal drugs, medications or other substances. Furthermore, we would like to make clear that Mr. Rawson was not aware of Paul Booshang's questionable actions on the day under investigation."

A different reporter from a national network got her question in.

"Why did Paul Booshang implicate you, Ajax?"

Ajax stepped forward while his family arced around him. "You'd have to ask him. It seems bizarre and a total waste of time to me."

"Today Booshang implicated another big stable owner in multiple past misdeeds dating back decades," the same reporter said. "Will Drake Darnel be investigated?"

Hux fielded the question. "We can't speak for anyone else." He clapped Ajax on the shoulder. "We're just glad to get back to business as usual."

There were a few more questions asked and answered before Jacob stepped in again and closed the session.

"Well done," Hux said, shaking both his sons' hands as the reporters began to drift away. "And now that we're all law-and-ordered out, I suggest we put on our feed bags."

Wearing a smart pantsuit, Lanie piped up, "There's a new place opened around the corner. Grape pie's on the menu, I hear." She found Susan's gaze. "Not anywhere near as good as yours, of course. But it is the man of the hour's favorite."

Ajax loved grape pie almost as much as he loved the support his family was showing him. He couldn't have been more pleased with the outcome. But for once he wasn't particularly hungry. He was thinking about Veda. He couldn't get her out of his mind.

Jacob was hugging the women goodbye. "I gotta go. I promised Buddy and Tea I'd cook my world's best ever spaghetti tonight. Pasta from scratch. Sauce to die for."

Susan planted a big kiss on his cheek. "You need to give me the recipe."

"And we need to see the rest of the family up here again soon," Hux added as he drew Susan close. "There's nothing better."

Clearly Hux and Susan were in love—had been for many years. There was a familiarity and trust that radiated whenever they were together, and it didn't matter that they weren't as young as they once were. That kind of love just grew and grew. It was real and it was lasting.

"I'm going to shoot off, too," Griff said, checking his wristwatch.

"Big date tonight?" Jacob asked, nudging Ajax in the ribs as if to say, *We know this dude's game.*

"As a matter of fact...none of your business." Griff gave a wink as he headed off.

Which left four to enjoy that new place Lanie had recommended.

"Ajax, I need to apologize," Hux said as the women walked off ahead of them.

Ajax wasn't sure this was the right place or time.

"We can talk later, Dad."

"It's been weighing on my mind...how I expected too much of you, and even learned to depend on you. You're right. I don't show nearly enough gratitude for what you do. I haven't truly acknowledged how much you've sacrificed."

Ajax felt as if his chest just puffed out ten inches. He and Hux had said some things to each other they shouldn't have. It was good to hear his father open up this way.

"We wouldn't be nearly as successful," Hux went on, "if it weren't for all the hours you put in every week."

"Well, I love taking care of my team."

Susan was calling out, "You guys coming?"

Hux replied, "Be right there." Then he caught Ajax's gaze again and gave a definitive nod. "Jacob has his career. Griff and Lanie, too. And you, Ajax, have made a real name for yourself in this industry, not only as a trainer and businessman but as a gentleman."

Ajax ran a finger around the inside of his collar. "I wouldn't go that far."

"People enjoy your company. They want to work with you. Yes, we've had some losses these past weeks, but that won't take away from your legacy."

Legacy? "I'm not that old, am I?"

"Well, you're old enough for this." Hux reached into his jacket's inner pocket and drew out a folded document. "You deserve this, son. I should have taken care of it sooner."

When Ajax unfolded the paperwork, his stomach did a flip. He could barely believe his eyes. "This is a partnership agreement."

"Between you and me for the farm."

Ajax coughed out a laugh. This was precisely what he'd wanted. What he had decided to demand as long overdue. Inside he was kicking his heels, pumping both fists, because he was legitimately happy.

Yep.

He really was.

"It needs your signature," Hux explained as Ajax handed the contract back.

"Sure." He blew out a shaky breath over a smile and added, "Thanks. I really mean that."

"I know you do." Hux hesitated. "But I can see you're focused on something else right now."

Ajax rolled back his shoulders, shook his head. "You don't want to know."

"Let me guess. Veda Darnel." When Ajax nodded, Hux's expression deepened. "I owe you an apology there, too. I attacked that girl's character when, of course, she wasn't involved in the Booshang mess. Veda Darnel is important to you. I should have given that more consideration before running my mouth off. I was just pissed at her father shooting *his* mouth off to the press…pointing fingers…"

A reporter rushed over—the same guy who had asked about their next move.

"A heads-up," the reporter said. "We're all shooting over to get a statement from Darnel."

"You're out of luck," Ajax said. "Drake Darnel is in the hospital."

"Negative. My sources say he got out this morning. I'm not sure that he knows he's been implicated in the wrongdoing today." The reporter was striding away. "We're about to find out."

"They never let up," Hux said, removing his hat to dab his brow with a monogrammed handkerchief. "Hell, I almost feel sorry for Drake having to face it alone, and with no warning."

Ajax didn't care about Drake Darnel. As that reporter jumped into a news van and sped off, he was thinking about the one person who didn't deserve a grilling. The only person he cared about right now.

Veda.

Earlier that morning, when Veda had arrived, the doctor had yet to finish his rounds and give her father a green light to leave. In the waiting room, Veda had taken the time to reaffirm her decision, effective as of today.

To say Drake Darnel was a difficult man was an understatement. This week he had provoked not one but two significant disagreements. Rarely did he show that he cared. As far as fatherly affection was concerned, he'd missed practically every class. But that was on him.

Veda had her own life now.

The drive home from the hospital had been strained. Now as Drake walked into the house and headed for the kitchen, Veda took in his lanky figure. He was getting older...more gray hair and even more impatience. When she was a little girl, of course she had respected him. Growing up, she had no choice but to endure his miserable moods. Even as an adult, she had taken his BS. But now, if Drake wasn't on board with the whole mutual respect thing—if he wanted to continue with this crazy controlling crap—then she didn't need to be around him anymore.

She was done.

In the kitchen, he found his favorite Wedgwood cup and saucer. After the water boiled, he brewed his pungent green tea without a word or a look. She knew the drill. Her father dished out his silent treatment as often as sharks shed teeth.

As he lifted the cup, he sniffed and said, "Thank you for collecting me this morning."

Veda's reply was hollow. Automatic.

"You're welcome."

"The doctor said that I'm well enough to drive again now."

Meaning he didn't need her to taxi him around in one of his many cars housed in that huge, pristine garage.

Wonderful.

He took his time slicing a lemon and squeezing just enough into the brew before his gaze lifted to meet hers for the first time that day.

"This hasn't been a good week," he said.

"Tell me about it."

He grunted and squeezed some more lemon.

"Veda, are you still seeing that man?"

She stiffened. Firstly, she didn't want to think about Ajax right now. She wished she never had to think about him again. Secondly, her father needed to back off.

"I won't discuss Ajax Rawson with you," she replied.

"I think we need to talk about it," he said.

"I really don't."

"Come into the living room and we'll sit down."

As he moved toward her, Veda's patience expired and she held up her hand for him to stop.

"I won't do this anymore."

He frowned. "Do what?"

"I need to walk away. I mean *really* walk away. I should have done it a long time ago."

His brow furrowed before he scratched an ear and set his cup and saucer back down on the counter.

"I need to show you something," he said. "Something I see every day and yet never want to acknowledge."

Veda pushed out a heavy breath. "You're talking in riddles." Trying to manipulate her.

"A riddle… I suppose it is. Maybe we can solve it together."

Veda narrowed her eyes at him. She hadn't heard him use this tone before, or this tactic. "You aren't making any sense."

"Why don't you come and see for yourself?" When she continued to study him, trying to work out the trap, his eyebrows pinched before a small smile hooked one side of his mouth.

"Please, Veda?" he asked.

She couldn't remember a time when Drake had looked anything close to vulnerable. Whatever this riddle was, she had to see it.

She followed him through to the den, a large, well-appointed room with its own library, wet bar and assortment of fine art, including a full-sized bronze horse sculpture at the dead center of the room. Drake went to stand behind his ultra-tidy desk and waited for her to join him. When they were side by side, he slid open the top left-hand drawer, reached inside and pulled out three items…a pair of gold wedding rings and a photograph. A family photograph from when Veda was a little girl, prior to going to school.

He laid the rings in his palm and flipped over the

photo—the inscription on the back read, "Veda's three!"—before placing it faceup on the desk. In awe, she took in the image of father, mother and daughter sitting on the chesterfield in the living room. Drake was so young, with dark hair and no scowl lines. With her cheek pressed against Veda's, her beautiful mom was beaming. The room was packed with people smiling for the camera or looking adoringly at the lucky girl with her striking cloud of red curls. Drake was holding a kids' picture book—a birthday gift, Veda assumed.

As she let the image sink in, Veda's throat ached with emotion. There was gratitude that she had once known this kind of support coupled with a near-desperate longing to know it again. She was still digesting the fact that Drake had kept those wedding rings and this happy family snapshot when he drew a fourth item from the drawer. It was an old book.

The one in the photo.

"I wanted you to grow up to be smart and happy," he said, focusing on the cartoon barn animal scene on the book's cover.

Absorbing every detail of the cover, with its two horses, cow, three pigs and fluffy little dog, Veda got this warm, rippling feeling. She couldn't be sure, but it was so similar to the picture she'd had in her mind for so long...an image of how her own animal farm might look.

Her father cleared his throat but then studied the photograph again with a smile she had never seen on him before...like he not only remembered but also cherished having had that joy in his life.

"I spent practically all my time on the business," he said, "making sure you were both well provided for...that you could grow up with everything you needed and deserved. The trouble started the day after this party. She asked me to spend more time with you both. As the years went by, her patience turned into irritation and, ultimately, despair."

Veda picked up the musty-smelling photo and looked into her mother's smiling eyes. So many times she remembered her saying that she had only ever wanted three things: a happy child, a nice home and a good husband. Was that too much to ask?

"The more your mom insisted I put work second," he went on, "the more I retreated and looked back, clutching on to something—some*one*—who had never truly been mine. To take my mind off fixing a real problem, being less selfish, I began to focus on that aspect of my life. I picked and picked until I felt it like a scab on my heart."

He was talking about the woman Hux Rawson had fallen in love with and married. The mother Ajax had lost around the same time Veda's own mom had died.

"I was an uncompromising fool, stuck in my ways." Drake eyes were glistening. "I threw it all away."

Veda had never heard her father speak like this before... with insight and humility. Like a human being rather than a cracked and bitter shell.

"I saw you slap her once," she said.

He cringed like he remembered it well. "She had stopped talking to me. Stopping caring altogether. I thought she might have someone else." He shook his head hard. "I was wrong. There's no excuse. None."

Veda had half expected him to deny the entire incident, so she got something else off her chest. "I can't remember you ever really talking to me."

"I kept it all in. Blocked everyone out. And this week, I've pushed you even further away. I know if I don't change, and change now, I'll lose you again, and this time for good." Holding that book to his chest, he turned more toward her and lowered his chin. "I don't want that to happen. Veda.

It's hard for me to say, but—" he swallowed deeply "—I need your help."

This conversation just kept getting weirder. "You want *my* help?"

"I see from your blog, you're a bit of an expert at that."

Veda's mouth dropped open. She must have heard wrong. "You read my blog?"

"Every post. It's to the point. Extremely informative." His eyes shone as he smiled. "I haven't told you for so many years. I'm proud of you, Veda. I know your mother would be proud of you, too."

Those words... The night of that party, she remembered Hux saying them to Lanie.

The right thing to do was wrap her arms around her father and tell him everything was forgiven...to let go of the uncertainty, the fear and all the frustration. Letting go was a choice, after all. But she needed time to come to terms with this sudden change of heart and accept that her father might actually, well, love her.

So she held off on gushing. Instead, she returned her father's smile and nodded as if to say, *Let's see what happens from here. Fingers crossed.*

A speculative gleam appeared in his eye.

"Now we really do need to speak about Ajax Rawson."

She groaned. "Dad, can we not?"

"I was only going to say that we should have him over for dinner sometime." He anticipated her reaction. "Yes, it will be a little awkward. The Rawsons and Darnels are far from friends. I've done some things I'm ashamed of, particularly this week. I'm not sure Ajax would even accept an invitation. But I can try, Veda. *We* can try."

If the offer had come a week earlier, she would have considered it. But her on-again, off-again relationship with Ajax had been permanently laid to rest. Any notion of extending olive branches between the families was too late.

So, should she let her father know about the breakup? Would his eyes fill with sympathy—support—or would he simply say *I told you so*?

The sound of the knocker hitting the front door echoed through the house. But her father didn't react. He had more to say.

"How does a man who has lost what's most important get it back?" he asked. "That's the riddle."

She didn't have the whole answer, but said, "He starts by saying I'm sorry and meaning it."

Drake hung his head before finding her eyes again. "I'm so sorry, Veda. Sorry for driving your mother away. Sorry for putting up that wall and not appreciating what I had."

The knocker sounded again.

Veda swept away a tear before it fell. "We should probably get that."

He tried on a smile. "To be continued, then?"

Before she could answer, Veda's ears pricked up to a different sound. "Do you hear that?"

Drake's eyes narrowed as he looked out the den's window, which gave a partial view of the front of the house. "There are vans pulling up." He headed for the door. "I'll go see what's happening."

Veda set the photograph down and told him, "I'm going with you."

Out in front of the Darnel mansion, the Rawson truck skidded to a stop. With Hux riding shotgun—Lanie and Susan had decided to stay in town and leave this showdown to the men—Ajax had arrived here in record time but, unfortunately, not soon enough.

Reporters were congregated on the lawn, the same pack Jacob had handled so well earlier. Cameras were pointed like cannons at the front door, and questions were being thrown like knives. Facing the onslaught, standing at the center of his extravagant stone porch, Drake Darnel looked completely blindsided.

Ajax didn't care about Drake. Only Veda. She was standing beside her father, chin high, loyal to the bitter end.

Ajax threw open the car door, growling, "I'm going to save my girl."

"This all ends now," Hux replied, growling, too. "*All* of it."

Together, father and son strode up and cut through the media mob. Ajax was ready to tell them all to back the hell off and go home. But then Hux did something downright extraordinary. Something that had Ajax doubting his own eyes and ears.

Hux trotted up those porch steps. When he came to stand beside his old enemy, Drake's shocked expression deepened and Veda's eyes practically popped out of her skull. Then, turning to confront the mob, Hux waved his arms. When the barrage of questions quietened, he took a breath while Drake and Veda gaped on.

"My family spoke with you people earlier," Hux said. "You all know the score on those dud test results. As you are all obviously aware, this morning Paul Booshang, a former employee, went on to implicate Drake Darnel in similar illegal activities."

"Mr. Darnel!" a reporter called out. "Sir, what is your relationship with Paul Booshang?"

"Has the State Gaming Commission been in touch regarding this matter?" asked another.

Drake took a halting step forward. "The Darnel Stables... I have never...would...never..."

Hux edged closer to Drake's side and, catching his gaze, tried to share a stalwart smile.

"Let me be honest here. These stables are among the best and most reputable in the state," Hux said. "In the country." His voice took on a solemn tone. "Our families have known each other many years. I would like to go on the record as standing alongside our neighbors against these baseless allegations."

Ajax was watching Veda watching Hux. She looked like a child tasting ice cream for the first time—there was a second of surprise quickly followed by delight.

Hux went on. "Mr. Darnel has returned from the hospital only a short time ago. I'm sure you all agree, we need to walk it back and respect his privacy right now." He offered a meaningful smile to Drake. "It's time we all moved on."

Talk about taking the high road.

As the reporters and cameramen drifted off toward their vehicles, Ajax made his way up the porch steps. He wasn't sure what he was going to say to Hux, let alone Drake; this morning had certainly been one for the books.

But more importantly, he needed to talk with Veda. The last time they had spoken, she hadn't pulled any punches. He didn't have what she needed, and he would move on soon enough.

Ajax hadn't agreed then, and he didn't agree now. He needed one more chance to have her hear why.

Hux put out his arm to welcome his son as he climbed the steps. "Drake, I don't know if you've had the pleasure of meeting my boy."

As the other man's watery gaze narrowed, Ajax held his breath. Drake knew he had been seeing Veda. Given Drake's screwy way of looking at the world, he might view that as stealing his daughter, just as Hux had "stolen" the woman Drake had loved so many years ago.

But now Drake only surrendered a genuine smile and put out his hand.

"I'm pleased to meet you… Ajax, isn't it?"

Ajax's knees almost buckled. He had to be dreaming.

But when Drake's smile not only held but grew, Ajax accepted the fact that miracles did happen. Which was great news, because he sure as hell could use another one right about now.

There was a brief exchange about this morning's meeting and Hux's handling of the media before Drake invited them all inside for a cool drink. Ajax had felt Veda's eyes on him the entire time. Had this unfolding scene softened her stand against him? Ready or not, time to find out.

"A cool drink would be nice," he told Drake before focusing on Veda. "But I'd like to speak with your daughter first, if that's all right."

After an awkward beat, in which Drake and Veda exchanged looks, Drake headed for the open front door, tossing over his shoulder, "Huxley, shall we?"

When he and Veda were alone, Ajax tried on a *well, here we all are smile* while she scooped her hair back behind her ear, searching his eyes, looking more beautiful than ever before.

"I appreciate you and Hux coming today," she said. "We were totally unprepared for reporters."

"They'd just finished with us when we got word they were on their way here."

She titled her head. "So, congratulations on the test results."

"Yeah, well, it was an experience, and not without consequences."

"Have any more clients bailed?"

"One. But we've had a lot of support, as well."

She nodded. "Full steam ahead then."

"Which brings me to some other news. You remember how I wanted Hux to consider a partnership? I was saving the discussion until this was all over, but Dad was a step ahead of me. Right after the meeting this morning, he presented me with a document—fifty-fifty."

Her eyebrows edged up. "Bet you couldn't find a pen fast enough."

A week ago, that would have been the smart bet. As it turned out, he had handed the contract back, leaving it unsigned. For now.

When Veda slid a look toward the front door, he anticipated her next words. She would either suggest that they join their fathers or, more likely, that she would leave the men alone to talk. Neither option worked. He wanted more time with her alone. He needed to somehow make this right.

He spoke again before she could.

"So your dad got the all clear from the doctor?"

She nodded an unusually long time as if she wasn't sure if she should fill him in more.

"Actually, Dad and I had a discussion this morning," she finally said. "A real talk like I can't remember ever happening before."

"That's *huge*. Seems like it's a day for progress."

"Well, it's a start." She surrendered a smile. "I think a good start."

There was another loaded silence during which Ajax thought he saw a glimmer of anticipation in her eyes…a spark of *Say the right thing now and maybe I'll agree to see where this goes.* He had nothing to lose and pretty much everything to gain.

He'd get the tricky part out of the way first.

"Fallon's gone. She wanted me to pass on that she's sorry if she caused any trouble between you and me."

Other than crossing her arms, Veda gave no response. Not a word.

He forced the admission out. "I want to tell you that years ago, she and I spent a night together. Just one."

"I know."

"You…know?"

"Lanie told me."

"How did she—?"

"Griff."

He grunted. "So much for a brother's confidence."

"Oh, Ajax, I'm sure he's not the only one who knew."

He got back to the point. "Now Fallon is a friend," he said. "That's it. Friend. Period."

When Veda continued with the bland stare, he pushed on. He could feel his time running out. He needed to act, bring her close, show her just how he felt.

"Veda, I want to see you again."

Her jaw tightened before she shook her head.

No?

"Our fathers have put aside their differences," he said. "Can't we at least try to do the same?"

"I'm glad everyone's talking again. Dad and Hux. Me and my father. You and your dad."

He stepped forward, close enough to feel her warmth and for her to feel his.

"I'm way more interested in the two of us," he said.

She shook her head again.

"It's just... I feel very strongly about this," he went on. "About us."

"I know it's hard when you're so used to winning."

Every muscle in his body tensed. He had never known a woman like her. She never gave him a pass.

And then, as if she wanted to prove him wrong, she unfolded her arms and made a concession.

"I believe you about Fallon Kelly," she said.

He sparked up. "You do?"

When she looked almost disappointed, like she thought he was surprised that he had pulled the wool over her eyes, he took it down a notch.

"It's the truth. Veda, I would never do that to you."

She seemed to gather her thoughts before moving to the railing. When he joined her, her eyes were narrowed on the horizon like she was trying to see into the future. Or maybe back into the past.

"I'm not a fan of cowboys," she said. "Particularly the smooth-talking kind."

"You've made that pretty clear."

"Do you want to know why? The truest, deepest, most terrifying reason?"

As she faced him, he searched her resigned expression and nodded. "I really do."

"You know that my mother died in a car accident," she began.

"That was the word at the time."

"I was in the back seat."

He straightened as his stomach pitched. "God, Veda... were you hurt?"

"Not a scratch." Her grin was wry. "Isn't that something?"

More than ever, he wanted to reassure her somehow. But the best way to do that now was to sit tight and listen.

"After Mom left my dad, she hooked up with a man. A cowboy with a silver tongue. Or at least where my mother was concerned. Dad didn't keep in touch as such, but he sent money. Lots of it. Her cowboy was as sweet as he needed to be to get Mom to pay all the bills, including his gambling debts."

Ajax shuddered. He knew about Veda's problems with her dad and dyslexia. But this story was shaping up to be even worse.

"There were times when I was alone with him. He was nice until he started drinking. When he found out I couldn't read that well, he liked to put me down. He'd make out like he was joking, calling me Dumbo, flapping his hands at the sides of his head."

Oh, Ajax was mad now. Was this asshole still alive? He wanted to track him down and teach him a lesson about picking on someone his own size.

"The night of the accident," Veda went on, "he was

drinking from a flask with a pair of bull's horns etched into the tin. Mom was driving. He wanted to see Vegas, so Vegas it was. He'd never been mean to me in front of her before. Only ever sweet like he was with her, even when she accused him of being with another woman. *It's all in your head, darlin'. I would never do that to you.* But he told me once—said it straight-out—Mom was just his latest."

Ajax felt as if he were shrinking into the floor. The link was obvious.

But he wasn't that cowboy. He wasn't that kind of man.

He dug his hands deeper into his pockets. "You didn't tell your mom how he was with you?"

"I wanted to, but I didn't want to take her happiness away. She was so in love with the guy."

The absolute wrong guy.

While Ajax ground his teeth, Veda continued her story.

"We were in the car that night when he started on about my grades. I needed to try harder, he said. Do better. Then he called me Dumbo, softly at first, but getting louder. Growing meaner."

Veda's hands were laced together so tight, the knuckles were white.

"I didn't want to cry," she said. "I wanted to tell him to shut up. That he wasn't any better than me. But I was frozen...couldn't get the words out. Mom was ripping into him, though. Telling him to back off or get out."

Ajax felt sick to his stomach. There really were some first-class pricks in the world. Men who got their kicks from hurting kids and women. Lowlifes who had zero respect for themselves or anyone else.

"I was sitting in the back seat," Veda said, "throat closed, only choked sobs getting out. Then...all I remember is the bull horns on that flask and the oncoming headlights getting closer through the rain."

Ajax had heard enough. He brought Veda close and held her until she had finished shaking.

"The thing is," she went on, "when we lived here, I blamed myself for my mother being unhappy so much of the time. She wanted to keep the family together. I was the reason she stayed so long. And, of course, I blamed myself for the accident. For her death. She'd been distracted, trying to protect the dumb, mute weirdo who had never learned to defend herself."

Ajax dredged up a heavy smile. "But, boy, you can stand up for yourself now."

She straightened. "I know who I am. Even if it's hard sometimes, I know what I need to feel good about myself, and I can't afford to ever go back." Cupping his cheek, she searched his eyes and told him, "Ajax, not even for you."

Fifteen

Since that afternoon two weeks ago when she and Ajax
Rawson had said goodbye for good, Veda had fallen into
a slump. She had gotten involved with the wrong man and
fallen in love. Now she was paying the price.

Today, after seeing off a new client at the door of her
Jersey condo, Veda pulled up her sleeves and made a decision. She needed to regain a sense of control and, as nervous as she was about it, she thought she knew how. Time
to step up, put it out there and reclaim that final piece of
her power.

Veda opened her laptop and pulled up her Best Life Now
blog on the screen. Over the years, she had discussed life's
many challenges here: family, health, education and, of
course, relationship issues. But this morning's post would
go deeper and hopefully help even more.

I always try to be honest, Veda wrote under the header
"A Life Coach's Best Advice." *That's the way to build trust
in relationships and get good results. Except I haven't been*

completely open here. I have a big secret, you see. One that I'm finally ready to share.

My brain has trouble with letters and associated sounds. Things can get jumbled and blend together all wrong. In school, I really struggled to read. Then, whenever I got stressed, I would freeze up. Zone out.

Think of a possum playing dead. Nothing to see here, folks!

Once I got my dyslexia diagnosis, things improved. I had a word and reason that explained my daily struggles, as well as tools to help me cope. After some hard work, I found my way out of that hole. Now I try to help others climb out of theirs. And guess what. Some of my Best Life Now clients have been dyslexic just like me.

But here's the kicker. The bare bones truth without a wrapper.

I never let any of them know. A part of me was still embarrassed. Ashamed. And yes, even scared.

I won't do that anymore.

So, what's this life coach's best advice?

When you feel like hiding away or flat-out giving up, remind yourself that none of us is perfect. Everyone is spectacularly unique. Then stand up, fill your lungs and shout from the rooftops.

If I want to be free, I need to be me!

Ajax and his team were finishing up for the afternoon when Hux walked into the stables.

"Another blistering win for this one last week," Hux said, eyeing Someone's Prince Charming's whiteboard chart. "Good job, son."

After making a note about feed, Ajax set down the pen. "Things are certainly getting back to normal."

Hux entered the stall to check Prince's hooves.

"I heard from Matt today," he said, rubbing a fingertip around one of the plates. "Paul Booshang finally came clean. Apparently over the years, he'd lost everything at the track. He said if he couldn't take down horse racing in its entirety, he wanted to at least cause a stir for some guys at the top. He had a personal gripe with Darnel...the way he'd treated his family...something about a tree house." Hux straightened. "Apparently a TV network has offered him a fortune for the story."

Ajax recalled one of Veda's arguments against the industry. "Losing your shirt... I wonder how many people can identify."

"Son, you can't help people like that. They have no control."

That's what Ajax had always thought, but that was kind of the point, wasn't it? "You have to admit we're at least part of the problem."

"We don't twist anyone's arm. We don't force anyone to get into bed with a loan shark."

Ajax paraphrased Veda. "A drug dealer doesn't force an addict to keep using, either."

Hux was on to the last hoof. "Hardly the same thing. Horse racing generates billions of dollars for the state's economy. It's a tradition." Joining Ajax again, Hux pushed on with another topic of conversation as he looked up and down the stalls. "So, update me on any new plans you have, partner."

Ajax had signed that contract. Half the land and half the profits were now his. A huge achievement, particularly knowing that he truly had his father's respect.

Only...he had thought it would feel better than this. That he might feel, well, really whole now. Complete.

"The new walker's almost finished," he said, grabbing his hat and heading to the door with Hux. "I put on another vet this morning. The very best credentials, and we're on the same page with regard to overmedicating."

All too often in the industry, horses were given powerful medications that allowed them to race despite their injuries.

Hux dropped his hat on his head. "Good. Good. We want a fair race."

"And healthy horses."

Hux's smile deepened as they headed out into the sunshine. "I'm so fortunate to have a son who wants nothing more than to carry on the family tradition. You've always been so dedicated. Such a natural."

Looking around the place, Ajax held his hat in his hands. "I've been at it a long time."

"And will be for a long time to come."

That had always been the plan, and Ajax hadn't wanted anything more. Now... Well, he had other things on his mind, all to do with a strong-minded redhead who had put up a wall he couldn't find a way to break down.

"Something troubling you?" Hux asked. "Maybe something to do with Veda Darnel?"

Ajax tried to shrug it off. "I'm good."

Hux gave a thoughtful nod. "Well, you know what they say."

"No. What do they say?"

"Plenty more fish in the sea."

Ajax shut one eye as he winced. "I don't see Veda as a fish."

"I'm only saying that she must not be the one. But one day you'll find your special someone, no doubt about it. And when you do, you'll know. And so will she."

When Hux hailed a groom on his way to a tack room, Ajax headed back to the office with his father's words still ringing in his ears. Hux didn't know what he and Veda had discussed that day on Drake's porch. Her story was as private, and haunting, as they come. Ajax couldn't stop thinking about the circumstances surrounding her mom's death. That cowboy had been lower than a bottom-feeder. No wonder Veda had developed a lifelong aversion to that type.

But Ajax reassured himself again: he was nothing like that. He could never treat anyone that way. *Never.*

And yet those lines kept circling.

It's all in your head, darlin'.

I would never do that to you.

Yes, he had known a few women in his life, but as he had explained to Veda, he had never parted with anyone on bad terms. Fallon Kelly was a case in point. Except...

If he were to be 100 percent honest, he had always gotten out early for just that reason—to avoid the possibility of an ugly breakup. Put another way: he liked to have his cake and eat it, too. He wanted to enjoy the intimate company of a beautiful, engaging woman without the drag of making anything official.

But with Veda, that way of thinking—of feeling—just didn't seem to fit. Where she was concerned, the idea of commitment didn't spook him. In fact, he couldn't fathom a time when he didn't want to be with her, and only her.

Things had changed.

He had changed.

As Ajax reached the main paddock, Chester came trotting down from the house like he usually did this time of day. Trying to clear his head, Ajax deliberated on a chestnut prancing about, tossing her mane, while a buckskin colt capered up, his tail elevated and strong neck curved. Farther down, in the next paddock, two retired horses were grazing, stomping a hoof every now and then to shoo away flies. Over the years, he'd given away others to good and caring homes.

Scenes like this had filled and shaped his life. He'd grown up hankering for the next bustling day at the track. From a young age, he'd always leaped out of bed before the birds to start the day. The horses in his care had grade-A food and exercise, as well as the best grooms, riders, farriers and veterinary care.

He loved his horses. They were treated like kings.

But there were still injuries, some of them fatal. More than once he had watched, heartsick, as one of his own had gone down. The latest statistics said over fifty horses had died or been euthanized on New York State racecourses just this year.

He'd been one of the blinder-wearing crowd who argued that those numbers were built into the system. But what did that mean exactly? For the owners…for the horses…

Which side was he really on?

When Chester started wagging his tail, Ajax realized they had company. Susan was strolling over, a covered plate in her hand. He could smell the pie from here.

"Just pulled this out of the oven," she said, removing the cover to reveal a fat slice of his favorite: grape pie.

Ajax accepted the plate. "You're a honey, do you know that?"

Susan gave a big dimpled grin before she turned to study the horses.

"Sometimes I still can't believe I actually found my way here," she said. "This truly is my safe haven home."

Ajax had always believed this was his safe haven, too. That he would always feel rooted and cared for here. But lately trying to hold on to that had left a cold, heavy knot in his gut. He was hardly a kid anymore but still a long way from hanging up his reins. Was there more for him somewhere out there?

"You must be glad all that doping business is behind you," she said, leaning down to ruffle Chester's ears while his tail batted the ground. "And I'm so relieved that feud between Hux and Drake Darnel is finally over," she added. "Just goes to show. Differences can be worked out even when we might think there's no hope." She slid him a look. "I'm sure Veda would agree. She seems like a lovely girl."

"She is lovely. And smart." He paused, then added, "And strong."

"Yes, indeed," Susan said, looking out over the paddock again. "Diamonds are definitely out there. My ex-husband, however…well, he was a grimy lump of coal."

Ajax recalled that Veda's mother had stayed with Drake for the sake of the family. But Susan hadn't had children with her ex-husband. Why had she stayed so long? He hoped she wouldn't mind if he asked.

"Why didn't you leave the guy sooner?"

"Well, I married young. Taking those vows… I thought I had to stay. But over the years, of course the abuse wore me down, to the point I could barely think straight. Hux helped bring me back. I truly am a different person because of his love." She thought that through more and added, "Or maybe not different so much as… I think the right word is authentic. He's so lovely. And smart. And strong."

Ajax grinned. *Lovely. Smart. Strong.* Those words were a common link between Susan's love for Hux and his own thoughts on Veda. And Hux might have helped Susan, but she'd done just as much for him. Maybe more.

So, what would have happened to Hux, to their family, if Susan hadn't come along? Ajax wanted to believe that his father would have come out of that thick dark fog on his own. But he wondered….

And if *he* fell in love, married, had kids, and something happened to his wife—if she died… How would he deal? Would he cope or simply want to give in?

After Susan left with Chester bounding off ahead of her, Ajax took his pie into the office. As he sat behind his desk and opened his laptop, he mulled over Susan's words.

She had helped settle what he'd been struggling with for weeks. He needed to reach out to Veda again because he couldn't dance around the truth anymore. Earlier Hux had given sound advice about a person knowing when they had found their special someone. Ajax *did* know. He had to believe that Veda knew, too.

But he'd run out of things to say.

What could he do to convince her?

He set the pie aside to search Best Life Now. The link to Veda's website popped up. He checked out each page and ended up on her blog. The latest post had him riveted. He could literally hear her speaking to him, giving him advice.

If I want to be free, I need to be me.

Ajax thought back on those words the following weekend at the track. Someone's Prince Charming was two lengths ahead when he stumbled and broke down.

The examining veterinarian reported catastrophic fractures to both front ankles. The jockey, who had sustained serious injuries, was carried away on a stretcher. When the order was given to euthanize the horse, Ajax was there, kneeling at his friend's side.

On the drive home, his chest and eyes were burning so much, Ajax had to pull over. A bottle of Scotch kept him company through the night. By morning, he'd crossed that line and made up his mind.

To hell with anyone who didn't agree.

Sixteen

Veda heard it first from her dad.

The previous week when they'd talked on FaceTime, Drake had mentioned the "big news concerning the Rawsons." Veda had coughed out a laugh and told him point-blank he was wrong. But her father insisted; a Darnel farrier had confirmed the rumor just that day.

Ajax Rawson was no longer associated with Rawson Studs. No one knew for sure what big plans he had for himself, although talk was that he was still on the property working things through.

Veda hadn't spoken with Ajax since that day on her father's porch two whole months ago when she had opened up more about her past and made her position crystal clear. She had survived some tough breaks. Now that she was in a good place, there was no turning back, only going forward.

At the time, Ajax had looked disappointed, but obviously he had accepted her decision and moved on. Of course, the breakup had brought her down. Coming out on her blog had helped build her sense of self up again, as did personally sharing her dyslexia experiences later with each of her clients. And if she ever felt like curling up into a ball, she reminded herself that she wouldn't feel this way forever. Over time, her love for Ajax would fade.

Unfortunately she couldn't see that happening anytime soon.

Before ending that FaceTime call, Drake had suggested she visit again. How about this weekend? She had smiled and said good idea. It felt weird actually looking forward to spending time with her dad. Even weirder to anticipate driving right past the Rawson property knowing that Ajax was probably still there.

Now, as she traveled on the interstate, getting closer to the Rawsons' connecting road, Veda told her heart to quit pumping so hard. But memories from the night her car had spun out were coming thick and fast. Ajax racing down through the rain to rescue her still felt like something out of a dream.

Her hands were damp on the steering wheel by the time the Rawsons' billboard-size sign came into view. Would things have been different between her and Ajax if that doping scandal hadn't hit? But of course, realistically, they were never going to make it. He had his life and, yes, she had hers.

Veda stepped on the accelerator and forced herself to look straight ahead. She was going to visit her father. When she arrived, Drake would welcome her with a smile and perhaps even a hug. Going through to the kitchen, he would brew his tea while she poured herself a wine. Then they would venture out to the same spot where she and Ajax had relaxed after he had driven her home from the hospital that day. She could see the tree house from there.

Veda slammed on the brakes and caught her breath as another *new* sign came into view.

Welcome to Giddy Up Safe Haven.

The letters were multicolored and cartoonish like the ones from that old birthday book. A drawing of a grinning horse, standing with his front legs crossed, made her smile even harder. Then she spotted something else in a corner. A blue bucket with a dog sitting up inside it. It was small and fluffy with apricot dots on each cheek.

A blasting horn sent Veda jumping out of her seat. As the flatbed truck swerved around her, she turned onto the shoulder of the entrance road. Her heart was slamming against her ribs, and she couldn't contain the grin because this was more than a coincidence.

The Rawsons owned hundreds of acres, including this hill. Ajax knew she had a dream of having a farm where animals didn't have to work or breed or die. A sanctuary. A safe haven. That puppy—little Gus in his bucket—was the bow that tied this all together.

Ajax had created Giddy Up Safe Haven, and he'd done it with her in mind.

Bubbling with excitement, she turned into the entrance road and drove to the crest of that hill. On the plateau, a freshly painted Cape Cod cabin appeared, as well as post-and-rail paddocks, a big old barn and then...

Well, suddenly all those warm, bubbly feelings began to pop and evaporate because on top of being a magnificent example of the male species, Veda knew the truth. Ajax was also a pro in the art of seduction. Lanie had said that he was all about the chase. And it had certainly been true where they were concerned. So, what was really going on here?

Braking, Veda saw movement up ahead. Three horses— a gray, a brindle and a cream—were trotting up to a fence. Ajax was holding two buckets, presumably full of feed. But beneath the wide brim of his black hat, his undivided attention was fixed on her approach.

A yearning, almost desperate heat filled Veda in an instant. In his white button-down, his shoulders looked even bigger. The vee below his open collar was definitely more bronzed. The weight of the buckets strained his gorgeous forearms, highlighting the corded muscle. She could imagine his crooning voice now, saying how beautiful she was, how good she smelled, how much he had missed her and…

"Well, dang, Veda baby. I knew you'd be back."

He had promoted a rumor that suggested he had given up the Rawson brand, his career and the prestige. But seriously? A couple of rescue horses and a rickety old cabin wouldn't hold his attention. That said, she was almost flattered that he'd gone to so much trouble to set up such an elaborate prop.

As he set down the buckets and sauntered over, rocking a pair of worn blue jeans like no other man could, Veda bit her lip to divert the pain that was filling her all the way to the top. He thought he could charm her, fool her, by using a dream she held so dear to her heart?

Setting her jaw, she threw open the car door.

Sorry, cowboy.

Guess again.

As Ajax dropped the buckets and headed over to the Best Life Now vehicle, his thumping heart nearly burst out of his chest. Veda must have seen the Giddy Up sign on her way to her father's place. Her showing up out of the blue gave this move a special seal of approval. He knew his mom was smiling down, cheering him on, giving her blessing.

Just as Hux had done when Ajax had explained why he needed to move on.

He had loved his life growing up. He would always hold dear memories of the farm through his years from a child to a man. But now more than ever, he knew he'd made the right choice. And as Veda got out of the car and

er gaze meshed with his, it all felt so damn good, he
roke into a jog.

Drawing closer, he watched the breeze play through her
air, making it dance while it pushed that summer dress
against her body, emphasizing every delicious sweep and
urve. Her green eyes were sparkling in the sunshine, and
he beautiful lips he longed to taste again were…

Turned down?

Ajax pulled back.

Veda had found her way here but she wasn't happy?
urely it wasn't anything he could have done. Not this time.
erhaps she'd had another argument with Drake. Maybe
here'd been bad news with regard to her business.

Well, if she was looking for a shoulder to lean on, two
rms to bring her close and lift her up, she had come to
he right place.

He picked up the pace again until he was running right
t her. As he swept by, he grabbed her around the waist,
oisted her up against him and twirled her around. He felt
er stiffen because of course she was caught off guard. And
vhen he stopped spinning and let her slide down against
im, he kept the surprises coming. As soon as her mouth
vas within range, he kissed her like he'd dreamed of doing
very minute of every day since he'd let her walk away.

Now she was back.

You'd better believe she was here to stay.

Ajax worked the kiss, cupping the back of her head while
e held her snug against him. Feeling her feet flap in the air,
e pressed in deeper as every starving part of him hardened
nd cried out for more. Veda was gripping what she could
f his shoulders, her fingers digging into his shirt while
er lower half pressed against his belt. While working on
his place these past weeks, he had routinely lost himself
n daydreams about a reunion…how steamy and flat-out
oyous the makeup sex would be. But this moment was

about way more than anything physical. This connection was real, and no matter how many challenges the future threw their way, they would make it through together. To the depths of his soul, he knew that.

But then…

Well, something changed.

Veda didn't seem to be gripping his shirt so much as trying to shove him away. And while he was certain she'd been kissing him back a moment ago, now her mouth was closed, shutting him out.

Pulling back, he searched her eyes. They were shining with emotion. But he wouldn't call it love.

"Let me down!" She pushed him again. "What are you doing? Are you crazy?"

It took another second for those words to sink in. After setting her down, he tried to figure out how the hell he had read it so wrong.

"I get out of my car and you literally jump on me," she was saying. "You really have a problem, you know that?"

He blinked several times, rubbed his brow. "I presumed you were here to see me."

"I was curious," she said, rearranging her dress, which was askew after that amazing midair kiss.

His lips were still burning, begging for more. But he needed to stay focused and rewind to a time before he had believed she had actually wanted him to sweep her off her feet.

"Okay." Holding up both hands, he took in a deep breath, blew it out. "What's going on?"

"I was driving by," she explained, "when I saw the sign. I'd heard rumors."

"That I'd walked away from Rawsons. Correct."

Her eyes widened. "You really did?"

"I decided that I needed to do something different. Something where I could be around horses but…"

His words trailed off because this had all taken such a sharp turn in the wrong direction. What was she so pissed about? What had he done wrong now?

He threw a glance at the new paddock railings he'd put up, then at the cabin roof he'd almost finished repairing. The old barn was big enough to house twenty retired racehorses.

Veda was looking around, too, like she was waiting to be ambushed or expecting a big rock to crash on her head.

"You've really put a lot of work into this," she finally said, obviously remembering the pictures he'd shown her on his phone.

"Yeah." His mouth twisted as the backs of his eyes kind of prickled. "I did."

She crossed her arms. "But if this is all for me, you shouldn't have bothered."

He just looked at her now because…*wow.*

Just.

Wow.

"If you want to know, this wasn't just for you," he said over the god-awful lump in his throat. "It was for *us.* You were the one who said to go after the things that matter most. I thought I could make us both happy. In fact, when I set my mind to it, I felt so good, so sure, I thought you'd be blown away."

She hesitated, then said, "You really thought that I'd trust you?"

"Right." He stepped back into her space. "Because if this is going to work, and I know that it can, we need to trust each other. That's what love is about, damn it!"

He clenched his jaw and dialed it back. She obviously wasn't ready for this. Would she ever be?

Raking a hand through his hair, he groaned. "I need to shut up now—"

"No," she said as quick as a whip. Then the corners of

her mouth twitched. It wasn't exactly a smile but not an outright scowl, either.

He tried to corral the emotions needing to break free. But he couldn't contain the way he felt about her. Right now, this minute, he needed her to know it all.

"I enrolled in college. A bachelor's degree in animal biology. Vet school is another four years at least on top of that, so maybe not—"

"Maybe *yes*." She came forward. "That's so amazing. You always wanted to do that."

Ajax remembered the day when Someone's Prince Charming had broken down. He hadn't been able to save him. But he'd made his decision very soon after that.

"And I took some advice from your blog," he said.

Her eyes widened. "You read my blog?"

"I've done way more than that." He let it all out. "I've fallen in love with you, Veda. But it's more than that, too." He held her arms. "I know I want to spend the rest of my days with you."

When her lips quivered with a growing smile and her eyes filled with what he hoped were happy tears, he looped his arms around her waist and tugged her close again.

"I've brought over my retirees," he said, flickering a glance at the trio. "There'll be more to come. And there's plenty of room for pet pigs and sheep and a fluffy little dog we'll call Gus, too."

She still wasn't talking. Not a croak. Not a peep.

But the tears in her eyes were close to falling, and her lips were definitely calling to him again. So he leaned that bit closer, held her that much tighter and laid out the last of his speech.

"This is who I am," he told her. "This is who I want to be. With you every damn day for as long as we live."

This time when they kissed, Ajax felt a sense of certainty spiral through him, filling him up in a way that reaffirmed what he already knew. He had made the right choice. Veda would always be his sweetheart.

Veda was "the one."

When he slowly broke the kiss, her eyes were heavy with the same wonderful emotions he was feeling.

"Veda," he said, "you are the best thing that's ever happened to me."

"You really mean that? The *best*?"

She looked too choked up to get more words out. But then she took a breath, and asked in a near whisper, "Ajax?"

He smiled and brought her closer. "Yes, Veda."

"I love you, too. I'm pretty sure I loved you from the start."

Then he was kissing her again, lifting her higher, loving her even more. And he knew this time they had done it.

Theirs would be the best life ever.

The best there ever was.

* * * * *

MILLS & BOON

THE HEART OF ROMANCE

A ROMANCE FOR EVERY READER

MODERN

Prepare to be swept off your feet by sophisticated, sexy and seductive heroes, in some of the world's most glamourous and roma locations, where power and passion collide.

HISTORICAL

Escape with historical heroes from time gone by. Whether your passio for wicked Regency Rakes, muscled Vikings or rugged Highlanders, a the romance of the past.

MEDICAL

Set your pulse racing with dedicated, delectable doctors in the high-p sure world of medicine, where emotions run high and passion, comfo love are the best medicine.

True Love

Celebrate true love with tender stories of heartfelt romance, from th rush of falling in love to the joy a new baby can bring, and a focus o emotional heart of a relationship.

Desire

Indulge in secrets and scandal, intense drama and plenty of sizzling action with powerful and passionate heroes who have it all: wealth, st good looks…everything but the right woman.

HEROES

Experience all the excitement of a gripping thriller, with an intense r mance at its heart. Resourceful, true-to-life women and strong, fearle face danger and desire - a killer combination!

To see which titles are coming soon, please visit

millsandboon.co.uk/nextmonth

LET'S TALK
Romance

For exclusive extracts, competitions
and special offers, find us online:

JOIN US ON SOCIAL MEDIA!

Stay up to date with our latest releases, author news and gossip, special offers and discounts, and all the behind-the-scenes action from Mills & Boon...

 @millsandboon

 @millsandboonuk

 facebook.com/millsandboon

 @millsandboonuk

It might just be true love...

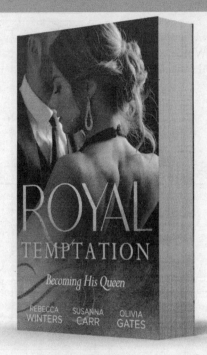